H. G. Wells

THE RED ROOM
and other stories

Selected by JOHN HAMMOND

PHŒNIX

A PHOENIX PAPERBACK

First published in 1998
by Phoenix, a division of Orion Books Ltd
Orion House, 5 Upper St Martin's Lane, London WC2H 9EA

A CIP catalogue record for this book
is available from the British Library.

ISBN 0 75380 453 0

Typeset by Deltatype Ltd, Birkenhead, Merseyside
Printed in Great Britain by
The Guernsey Press Co. Ltd., Guernsey, C. I.

Contents

Note on the Author and Editor

HERBERT GEORGE WELLS (1866–1946) was born in Bromley, Kent, the son of a gardener and a lady's maid. After several 'false starts' in life, including a two-year apprenticeship in a drapers shop, he won a scholarship to the Normal School of Science at South Kensington (now Imperial College, University of London) where he studied biology under T. H. Huxley.

After gaining his degree in 1890, his subsequent career as a teacher was cut short by ill health. While convalescing after a breakdown in 1893 he began writing articles and short stories and was soon earning his living as a journalist. Meanwhile his marriage to his cousin Isabel (1891) ended in failure, but a second marriage to Amy Catherine Robbins (1895) ended only with her death in 1927.

His first novel, *The Time Machine* (1895) was quickly followed by *The Invisible Man* (1897), *The War of the Worlds* (1898), *The First Men in the Moon* (1901) and other scientific romances. Simultaneously he was writing novels in the Dickensian tradition including *The Wheels of Chance, Love and Mr Lewisham* (1900), *Kipps* (1905), *Tono-Bungay* (1909) and *The History of Mr Polly* (1910).

He continued to write novels, short stories, science fiction and a wide range of non-fiction until his death in 1946. His *Experiment in Autobiography* (1934) reviews his life, work and thought.

JOHN HAMMOND is the founder and the president of the H. G. Wells Society. He has written and lectured extensively on Wells and is the author of *An H. G. Wells Companion, H. G. Wells and the Modern Novel* and *H. G. Wells and Rebecca West*. He has edited *H. G. Wells: Interviews and Recollections* and a collection of Wells's unreprinted short stories. His most recent publications are a critical study of Wells's short stories and *A Defoe Companion*. He is a Research fellow at Nottingham Trent University.

Introduction

Wells produced some of the finest short stories in the English language. His earliest published short stories, 'Walcote' and 'The Devotee of Art', appeared in 1888 when he was twenty-two, and his last, 'Answer to Prayer', was published in 1937. He was thus writing short stories for almost exactly fifty years. However, he never sought any precise definition of the short story as a genre, contenting himself with the statement that 'it may be horrible or pathetic or funny or beautiful or profoundly illuminating, having only this essential, that it should take from fifteen to fifty minutes to read aloud'.

Despite the long span over which Wells was writing, the great bulk of his short stories dates from the period 1894–7, when he was at the very beginning of his literary career. This was a time when, in his own words, 'life bubbled with short stories', and when he was simultaneously at work on his early scientific romances including *The Time Machine* (1895), *The Island of Doctor Moreau* (1896) and *The Invisible Man* (1897). Many of his stories appeared in the *Pall Mall Gazette* and its weekly offshoot the *Pall Mall Budget*, journals which were eager to publish lively and original pieces written by a young man with a scientific background and a fresh and stimulating approach.

Wells is principally remembered today as the father of science fiction, but it is a mistake to regard him simply as a writer of scientific fantasias. His short stories range over widely differing styles and themes – including horror ('Pollock and the Porroh Man'), adventure ('The Valley of Spiders'), metaphysics ('Under the Knife') and romance ('Mr Skelmersdale in Fairyland'). One of his characteristics as a writer is his ability not only to engage in exhilarating flights of fancy but to portray everyday people going about their daily lives in recognisably familiar surroundings. The suburban settings of, for example, 'A Catastrophe', 'The Purple Pileus' and 'How Gabriel Became Thompson' display this gift; while in 'Through a Window' and 'The Crystal Egg' we observe totally believable characters deflected from their normal routines by unforeseen circumstances.

Wells's mystical, almost poetic, vision is illustrated by such tales as 'Mr Skelmersdale in Fairyland', 'The Country of the Blind' and 'The Door in the Wall'. In each of these stories the central character is haunted by an elusive vision of beauty and desire which beckons and intrigues, rendering everyday existence colourless by comparison. The tension – the contradiction between duty and desire, between rational and imaginative drives – is one which fractures all of Wells's work and yet which is paradoxically one of his greatest strengths. The typical Wells hero is an inconspicuous figure who spends much of his life in humdrum surroundings, yet is continually beckoned by a vision of happiness and beauty beyond his reach.

Wells the short-story writer was described by H. E. Bates as 'the product of a union between Dickens and Poe'. It is certainly possible to detect the influence of both these writers upon his work, but in the final analysis Wells's stories have a distinctive quality which gives them a flavour peculiar to himself: the ability to stimulate thought, to suggest new possibilities of action, to hint at novel horizons of behaviour or experience. It is this sense of *exhilaration*, of the infinite possibilities inherent in life, which gives Wells's stories their quality of freshness.

The reader who is already familiar with Wells as a novelist or science-fiction writer will find much of interest in these shorter pieces. Implicit throughout the stories are themes and ideas he develops in the full-length fiction. 'The Purple Pileus', for example, anticipates themes which he depicted on a much fuller canvas in *The History of Mr Polly*. 'The Sea Raiders' and 'The Crystal Egg' offer a foretaste of the alien invasion theme of *The War of the Worlds*. 'How Gabriel Became Thompson' hints at motifs elaborated in *Love and Mr Lewisham*, and so on. The potentialities of science for good or evil, the conflict between domesticity and romantic longings, the importance of chance in human affairs: all are explored first in the short stories. At the same time Wells insists that a short story is not a novel in miniature but a genre in its own right, demanding concentration on a single effect or impression that will remain in the reader's mind.

This edition brings together a representative selection that will give a flavour of Wells as a writer of short stories. Whether your preference is for ghost stories, mystery, humour, adventure, pathos or tales of alien worlds you will find something here to meet your taste. Wells himself described his short stories as 'a miscellany of inventions, many of which were very pleasant to write', and added that his end was more than attained 'if some of them are refreshing and agreeable to read'. At his best Wells was a stimulating exponent of the art of the short story, and the finest of his work stands comparison with other masters of the genre.

In a sense each tale is a window on human life. To read them is to enter into a world rich in possibilities and to share with their author a sense of wonder at the unpredictability of experience.

JOHN HAMMOND

THE RED ROOM
and other stories

Through a Window

After his legs were set, they carried Bailey into the study and put
him on a couch before the open window. There he lay, a live –
even a feverish man down to the loins, and below that a double-
barrelled mummy swathed in white wrappings. He tried to read,
even tried to write a little, but most of the time he looked out of
the window.

He had thought the window cheerful to begin with, but now
he thanked God for it many times a day. Within, the room was
dim and grey, and in the reflected light the wear of the furniture
showed plainly. His medicine and drink stood on the little table,
with such litter as the bare branches of a bunch of grapes or the
ashes of a cigar upon a green plate, or a day old evening paper.
The view outside was flooded with light, and across the corner of
it came the head of the acacia, and at the foot the top of the
balcony-railing of hammered iron. In the foreground was the
weltering silver of the river, never quiet and yet never tiresome.
Beyond was the reedy bank, a broad stretch of meadow land, and
then a dark line of trees ending in a group of poplars at the
distant bend of the river, and, upstanding behind them, a square
church tower.

Up and down the river, all day long, things were passing. Now
a string of barges drifting down to London, piled with lime or
barrels of beer; then a steam-launch, disengaging heavy masses
of black smoke, and disturbing the whole width of the river with
long rolling waves; then an impetuous electric launch, and then
a boatload of pleasure-seekers, a solitary sculler, or a four from
some rowing club. Perhaps the river was quietest of a morning or
late at night. One moonlight night some people drifted down
singing, and with a zither playing – it sounded very pleasantly
across the water.

In a few days Bailey began to recognise some of the craft; in a
week he knew the intimate history of half-a-dozen. The launch
Luzon, from Fitzgibbon's, two miles up, would go fretting by,
sometimes three or four times a day, conspicuous with its

colouring of Indian-red and yellow, and its two Oriental attendants; and one day, to Bailey's vast amusement, the house-boat
Purple Emperor came to a stop outside, and breakfasted in the
most shameless domesticity. Then one afternoon, the captain of a
slow-moving barge began a quarrel with his wife as they came
into sight from the left, and had carried it to personal violence
before he vanished behind the window-frame to the right. Bailey
regarded all this as an entertainment got up to while away his
illness, and applauded all the more moving incidents. Mrs Green,
coming in at rare intervals with his meals, would catch him
clapping his hands or softly crying, 'Encore!' But the river players
had other engagements, and his encore went unheeded.

'I should never have thought I could take such an interest in
things that did not concern me,' said Bailey to Wilderspin, who
used to come in in his nervous, friendly way and try to comfort
the sufferer by being talked to. 'I thought this idle capacity was
distinctive of little children and old maids. But it's just circumstances. I simply can't work, and things have to drift; it's no good
to fret and struggle. And so I lie here and am as amused as a
baby with a rattle, at this river and its affairs.

'Sometimes, of course, it gets a bit dull, but not often.

'I would give anything, Wilderspin, for a swamp – just one
swamp – once. Heads swimming and a steam launch to the
rescue, and a chap or so hauled out with a boat-hook.... There
goes Fitzgibbon's launch! They have a new boat-hook, I see, and
the little blackie is still in the dumps. I don't think he's very well,
Wilderspin. He's been like that for two or three days, squatting
sulky-fashion and meditating over the churning of the water.
Unwholesome for him to be always staring at the frothy water
running away from the stern.'

They watched the little steamer fuss across the patch of sunlit
river, suffer momentary occultation from the acacia, and glide
out of sight behind the dark window-frame.

'I'm getting a wonderful eye for details,' said Bailey: 'I spotted
that new boat-hook at once. The other nigger is a funny little
chap. He never used to swagger with the old boat-hook like that.'

'Malays, aren't they?' said Wilderspin.

'Don't know,' said Bailey. 'I thought one called all that sort of
mariner Lascar.'

Then he began to tell Wilderspin what he knew of the private affairs of the house-boat, *Purple Emperor*. 'Funny,' he said, 'how these people come from all points of the compass – from Oxford and Windsor, from Asia and Africa – and gather and pass opposite the window just to entertain me. One man floated out of the infinite the day before yesterday, caught one perfect crab opposite, lost and recovered a scull, and passed on again. Probably he will never come into my life again. So far as I am concerned, he has lived and had his little troubles, perhaps thirty – perhaps forty – years on the earth, merely to make an ass of himself for three minutes in front of my window. Wonderful thing, Wilderspin, if you come to think of it.'

'Yes,' said Wilderspin; '*isn't* it?'

A day or two after this Bailey had a brilliant morning. Indeed, towards the end of the affair, it became almost as exciting as any window show very well could be. We will, however, begin at the beginning.

Bailey was all alone in the house, for his housekeeper had gone into the town three miles away to pay bills, and the servant had her holiday. The morning began dull. A canoe went up about half-past nine, and later a boat-load of camping men came down. But this was mere margin. Things became cheerful about ten o'clock.

It began with something white fluttering in the remote distance where the three poplars marked the river bend. 'Pocket-handkerchief,' said Bailey, when he saw it. 'No. Too big! Flag perhaps.'

However, it was not a flag, for it jumped about. 'Man in whites running fast, and this way,' said Bailey. 'That's luck! But his whites are precious loose!'

Then a singular thing happened. There was a minute pink gleam among the dark trees in the distance, and a little puff of pale grey that began to drift and vanish eastward. The man in white jumped and continued running. Presently the report of the shot arrived.

'What the devil!' said Bailey. 'Looks as if someone was shooting at him.'

He sat up stiffly and stared hard. The white figure was coming along the pathway through the corn. 'It's one of those niggers from the Fitzgibbon's,' said Bailey; 'or may I be hanged! I wonder why he keeps sawing with his arm.'

Then three other figures became indistinctly visible against the dark background of the trees.

Abruptly on the opposite bank a man walked into the picture. He was black-bearded, dressed in flannels, had a red belt, and a vast grey felt hat. He walked, leaning very much forward and with his hands swinging before him. Behind him one could see the grass swept by the towing-rope of the boat he was dragging. He was steadfastly regarding the white figure that was hurrying through the corn. Suddenly he stopped. Then, with a peculiar gesture, Bailey could see that he began pulling in the tow-rope hand over hand. Over the water could be heard the voices of the people in the still invisible boat.

'What are you after, Hagshot?' said someone.

The individual with the red belt shouted something that was inaudible, and went on lugging in the rope, looking over his shoulder at the advancing white figure as he did so. He came down the bank, and the rope bent a lane among the reeds and lashed the water between his pulls.

Then just the bows of the boat came into view, with the towing-mast and a tall, fair-haired man standing up and trying to see over the bank. The boat bumped unexpectedly among the reeds, and the tall, fair-haired man disappeared suddenly, having apparently fallen back into the invisible part of the boat. There was a curse and some indistinct laughter. Hagshot did not laugh, but hastily clambered into the boat and pushed off. Abruptly the boat passed out of Bailey's sight.

But it was still audible. The melody of voices suggested that its occupants were busy telling each other what to do.

The running figure was drawing near the bank. Bailey could now see clearly that it was one of Fitzgibbon's Orientals, and began to realise what the sinuous thing the man carried in his hand might be. Three other men followed one another through the corn, and the foremost carried what was probably the gun. They were perhaps two hundred yards or more behind the Malay.

'It's a man hunt, by all that's holy!' said Bailey.

The Malay stopped for a moment and surveyed the bank to the right. Then he left the path, and, breaking through the corn, vanished in that direction. The three pursuers followed suit, and their heads and gesticulating arms above the corn, after a brief interval, also went out of Bailey's field of vision.

Bailey so far forgot himself as to swear. 'Just as things were getting lively!' he said. Something like a woman's shriek came through the air. Then shouts, a howl, a dull whack upon the balcony outside that made Bailey jump, and then the report of a gun.

'This is precious hard on an invalid,' said Bailey.

But more was to happen yet in his picture. In fact, a great deal more. The Malay appeared again, running now along the bank up stream. His stride had more swing and less pace in it than before. He was threatening someone ahead with the ugly krees he carried. The blade, Bailey noticed, was dull – it did not shine as steel should.

Then came the tall, fair man, brandishing a boathook, and after him three other men in boating costume running clumsily with oars. The man with the grey hat and red belt was not with them. After an interval the three men with the gun reappeared, still in the corn, but now near the river bank. They emerged upon the towing-path, and hurried after the others. The opposite bank was left blank and desolate again.

The sick-room was disgraced by more profanity. 'I would give my life to see the end of this,' said Bailey. There were indistinct shouts up stream. Once they seemed to be coming nearer, but they disappointed him.

Bailey sat and grumbled. He was still grumbling when his eye caught something black and round among the waves. 'Hullo!' he said. He looked narrowly and saw two triangular black bodies frothing every now and then about a yard in front of this.

He was still doubtful when the little band of pursuers came into sight again, and began to point to this floating object. They were talking eagerly. Then the man with the gun took aim.

'He's swimming the river, by George!' said Bailey.

The Malay looked round, saw the gun, and went under. He came up so close to Bailey's bank of the river that one of the bars of the balcony hid him for a moment. As he emerged the man with the gun fired. The Malay kept steadily onward – Bailey could see the wet hair on his forehead now and the krees between his teeth – and was presently hidden by the balcony.

This seemed to Bailey an unendurable wrong. The man was

lost to him for ever now, so he thought. Why couldn't the brute have got himself decently caught on the opposite bank, or shot in the water?

'It's worse than Edwin Drood,' said Bailey.

Over the river, too, things had become an absolute blank. All seven men had gone down stream again, probably to get the boat and follow across. Bailey listened and waited. There was silence. 'Surely it's not over like this,' said Bailey.

Five minutes passed – ten minutes. Then a tug with two barges went up stream. The attitudes of the men upon these were the attitudes of those who see nothing remarkable in earth, water, or sky. Clearly the whole affair had passed out of sight of the river. Probably the hunt had gone into the beech woods behind the house.

'Confound it!' said Bailey. 'To be continued again, and no chance this time of the sequel. But this is hard on a sick man.'

He heard a step on the staircase behind him, and looking round saw the door open. Mrs Green came in and sat down, panting. She still had her bonnet on, her purse in her hand, and her little brown basket upon her arm. 'Oh, there!' she said, and left Bailey to imagine the rest.

'Have a little whisky and water, Mrs Green, and tell me about it,' said Bailey.

Sipping a little, the lady began to recover her powers of explanation.

One of those black creatures at the Fitzgibbon's had gone mad, and was running about with a big knife, stabbing people. He had killed a groom, and stabbed the under-butler, and almost cut the arm off a boating gentleman.

'Running amuck with a krees,' said Bailey. 'I thought that was it.'

And he was hiding in the wood when she came through it from the town.

'What! Did he run after you?' asked Bailey, with a certain touch of glee in his voice.

'No, that was the horrible part of it,' Mrs Green explained. She had been right through the woods and had *never known he was there*. It was only when she met young Mr Fitzgibbon carrying his gun in the shrubbery that she heard anything about it. Apparently, what upset Mrs Green was the lost opportunity for emotion. She was determined, however, to make the most of what was left her.

'To think he was there all the time!' she said, over and over again.

Bailey endured this patiently enough for perhaps ten minutes. At last he thought it advisable to assert himself. 'It's twenty past one, Mrs Green,' he said. 'Don't you think it time you got me something to eat?'

This brought Mrs Green suddenly to her knees.

'Oh Lord, sir!' she said. 'Oh! don't go making me go out of this room, sir, till I know he's caught. He might have got into the house, sir. He might be creeping, creeping, with that knife of his, along the passage this very—'

She broke off suddenly and glared over him at the window. Her lower jaw dropped. Bailey turned his head sharply.

For the space of half a second things seemed just as they were. There was the tree, the balcony, the shining river, the distant church tower. Then he noticed that the acacia was displaced about a foot to the right, and that it was quivering, and the leaves were rustling. The tree was shaken violently, and a heavy panting was audible.

In another moment a hairy brown hand had appeared and clutched the balcony railings, and in another the face of the Malay was peering through these at the man on the couch. His expression was an unpleasant grin, by reason of the krees he held between his teeth, and he was bleeding from an ugly wound in his cheek. His hair wet to drying stuck out like horns from his head. His body was bare save for the wet trousers that clung to him. Bailey's first impulse was to spring from the couch, but his legs reminded him that this was impossible.

By means of the balcony and tree the man slowly raised himself until he was visible to Mrs Green. With a choking cry she made for the door and fumbled with the handle.

Bailey thought swiftly and clutched a medicine bottle in either hand. One he flung, and it smashed against the acacia. Silently and deliberately, and keeping his bright eyes fixed on Bailey, the Malay clambered into the balcony. Bailey, still clutching his second bottle, but with a sickening, sinking feeling about his heart, watched first one leg come over the railing and then the other.

It was Bailey's impression that the Malay took about an hour to get his second leg over the rail. The period that elapsed before the sitting position was changed to a standing one seemed enormous – days, weeks, possibly a year or so. Yet Bailey had no clear impression of anything going on in his mind during that vast period, except a vague wonder at his inability to throw the second medicine bottle. Suddenly the Malay glanced over his shoulder. There was the crack of a rifle. He flung up his arms and came down upon the couch. Mrs Green began a dismal shriek that seemed likely to last until Doomsday. Bailey stared at the brown body with its shoulder blade driven in, that writhed painfully across his legs and rapidly staining and soaking the spotless bandages. Then he looked at the long krees, with the reddish streaks upon its blade, that lay an inch beyond the trembling brown fingers upon the floor. Then at Mrs Green, who had backed hard against the door and was staring at the body and shrieking in gusty outbursts as if she would wake the dead. And then the body was shaken by one last convulsive effort.

The Malay gripped the krees, tried to raise himself with his left hand, and collapsed. Then he raised his head, stared for a moment at Mrs Green, and twisting his face round looked at Bailey. With a gasping groan the dying man succeeded in clutching the bed clothes with his disabled hand, and by a violent effort, which hurt Bailey's legs exceedingly, writhed sideways towards what must be his last victim. Then something seemed released in Bailey's mind and he brought down the second bottle with all his strength on to the Malay's face. The krees fell heavily upon the floor.

'Easy with those legs,' said Bailey, as young Fitzgibbon and one of the boating party lifted the body off him.

Young Fitzgibbon was very white in the face. 'I didn't mean to kill him,' he said.

'It's just as well,' said Bailey.

The Purple Pileus

Mr Coombes was sick of life. He walked away from his unhappy
home, and, sick not only of his own existence but of everybody
else's, turned aside down Gaswork Lane to avoid the town, and,
crossing the wooden bridge that goes over the canal to Starling's
Cottages, was presently alone in the damp pine woods and out of
sight and sound of human habitation. He would stand it no
longer. He repeated aloud with blasphemies unusual to him that
he would stand it no longer.

He was a pale-faced little man, with dark eyes and a fine and
very black moustache. He had a very stiff, upright collar slightly
frayed, that gave him an illusory double chin, and his overcoat
(albeit shabby) was trimmed with astrachan. His gloves were a
bright brown with black stripes over the knuckles, and split at the
finger ends. His appearance, his wife had said once in the dear,
dead days beyond recall – before he married her, that is – was
military. But now she called him – it seems a dreadful thing to tell
of between husband and wife, but she called him 'a little grub'. It
wasn't the only thing she had called him, either.

The row had arisen about that beastly Jennie again. Jennie was
his wife's friend, and, by no invitation of Mr Coombes, she came
in every blessed Sunday to dinner, and made a shindy all the
afternoon. She was a big, noisy girl, with a taste for loud colours
and a strident laugh; and this Sunday she had outdone all her
previous intrusions by bringing in a fellow with her, a chap as
showy as herself. And Mr Coombes, in a starchy, clean collar and
his Sunday frock-coat, had sat dumb and wrathful at his own
table, while his wife and her guests talked foolishly and
undesirably, and laughed aloud. Well, he stood that, and after
dinner (which, 'as usual', was late), what must Miss Jennie do
but go to the piano and play banjo tunes, for all the world as if it
were a week-day! Flesh and blood could not endure such goings
on. They would hear next door, they would hear in the road, it
was a public announcement of their disrepute. He had to speak.

He had felt himself go pale, and a kind of rigour had affected his respiration as he delivered himself. He had been sitting on one of the chairs by the window – the new guest had taken possession of the arm-chair. He turned his head. 'Sun Day!' he said over the collar, in the voice of one who warns. 'Sun Day!' What people call a 'nasty' tone, it was.

Jennie had kept on playing, but his wife, who was looking through some music that was piled on the top of the piano, had stared at him. 'What's wrong now?' she said; 'can't people enjoy themselves?'

'I don't mind rational 'njoyment, at all,' said little Coombes, 'but I ain't a-going to have week-day tunes playing on a Sunday in this house.'

'What's wrong with my playing now?' said Jennie, stopping and twirling round on the music-stool with a monstrous rustle of flounces.

Coombes saw it was going to be a row, and opened too vigorously, as is common with your timid, nervous men all the world over. 'Steady on with that music-stool!' said he; 'it ain't made for 'eavy-weights.'

'Never you mind about weights,' said Jennie, incensed. 'What was you saying behind my back about my playing?'

'Surely you don't 'old with not having a bit of music on a Sunday, Mr Coombes?' said the new guest, learning back in the arm-chair, blowing a cloud of cigarette smoke and smiling in a kind of pitying way. And simultaneously his wife said something to Jennie about 'Never mind 'im. You go on, Jinny.'

'I do,' said Mr Coombes, addressing the new guest.

'May I arst why?' said the new guest, evidently enjoying both his cigarette and the prospect of an argument. He was, by-the-by, a lank young man, very stylishly dressed in bright drab, with a white cravat and a pearl and silver pin. It had been better taste to come in a black coat, Mr Coombes thought.

'Because,' began Mr Coombes, 'it don't suit me. I'm a business man. I 'ave to study my connection. Rational 'njoyment—'

'His connection!' said Mrs Coombes scornfully. 'That's what he's always a-saying. We got to do this, and we got to do that—'

'If you don't mean to study my connection,' said Mr Coombes, 'what did you marry me for?'

'I wonder,' said Jennie, and turned back to the piano.

'I never saw such a man as you,' said Mrs Coombes.

'You've altered all round since we were married. Before—'
Then Jennie began at the tum, tum, tum again.

'Look here!' said Mr Coombes, driven at last to revolt, standing
up and raising his voice. 'I tell you I won't have that.' The frock-
coat heaved with his indignation.

'No vi'lence, now,' said the long young man in drab, sitting up.

'Who the juice are you?' said Mr Coombes fiercely.

Whereupon they all began talking at once. The new guest said
he was Jennie's 'intended,' and meant to protect her, and Mr
Coombes said he was welcome to do so anywhere but in his (Mr
Coombes') house; and Mrs Coombes said he ought to be ashamed
of insulting his guests, and (as I have already mentioned) that he
was getting a regular little grub; and the end was, that Mr
Coombes ordered his visitors out of the house, and they wouldn't
go, and so he said he would go himself. With his face burning
and tears of excitement in his eyes, he went into the passage, and
as he struggled with his overcoat – his frock-coat sleeves got
concertinaed up his arm – and gave a brush at his silk hat, Jennie
began again at the piano, and strummed him insultingly out of
the house. Tum, tum, tum. He slammed the shop door so that the
house quivered. That, briefly, was the immediate making of his
mood. You will perhaps begin to understand his disgust with
existence.

As he walked along the muddy path under the firs, – it was late
October, and the ditches and heaps of fir needles were gorgeous
with clumps of fungi, – recapitulated the melancholy history of
his marriage. It was brief and commonplace enough. He now
perceived with sufficient clearness that his wife had married him
out of a natural curiosity and in order to escape from her
worrying, laborious, and uncertain life in the workroom; and,
like the majority of her class, she was far too stupid to realise that
it was her duty to co-operate with him in his business. She was
greedy of enjoyment, loquacious, and socially-minded, and
evidently disappointed to find the restraints of poverty still
hanging about her. His worries exasperated her, and the slightest
attempt to control her proceedings resulted in a charge of
'grumbling'. Why couldn't he be nice – as he used to be? And
Coombes was such a harmless little man, too, nourished mentally
on *Self-Help*, and with a meagre ambition of self-denial and
competition, that was to end in a 'sufficiency'. Then Jennie came

in as a female Mephistopheles, a gabbling chronicle of 'fellers',
and was always wanting his wife to go to theatres, and 'all that'.
And in addition were aunts of his wife, and cousins (male and
female) to eat up capital, insult him personally, upset business
arrangements, annoy good customers, and generally blight his
life. It was not the first occasion by many that Mr Coombes had
fled his home in wrath and indignation, and something like fear,
vowing furiously and even aloud that he wouldn't stand it, and
so frothing away his energy along the line of least resistance. But
never before had he been quite so sick of life as on this particular
Sunday afternoon. The Sunday dinner may have had its share in
his despair – and the greyness of the sky. Perhaps, too, he was
beginning to realise his unendurable frustration as a business
man as the consequence of his marriage. Presently bankruptcy,
and after that – Perhaps she might have reason to repent when it
was too late. And destiny, as I have already intimated, had
planted the path through the wood with evil-smelling fungi,
thickly and variously planted it, not only on the right side, but on
the left.

A small shopman is in such a melancholy position, if his wife
turns out a disloyal partner. His capital is all tied up in his
business, and to leave her means to join the unemployed in some
strange part of the earth. The luxuries of divorce are beyond him
altogether. So that the good old tradition of marriage for better or
worse holds inexorably for him, and things work up to tragic
culminations. Bricklayers kick their wives to death, and dukes
betray theirs; but it is among the small clerks and shopkeepers
nowadays that it comes most often to a cutting of throats. Under
the circumstances it is not so very remarkable – and you must
take it as charitably as you can – that the mind of Mr Coombes
ran for a while on some such glorious close to his disappointed
hopes, and that he thought of razors, pistols, bread-knives, and
touching letters to the coroner denouncing his enemies by name,
and praying piously for forgiveness. After a time his fierceness
gave way to melancholia. He had been married in this very
overcoat, in his first and only frock-coat that was buttoned up
beneath it. He began to recall their courting along this very walk,
his years of penurious saving to get capital, and the bright
hopefulness of his marrying days. For it all to work out like this!

Was there no sympathetic ruler anywhere in the world? He reverted to death as a topic.

He thought of the canal he had just crossed, and doubted whether he shouldn't stand with his head out, even in the middle, and it was while drowning was in his mind that the purple pileus caught his eye. He looked at it mechanically for a moment, and stopped and stooped towards it to pick it up, under the impression that it was some such small leather object as a purse. Then he saw that it was the purple top of a fungus, a peculiarly poisonous-looking purple: slimy, shiny, and emitting a sour odour. He hesitated with his hand an inch or so from it, and the thought of poison crossed his mind. With that he picked the thing, and stood up again with it in his hand.

The odour was certainly strong – acrid, but by no means disgusting. He broke off a piece, and the fresh surface was a creamy white, that changed like magic in the space of ten seconds to a yellowish-green colour. It was even an inviting-looking change. He broke off two other pieces to see it repeated. They were wonderful things these fungi, thought Mr Coombes, and all of them the deadliest poisons, as his father had often told him. Deadly poisons!

There is no time like the present for a rash resolve. Why not here and now? thought Mr Coombes. He tasted a little piece, a very little piece indeed – a mere crumb. It was so pungent that he almost spat it out again, then merely hot and full-flavoured: a kind of German mustard with a touch of horse-radish and – well, mushroom. He swallowed it in the excitement of the moment. Did he like it or did he not? His mind was curiously careless. He would try another bit. It really wasn't bad – it was good. He forgot his troubles in the interest of the immediate moment. Playing with death it was. He took another bite, and then deliberately finished a mouthful. A curious, tingling sensation began in his finger-tips and toes. His pulse began to move faster. The blood in his ears sounded like a mill-race. 'Try bi' more,' said Mr Coombes. He turned and looked about him, and found his feet unsteady. He saw, and struggled towards, a little patch of purple a dozen yards away. 'Jol' goo' stuff,' said Mr Coombes. 'E – lomore ye'.' He pitched forward and fell on his face, his hands outstretched towards the cluster of pilei. But he did not eat any more of them. He forgot forthwith.

He rolled over and sat up with a look of astonishment on his face. His carefully brushed silk hat had rolled away towards the ditch. He pressed his hand to his brow. Something had happened, but he could not rightly determine what it was. Anyhow, he was no longer dull – he felt bright, cheerful. And his throat was afire. He laughed in the sudden gaiety of his heart. Had he been dull? He did not know; but at anyrate he would be dull no longer. He got up and stood unsteadily, regarding the universe with an agreeable smile. He began to remember. He could not remember very well, because of a steam roundabout that was beginning in his head. And he knew he had been disagreeable at home, just because they wanted to be happy. They were quite right; life should be as gay as possible. He would go home and make it up, and reassure them. And why not take some of this delightful toadstool with him, for them to eat? A hatful, no less. Some of those red ones with white spots as well, and a few yellow. He had been a dull dog, an enemy to merriment; he would make up for it. It would be gay to turn his coat-sleeves inside out, and stick some yellow gorse into his waistcoat pockets. Then home – singing – for a jolly evening.

After the departure of Mr Coombes, Jennie discontinued playing, and turned round on the music-stool again. 'What a fuss about nothing!' said Jennie.

'You see, Mr Clarence, what I've got to put up with,' said Mrs Coombes.

'He is a bit hasty,' said Mr Clarence judicially.

'He ain't got the slightest sense of our position,' said Mrs Coombes; 'that's what I complain of. He cares for nothing but his old shop; and if I have a bit of company, or buy anything to keep myself decent, or get any little thing I want out of the housekeeping money, there's disagreeables. "Economy," he says; "struggle for life", and all that. He lies awake of nights about it, worrying how he can screw me out of a shilling. He wanted us to eat Dorset butter once. If once I was to give in to him – there!'

'Of course,' said Jennie.

'If a man values a woman,' said Mr Clarence, lounging back in the arm-chair, 'he must be prepared to make sacrifices for her. For my own part,' said Mr Clarence, with his eye on Jennie, 'I shouldn't think of marrying till I was in a position to do the thing in style. It's downright selfishness. A man ought to go through the rough-and-tumble by himself, and not drag her—'

'I don't agree altogether with that,' said Jennie. 'I don't see why a man shouldn't have a woman's help, provided he doesn't treat her meanly, you know. It's meanness—'

'You wouldn't believe,' said Mrs Coombes. 'But I was a fool to 'ave 'im. I might 'ave known. If it 'adn't been for my father, we shouldn't 'ave 'ad not a carriage to our wedding.'

'Lord! he didn't stick out at that?' said Mr Clarence, quite shocked.

'Said he wanted the money for his stock, or some such rubbish. Why, he wouldn't have a woman in to help me once a week if it wasn't for my standing out plucky. And the fusses he makes about money – comes to me, well, pretty near crying, with sheets of paper and figgers. "If only we can tide over this year," he says, "the business is bound to go." "If only we can tide over this year," I says; "then it'll be, if only we can tide over next year. I know you," I says. "And you don't catch me screwing myself lean and ugly. Why didn't you marry a slavey?" I says, "if you wanted one – instead of a respectable girl," I says.'

So Mrs Coombes. But we will not follow this unedifying conversation further. Suffice it that Mr Coombes was very satisfactorily disposed of, and they had a snug little time round the fire. Then Mrs Coombes went to get the tea, and Jennie sat coquettishly on the arm of Mr Clarence's chair until the tea-things clattered outside. 'What was that I heard?' asked Mrs Coombes playfully, as she entered, and there was badinage about kissing. They were just sitting down to the little circular table when the first intimation of Mr Coombes' return was heard.

This was a fumbling at the latch of the front door.

"Ere's my lord,' said Mrs Coombes. 'Went out like a lion and comes back like a lamb, I'll lay.'

Something fell over in the shop: a chair, it sounded like. Then there was a sound as of some complicated step exercise in the passage. Then the door opened and Coombes appeared. But it was Coombes transfigured. The immaculate collar had been torn carelessly from his throat. His carefully-brushed silk hat, half-full of a crush of fungi, was under one arm; his coat was inside out, and his waistcoat adorned with bunches of yellow-blossomed furze. These little eccentricities of Sunday costume, however, were quite overshadowed by the change in his face; it was livid white, his eyes were unnaturally large and bright, and his pale blue lips were drawn back in a cheerless grin. 'Merry!' he said. He had stopped dancing to open the door. 'Rational 'njoyment. Dance.' He made three fantastic steps into the room, and stood bowing.

'Jim!' shrieked Mrs Coombes, and Mr Clarence sat petrified, with a dropping lower jaw.

'Tea,' said Mr Coombes. 'Jol' thing, tea. Tose-stools, too. Brosher.'

'He's drunk,' said Jennie in a weak voice. Never before had she seen this intense pallor in a drunken man, or such shining, dilated eyes.

Mr Coombes held out a handful of scarlet agaric to Mr Clarence. 'Jo' stuff,' said he; 'ta' some.'

At that moment he was genial. Then at the sight of their startled faces he changed, with the swift transition of insanity, into overbearing fury. And it seemed as if he had suddenly recalled the quarrel of his departure. In such a huge voice as Mrs Coombes had never heard before, he shouted, 'My house. I'm master 'ere. Eat what I give yer!' He bawled this, as it seemed, without an effort, without a violent gesture, standing there as motionless as one who whispers, holding out a handful of fungus.

Clarence approved himself a coward. He could not meet the mad fury in Coombes' eyes; he rose to his feet, pushing back his chair, and turned, stooping. At that Coombes rushed at him. Jennie saw her opportunity, and, with the ghost of a shriek, made for the door. Mrs Coombes followed her. Clarence tried to dodge. Over went the tea-table with a smash as Coombes clutched him by the collar and tried to thrust the fungus into his mouth. Clarence was content to leave his collar behind him, and shot out into the passage with red patches of fly agaric still adherent to his face. 'Shut 'im in!' cried Mrs Coombes, and would have closed the door, but her supports deserted her; Jennie saw the shop door open, and vanished thereby, locking it behind her, while Clarence went on hastily into the kitchen. Mr Coombes came heavily against the door, and Mrs Coombes, finding the key was inside, fled upstairs and locked herself in the spare bedroom.

So the new convert to *joie de vivre* emerged upon the passage, his decorations a little scattered, but that respectable hatful of fungi still under his arm. He hesitated at the three ways, and decided on the kitchen. Whereupon Clarence, who was fumbling with the key, gave up the attempt to imprison his host, and fled into the scullery, only to be captured before he could open the door into the yard. Mr Clarence is singularly reticent of the details of what occurred. It seems that Mr Coombes' transitory irritation had vanished again, and he was once more a genial playfellow. And as there were knives and meat choppers about, Clarence very generously resolved to humour him and so avoid anything tragic. It is beyond dispute that Mr Coombes played with Mr Clarence to his heart's content; they could not have been more playful and familiar if they had known each other for years. He insisted gaily on Clarence trying the fungi, and, after a friendly tussle, was smitten with remorse at the mess he was making of his guest's face. It also appears that Clarence was dragged under the sink and his face scrubbed with the blacking brush – he being still resolved to humour the lunatic at any cost – and that finally, in a somewhat dishevelled, chipped, and discoloured condition, he was assisted to his coat and shown out by the back door, the shopway being barred by Jennie. Mr Coombes' wandering thoughts then turned to Jennie. Jennie had been unable to unfasten the shop door, but she shot the bolts against Mr Coombes' latch-key, and remained in possession of the shop for the rest of the evening.

It would appear that Mr Coombes then returned to the kitchen, still in pursuit of gaiety, and, albeit a strict Good Templar, drank (or spilt down the front of the first and only frock-coat) no less than five bottles of the stout Mrs Coombes insisted upon having for her health's sake. He made cheerful noises by breaking off the necks of the bottles with several of his wife's wedding-present dinner-plates, and during the earlier part of this great drunk he sang divers merry ballads. He cut his finger rather badly with one of the bottles – the only bloodshed in this story – and what with that, and the systematic convulsion of his inexperienced physiology by the liquorish brand of Mrs Coombes' stout, it may be the evil of the fungus poison was somehow allayed. But we prefer to draw a veil over the concluding incidents of this Sunday afternoon. They ended in the coal cellar, in a deep and healing sleep.

* * *

An interval of five years elapsed. Again it was a Sunday afternoon in October, and again Mr Coombes walked through the pine wood beyond the canal. He was still the same dark-eyed, black-moustached little man that he was at the outset of the story, but his double chin was now scarcely so illusory as it had been. His overcoat was new, with a velvet lapel, and a stylish collar with turn-down corners, free of any coarse starchiness, had replaced the original all-round article. His hat was glossy, his gloves newish – though one finger had split and been carefully mended. And a casual observer would have noticed about him a certain rectitude of bearing, a certain erectness of head that marks the man who thinks well of himself. He was a master now, with three assistants. Beside him walked a larger sunburnt parody of himself, his brother Tom, just back from Australia. They were recapitulating their early struggles, and Mr Coombes had just been making a financial statement.

'It's a very nice little business, Jim,' said brother Tom. 'In these days of competition you're jolly lucky to have worked it up so. And you're jolly lucky, too, to have a wife who's willing to help like yours does.'

'Between ourselves,' said Mr Coombes, 'it wasn't always so. It wasn't always like this. To begin with, the missus was a bit giddy. Girls are funny creatures.'

'Dear me!'

'Yes. You'd hardly think it, but she was downright extravagant, and always having slaps at me. I was a bit too easy and loving, and all that, and she thought the whole blessed show was run for her. Turned the 'ouse into a regular caravansery, always having her relations and girls from business in, and their chaps. Comic songs a' Sunday, it was getting to, and driving trade away. And she was making eyes at the chaps, too! I tell you, Tom, the place wasn't my own.'

'Shouldn't 'a' thought it.'

'It was so. Well – I reasoned with her. I said, "I ain't a duke, to keep a wife like a pet animal. I married you for 'elp and company." I said, "You got to 'elp and pull the business through." She wouldn't 'ear of it. "Very well," I says; "I'm a mild man till I'm roused," I says, "and it's getting to that." But she wouldn't 'ear of no warnings.'

'Well?'

'It's the way with women. She didn't think I 'ad it in me to be roused. Women of her sort (between ourselves, Tom) don't respect a man until they're a bit afraid of him. So I just broke out to show her. In comes a girl named Jennie, that used to work with her, and her chap. We 'ad a bit of a row, and I came out 'ere – it was just such another day as this – and I thought it all out. Then I went back and pitched into them.'

'You did?'

'I did. I was mad, I can tell you. I wasn't going to 'it 'er, if I could 'elp it, so I went back and licked into this chap, just to show 'er what I could do. 'E was a big chap, too. Well, I chucked him, and smashed things about, and gave 'er a scaring, and she ran up and locked 'erself into the spare room.'

'Well?'

'That's all. I says to 'er the next morning, "Now you know," I says, "what I'm like when I'm roused." And I didn't have to say anything more.'

'And you've been happy ever after, eh?'

'So to speak. There's nothing like putting your foot down with them. If it 'adn't been for that afternoon I should 'a' been tramping the roads now, and she'd 'a' been grumbling at me, and all her family grumbling for bringing her to poverty – I know their little ways. But we're all right now. And it's a very decent little business, as you say.'

They proceeded on their way meditatively. 'Women are funny creatures,' said Brother Tom.

'They want a firm hand,' says Coombes.

'What a lot of these funguses there are about here!' remarked Brother Tom presently. 'I can't see what use they are in the world.'

Mr Coombes looked. 'I dessay they're sent for some wise purpose,' said Mr Coombes.

And that was as much thanks as the purple pileus ever got for maddening this absurd little man to the pitch of decisive action, and so altering the whole course of his life.

A Catastrophe

The little shop was not paying. The realisation came insensibly. Winslow was not the man for definite addition and subtraction and sudden discovery. He became aware of the truth in his mind gradually, as though it had always been there. A lot of facts had converged and led him there. There was that line of cretonnes – four half-pieces – untouched, save for half a yard sold to cover a stool. There were those shirtings at $4\frac{3}{4}$d. – Bandersnatch, in the Broadway, was selling them at $2\frac{3}{4}$d. – under cost, in fact. (Surely Bandersnatch might let a man live!) Those servants' caps, a selling line, needed replenishing, and that brought back the memory of Winslow's sole wholesale dealers, Helter, Skelter, & Grab. Why! how about their account?

Winslow stood with a big green box open on the counter before him when he thought of it. His pale grey eyes grew a little rounder; his pale, straggling moustache twitched. He had been drifting along, day after day. He went round to the ramshackle cash-desk in the corner – it was Winslow's weakness to sell his goods over the counter, give his customers a duplicate bill, and then dodge into the desk to receive the money, as though he doubted his own honesty. His lank forefinger, with the prominent joints, ran down the bright little calendar ('Clack's Cottons last for All Time'). 'One – two – three; three weeks an' a day!' said Winslow, staring. 'March! Only three weeks and a day. It *can't* be.'

'Tea, dear,' said Mrs Winslow, opening the door with the glass window and the white blind that communicated with the parlour.

'One minute,' said Winslow, and began unlocking the desk.

An irritable old gentleman, very hot and red about the face, and in a heavy fur-lined coat, came in noisily. Mrs Winslow vanished.

'Ugh!' said the old gentleman. 'Pocket-handkerchief.'

'Yes, sir,' said Winslow. 'About what price' –

'Ugh!' said the old gentleman. 'Poggit-handkerchief, quig!'

Winslow began to feel flustered. He produced two boxes.

'These sir' – began Winslow.

'Sheed tin!' said the old gentleman, clutching the stiffness of the linen. 'Wad to blow my nose – not haggit about.'

'A cotton one, p'raps, sir?' said Winslow.

'How much?' said the old gentleman over the handkerchief.

'Sevenpence, sir. There's nothing more I can show you? No ties, braces –?'

'Damn!' said the old gentleman, fumbling in his ticket-pocket, and finally producing half a crown. Winslow looked round for his metallic duplicate-book which he kept in various fixtures, according to circumstances, and then he caught the old gentleman's eye. He went straight to the desk at once and got the change, with an entire disregard of the routine of the shop.

Winslow was always more or less excited by a customer. But the open desk reminded him of his trouble. It did not come back to him all at once. He heard a finger-nail softly tapping on the glass, and, looking up, saw Minnie's eyes over the blind. It seemed like retreat opening. He shut and locked the desk, and went into the back room to tea.

But he was preoccupied. Three weeks and a day! He took unusually large bites of his bread and butter, and stared hard at the little pot of jam. He answered Minnie's conversational advances distractedly. The shadow of Helter, Skelter, & Grab lay upon the tea-table. He was struggling with this new idea of failure, the tangible realisation that was taking shape and substance, condensing, as it were, out of the misty uneasiness of many days. At present it was simply one concrete fact: there were thirty-nine pounds left in the bank, and that day three weeks Messrs Helter, Skelter, & Grab, those enterprising outfitters of young men, would demand their eighty pounds.

After tea there was a customer or so – small purchases: some muslin and buckram, dress-protectors, tape, and a pair of Lisle hose. Then, knowing that Black Care was lurking in the dusky corners of the shop, he lit the three lamps early and set to, refolding his cotton prints, the most vigorous and least meditative proceeding of which he could think. He could see Minnie's shadow in the other room as she moved about the table. She was busy turning an old dress. He had a walk after supper, looked in at the Y.M.C.A., but found no one to talk to, and finally went to bed. Minnie was already there. And there, too, waiting for him, nudging him gently, until about midnight he was hopelessly awake, sat Black Care.

He had had one or two nights lately in that company, but this was much worse. First came Messrs Helter, Skelter, & Grab, and their demand for eighty pounds – an enormous sum when your original capital was only a hundred and seventy. They camped, as it were, before him, sat down and beleaguered him. He clutched feebly at the circumambient darkness for expedients. Suppose he had a sale, sold things for almost anything? He tried to imagine a sale miraculously successful in some unexpected manner, and mildly profitable, in spite of reductions below cost. Then Bandersnatch Limited, 101, 102, 103, 105, 106, 107 Broadway, joined the siege, a long caterpillar of frontage, a battery of shop fronts, wherein things were sold at a farthing above cost. How could he fight such an establishment? Besides, what had he to sell? He began to review his resources. What taking line was there to bait the sale? Then straightway came those pieces of cretonne, yellow and black, with a bluish-green flower; those discredited skirtings, prints without buoyancy, skirmishing haberdashery, some despairful four-button gloves by an inferior maker – a hopeless crew. And that was his force against Bandersnatch, Helter, Skelter, & Grab, and the pitiless world behind them. Whatever had made him think a mortal would buy such things? Why had he bought this and neglected that? He suddenly realised the intensity of his hatred for Helter, Skelter, & Grab's salesman. Then he drove towards an agony of self-reproach. He had spent too much on that cash-desk. What real need was there of a desk? He saw his vanity of that desk in a lurid glow of self-discovery. And the lamps? Five pounds! Then suddenly, with what was almost physical pain, he remembered the rent.

He groaned and turned over. And there, dim in the darkness, was the hummock of Mrs Winslow's shoulder. That set him off in another direction. He became acutely sensible of Minnie's want of feeling. Here he was, worried to death about business, and she sleeping like a little child. He regretted having married, with that infinite bitterness that only comes to the human heart in the small hours of the morning. That hummock of white seemed absolutely without helpfulness, a burden, a responsibility. What

fools men were to marry! Minnie's inert repose irritated him so
much that he was almost provoked to wake her up and tell her
that they were 'Ruined.' She would have to go back to her uncle;
her uncle had always been against him: and as for his own
future, Winslow was exceedingly uncertain. A shop assistant
who has once set up for himself finds the utmost difficulty in
getting into a situation again. He began to figure himself 'crib-
hunting' once more, going from this wholesale house to that,
writing innumerable letters. How he hated writing letters! 'Sir, –
Referring to your advertisement in the *Christian World*.' He
beheld an infinite vista of discomfort and disappointment, ending
– in a gulf.

He dressed, yawning, and went down to open the shop. He felt
tired before the day began. As he carried the shutters in, he kept
asking himself what good he was doing. The end was inevitable,
whether he bothered or not. The clear daylight smote into the
place, and showed how old and rough and splintered was
the floor, how shabby the second-hand counter, how hopeless the
whole enterprise. He had been dreaming these past six months of
a bright shop, of a happy couple, of a modest but comely profit
flowing in. He had suddenly awakened from his dream. The braid
that bound his decent black coat – it was a trifle loose – caught
against the catch of the shop door, and was torn away. This
suddenly turned his wretchedness to wrath. He stood quivering
for a moment, then, with a spiteful clutch, tore the braid looser,
and went in to Minnie.

'Here,' he said, with infinite reproach; 'look here! You might
look after a chap a bit.'

'I didn't see it was torn,' said Minnie.

'You never do,' said Winslow, with gross injustice, 'until things
are too late.'

Minnie looked suddenly at his face. 'I'll sew it now, Sid, if you
like.'

'Let's have breakfast first,' said Winslow, 'and do things at
their proper time.'

He was preoccupied at breakfast, and Minnie watched him
anxiously. His only remark was to declare his egg a bad one. It
wasn't; it was flavoury, – being one of those at fifteen a shilling, –
but quite nice. He pushed it away from him, and then, having

eaten a slice of bread and butter, admitted himself in the wrong by resuming the egg.

'Sid,' said Minnie, as he stood up to go into the shop again, 'you're not well.'

'I'm *well* enough.' He looked at her as though he hated her.

'Then there's something else the matter. You aren't angry with me, Sid, are you, about that braid? *Do* tell me what's the matter. You were just like this at tea yesterday, and at supper-time. It wasn't the braid then.'

'And I'm likely to be.'

She looked interrogation. 'Oh, what *is* the matter?' she said.

It was too good a chance to miss, and he brought the evil news out with dramatic force. 'Matter?' he said. 'I done my best, and here we are. That's the matter! If I can't pay Helter, Skelter & Grab eighty pounds, this day three weeks' – Pause. 'We shall be sold up! Sold up! That's the matter, Min! SOLD UP!'

'Oh, Sid!' began Minnie.

He slammed the door. For the moment he felt relieved of at least half his misery. He began dusting boxes that did not require dusting, and then reblocked a cretonne already faultlessly blocked. He was in a state of grim wretchedness; a martyr under the harrow of fate. At anyrate, it should not be said he failed for want of industry. And how he had planned and contrived and worked! All to this end! He felt horrible doubts. Providence and Bandersnatch – surely they were incompatible! Perhaps he was being 'tried'? That sent him off upon a new tack, a very comforting one. The martyr pose, the gold-in-the-furnace attitude, lasted all the morning.

At dinner – 'potato pie' – he looked up suddenly, and saw Minnie's face regarding him. Pale she looked, and a little red about the eyes. Something caught him suddenly with a queer effect upon his throat. All his thoughts seemed to wheel round into quite a new direction.

He pushed back his plate and stared at her blankly. Then he got up, went round the table to her – she staring at him. He dropped on his knees beside her without a word. 'Oh, Minnie!' he said, and suddenly she knew it was peace, and put her arms about him, as he began to sob and weep.

He cried like a little boy, slobbering on her shoulder that he was a knave to have married her and brought her to this, that he hadn't the wits to be trusted with a penny, that it was all his fault, that he '*had* hoped *so*' – ending in a howl. And she, crying gently herself, patting his shoulders, said '*Ssh!*' softly to his noisy weeping, and so soothed the outbreak. Then suddenly the crazy bell upon the shop door began, and Winslow had to jump to his feet, and be a man again.

After that scene they 'talked it over' at tea, at supper, in bed, at every possible interval in between, solemnly – quite inconclusively – with set faces and eyes for the most part staring in front of them – and yet with a certain mutual comfort. 'What to do I don't know,' was Winslow's main proposition. Minnie tried to take a cheerful view of service – with a probable baby. But she found she needed all her courage. And her uncle would help her again, perhaps, just at the critical time. It didn't do for folks to be too proud. Besides, 'something might happen', a favourite formula with her.

One hopeful line was to anticipate a sudden afflux of customers. 'Perhaps,' said Minnie, 'you might get together fifty. They know you well enough to trust you a bit.' They debated that point. Once the possibility of Helter, Skelter, & Grab giving credit was admitted, it was pleasant to begin sweating the acceptable minimum. For some half-hour over tea the second day after Winslow's discoveries they were quite cheerful again, laughing even at their terrific fears. Even twenty pounds to go on with might be considered enough. Then in some mysterious way the pleasant prospect of Messrs Helter, Skelter, & Grab tempering the wind to the shorn retailer vanished – vanished absolutely, and Winslow found himself again in the pit of despair.

He began looking about at the furniture, and wondering idly what it would fetch. The chiffonier was good, anyhow, and there were Minnie's old plates that her mother used to have. Then he began to think of desperate expedients for putting off the evil day. He had heard somewhere of Bills of Sale – there was to his ears something comfortingly substantial in the phrase. Then, why not 'Go to the Money-Lenders'?

One cheering thing happened on Thursday afternoon a little girl came in with a pattern of 'print', and he was able to match it. He had not been able to match anything out of his meagre stock before. He went in and told Minnie. The incident is mentioned lest the reader should imagine it was uniform despair with him.

The next morning, and the next, after the discovery, Winslow opened shop late. When one has been awake most of the night, and has no hope, what *is* the good of getting up punctually? But as he went into the dark shop on Friday he saw something lying on the floor, something lit by the bright light that came under the ill-fitting door – a black oblong. He stooped and picked up an envelope with a deep mourning edge. It was addressed to his wife. Clearly a death in her family – perhaps her uncle. He knew the man too well to have expectations. And they would have to get mourning and go to the funeral. The brutal cruelty of people dying! He saw it all in a flash – he always visualised his thoughts. Black trousers to get, black crape, black gloves – none in stock – the railway fares, the shop closed for the day.

'I'm afraid there's bad news, Minnie,' he said.

She was kneeling before the fireplace, blowing the fire. She had her housemaid's gloves on and the old country sun-bonnet she wore of a morning, to keep the dust out of her hair. She turned, saw the envelope, gave a gasp, and pressed two bloodless lips together.

'I'm afraid it's uncle,' she said, holding the letter and staring with eyes wide open into Winslow's face. *'It's a strange hand!'*

'The postmark's Hull,' said Winslow.

'The postmark's Hull.'

Minnie opened the letter slowly, drew it out, hesitated, turned it over, saw the signature. 'It's Mr Speight!'

'What does he say?' said Winslow.

Minnie began to read. *'Oh!'* she screamed. She dropped the letter, collapsed into a crouching heap, her hands covering her eyes. Winslow snatched at it. 'A most terrible accident has occurred,' he read; 'Melchior's chimney fell down yesterday evening right on the top of your uncle's house, and every living soul was killed – your uncle, your cousin Mary, Will and Ned, and the girl – every one of them, and smashed – you would hardly know them. I'm writing to you to break the news before you see it in the papers' – The letter fluttered from Winslow's fingers. He put out his hand against the mantel to steady himself.

All of them dead! Then he saw, as in a vision, a row of seven cottages, each let at seven shillings a week, a timber yard, two villas, and the ruins – still marketable – of the avuncular residence. He tried to feel a sense of loss and could not. They were sure to have been left to Minnie's aunt. All dead! $7 \times 7 \times 52 \div 20$ began insensibly to work itself out in his mind, but discipline was ever weak in his mental arithmetic; figures kept moving from one line to another, like children playing at Widdy, Widdy Way. Was it two hundred pounds about – or one hundred pounds? Presently he picked up the letter again, and finished reading it. 'You being the next of kin,' said Mr Speight.

'How *awful*!' said Minnie in a horror-struck whisper, and looking up at last. Winslow stared back at her, shaking his head solemnly. There were a thousand things running through his mind, but none that, even to his dull sense, seemed appropriate as a remark. 'It was the Lord's will,' he said at last.

'It seems so very, very terrible,' said Minnie; 'auntie, dear auntie – Ted – poor, dear uncle' –

'It was the Lord's will, Minnie,' said Winslow, with infinite feeling. A long silence.

'Yes,' said Minnie, very slowly, staring thoughtfully at the crackling black paper in the grate. The fire had gone out. 'Yes, perhaps it was the Lord's will.'

They looked gravely at one another. Each would have been terribly shocked at any mention of the property by the other. She turned to the dark fire-place and began tearing up an old newspaper slowly. Whatever our losses may be, the world's work still waits for us. Winslow gave a deep sigh and walked in a hushed manner towards the front door. As he opened it, a flood of sunlight came streaming into the dark shadows of the closed shop. Bandersnatch, Helter, Skelter, & Grab, had vanished out of his mind like the mists before the rising sun.

Presently he was carrying in the shutters, and in the briskest way, the fire in the kitchen was crackling exhilaratingly, with a little saucepan walloping above it, for Minnie was boiling two eggs, – one for herself this morning, as well as one for him, – and Minnie herself was audible, laying breakfast with the greatest *éclat*. The blow was a sudden and terrible one – but it behoves us to face such things bravely in this sad, unaccountable world. It was quite midday before either of them mentioned the cottages.

Æpyornis Island

The man with the scarred face leant over the table and looked at my bundle.

'Orchids?' he asked.

'A few,' I said.

'Cypripediums,' he said.

'Chiefly,' said I.

'Anything new? I thought not. I did these islands twenty-five – twenty-seven years ago. If you find anything new here – well, it's brand new. I didn't leave much.'

'I'm not a collector,' said I.

'I was young then,' he went on. 'Lord! how I used to fly round.' He seemed to take my measure. 'I was in the East Indies two years, and in Brazil seven. Then I went to Madagascar.'

'I know a few explorers by name,' I said, anticipating a yarn. 'Whom did you collect for?'

'Dawson's. I wonder if you've heard the name of Butcher ever?'

'Butcher – Butcher?' The name seemed vaguely present in my memory; then I recalled *Butcher* v. *Dawson*. 'Why!' said I, 'you are the man who sued them for four years' salary – got cast away on a desert island ...'

'Your servant,' said the man with the scar, bowing. 'Funny case, wasn't it? Here was me, making a little fortune on that island, doing nothing for it neither, and them quite unable to give me notice. It often used to amuse me thinking over it while I was there. I did calculations of it – big – all over the blessed atoll in ornamental figuring.'

'How did it happen?' said I. 'I don't rightly remember the case.'

'Well.... You've heard of the Æpyornis?'

'Rather. Andrews was telling me of a new species he was working on only a month or so ago. Just before I sailed. They've got a thigh bone, it seems, nearly a yard long. Monster the thing must have been!'

'I believe you,' said the man with the scar. 'It *was* a monster.

Sindbad's roc was just a legend of 'em. But when did they find these bones?'

'Three or four years ago – '91, I fancy. Why?'

'Why? Because *I* found them – Lord! – it's nearly twenty years ago. If Dawson's hadn't been silly about that salary they might have made a perfect ring in 'em.... *I* couldn't help the infernal boat going adrift.'

He paused. 'I suppose it's the same place. A kind of swamp about ninety miles north of Antananarivo. Do you happen to know? You have to go to it along the coast by boats. You don't happen to remember, perhaps?'

'I don't. I fancy Andrews said something about a swamp.'

'It must be the same. It's on the east coast. And somehow there's something in the water that keeps things from decaying. Like creosote it smells. It reminded me of Trinidad. Did they get any more eggs? Some of the eggs I found were a foot-and-a-half long. The swamp goes circling round, you know, and cuts off this bit. It's mostly salt, too. Well.... What a time I had of it! I found the things quite by accident. We went for eggs, me and two native chaps, in one of those rum canoes all tied together, and found the bones at the same time. We had a tent and provisions for four days, and we pitched on one of the firmer places. To think of it brings that odd tarry smell back even now. It's funny work. You go probing into the mud with iron rods, you know. Usually the egg gets smashed. I wonder how long it is since these Æpyornises really lived. The missionaries say the natives have legends about when they were alive, but I never heard any such stories myself.* But certainly those eggs we got were as fresh as if they had been new laid. Fresh! Carrying them down to the boat one of my nigger chaps dropped one on a rock and it smashed. How I lammed into the beggar! But sweet it was, as if it was new laid, not even smelly, and its mother dead these four hundred years, perhaps. Said a centipede had bit him. However, I'm getting off the straight with the story. It had taken us all day to dig into the slush and get these eggs out unbroken, and we were all covered with beastly black mud, and naturally I was cross. So far as I knew they were the only eggs that have ever been got out

---

* No European is known to have seen a live Æpyornis, with the doubtful exception of Macer, who visited Madagascar in 1745. – H. G. W.

not even cracked. I went afterwards to see the ones they have at the Natural History Museum in London; all of them were cracked and just stuck together like a mosaic, and bits missing. Mine were perfect, and I meant to blow them when I got back. Naturally I was annoyed at the silly duffer dropping three hours' work just on account of a centipede. I hit him about rather.'

The man with the scar took out a clay pipe. I placed my pouch before him. He filled up absent-mindedly.

'How about the others? Did you get those home? I don't remember—'

'That's the queer part of the story. I had three others. Perfectly fresh eggs. Well, we put 'em in the boat, and then I went up to the tent to make some coffee, leaving my two heathens down by the beach – the one fooling about with his sting and the other helping him. It never occurred to me that the beggars would take advantage of the peculiar position I was in to pick a quarrel. But I suppose the centipede poison and the kicking I had given him had upset the one – he was always a cantankerous sort – and he persuaded the other.

'I remember I was sitting and smoking and boiling up the water over a spirit-lamp business I used to take on these expeditions. Incidentally I was admiring the swamp under the sunset. All black and blood-red it was, in streaks – a beautiful sight. And up beyond the land rose grey and hazy to the hills, and the sky behind them red, like a furnace mouth. And fifty yards behind the back of me was these blessed heathen – quite regardless of the tranquil air of things – plotting to cut off with the boat and leave me all alone with three days' provisions and a canvas tent, and nothing to drink whatsoever beyond a little keg of water. I heard a kind of yelp behind me, and there they were in this canoe affair – it wasn't properly a boat – and, perhaps, twenty yards from land. I realised what was up in a moment. My gun was in the tent, and, besides, I had no bullets – only duck shot. They knew that. But I had a little revolver in my pocket, and I pulled that out as I ran down to the beach.

'"Come back!"' says I, flourishing it.

'They jabbered something at me, and the man that broke the egg jeered. I aimed at the other – because he was unwounded and had the paddle, and I missed. They laughed. However, I wasn't beat. I knew I had to keep cool, and I tried him again and made him jump with the whang of it. He didn't laugh that time. The third time I got his head, and over he went, and the paddle with him. It was a precious lucky shot for a revolver. I reckon it was fifty yards. He went right under. I don't know if he was shot, or simply stunned and drowned. Then I began to shout to the other chap to come back, but he huddled up in the canoe and refused to answer. So I fired out my revolver at him and never got near him.

'I felt a precious fool, I can tell you. There I was on this rotten, black beach, flat swamp all behind me, and the flat sea, cold after the sun set, and just this black canoe drifting steadily out to sea. I tell you I damned Dawson's and Jamrach's and Museums and all the rest of it just to rights. I bawled to this nigger to come back, until my voice went up into a scream.

'There was nothing for it but to swim after him and take my luck with the sharks. So I opened my clasp-knife and put it in my mouth, and took off my clothes and waded in. As soon as I was in the water I lost sight of the canoe, but I aimed, as I judged, to head it off. I hoped the man in it was too bad to navigate it, and that it would keep on drifting in the same direction. Presently it came up over the horizon again to the south-westward about. The afterglow of sunset was well over now and the dim of night creeping up. The stars were coming through the blue. I swum like a champion, though my legs and arms were soon aching.

'However, I came up to him by the time the stars were fairly out. As it got darker I began to see all manner of glowing things in the water – phosphorescence, you know. At times it made me giddy. I hardly knew which was stars and which was phosphorescence, and whether I was swimming on my head or my heels. The canoe was as black as sin, and the ripple under the bows like liquid fire. I was naturally chary of clambering up into it. I was anxious to see what he was up to first. He seemed to be lying cuddled up in a lump in the bows, and the stern was all out of water. The thing kept turning round slowly as it drifted – kind of waltzing, don't you know. I went to the stern and pulled it down, expecting him to wake up. Then I began to clamber in with my knife in my hand, and ready for a rush. But he never stirred. So there I sat in the stern of the little canoe, drifting away over the calm phosphorescent sea, and with all the host of the stars above me, waiting for something to happen.

'After a long time I called him by name, but he never answered. I was too tired to take any risks by going along to him. So we sat there. I fancy I dozed once or twice. When the dawn came I saw he was as dead as a doornail and all puffed up and purple. My three eggs and the bones were lying in the middle of the canoe, and the keg of water and some coffee and biscuits wrapped in a Cape *Argus* by his feet, and a tin of methylated spirit underneath him. There was no paddle, nor, in fact, anything except the spirit-tin that I could use as one, so I settled to drift until I was picked up. I held an inquest on him, brought in a verdict against some snake, scorpion, or centipede unknown, and sent him overboard.

'After that I had a drink of water and a few biscuits, and took a look round. I suppose a man low down as I was don't see very far; leastways, Madagascar was clean out of sight, and any trace of land at all. I saw a sail going south-westward – looked like a schooner but her hull never came up. Presently the sun got high in the sky and began to beat down upon me. Lord! it pretty near made my brains boil. I tried dipping my head in the sea, but after a while my eye fell on the Cape *Argus*, and I lay down flat in the canoe and spread this over me. Wonderful things these newspapers! I never read one through thoroughly before, but it's odd what you get up to when you're alone, as I was. I suppose I read that blessed old Cape *Argus* twenty times. The pitch in the canoe simply reeked with the heat and rose up into big blisters.

'I drifted ten days,' said the man with the scar. 'It's a little thing in the telling, isn't it? Every day was like the last. Except in the morning and the evening I never kept a look-out even – the blaze was so infernal. I didn't see a sail after the first three days, and those I saw took no notice of me. About the sixth night a ship went by scarcely half a mile away from me, with all its lights ablaze and its ports open, looking like a big firefly. There was music aboard. I stood up and shouted and screamed at it. The second day I broached one of the Æpyornis eggs, scraped the shell away at the end bit by bit, and tried it, and I was glad to find it was good enough to eat. A bit flavoury – not bad, I mean – but with something of the taste of a duck's egg. There was a kind of circular patch, about six inches across, on one side of the yoke, and with streaks of blood and a white mark like a ladder in it that I thought queer, but I did not understand what this meant at the

time, and I wasn't inclined to be particular. The egg lasted me
three days, with biscuits and a drink of water. I chewed coffee
berries too – invigorating stuff. The second egg I opened about
the eighth day, and it scared me.'

The man with the scar paused. 'Yes,' he said, 'developing.'

'I daresay you find it hard to believe. *I* did, with the thing
before me. There the egg had been, sunk in that cold black mud,
perhaps three hundred years. But there was no mistaking it.
There was the – what is it? – embryo, with its big head and
curved back, and its heart beating under its throat, and the yolk
shrivelled up and great membranes spreading inside of the shell
and all over the yolk. Here was I hatching out the eggs of the
biggest of all extinct birds, in a little canoe in the midst of the
Indian Ocean. If old Dawson had known that! It was worth four
years' salary. What do *you* think?

'However, I had to eat that precious thing up, every bit of it,
before I sighted the reef, and some of the mouthfuls were beastly
unpleasant. I left the third one alone. I held it up to the light, but
the shell was too thick for me to get any notion of what might be
happening inside; and though I fancied I heard blood pulsing it
might have been the rustle in my own ears, like what you listen
to in a seashell.

'Then came the atoll. Came out of the sunrise, as it were,
suddenly, close up to me. I drifted straight towards it until I was
about half a mile from shore, not more, and then the current took
a turn, and I had to paddle as hard as I could with my hands and
bits of the Æpyornis shell to make the place. However, I got there.
It was just a common atoll about four miles round, with a few
trees growing and a spring in one place, and the lagoon full of
parrot-fish. I took the egg ashore and put it in a good place, well
above the tide lines and in the sun, to give it all the chance I
could, and pulled the canoe up safe, and loafed about prospec-
ting. It's rum how dull an atoll is. As soon as I had found a spring
all the interest seemed to vanish. When I was a kid I thought
nothing could be finer or more adventurous than the Robinson
Crusoe business, but that place was as monotonous as a book of
sermons. I went round finding eatable things and generally
thinking; but I tell you I was bored to death before the first day
was out. It shows my luck – the very day I landed the weather
changed. A thunderstorm went by to the north and flicked its

wing over the island, and in the night there came a drencher and
a howling wind slap over us. It wouldn't have taken much, you
know, to upset that canoe.

'I was sleeping under the canoe, and the egg was luckily
among the sand higher up the beach, and the first thing I
remember was a sound like a hundred pebbles hitting the boat at
once, and a rush of water over my body. I'd been dreaming of
Antananarivo, and I sat up and holloaed to Intoshi to ask her
what the devil was up, and clawed out at the chair where the
matches used to be. Then I remembered where I was. There were
phosphorescent waves rolling up as if they meant to eat me, and
all the rest of the night as black as pitch. The air was simply
yelling. The clouds seemed down on your head almost, and the
rain fell as if heaven was sinking and they were baling out the
waters above the firmament. One great roller came writhing at
me, like a fiery serpent, and I bolted. Then I thought of the canoe,
and ran down to it as the water went hissing back again; but the
thing had gone. I wondered about the egg then, and felt my way
to it. It was all right and well out of reach of the maddest waves,
so I sat down beside it and cuddled it for company. Lord! what a
night that was!

'The storm was over before the morning. There wasn't a rag of
cloud left in the sky when the dawn came, and all along the
beach there were bits of plank scattered – which was the
disarticulated skeleton, so to speak, of my canoe. However, that
gave me something to do, for, taking advantage of two of the
trees being together, I rigged up a kind of storm-shelter with
these vestiges. And that day the egg hatched.

'Hatched, sir, when my head was pillowed on it and I was
asleep. I heard a whack and felt a jar and sat up, and there was
the end of the egg pecked out and a rum little brown head
looking out at me. "Lord!" I said, "you're welcome"; and with a
little difficulty he came out.

'He was a nice friendly little chap at first, about the size of a
small hen – very much like most other young birds, only bigger.
His plumage was a dirty brown to begin with, with a sort of grey
scab that fell off it very soon, and scarcely feathers – a kind of
downy hair. I can hardly express how pleased I was to see him. I
tell you, Robinson Crusoe don't make near enough of his
loneliness. But here was interesting company. He looked at me

and winked his eye from the front backwards, like a hen, and gave a chirp and began to peck about at once, as though being hatched three hundred years too late was just nothing. "Glad to see you, Man Friday!" says I, for I had naturally settled he was to be called Man Friday if ever he was hatched, as soon as ever I found the egg in the canoe had developed. I was a bit anxious about his feed, so I gave him a lump of raw parrot-fish at once. He took it, and opened his beak for more. I was glad of that for, under the circumstances, if he'd been at all fanciful, I should have had to eat him after all.

'You'd be surprised what an interesting bird that Æpyornis chick was. He followed me about from the very beginning. He used to stand by me and watch while I fished in the lagoon, and go shares in anything I caught. And he was sensible, too. There were nasty green warty things, like pickled gherkins, used to lie about on the beach, and he tried one of these and it upset him. He never even looked at any of them again.

'And he grew. You could almost see him grow. And as I was never much of a society man, his quiet, friendly ways suited me to a T. For nearly two years we were as happy as we could be on that island. I had no business worries, for I knew my salary was mounting up at Dawson's. We would see a sail now and then, but nothing ever came near us. I amused myself, too, by decorating the island with designs worked in sea-urchins and fancy shells of various kinds. I put ÆPYORNIS ISLAND all round the place very nearly, in big letters, like what you see done with coloured stones at railway stations in the old country, and mathematical calculations and drawings of various sorts. And I used to lie watching the blessed bird stalking round and growing, growing; and think how I could make a living out of him by showing him about if I ever got taken off. After his first moult he began to get handsome, with a crest and a blue wattle, and a lot of green feathers at the behind of him. And then I used to puzzle whether Dawson's had any right to claim him or not. Stormy weather and in the rainy season we lay snug under the shelter I had made out of the old canoe, and I used to tell him lies about my friends at home. And after a storm we would go round the island together to see if there was any drift. It was a kind of idyll, you might say. If only I had had some tobacco it would have been simply just like heaven.

'It was about the end of the second year our little paradise went wrong. Friday was then about fourteen feet high to the bill of him, with a big, broad head like the end of a pickaxe, and two huge brown eyes with yellow rims, set together like a man's – not out of sight of each other like a hen's. His plumage was fine – none of the half-mourning style of your ostrich – more like a cassowary as far as colour and texture go. And then it was he began to cock his comb at me and give himself airs, and show signs of a nasty temper....

'At last came a time when my fishing had been rather unlucky, and he began to hang about me in a queer, meditative way. I thought he might have been eating sea-cucumbers or something, but it was really just discontent on his part. I was hungry too, and when at last I landed a fish I wanted it for myself. Tempers were short that morning on both sides. He pecked at it and grabbed it, and I gave him a whack on the head to make him leave go. And at that he went for me. Lord! ...

'He gave me this in the face.' The man indicated his scar. 'Then he kicked me. It was like a carthorse. I got up, and seeing he hadn't finished, I started off full tilt with my arms doubled up over my face. But he ran on those gawky legs of his faster than a racehorse, and kept landing out at me with sledgehammer kicks, and bringing his pickaxe down on the back of my head. I made for the lagoon, and went in up to my neck. He stopped at the water, for he hated getting his feet wet, and began to make a shindy, something like a peacock's, only hoarser. He started strutting up and down the beach. I'll admit I felt small to see this blessed fossil lording it there. And my head and face were all bleeding, and – well, my body just one jelly of bruises.

'I decided to swim across the lagoon and leave him alone for a bit, until the affair blew over. I shinned up the tallest palm-tree, and sat there thinking of it all. I don't suppose I ever felt so hurt by anything before or since. It was the brutal ingratitude of the creature. I'd been more than a brother to him. I'd hatched him, educated him. A great gawky, out-of-date bird! And me a human being – heir of the ages and all that.

'I thought after a time he'd begin to see things in that light himself, and feel a little sorry for his behaviour. I thought if I was to catch some nice little bits of fish, perhaps, and go to him presently in a casual kind of way, and offer them to him, he might do the sensible thing. It took me some time to learn how unforgiving and cantankerous an extinct bird can be. Malice!

'I won't tell you all the little devices I tried to get that bird round again. I simply can't. It makes my cheek burn with shame even now to think of the snubs and buffets I had from this infernal curiosity. I tried violence. I chucked lumps of coral at him from a safe distance, but he only swallowed them. I shied my open knife at him and almost lost it, though it was too big for him to swallow. I tried starving him out and struck fishing, but he took to picking along the beach at low water after worms, and rubbed along on that. Half my time I spent up to my neck in the lagoon, and the rest up the palm-trees. One of them was scarcely high enough, and when he caught me up it he had a regular Bank Holiday with the calves of my legs. It got unbearable. I don't know if you have ever tried sleeping up a palm-tree. It gave me the most horrible nightmares. Think of the shame of it, too! Here was this extinct animal mooning about my island like a sulky duke, and me not allowed to rest the sole of my foot on the place. I used to cry with weariness and vexation. I told him straight that I didn't mean to be chased about a desert island by any damned anachronisms. I told him to go and peck a navigator of his own age. But he only snapped his beak at me. Great ugly bird, all legs and neck!

'I shouldn't like to say how long that went on altogether. I'd have killed him sooner if I'd known how. However, I hit on a way of settling him at last. It is a South American dodge. I joined all my fishing-lines together with stems of seaweed and things, and made a stoutish string, perhaps twelve yards in length or more, and I fastened two lumps of coral rock to the ends of this. It took me some time to do, because every now and then I had to go into the lagoon or up a tree as the fancy took me. This I whirled rapidly round my head, and then let it go at him. The first time I missed, but the next time the string caught his legs beautifully, and wrapped round them again and again. Over he went. I threw it standing waist-deep in the lagoon, and as soon as he went down I was out of the water and sawing at his neck with my knife ...

'I don't like to think of that even now. I felt like a murderer while I did it, though my anger was hot against him. When I stood over him and saw him bleeding on the white sand, and his beautiful great legs and neck writhing in his last agony ... Pah!

'With that tragedy loneliness came upon me like a curse. Good Lord! you can't imagine how I missed that bird. I sat by his corpse and sorrowed over him, and shivered as I looked round the desolate, silent reef. I thought of what a jolly little bird he had been when he was hatched, and of a thousand pleasant tricks he had played before he went wrong. I thought if I'd only wounded him I might have nursed him round into a better understanding. If I'd had any means of digging into the coral rock I'd have buried him. I felt exactly as if he was human. As it was, I couldn't think of eating him, so I put him in the lagoon, and the little fishes picked him clean. I didn't even save the feathers. Then one day a chap cruising about in a yacht had a fancy to see if my atoll still existed.

'He didn't come a moment too soon, for I was about sick enough of the desolation of it, and only hesitating whether I should walk out into the sea and finish up the business that way, or fall back on the green things ...

'I sold the bones to a man named Winslow – a dealer near the British Museum, and he says he sold them to old Havers. It seems Havers didn't understand they were extra large, and it was only after his death they attracted attention. They called 'em Æpyornis – what was it?'

'*Æpyornis vastus*,' said I. 'It's funny, the very thing was mentioned to me by a friend of mine. When they found an Æpyornis, with a thigh a yard long, they thought they had reached the top of the scale, and called him *Æpyornis maximus*. Then some one turned up another thigh-bone four feet six or more, and that they called *Æpyornis Titan*. Then your *vastus* was found after old Havers died, in his collection, and then a *vastissimus* turned up.'

'Winslow was telling me as much,' said the man with the scar. 'If they get any more Æpyornises, he reckons some scientific swell will go and burst a blood-vessel. But it was a queer thing to happen to a man; wasn't it – altogether?'

The Sea Raiders

1

Until the extraordinary affair at Sidmouth, the peculiar species *Haploteuthis ferox* was known to science only generically, on the strength of a half-digested tentacle obtained near the Azores, and a decaying body pecked by birds and nibbled by fish, found early in 1896 by Mr Jennings, near Land's End.

In no department of zoological science, indeed, are we quite so much in the dark as with regard to the deep-sea cephalopods. A mere accident, for instance, it was that led to the Prince of Monaco's discovery of nearly a dozen new forms in the summer of 1895, a discovery in which the before-mentioned tentacle was included. It chanced that a cachalot was killed off Terceira by some sperm whalers, and in its last struggles charged almost to the Prince's yacht, missed it, rolled under, and died within twenty yards of his rudder. And in its agony it threw up a number of large objects, which the Prince, dimly perceiving they were strange and important, was, by a happy expedient, able to secure before they sank. He set his screws in motion, and kept them circling in the vortices thus created until a boat could be lowered. And these specimens were whole cephalopods and fragments of cephalopods, some of gigantic proportions, and almost all of them unknown to science!

It would seem, indeed, that these large and agile creatures, living in the middle depths of the sea, must, to a large extent, for ever remain unknown to us, since under water they are too nimble for nets, and it is only by such rare, unlooked-for accidents that specimens can be obtained. In the case of *Haploteuthis ferox*, for instance, we are still altogether ignorant of its habitat, as ignorant as we are of the breeding-ground of the herring or the sea-ways of the salmon. And zoologists are altogether at a loss to account for its sudden appearance on our coast. Possibly it was the stress of a hunger migration that drove it hither out of the deep. But it will be, perhaps, better to avoid necessarily inconclusive discussion, and to proceed at once with our narrative.

The first human being to set eyes upon a living *Haploteuthis* – the first human being to survive, that is, for there can be little doubt now that the wave of bathing fatalities and boating accidents that travelled along the coast of Cornwall and Devon in early May was due to this cause – was a retired tea-dealer of the name of Fison, who was stopping at a Sidmouth boarding-house. It was in the afternoon, and he was walking along the cliff path between Sidmouth and Ladram Bay. The cliffs in this direction are very high, but down the red face of them in one place a kind of ladder staircase has been made. He was near this when his attention was attracted by what at first he thought to be a cluster of birds struggling over a fragment of food that caught the sunlight, and glistened pinkish-white. The tide was right out, and this object was not only far below him, but remote across a broad waste of rock reefs covered with dark seaweed and interspersed with silvery shining tidal pools. And he was, moreover, dazzled by the brightness of the further water.

In a minute, regarding this again, he perceived that his judgment was in fault, for over this struggle circled a number of birds, jackdaws and gulls for the most part, the latter gleaming blindingly when the sunlight smote their wings, and they seemed minute in comparison with it. And his curiosity was, perhaps, aroused all the more strongly because of his first insufficient explanations.

As he had nothing better to do than amuse himself, he decided to make this object, whatever it was, the goal of his afternoon walk, instead of Ladram Bay, conceiving it might perhaps be a great fish of some sort, stranded by some chance, and flapping about in its distress. And so he hurried down the long steep ladder, stopping at intervals of thirty feet or so to take breath and scan the mysterious movement.

At the foot of the cliff he was, of course, nearer his object than he had been; but, on the other hand, it now came up against the incandescent sky, beneath the sun, so as to seem dark and indistinct. Whatever was pinkish of it was now hidden by a skerry of weedy boulders. But he perceived that it was made up of seven rounded bodies distinct or connected, and that the birds kept up a constant croaking and screaming but seemed afraid to approach it too closely.

Mr Fison, torn by curiosity, began picking his way across the wave-worn rocks, and finding the wet seaweed that covered them thickly rendered them extremely slippery, he stopped, removed his shoes and socks, and rolled his trousers above his knees. His object was, of course, merely to avoid stumbling into the rocky pools about him, and perhaps he was rather glad, as all men are, of an excuse to resume, even for a moment, the sensations of his boyhood. At any rate, it is to this, no doubt, that he owes his life.

He approached his mark with all the assurance which the absolute security of this country against all forms of animal life gives its inhabitants. The round bodies moved to and fro, but it was only when he surmounted the skerry of boulders I have mentioned that he realised the horrible nature of the discovery. It came upon him with some suddenness.

The rounded bodies fell apart as he came into sight over the ridge, and displayed the pinkish object to be the partially devoured body of a human being, but whether of a man or woman he was unable to say. And the rounded bodies were new and ghastly-looking creatures, in shape somewhat resembling an octopus, with huge and very long and flexible tentacles, coiled copiously on the ground. The skin had a glistening texture, unpleasant to see, like shiny leather. The downward bend of the tentacle-surrounded mouth, the curious excrescence at the bend, the tentacles, and the large intelligent eyes, gave the creatures a grotesque suggestion of a face. They were the size of a fair-sized swine about the body, and the tentacles seemed to him to be many feet in length. There were, he thinks, seven or eight at least of the creatures. Twenty yards beyond them, amid the surf of the now returning tide, two others were emerging from the sea.

Their bodies lay flatly on the rocks, and their eyes regarded him with evil interest; but it does not appear that Mr Fison was afraid, or that he realised that he was in any danger. Possibly his confidence is to be ascribed to the limpness of their attitudes. But he was horrified, of course, and intensely excited and indignant, at such revolting creatures preying upon human flesh. He thought they had chanced upon a drowned body. He shouted to them, with the idea of driving them off, and finding they did not budge, cast about him, picked up a big rounded lump of rock, and flung it at one.

And then, slowly uncoiling their tentacles, they all began moving towards him – creeping at first deliberately, and making a soft purring sound to each other.

In a moment Mr Fison realised that he was in danger. He shouted again, threw both his boots, and started off, with a leap, forthwith. Twenty yards off he stopped and faced about, judging them slow, and behold! the tentacles of their leader were already pouring over the rocky ridge on which he had just been standing!

At that he shouted again, but this time not threatening, but a cry of dismay, and began jumping, striding, slipping, wading across the uneven expanse between him and the beach. The tall red cliffs seemed suddenly at a vast distance, and he saw, as though they were creatures in another world, two minute workmen engaged in the repair of the ladder-way, and little suspecting the race for life that was beginning below them. At one time he could hear the creatures splashing in the pools not a dozen feet behind him, and once he slipped and almost fell.

They chased him to the very foot of the cliffs, and desisted only when he had been joined by the workmen at the foot of the ladder-way up the cliff. All three of the men pelted them with stones for a time, and then hurried to the cliff top and along the path towards Sidmouth, to secure assistance and a boat, and to rescue the desecrated body from the clutches of these abominable creatures.

2

And, as if he had not already been in sufficient peril that day, Mr Fison went with the boat to point out the exact spot of his adventure.

As the tide was down, it required a considerable detour to reach the spot, and when at last they came off the ladder-way, the mangled body had disappeared. The water was now running in, submerging first one slab of slimy rock and then another, and the four men in the boat – the workmen, that is, the boatman, and Mr Fison – now turned their attention from the bearings off shore to the water beneath the keel.

At first they could see little below them, save a dark jungle of laminaria, with an occasional darting fish. Their minds were set on adventure, and they expressed their disappointment freely. But presently they saw one of the monsters swimming through the water seaward, with a curious rolling motion that suggested to Mr Fison the spinning roll of a captive balloon. Almost immediately after, the waving streamers of laminaria were extraordinarily perturbed, parted for a moment, and three of these beasts became darkly visible, struggling for what was probably some fragment of the drowned man. In a moment the copious olive-green ribbons had poured again over this writhing group.

At that all four men, greatly excited, began beating the water with oars and shouting, and immediately they saw a tumultuous movement among the weeds. They desisted to see more clearly, and as soon as the water was smooth, they saw, as it seemed to them, the whole sea bottom among the weeds set with eyes.

'Ugly swine!' cried one of the men. 'Why, there's dozens!'

And forthwith the things began to rise through the water about them. Mr Fison has since described to the writer this startling eruption out of the waving laminaria meadows. To him it seemed to occupy a considerable time, but it is probable that really it was an affair of a few seconds only. For a time nothing but eyes, and then he speaks of tentacles streaming out and parting the weed fronds this way and that. Then these things, growing larger, until at last the bottom was hidden by their intercoiling forms, and the tips of tentacles rose darkly here and there into the air above the swell of the waters.

One came up boldly to the side of the boat, and clinging to this with three of its sucker-set tentacles, threw four others over the gunwale, as if with an intention either of oversetting the boat or of clambering into it. Mr Fison at once caught up the boat-hook, and, jabbing furiously at the soft tentacles, forced it to desist. He was struck in the back and almost pitched overboard by the boatman, who was using his oar to resist a similar attack on the other side of the boat. But the tentacles on either side at once relaxed their hold, slid out of sight, and splashed into the water.

'We'd better get out of this,' said Mr Fison, who was trembling violently. He went to the tiller, while the boatman and one of the workmen seated themselves and began rowing. The other workman stood up in the fore part of the boat, with the boat-hook, ready to strike any more tentacles that might appear. Nothing else seems to have been said. Mr Fison had expressed the common feeling beyond amendment. In a hushed, scared mood, with faces white and drawn, they set about escaping from the position into which they had so recklessly blundered.

But the oars had scarcely dropped into the water before dark, tapering, serpentine ropes had bound them, and were about the rudder; and creeping up the sides of the boat with a looping motion came the suckers again. The men gripped their oars and pulled, but it was like trying to move a boat in a floating raft of weeds. 'Help here!' cried the boatman, and Mr Fison and the second workman rushed to help lug at the oar.

Then the man with the boat-hook – his name was Ewan, or Ewen – sprang up with a curse and began striking downward over the side, as far as he could reach, at the bank of tentacles that now clustered along the boat's bottom. And, at the same time, the two rowers stood up to get a better purchase for the recovery of their oars. The boatman handed his to Mr Fison, who lugged desperately, and, meanwhile, the boatman opened a big clasp-knife, and leaning over the side of the boat, began hacking at the spiring arms upon the oar shaft.

Mr Fison, staggering with the quivering rocking of the boat, his teeth set, his breath coming short, and the veins starting on his hands as he pulled at his oar, suddenly cast his eyes seaward. And there, not fifty yards off, across the long rollers of the incoming tide, was a large boat standing in towards them, with three women and a little child in it. A boatman was rowing, and a little man in a pink-ribboned straw hat and whites stood in the stern hailing them. For a moment, of course, Mr Fison thought of help, and then he thought of the child. He abandoned his oar forthwith, threw up his arms in a frantic gesture, and screamed to the party in the boat to keep away 'for God's sake!' It says much for the modesty and courage of Mr Fison that he does not seem to be aware that there was any quality of heroism in his action at this juncture. The oar he had abandoned was at once drawn under, and presently reappeared floating about twenty yards away.

At the same moment Mr Fison felt the boat under him lurch violently, and a hoarse scream, a prolonged cry of terror from Hill, the boatman, caused him to forget the party of excursionists altogether. He turned, and saw Hill crouching by the forward row-lock, his face convulsed with terror, and his right arm over the side and drawn tightly down. He gave now a succession of short, sharp cries, 'Oh! oh! oh! – oh!' Mr Fison believes that he must have been hacking at the tentacles below the water-line, and have been grasped by them, but, of course, it is quite impossible to say now certainly what had happened. The boat was heeling over, so that the gunwale was within ten inches of the water, and both Ewan and the other labourer were striking down into the water, with oar and boat-hook, on either side of Hill's arm. Mr Fison instinctively placed himself to counterpoise them.

Then Hill, who was a burly, powerful man, made a strenuous effort, and rose almost to a standing position. He lifted his arm, indeed, clean out of the water. Hanging to it was a complicated tangle of brown ropes, and the eyes of one of the brutes that had hold of him, glaring straight and resolute, showed momentarily above the surface. The boat heeled more and more, and the green-brown water came pouring in a cascade over the side. Then Hill slipped and fell with his ribs across the side, and his arm and the mass of tentacles about it splashed back into the water. He rolled over; his boot kicked Mr Fison's knee as that gentleman rushed forward to seize him, and in another moment fresh tentacles had whipped about his waist and neck, and after a brief, convulsive struggle, in which the boat was nearly capsized, Hill was lugged overboard. The boat righted with a violent jerk that all but sent Mr Fison over the other side, and hid the struggle in the water from his eyes.

He stood staggering to recover his balance for a moment, and as he did so he became aware that the struggle and the inflowing tide had carried them close upon the weedy rocks again. Not four yards off a table of rock still rose in rhythmic movements above the in-wash of the tide. In a moment Mr Fison seized the oar from Ewan, gave one vigorous stroke, then dropping it, ran to the bows and leapt. He felt his feet slide over the rock, and, by a frantic effort, leapt again towards a further mass. He stumbled over this, came to his knees, and rose again.

'Look out!' cried someone, and a large drab body struck him. He was knocked flat into a tidal pool by one of the workmen, and as he went down he heard smothered, choking cries, that he believed at the time came from Hill. Then he found himself marvelling at the shrillness and variety of Hill's voice. Someone jumped over him, and a curving rush of foamy water poured over him, and passed. He scrambled to his feet dripping, and without looking seaward, ran as fast as his terror would let him shoreward. Before him, over the flat space of scattered rocks, stumbled the two workmen – one a dozen yards in front of the other.

He looked over his shoulder at last, and seeing that he was not pursued, faced about. He was astonished. From the moment of the rising of the cephalopods out of the water he had been acting too swiftly to fully comprehend his actions. Now it seemed to him as if he had suddenly jumped out of an evil dream.

For there were the sky, cloudless and blazing with the afternoon sun, the sea weltering under its pitiless brightness, the soft creamy foam of the breaking water, and the low, long, dark ridges of rock. The righted boat floated, rising and falling gently on the swell about a dozen yards from shore. Hill and the monsters, all the stress and tumult of that fierce fight for life, had vanished as though they had never been.

Mr Fison's heart was beating violently; he was throbbing to the finger-tips, and his breath came deep.

There was something missing. For some seconds he could not think clearly enough what this might be. Sun, sky, sea, rocks – what was it? Then he remembered the boat-load of excursionists. It had vanished. He wondered whether he had imagined it. He turned, and saw the two workmen standing side by side under the projecting masses of the tall pink cliffs. He hesitated whether he should make one last attempt to save the man Hill. His physical excitement seemed to desert him suddenly, and leave him aimless and helpless. He turned shoreward, stumbling and wading towards his two companions.

He looked back again, and there were now two boats floating, and the one farthest out at sea pitched clumsily, bottom upward.

3

So it was *Haploteuthis ferox* made its appearance upon the Devonshire coast. So far, this has been its most serious aggression. Mr Fison's account, taken together with the wave of boating and bathing casualties to which I have already alluded, and the absence of fish from the Cornish coasts that year, points clearly to a shoal of these voracious deep-sea monsters prowling slowly along the sub-tidal coast-line. Hunger migration, has, I know, been suggested as the force that drove them hither; but, for my own part, I prefer to believe the alternative theory of Hemsley. Hemsley holds that a pack or shoal of these creatures may have become enamoured of human flesh by the accident of a foundered ship sinking among them, and have wandered in search of it out of their accustomed zone; first waylaying and following ships, and so coming to our shores in the wake of the Atlantic traffic. But to discuss Hemsley's cogent and admirably-stated arguments would be out of place here.

It would seem that the appetites of the shoal were satisfied by the catch of eleven people – for, so far as can be ascertained, there were ten people in the second boat, and certainly these creatures gave no further signs of their presence off Sidmouth that day. The coast between Seaton and Budleigh Salterton was patrolled all that evening and night by four Preventive Service boats, the men in which were armed with harpoons and cutlasses, and as the evening advanced, a number of more or less similarly equipped expeditions, organised by private individuals, joined them. Mr Fison took no part in any of these expeditions.

About midnight excited hails were heard from a boat about a couple of miles out at sea to the south-east of Sidmouth, and a lantern was seen waving in a strange manner to and fro and up and down. The nearer boats at once hurried towards the alarm. The venturesome occupants of the boat – a seaman, a curate, and two schoolboys – had actually seen the monsters passing under their boat. The creatures, it seems, like most deep-sea organisms, were phosphorescent, and they had been floating, five fathoms deep or so, like creatures of moonshine through the blackness of the water, their tentacles retracted and as if asleep, rolling over and over, and moving slowly in a wedge-like formation towards the south-east.

These people told their story in gesticulated fragments, as first one boat drew alongside and then another. At last there was a little fleet of eight or nine boats collected together, and from them a tumult, like the chatter of a market-place, rose into the stillness of the night. There was little or no disposition to pursue the shoal, the people had neither weapons nor experience for such a dubious chase, and presently – even with a certain relief, it may be – the boats turned shoreward.

And now to tell what is perhaps the most astonishing fact in this whole astonishing raid. We have not the slightest knowledge of the subsequent movements of the shoal, although the whole south-west coast was now alert for it. But it may, perhaps, be significant that a cachalot was stranded off Sark on June 3. Two weeks and three days after this Sidmouth affair, a living *Haploteuthis* came ashore on Calais sands. It was alive, because several witnesses saw its tentacles moving in a convulsive way. But it is probable that it was dying. A gentleman named Pouchet obtained a rifle and shot it.

That was the last appearance of a living *Haploteuthis*. No others were seen on the French coast. On the 15th of June a dead carcass, almost complete, was washed ashore near Torquay, and a few days later a boat from the Marine Biological station, engaged in dredging off Plymouth, picked up a rotting specimen, slashed deeply with a cutlass wound. How the former had come by its death it is impossible to say. And on the last day of June, Mr Egbert Caine, an artist, bathing near Newlyn, threw up his arms, shrieked, and was drawn under. A friend bathing with him made no attempt to save him, but swam at once for the shore. This is the last fact to tell of this extraordinary raid from the deeper sea. Whether it is really the last of these horrible creatures it is, as yet, premature to say. But it is believed, and certainly it is to be hoped, that they have returned now, and returned for good, to the sunless depths of the middle seas, out of which they have so strangely and so mysteriously arisen.

The Crystal Egg

There was, until a year ago, a little and very grimy-looking shop near Seven Dials, over which, in weather-worn yellow lettering, the name of 'C. Cave, Naturalist and Dealer in Antiquities', was inscribed. The contents of its window were curiously variegated. They comprised some elephant tusks and an imperfect set of chessmen, beads and weapons, a box of eyes, two skulls of tigers and one human, several moth-eaten stuffed monkeys (one holding a lamp), an old-fashioned cabinet, a fly-blown ostrich egg or so, some fishing-tackle, and an extraordinarily dirty, empty glass fish-tank. There was also, at the moment the story begins, a mass of crystal, worked into the shape of an egg and brilliantly polished. And at that two people who stood outside the window were looking, one of them a tall, thin clergyman, the other a black-bearded young man of dusky complexion and unobtrusive costume. The dusky young man spoke with eager gesticulation, and seemed anxious for his companion to purchase the article.

While they were there, Mr Cave came into his shop, his beard still wagging with the bread and butter of his tea. When he saw these men and the object of their regard, his countenance fell. He glanced guiltily over his shoulder, and softly shut the door. He was a little old man, with pale face and peculiar watery blue eyes; his hair was a dirty grey, and he wore a shabby blue frock-coat, an ancient silk hat, and carpet slippers very much down at heel. He remained watching the two men as they talked. The clergyman went deep into his trouser pocket, examined a handful of money, and showed his teeth in an agreeable smile. Mr Cave seemed still more depressed when they came into the shop.

The clergyman, without any ceremony, asked the price of the crystal egg. Mr Cave glanced nervously towards the door leading into the parlour, and said five pounds. The clergyman protested that the price was high, to his companion as well as to Mr Cave – it was, indeed, very much more than Mr Cave had intended to ask when he had stocked the article – and an attempt at bargaining ensued. Mr Cave stepped to the shop door, and held it open. 'Five pounds is my price,' he said, as though he wished to save himself the trouble of unprofitable discussion. As he did so, the upper portion of a woman's face appeared above the blind in the glass upper panel of the door leading into the parlour, and stared curiously at the two customers. 'Five pounds is my price,' said Mr Cave, with a quiver in his voice.

The swarthy young man had so far remained a spectator, watching Cave keenly. Now he spoke. 'Give him five pounds,' he said. The clergyman glanced at him to see if he were in earnest, and when he looked at Mr Cave again, he saw that the latter's face was white. 'It's a lot of money,' said the clergyman, and, diving into his pocket, began counting his resources. He had little more than thirty shillings, and he appealed to his companion, with whom he seemed to be on terms of considerable intimacy. This gave Mr Cave an opportunity of collecting his thoughts, and he began to explain in an agitated manner that the crystal was not, as a matter of fact, entirely free for sale. His two customers were naturally surprised at this, and inquired why he had not thought of that before he began to bargain. Mr Cave became confused, but he stuck to his story, that the crystal was not in the market that afternoon, that a probable purchaser of it had already appeared. The two, treating this as an attempt to raise the price still further, made as if they would leave the shop. But at this point the parlour door opened, and the owner of the dark fringe and the little eyes appeared.

She was a coarse-featured, corpulent woman, younger and very much larger than Mr Cave; she walked heavily and her face was flushed. 'That crystal *is* for sale,' she said. 'And five pounds is a good enough price for it. I can't think what you're about, Cave, not to take the gentleman's offer!'

Mr Cave, greatly perturbed by the irruption, looked angrily at her over the rims of his spectacles, and, without excessive assurance, asserted his right to manage his business in his own way. An altercation began. The two customers watched the scene with interest and some amusement, occasionally assisting Mrs Cave with suggestions. Mr Cave, hard driven, persisted in a confused and impossible story of an inquiry for the crystal that morning, and his agitation became painful. But he stuck to his point with extraordinary persistence. It was the young Oriental who ended this curious controversy. He proposed that they should call again in the course of two days – so as to give the alleged inquirer a fair chance. 'And then we must insist,' said the clergyman. 'Five pounds.' Mrs Cave took it on herself to apologise for her husband, explaining that he was sometimes 'a little odd', and as the two customers left, the couple prepared for a free discussion of the incident in all its bearings.

Mrs Cave talked to her husband with singular directness. The poor little man, quivering with emotion, muddled himself between his stories, maintaining on the one hand that he had another customer in view, and on the other asserting that the crystal was honestly worth ten guineas. 'Why did you ask five pounds?' said his wife. '*Do* let me manage my business my own way!' said Mr Cave.

Mr Cave had living with him a step-daughter and a step-son, and at supper that night the transaction was re-discussed. None of them had a high opinion of Mr Cave's business methods, and this action seemed a culminating folly.

'It's my opinion he's refused that crystal before,' said the step-son, a loose-limbed lout of eighteen.

'But *Five Pounds!*' said the step-daughter, an argumentative young woman of six-and-twenty.

Mr Cave's answers were wretched; he could only mumble weak assertions that he knew his own business best. They drove him from his half-eaten supper into the shop, to close it for the night, his ears aflame and tears of vexation behind his spectacles. Why had he left the crystal in the window so long? The folly of it! That was the trouble closest in his mind. For a time he could see no way of evading sale.

After supper his step-daughter and step-son smartened themselves up and went out and his wife retired upstairs to reflect upon the business aspects of the crystal, over a little sugar and lemon and so forth in hot water. Mr Cave went into the shop, and stayed there until late, ostensibly to make ornamental rockeries for gold-fish cases, but really for a private purpose that will be better explained later. The next day Mrs Cave found that the crystal had been removed from the window, and was lying behind some second-hand books on angling. She replaced it in a conspicuous position. But she did not argue further about it, as a nervous headache disinclined her from debate. Mr Cave was always disinclined. The day passed disagreeably. Mr Cave was, if anything, more absent-minded than usual, and uncommonly irritable withal. In the afternoon, when his wife was taking her customary sleep, he removed the crystal from the window again.

The next day Mr Cave had to deliver a consignment of dog-fish at one of the hospital schools, where they were needed for dissection. In his absence Mrs Cave's mind reverted to the topic of the crystal, and the methods of expenditure suitable to a windfall of five pounds. She had already devised some very agreeable expedients, among others a dress of green silk for herself and a trip to Richmond, when a jangling of the front door bell summoned her into the shop. The customer was an examination coach who came to complain of the non-delivery of certain frogs asked for the previous day. Mrs Cave did not approve of this particular branch of Mr Cave's business, and the gentleman, who had called in a somewhat aggressive mood, retired after a brief exchange of words – entirely civil, so far as he was concerned. Mrs Cave's eye then naturally turned to the window; for the sight of the crystal was an assurance of the five pounds and of her dreams. What was her surprise to find it gone!

She went to the place behind the locker on the counter, where she had discovered it the day before. It was not there; and she immediately began an eager search about the shop.

When Mr Cave returned from his business with the dog-fish, about a quarter to two in the afternoon, he found the shop in some confusion, and his wife, extremely exasperated and on her knees behind the counter, routing among his taxidermic material. Her face came up hot and angry over the counter, as the jangling bell announced his return, and she forthwith accused him of 'hiding it'.

'Hid *what?*' asked Mr Cave.

'The crystal!'

At that Mr Cave, apparently much surprised, rushed to the window. 'Isn't it here?' he said. 'Great Heavens! what has become of it?'

Just then Mr Cave's step-son re-entered the shop from the inner room – he had come home a minute or so before Mr Cave – and he was blaspheming freely. He was apprenticed to a second-hand furniture dealer down the road, but he had his meals at home, and he was naturally annoyed to find no dinner ready.

But when he heard of the loss of the crystal, he forgot his meal, and his anger was diverted from his mother to his step-father. Their first idea, of course, was that he had hidden it. But Mr Cave stoutly denied all knowledge of its fate, freely offering his bedabbled affidavit in the matter – and at last was worked up to the point of accusing, first, his wife and then his step-son of having taken it with a view to a private sale. So began an exceedingly acrimonious and emotional discussion, which ended for Mrs Cave in a peculiar nervous condition midway between hysterics and amuck, and caused the step-son to be half-an-hour late at the furniture establishment in the afternoon. Mr Cave took refuge from his wife's emotions in the shop.

In the evening the matter was resumed, with less passion and in a judicial spirit, under the presidency of the step-daughter. The supper passed unhappily and culminated in a painful scene. Mr Cave gave way at last to extreme exasperation, and went out banging the front door violently. The rest of the family, having discussed him with the freedom his absence warranted, hunted the house from garret to cellar, hoping to light upon the crystal.

The next day the two customers called again. They were received by Mrs Cave almost in tears. It transpired that no one *could* imagine all that she had stood from Cave at various times in her married pilgrimage.... She also gave a garbled account of the disappearance. The clergyman and the Oriental laughed silently at one another, and said it was very extraordinary. As Mrs Cave seemed disposed to give them the complete history of her life they made to leave the shop. Thereupon Mrs Cave, still clinging to hope, asked for the clergyman's address, so that, if she could get anything out of Cave, she might communicate it. The address was duly given, but apparently was afterwards mislaid. Mrs Cave can remember nothing about it.

In the evening of that day the Caves seem to have exhausted their emotions, and Mr Cave, who had been out in the afternoon, supped in a gloomy isolation that contrasted pleasantly with the impassioned controversy of the previous days. For some time matters were very badly strained in the Cave household, but neither crystal nor customer reappeared.

Now, without mincing the matter, we must admit that Mr Cave was a liar. He knew perfectly well where the crystal was. It was in the rooms of Mr Jacoby Wace, Assistant Demonstrator at St Catherine's Hospital, Westbourne Street. It stood on the sideboard partially covered by a black velvet cloth, and beside a decanter of American whisky. It is from Mr Wace, indeed, that the particulars upon which this narrative is based were derived. Cave had taken off the thing to the hospital hidden in the dog-fish sack, and there had pressed the young investigator to keep it for him. Mr Wace was a little dubious at first. His relationship to Cave was peculiar. He had a taste for singular characters, and he had more than once invited the old man to smoke and drink in his rooms, and to unfold his rather amusing views of life in general and of his wife in particular. Mr Wace had encountered Mrs Cave, too, on occasions when Mr Cave was not at home to attend to him. He knew the constant interference to which Cave was subjected, and having weighed the story judicially, he decided to give the crystal a refuge. Mr Cave promised to explain the reasons for his remarkable affection for the crystal more fully on a later occasion, but he spoke distinctly of seeing visions therein. He called on Mr Wace the same evening.

He told a complicated story. The crystal he said had come into his possession with other oddments at the forced sale of another curiosity dealer's effects, and not knowing what its value might be, he had ticketed it at ten shillings. It had hung upon his hands at that price for some months, and he was thinking of 'reducing the figure', when he made a singular discovery.

At that time his health was very bad – and it must be borne in mind that, throughout all this experience, his physical condition was one of ebb – and he was in considerable distress by reason of the negligence, the positive ill-treatment even, he received from his wife and step-children. His wife was vain, extravagant, unfeeling, and had a growing taste for private drinking; his step-daughter was mean and over-reaching; and his step-son had conceived a violent dislike for him, and lost no chance of showing it. The requirements of his business pressed heavily upon him, and Mr Wace does not think that he was altogether free from occasional intemperance. He had begun life in a comfortable position, he was a man of fair education, and he suffered, for weeks at a stretch, from melancholia and insomnia. Afraid to disturb his family, he would slip quietly from his wife's side, when his thoughts became intolerable, and wander about the house. And about three o'clock one morning, late in August, chance directed him into the shop.

The dirty little place was impenetrably black except in one spot, where he perceived an unusual glow of light. Approaching this, he discovered it to be the crystal egg, which was standing on the corner of the counter towards the window. A thin ray smote through a crack in the shutters, impinged upon the object, and seemed as it were to fill its entire interior.

It occurred to Mr Cave that this was not in accordance with the laws of optics as he had known them in his younger days. He could understand the rays being refracted by the crystal and coming to a focus in its interior, but this diffusion jarred with his physical conceptions. He approached the crystal nearly, peering into it and round it, with a transient revival of the scientific curiosity that in his youth had determined his choice of a calling. He was surprised to find the light not steady, but writhing within the substance of the egg, as though that object was a hollow sphere of some luminous vapour. In moving about to get different points of view, he suddenly found that he had come between it and the ray, and that the crystal none the less remained luminous. Greatly astonished, he lifted it out of the light ray and carried it to the darkest part of the shop. It remained bright for some four or five minutes, when it slowly faded and went out. He placed it in the thin streak of daylight, and its luminousness was almost immediately restored.

So far, at least, Mr Wace was able to verify the remarkable story of Mr Cave. He has himself repeatedly held this crystal in a ray of light (which had to be of a less diameter than one millimetre). And in a perfect darkness, such as could be produced by velvet wrapping, the crystal did undoubtedly appear very faintly phosphorescent. It would seem, however, that the luminousness was of some exceptional sort, and not equally visible to all eyes; for Mr Harbinger – whose name will be familiar to the scientific reader in connection with the Pasteur Institute – was quite unable to see any light whatever. And Mr Wace's own capacity for its appreciation was out of comparison inferior to that of Mr Cave's. Even with Mr Cave the power varied very considerably: his vision was most vivid during states of extreme weakness and fatigue.

Now, from the outset, this light in the crystal exercised a curious fascination upon Mr Cave. And it says more for his loneliness of soul than a volume of pathetic writing could do, that he told no human being of his curious observations. He seems to have been living in such an atmosphere of petty spite that to admit the existence of a pleasure would have been to risk the loss of it. He found that as the dawn advanced, and the amount of diffused light increased, the crystal became to all appearance non-luminous. And for some time he was unable to see anything in it, except at night-time, in dark corners of the shop.

But the use of an old velvet cloth, which he used as a background for a collection of minerals, occurred to him, and by doubling this, and putting it over his head and hands, he was able to get a sight of the luminous movement within the crystal even in the day-time. He was very cautious lest he should be thus discovered by his wife, and he practised this occupation only in the afternoons, while she was asleep upstairs, and then circum-spectly in a hollow under the counter. And one day, turning the crystal about in his hands, he saw something. It came and went like a flash, but it gave him the impression that the object had for a moment opened to him the view of a wide and spacious and strange country; and turning it about, he did, just as the light faded, see the same vision again.

Now it would be tedious and unnecessary to state all the phases of Mr Cave's discovery from this point. Suffice that the effect was this: the crystal, being peered into at an angle of about 137 degrees from the direction of the illuminating ray, gave a clear and consistent picture of a wide and peculiar country-side. It was not dreamlike at all: it produced a definite impression of reality, and the better the light the more real and solid it seemed. It was a moving picture: that is to say, certain objects moved in it, but slowly in an orderly manner like real things, and, according as the direction of the lighting and vision changed, the picture changed also. It must, indeed, have been like looking through an oval glass at a view, and turning the glass about to get at different aspects.

Mr Cave's statements, Mr Wace assures me, were extremely circumstantial, and entirely free from any of that emotional quality that taints hallucinatory impressions. But it must be remembered that all the efforts of Mr Wace to see any similar clarity in the faint opalescence of the crystal were wholly unsuccessful, try as he would. The difference in intensity of the impressions received by the two men was very great, and it is quite conceivable that what was a view to Mr Cave was a mere blurred nebulosity to Mr Wace.

The view, as Mr Cave described it, was invariably of an extensive plain, and he seemed always to be looking at it from a considerable height, as if from a tower or a mast. To the east and to the west the plain was bounded at a remote distance by vast reddish cliffs, which reminded him of those he had seen in some picture; but what the picture was Mr Wace was unable to ascertain. These cliffs passed north and south – he could tell the points of the compass by the stars that were visible of a night – receding in an almost illimitable perspective and fading into the mists of the distance before they met. He was nearer the eastern set of cliffs; on the occasion of his first vision the sun was rising over them, and black against the sunlight and pale against their shadow appeared a multitude of soaring forms that Mr Cave regarded as birds. A vast range of buildings spread below him; he seemed to be looking down upon them; and as they approached the blurred and refracted edge of the picture they became indistinct. There were also trees curious in shape, and in colouring a deep mossy green and an exquisite grey, beside a wide and shining canal. And something great and brilliantly coloured flew across the picture. But the first time Mr Cave saw these pictures he saw only in flashes, his hands shook, his head moved, the vision came and went, and grew foggy and indistinct. And at first he had the greatest difficulty in finding the picture again once the direction of it was lost.

His next clear vision, which came about a week after the first, the interval having yielded nothing but tantalising glimpses and some useful experience, showed him the view down the length of the valley. The view was different, but he had a curious persuasion, which his subsequent observations abundantly confirmed, that he was regarding the strange world from exactly the same spot, although he was looking in a different direction. The long façade of the great building, whose roof he had looked down upon before, was now receding in perspective. He recognised the roof. In the front of the façade was a terrace of massive proportions and extraordinary length, and down the middle of the terrace, at certain intervals, stood huge but very graceful masts, bearing small shiny objects which reflected the setting sun. The import of these small objects did not occur to Mr Cave until some time after, as he was describing the scene to Mr Wace. The terrace overhung a thicket of the most luxuriant and graceful vegetation, and beyond this was a wide grassy lawn on which certain broad creatures, in form like beetles but enormously larger, reposed. Beyond this again was a richly decorated causeway of pinkish stone; and beyond that, and lined with dense red weeds, and passing up the valley exactly parallel with the distant cliffs, was a broad and mirror-like expanse of water. The air seemed full of squadrons of great birds, manœuvring in stately curves; and across the river was a multitude of splendid buildings, richly coloured and glittering with metallic tracery and facets, among a forest of moss-like and lichenous trees. And suddenly something flapped repeatedly across the vision, like the fluttering of a jewelled fan or the beating of a wing, and a face, or rather the upper part of a face with very large eyes, came as it were close to his own and as if on the other side of the crystal. Mr Cave was so startled and so impressed by the absolute reality of these eyes that he drew his head back from the crystal to look behind it. He had become so absorbed in watching that he was quite surprised to find himself in the cool darkness of his little shop, with its familiar odour of methyl, mustiness, and decay. And, as he blinked about him, the glowing crystal faded and went out.

Such were the first general impressions of Mr Cave. The story is curiously direct and circumstantial. From the outset, when the valley first flashed momentarily on his senses, his imagination was strangely affected, and as he began to appreciate the details of the scene he saw, his wonder rose to the point of a passion. He went about his business listless and distraught, thinking only of the time when he should be able to return to his watching. And then a few weeks after his first sight of the valley came the two customers, the stress and excitement of their offer, and the narrow escape of the crystal from sale, as I have already told.

Now, while the thing was Mr Cave's secret, it remained a mere wonder, a thing to creep to covertly and peep at, as a child might peep upon a forbidden garden. But Mr Wace has, for a young scientific investigator, a particularly lucid and consecutive habit of mind. Directly the crystal and its story came to him, and he had satisfied himself, by seeing the phosphorescence with his own eyes, that there really was a certain evidence for Mr Cave's statements, he proceeded to develop the matter systematically. Mr Cave was only too eager to come and feast his eyes on this wonderland he saw, and he came every night from half-past eight until half-past ten, and sometimes, in Mr Wace's absence, during the day. On Sunday afternoons, also, he came. From the outset Mr Wace made copious notes, and it was due to his scientific method that the relation between the direction from which the initiating ray entered the crystal and the orientation of the picture were proved. And, by covering the crystal in a box perforated only with a small aperture to admit the exciting ray, and by substituting black holland for his buff blinds, he greatly improved the conditions of the observations; so that in a little while they were able to survey the valley in any direction they desired.

So having cleared the way, we may give a brief account of this visionary world within the crystal. The things were in all cases seen by Mr Cave, and the method of working was invariably for him to watch the crystal and report what he saw, while Mr Wace (who as a science student had learnt the trick of writing in the dark) wrote a brief note of his report. When the crystal faded, it was put into its box in the proper position and the electric light turned on. Mr Wace asked questions, and suggested observations to clear up difficult points. Nothing, indeed, could have been less visionary and more matter-of-fact.

The attention of Mr Cave had been speedily directed to the bird-like creatures he had seen so abundantly present in each of his earlier visions. His first impression was soon corrected, and he considered for a time that they might represent a diurnal species of bat. Then he thought, grotesquely enough, that they might be cherubs. Their heads were round and curiously human, and it was the eyes of one of them that had so startled him on his second observation. They had broad, silvery wings, not feathered, but glistening almost as brilliantly as new-killed fish and with the same subtle play of colour, and these wings were not built on the plan of bird-wing or bat, Mr Wace learned, but supported by curved ribs radiating from the body. (A sort of butterfly wing with curved ribs seems best to express their appearance.) The body was small, but fitted with two bunches of prehensile organs, like long tentacles, immediately under the mouth. Incredible as it appeared to Mr Wace, the persuasion at last became irresistible that it was these creatures which owned the great quasi-human buildings and the magnificent garden that made the broad valley so splendid. And Mr Cave perceived that the buildings, with other peculiarities, had no doors, but that the great circular windows, which opened freely, gave the creatures egress and entrance. They would alight upon their tentacles, fold their wings to a smallness almost rod-like, and hop into the interior. But among them was a multitude of smaller-winged creatures, like great dragon-flies and moths and flying beetles, and across the greensward brilliantly-coloured gigantic ground-beetles crawled lazily to and fro. Moreover, on the causeways and terraces, large-headed creatures similar to the greater winged flies, but wingless, were visible, hopping busily upon their hand-like tangle of tentacles.

Allusion has already been made to the glittering objects upon masts that stood upon the terrace of the nearer building. It dawned upon Mr Cave, after regarding one of these masts very fixedly on one particularly vivid day that the glittering object there was a crystal exactly like that into which he peered. And a still more careful scrutiny convinced him that each one in a vista of nearly twenty carried a similar object.

Occasionally one of the large flying creatures would flutter up to one, and folding its wings and coiling a number of its tentacles about the mast, would regard the crystal fixedly for a space, – sometimes for as long as fifteen minutes. And a series of observations, made at the suggestion of Mr Wace, convinced both watchers that, so far as this visionary world was concerned, the crystal into which they peered actually stood at the summit of the end-most mast on the terrace, and that on one occasion at least one of these inhabitants of this other world had looked into Mr Cave's face while he was making these observations.

So much for the essential facts of this very singular story. Unless we dismiss it all as the ingenious fabrication of Mr Wace, we have to believe one of two things: either that Mr Cave's crystal was in two worlds at once, and that while it was carried about in one, it remained stationary in the other, which seems altogether absurd; or else that it had some peculiar relation of sympathy with another and exactly similar crystal in this other world, so that what was seen in the interior of the one in this world was, under suitable conditions, visible to an observer in the corresponding crystal in the other world; and *vice versa*. At present, indeed, we do not know of any way in which two crystals could so come *en rapport*, but nowadays we know enough to understand that the thing is not altogether impossible. This view of the crystals as *en rapport* was the supposition that occurred to Mr Wace, and to me at least it seems extremely plausible....

And where was this other world? On this, also, the alert intelligence of Mr Wace speedily threw light. After sunset, the sky darkened rapidly – there was a very brief twilight interval indeed – and the stars shone out. They were recognisably the same as those we see, arranged in the same constellations. Mr Cave recognised the Bear, the Pleiades, Aldebaran, and Sirius; so that the other world must be somewhere in the solar system, and, at the utmost, only a few hundreds of millions of miles from our own. Following up this clue, Mr Wace learned that the midnight sky was a darker blue even than our midwinter sky, and that the sun seemed a little smaller. *And there were two small moons!* 'like our moon but smaller, and quite differently marked', one of which moved so rapidly that its motion was clearly visible as one regarded it. These moons were never high in the sky, but vanished as they rose: that is, every time they revolved they were eclipsed because they were so near their primary planet. And all this answers quite completely, although Mr Cave did not know it, to what must be the condition of things on Mars.

Indeed, it seems an exceedingly plausible conclusion that peering into this crystal Mr Cave did actually see the planet Mars and its inhabitants. And if that be the case, then the evening star that shone so brilliantly in the sky of that distant vision was neither more nor less than our own familiar earth.

For a time the Martians – if they were Martians – do not seem to have known of Mr Cave's inspection. Once or twice one would come to peer, and go away very shortly to some other mast, as though the vision was unsatisfactory. During this time Mr Cave was able to watch the proceedings of these winged people without being disturbed by their attentions, and although his report is necessarily vague and fragmentary, it is nevertheless very suggestive. Imagine the impression of humanity a Martian observer would get who, after a difficult process of preparation and with considerable fatigue to the eyes, was able to peer at

London from the steeple of St Martin's Church for stretches, at longest, of four minutes at a time. Mr Cave was unable to ascertain if the winged Martians were the same as the Martians who hopped about the causeways and terraces, and if the latter could put on wings at will. He several times saw certain clumsy bipeds, dimly suggestive of apes, white and partially translucent, feeding among certain of the lichenous trees, and once some of these fled before one of the hopping, round-headed Martians. The latter caught one in its tentacles, and then the picture faded suddenly and left Mr Cave most tantalisingly in the dark. On another occasion a vast thing, that Mr Cave thought at first was some gigantic insect, appeared advancing along the causeway beside the canal with extraordinary rapidity. As this drew nearer Mr Cave perceived that it was a mechanism of shining metals and of extraordinary complexity. And then, when he looked again, it had passed out of sight.

After a time Mr Wace aspired to attract the attention of the Martians, and the next time that the strange eyes of one of them appeared close to the crystal Mr Cave cried out and sprang away, and they immediately turned on the light and began to gesticulate in a manner suggestive of signalling. But when at last Mr Cave examined the crystal again the Martian had departed.

Thus far these observations had progressed in early November, and then Mr Cave, feeling that the suspicions of his family about the crystal were allayed, began to take it to and fro with him in order that, as occasion arose in the daytime or night, he might comfort himself with what was fast becoming the most real thing in his existence.

In December Mr Wace's work in connection with a forthcoming examination became heavy, the sittings were reluctantly suspended for a week, and for ten or eleven days – he is not quite sure which – he saw nothing of Cave. He then grew anxious to resume these investigations, and, the stress of his seasonal labours being abated, he went down to Seven Dials. At the corner he noticed a shutter before a bird fancier's window, and then another at a cobbler's. Mr Cave's shop was closed.

He rapped and the door was opened by the step-son in black. He at once called Mrs Cave, who was, Mr Wace could not but observe, in cheap but ample widow's weeds of the most imposing pattern. Without any very great surprise Mr Wace learnt that

Cave was dead and already buried. She was in tears, and her voice was a little thick. She had just returned from Highgate. Her mind seemed occupied with her own prospects and the honourable details of the obsequies, but Mr Wace was at last able to learn the particulars of Cave's death. He had been found dead in his shop in the early morning, the day after his last visit to Mr Wace, and the crystal had been clasped in his stone-cold hands. His face was smiling, said Mrs Cave, and the velvet cloth from the minerals lay on the floor at his feet. He must have been dead five or six hours when he was found.

This came as a great shock to Wace, and he began to reproach himself bitterly for having neglected the plain symptoms of the old man's ill-health. But his chief thought was of the crystal. He approached that topic in a gingerly manner, because he knew Mrs Cave's peculiarities. He was dumfounded to learn that it was sold.

Mrs Cave's first impulse, directly Cave's body had been taken upstairs, had been to write to the mad clergyman who had offered five pounds for the crystal, informing him of its recovery; but after a violent hunt, in which her daughter joined her, they were convinced of the loss of his address. As they were without the means required to mourn and bury Cave in the elaborate style the dignity of an old Seven Dials inhabitant demands, they had appealed to a friendly fellow-tradesman in Great Portland Street. He had very kindly taken over a portion of the stock at a valuation. The valuation was his own, and the crystal egg was included in one of the lots. Mr Wace, after a few suitable condolences, a little off-handedly proffered perhaps, hurried at once to Great Portland Street. But there he learned that the crystal egg had already been sold to a tall, dark man in grey. And there the material facts in this curious, and to me at least very suggestive, story come abruptly to an end. The Great Portland Street dealer did not know who the tall dark man in grey was, nor had he observed him with sufficient attention to describe him minutely. He did not even know which way this person had gone after leaving the shop. For a time Mr Wace remained in the shop, trying the dealer's patience with hopeless questions, venting his own exasperation. And at last, realising abruptly that the whole thing had passed out of his hands, had vanished like a vision of the night, he returned to his own rooms, a little astonished to find the notes he had made still tangible and visible upon his untidy table.

His annoyance and disappointment were naturally very great. He made a second call (equally ineffectual) upon the Great Portland Street dealer, and he resorted to advertisements in such periodicals as were likely to come into the hands of a *bric-a-brac* collector. He also wrote letters to *The Daily Chronicle* and *Nature*, but both those periodicals, suspecting a hoax, asked him to reconsider his action before they printed, and he was advised that such a strange story, unfortunately so bare of supporting evidence, might imperil his reputation as an investigator. Moreover, the calls of his proper work were urgent. So that after a month or so, save for an occasional reminder to certain dealers, he had reluctantly to abandon the quest for the crystal egg, and from that day to this it remains undiscovered. Occasionally, however, he tells me, and I can quite believe him, he has bursts of zeal, in which he abandons his more urgent occupation and resumes the search.

Whether or not it will remain lost for ever, with the material and origin of it, are things equally speculative at the present time. If the present purchaser is a collector, one would have expected the enquiries of Mr Wace to have reached him through the dealers. He has been able to discover Mr Cave's clergyman and 'Oriental' – no other than the Rev. James Parker and the young Prince of Bosso-Kuni in Java. I am obliged to them for certain particulars. The object of the Prince was simply curiosity – and extravagance. He was so eager to buy because Cave was so oddly reluctant to sell. It is just as possible that the buyer in the second instance was simply a casual purchaser and not a collector at all, and the crystal egg, for all I know, may at the present moment be within a mile of me, decorating a drawing-room or serving as a paper-weight – its remarkable functions all unknown. Indeed, it is partly with the idea of such a possibility that I have thrown this narrative into a form that will give it a chance of being read by the ordinary consumer of fiction.

My own ideas in the matter are practically identical with those of Mr Wace. I believe the crystal on the mast in Mars and the crystal egg of Mr Cave's to be in some physical, but at present quite inexplicable, way *en rapport*, and we both believe further that the terrestrial crystal must have been – possibly at some remote date – sent hither from that planet, in order to give the Martians a near view of our affairs. Possibly the fellows to the crystals on the other masts are also on our globe. No theory of hallucination suffices for the facts.

Under the Knife

'What if I die under it?' The thought recurred again and again, as I walked home from Haddon's. It was a purely personal question. I was spared the deep anxieties of a married man, and I knew there were few of my intimate friends but would find my death troublesome chiefly on account of their duty of regret. I was surprised indeed, and perhaps a little humiliated, as I turned the matter over, to think how few could possibly exceed the conventional requirement. Things came before me stripped of glamour, in a clear dry light, during that walk from Haddon's house over Primrose Hill. There were the friends of my youth: I perceived now that our affection was a tradition, which we foregathered rather laboriously to maintain. There were the rivals and helpers of my later career: I suppose I had been cold-blooded or undemonstrative – one perhaps implies the other. It may be that even the capacity for friendship is a question of physique. There had been a time in my own life when I had grieved bitterly enough at the loss of a friend; but as I walked home that afternoon the emotional side of my imagination was dormant. I could not pity myself, nor feel sorry for my friends, nor conceive of them as grieving for me.

I was interested in this deadness of my emotional nature – no doubt a concomitant of my stagnating physiology; and my thoughts wandered off along the line it suggested. Once before, in my hot youth, I had suffered a sudden loss of blood, and had been within an ace of death. I remembered now that my affections as well as my passions had drained out of me, leaving scarce anything but a tranquil resignation, a dreg of self-pity. It had been weeks before the old ambitions and tendernesses and all the complex moral interplay of a man had reasserted themselves. It occurred to me that the real meaning of this numbness might be a gradual slipping away from the pleasure-pain guidance of the animal man. It has been proven, I take it, as thoroughly as anything can be proven in this world, that the higher emotions, the moral feelings, even the subtle unselfishness of love, are evolved from the elemental desires and fears of the simple animal: they are the harness in which man's mental freedom goes. And it may be that as death overshadows us, as our possibility of acting diminishes, this complex growth of balanced impulse, propensity and aversion, whose interplay inspires our acts, goes with it. Leaving what?

I was suddenly brought back to reality by an imminent collision with the butcher-boy's tray. I found that I was crossing the bridge over the Regent's Park Canal, which runs parallel with that in the Zoological Gardens. The boy in blue had been looking over his shoulder at a black barge advancing slowly, towed by a gaunt white horse. In the Gardens a nurse was leading three happy little children over the bridge. The trees were bright green; the spring hopefulness was still unstained by the dusts of summer; the sky in the water was bright and clear, but broken by long waves, by quivering bands of black, as the barge drove through. The breeze was stirring; but it did not stir me as the spring breeze used to do.

Was this dulness of feeling in itself an anticipation? It was curious that I could reason and follow out a network of suggestion as clearly as ever: so, at least, it seemed to me. It was calmness rather than dulness that was coming upon me. Was there any ground for the belief in the presentiment of death? Did a man near to death begin instinctively to withdraw himself from the meshes of matter and sense, even before the cold hand was laid upon his? I felt strangely isolated – isolated without regret – from the life and existence about me. The children playing in the sun and gathering strength and experience for the business of life, the park-keeper gossiping with a nursemaid, the nursing mother, the young couple intent upon each other as they passed me, the trees by the wayside spreading new pleading leaves to the sunlight, the stir in their branches – I had been part of it all, but I had nearly done with it now.

Some way down the Broad Walk I perceived that I was tired, and that my feet were heavy. It was hot that afternoon, and I turned aside and sat down on one of the green chairs that line the way. In a minute I had dozed into a dream, and the tide of my thoughts washed up a vision of the resurrection. I was still sitting in the chair, but I thought myself actually dead, withered, tattered, dried, one eye (I saw) pecked out by birds. 'Awake!' cried a voice; and incontinently the dust of the path and the mould under the grass became insurgent. I had never before thought of Regent's Park as a cemetery, but now, through the trees, stretching as far as eye could see, I beheld a flat plain of writhing graves and heeling tombstones. There seemed to be some trouble: the rising dead appeared to stifle as they struggled upward, they bled in their struggles, the red flesh was torn away from the white bones. 'Awake!' cried a voice; but I determined I would not rise to such horrors. 'Awake!' They would not let me alone. 'Wike up!' said an angry voice. A cockney angel! The man who sells the tickets was shaking me, demanding my penny.

I paid my penny, pocketed my ticket, yawned, stretched my legs, and, feeling now rather less torpid, got up and walked on towards Langham Place. I speedily lost myself again in a shifting maze of thoughts about death. Going across Marylebone Road into that crescent at the end of Langham Place, I had the narrowest escape from the shaft of a cab, and went on my way with a palpitating heart and a bruised shoulder. It struck me that it would have been curious if my meditations on my death on the morrow had led to my death that day.

But I will not weary you with more of my experiences that day and the next. I knew more and more certainly that I should die under the operation; at times I think I was inclined to pose to myself. The doctors were coming at eleven, and I did not get up. It seemed scarce worth while to trouble about washing and dressing, and though I read my newspapers and the letters that came by the first post, I did not find them very interesting. There was a friendly note from Addison, my old schoolfriend, calling my attention to two discrepancies and a printer's error in my new book, with one from Langridge venting some vexation over Minton. The rest were business communications. I breakfasted in bed. The glow of pain at my side seemed more massive. I knew it was pain, and yet, if you can understand, I did not find it very painful. I had been awake and hot and thirsty in the night, but in the morning bed felt comfortable. In the night-time I had lain thinking of things that were past; in the morning I dozed over the question of immortality. Haddon came, punctual to the minute, with a neat black bag; and Mowbray soon followed. Their arrival stirred me up a little. I began to take a more personal interest in the proceedings. Haddon moved the little octagonal table close to the bedside, and, with his broad back to me, began taking things out of his bag. I heard the light click of steel upon steel. My imagination, I found, was not altogether stagnant. 'Will you hurt me much?' I said in an off-hand tone.

'Not a bit,' Haddon answered over his shoulder. 'We shall chloroform you. Your heart's as sound as a bell.' And as he spoke, I had a whiff of the pungent sweetness of the anæsthetic.

They stretched me out, with a convenient exposure of my side, and, almost before I realised what was happening, the chloroform was being administered. It stings the nostrils, and there is a suffocating sensation at first. I knew I should die – that this was the end of consciousness for me. And suddenly I felt that I was not prepared for death: I had a vague sense of a duty overlooked – I knew not what. What was it I had not done? I could think of nothing more to do, nothing desirable left in life; and yet I had the strangest disinclination for death. And the physical sensation was painfully oppressive. Of course the doctors did not know they were going to kill me. Possibly I struggled. Then I fell motionless, and a great silence, a monstrous silence, and an impenetrable blackness came upon me.

There must have been an interval of absolute unconsciousness, seconds or minutes. Then with a chilly, unemotional clearness, I perceived that I was not yet dead. I was still in my body; but all the multitudinous sensations that come sweeping from it to make up the background of consciousness had gone, leaving me free of it all. No, not free of it all; for as yet something still held me to the poor stark flesh upon the bed – held me, yet not so closely that I did not feel myself external to it, independent of it, straining away from it. I do not think I saw, I do not think I heard; but I perceived all that was going on, and it was as if I both heard and saw. Haddon was bending over me, Mowbray behind me; the scalpel – it was a large scalpel – was cutting my flesh at the side under the flying ribs. It was interesting to see myself cut like cheese, without a pang, without even a qualm. The interest was much of a quality with that one might feel in a game of chess between strangers. Haddon's face was firm and his hand steady; but I was surprised to perceive (*how* I know not) that he was feeling the gravest doubt as to his own wisdom in the conduct of the operation.

Mowbray's thoughts, too, I could see. He was thinking that

Haddon's manner showed too much of the specialist. New suggestions came up like bubbles through a stream of frothing meditation, and burst one after another in the little bright spot of his consciousness. He could not help noticing and admiring Haddon's swift dexterity, in spite of his envious quality and his disposition to detract. I saw my liver exposed. I was puzzled at my own condition. I did not feel that I was dead, but I was different in some way from my living self. The grey depression, that had weighed on me for a year or more and coloured all my thoughts, was gone. I perceived and thought without any emotional tint at all. I wondered if everyone perceived things in this way under chloroform, and forgot it again when he came out of it. It would be inconvenient to look into some heads, and not forget.

Although I did not think that I was dead, I still perceived quite clearly that I was soon to die. This brought me back to the consideration of Haddon's proceedings. I looked into his mind, and saw that he was afraid of cutting a branch of the portal vein. My attention was distracted from details by the curious changes going on in his mind. His consciousness was like the quivering little spot of light which is thrown by the mirror of a galvanometer. His thoughts ran under it like a stream, some through the focus bright and distinct, some shadowy in the half-light of the edge. Just now the little glow was steady; but the least movement on Mowbray's part, the slightest sound from outside, even a faint difference in the slow movement of the living flesh he was cutting, set the light-spot shivering and spinning. A new sense-impression came rushing up through the flow of thoughts; and lo! the light-spot jerked away towards it, swifter than a frightened fish. It was wonderful to think that upon that unstable, fitful thing depended all the complex motions of the man; that for the next five minutes, therefore, my life hung upon its movements. And he was growing more and more nervous in his work. It was as if a little picture of a cut vein grew brighter, and struggled to oust from his brain another picture of a cut falling short of the mark. He was afraid: his dread of cutting too little was battling with his dread of cutting too far.

Then, suddenly, like an escape of water from under a lock-gate, a great uprush of horrible realisation set all his thoughts swirling, and simultaneously I perceived that the vein was cut. He started back with a hoarse exclamation, and I saw the brown-purple blood gather in a swift bead, and run trickling. He was horrified. He pitched the red-stained scalpel on to the octagonal table; and instantly both doctors flung themselves upon me, making hasty and ill-conceived efforts to remedy the disaster. 'Ice!' said Mowbray, gasping. But I knew that I was killed, though my body still clung to me.

I will not describe their belated endeavours to save me, though I perceived every detail. My perceptions were sharper and swifter than they had ever been in life; my thoughts rushed through my mind with incredible swiftness, but with perfect definition. I can only compare their crowded clarity to the effects of a reasonable dose of opium. In a moment it would all be over, and I should be free. I knew I was immortal, but what would happen I did not know. Should I drift off presently, like a puff of smoke from a gun, in some kind of half-material body, an attenuated version of my material self? Should I find myself suddenly among the innumerable hosts of the dead, and know the world about me for the phantasmagoria it had always seemed? Should I drift to some spiritualistic *séance*, and there make foolish, incomprehensible attempts to affect a purblind medium? It was a state of unemotional curiosity, of colourless expectation. And then I realised a growing stress upon me, a feeling as though some huge human magnet was drawing me upward out of my body. The stress grew and grew. I seemed an atom for which monstrous forces were fighting. For one brief, terrible moment sensation came back to me. That feeling of falling headlong which comes in nightmares, that feeling a thousand times intensified, that and a black horror swept across my thoughts in a torrent. Then the two doctors, the naked body with its cut side, the little room, swept away from under me and vanished, as a speck of foam vanishes down an eddy.

I was in mild-air. Far below was the West End of London, receding rapidly, – for I seemed to be flying swiftly upward, – and as it receded, passing westward like a panorama. I could see, through the faint haze of smoke, the innumerable roofs chimney-set, the narrow roadways, stippled with people and conveyances, the little specks of squares, and the church steeples like thorns sticking out of the fabric. But it spun away as the earth rotated on its axis, and in a few seconds (as it seemed) I was over the scattered clumps of town about Ealing, the little Thames a thread of blue to the south, and the Chiltern Hills and the North Downs coming up like the rim of a basin, far away and faint with haze. Up I rushed. And at first I had not the faintest conception what this headlong rush upward could mean.

Every moment the circle of scenery beneath me grew wider and wider, and the details of town and field, of hill and valley, got more and more hazy and pale and indistinct, a luminous grey was mingled more and more with the blue of the hills and the green of the open meadows; and a little patch of cloud, low and far to the west, shone ever more dazzlingly white. Above, as the veil of atmosphere between myself and outer space grew thinner, the sky, which had been a fair springtime blue at first, grew deeper and richer in colour, passing steadily through the intervening shades, until presently it was as dark as the blue sky of midnight, and presently as black as the blackness of a frosty starlight, and at last as black as no blackness I had ever beheld. And first one star, and then many, and at last an innumerable host broke out upon the sky: more stars than anyone has ever seen from the face of the earth. For the blueness of the sky is the light of the sun and stars sifted and spread abroad blindingly: there is diffused light even in the darkest skies of winter, and we do not see the stars by day only because of the dazzling irradiation of the sun. But now I saw things – I know not how; assuredly with no mortal eyes – and that defect of bedazzlement blinded me no longer. The sun was incredibly strange and wonderful. The body of it was a disc of blinding white light: not yellowish, as it seems to those who live upon the earth, but livid white, all streaked with scarlet streaks and rimmed about with a fringe of writhing tongues of red fire. And shooting half-way across the heavens from either side of it and brighter than the Milky Way, were two pinions of silver white, making it look more like those winged globes I have seen in Egyptian sculpture than anything else I can remember upon earth. These I knew for the solar corona, though I had never seen anything of it but a picture during the days of my earthly life.

When my attention came back to the earth again, I saw that it had fallen very far away from me. Field and town were long since indistinguishable, and all the varied hues of the country were merging into a uniform bright grey, broken only by the brilliant white of the clouds that lay scattered in flocculent masses over

Ireland and the west of England. For now I could see the outlines of the north of France and Ireland, and all this Island of Britain, save where Scotland passed over the horizon to the north, or where the coast was blurred or obliterated by cloud. The sea was a dull grey, and darker than the land; and the whole panorama was rotating slowly towards the east.

All this had happened so swiftly that until I was some thousand miles or so from the earth I had no thought for myself. But now I perceived I had neither hands nor feet, neither parts nor organs, and that I felt neither alarm nor pain. All about me I perceived that the vacancy (for I had already left the air behind) was cold beyond the imagination of man; but it troubled me not. The sun's rays shot through the void, powerless to light or heat until they should strike on matter in their course. I saw things with a serene self-forgetfulness, even as if I were God. And down below there, rushing away from me, – countless miles in a second, – where a little dark spot on the grey marked the position of London, two doctors were struggling to restore life to the poor hacked and outworn shell I had abandoned. I felt then such release, such serenity as I can compare to no mortal delight I have ever known.

It was only after I had perceived all these things that the meaning of that headlong rush of the earth grew into comprehension. Yet it was so simple, so obvious, that I was amazed at my never anticipating the thing that was happening to me. I had suddenly been cut adrift from matter: all that was material of me was there upon earth, whirling away through space, held to the earth by gravitation, partaking of the earth-inertia, moving in its wreath of epicycles round the sun, and with the sun and the planets on their vast march through space. But the immaterial has no inertia, feels nothing of the pull of matter for matter: where it parts from its garment of flesh, there it remains (so far as space concerns it any longer) immovable in space. I was not leaving the earth: the earth was leaving *me*, and not only the earth but the whole solar system was streaming past. And about me in space, invisible to me, scattered in the wake of the earth upon its journey, there must be an innumerable multitude of souls, stripped like myself of the material, stripped like myself of the passions of the individual and the generous emotions of the gregarious brute, naked intelligences, things of new-born wonder

and thought, marvelling at the strange release that had suddenly
come on them!

As I receded faster and faster from the strange white sun in the
black heavens, and from the broad and shining earth upon
which my being had begun, I seemed to grow in some incredible
manner vast: vast as regards this world I had left, vast as regards
the moments and periods of a human life. Very soon I saw the full
circle of the earth, slightly gibbous, like the moon when she nears
her full, but very large; and the silvery shape of America was
now in the noonday blaze wherein (as it seemed) little England
had been basking but a few minutes ago. At first the earth was
large, and shone in the heavens, filling a great part of them; but
every moment she grew smaller and more distant. As she shrank,
the broad moon in its third quarter crept into view over the rim
of her disc. I looked for the constellations. Only that part of Aries
directly behind the sun and the Lion, which the earth covered,
were hidden. I recognised the tortuous, tattered band of the Milky
Way with Vega very bright between sun and earth; and Sirius
and Orion shone splendid against the unfathomable blackness in
the opposite quarter of the heavens. The Pole Star was overhead,
and the Great Bear hung over the circle of the earth. And away
beneath and beyond the shining corona of the sun were strange
groupings of stars I had never seen in my life – notably a dagger-
shaped group that I knew for the Southern Cross. All these were
no larger than when they had shone on earth, but the little stars
that one scarce sees shone now against the setting of black
vacancy as brightly as the first-magnitudes had done, while the
larger worlds were points of indescribable glory and colour.
Aldebaran was a spot of blood-red fire, and Sirius condensed to
one point the light of innumerable sapphires. And they shone
steadily: they did not scintillate, they were calmly glorious. My
impressions had an adamantine hardness and brightness: there
was no blurring softness, no atmosphere, nothing but infinite
darkness set with the myriads of these acute and brilliant points
and specks of light. Presently, when I looked again, the little
earth seemed no bigger than the sun, and it dwindled and turned
as I looked, until in a second's space (as it seemed to me), it was
halved; and so it went on swiftly dwindling. Far away in the
opposite direction, a little pinkish pin's head of light, shining
steadily, was the planet Mars. I swam motionless in vacancy,

and, without a trace of terror or astonishment, watched the speck of cosmic dust we call the world fall away from me.

Presently it dawned upon me that my sense of duration had changed; that my mind was moving not faster but infinitely slower, that between each separate impression there was a period of many days. The moon spun once round the earth as I noted this; and I perceived clearly the motion of Mars in his orbit. Moreover, it appeared as if the time between thought and thought grew steadily greater, until at last a thousand years was but a moment in my perception.

At first the constellations had shone motionless against the black background of infinite space; but presently it seemed as though the group of stars about Hercules and the Scorpion was contracting, while Orion and Aldebaran and their neighbours were scattering apart. Flashing suddenly out of the darkness there came a flying multitude of particles of rock, glittering like dust-specks in a sunbeam, and encompassed in a faintly luminous cloud. They swirled all about me, and vanished again in a twinkling far behind. And then I saw that a bright spot of light, that shone a little to one side of my path, was growing very rapidly larger, and perceived that it was the planet Saturn rushing towards me. Larger and larger it grew, swallowing up the heavens behind it, and hiding every moment a fresh multitude of stars. I perceived its flattened, whirling body, its disc-like belt, and seven of its little satellites. It grew and grew, till it towered enormous; and then I plunged amid a streaming multitude of clashing stones and dancing dust particles and gas-eddies, and saw for a moment the mighty triple belt like three concentric arches of moonlight above me, its shadow black on the boiling tumult below. These things happened in one-tenth of the time it takes to tell them. The planet went by like a flash of lightning; for a few seconds it blotted out the sun, and there and then became a mere black, dwindling, winged patch against the light. The earth, the mother mote of my being, I could no longer see.

So with a stately swiftness, in the profoundest silence, the solar system fell from me as it had been a garment, until the sun was a mere star amid the multitude of stars, with its eddy of planet-specks lost in the confused glittering of the remoter light. I was no longer a denizen of the solar system: I had come to the outer

Universe, I seemed to grasp and comprehend the whole world of matter. Ever more swiftly the stars closed in about the spot where Antares and Vega had vanished in a phosphorescent haze, until that part of the sky had the semblance of a whirling mass of nebulae, and ever before me yawned vaster gaps of vacant blackness, and the stars shone fewer and fewer. It seemed as if I moved towards a point between Orion's belt and sword; and the void about that region opened vaster and vaster every second, an incredible gulf of nothingness into which I was falling. Faster and ever faster the universe rushed by, a hurry of whirling motes at last, speeding silently into the void. Stars glowing brighter and brighter, with their circling planets catching the light in a ghostly fashion as I neared them, shone out and vanished again into inexistence; faint comets, clusters of meteorites, winking specks of matter, eddying light-points, whizzed past, some perhaps a hundred millions of miles or so from me at most, few nearer, travelling with unimaginable rapidity, shooting constellations, momentary darts of fire, through that black, enormous night. More than anything else it was like a dusty draught, sunbeam-lit. Broader and wider and deeper grew the starless space, the vacant Beyond, into which I was being drawn. At last a quarter of the heavens was black and blank, and the whole headlong rush of stellar universe closed in behind me like a veil of light that is gathered together. It drove away from me like a monstrous jack-o'-lantern driven by the wind. I had come out into the wilderness of space. Ever the vacant blackness grew broader, until the hosts of the stars seemed only like a swarm of fiery specks hurrying away from me, inconceivably remote, and the darkness, the nothingness and emptiness, was about me on every side. Soon the little universe of matter, the cage of points in which I had begun to be, was dwindling, now to a whirling disc of luminous glittering, and now to one minute disc of hazy light. In a little while it would shrink to a point, and at last would vanish altogether.

Suddenly feeling came back to me – feeling in the shape of overwhelming terror; such a dread of those dark vastitudes as no words can describe, a passionate resurgence of sympathy and social desire. Were there other souls, invisible to me as I to them, about me in the blackness? or was I indeed, even as I felt, alone? Had I passed out of being into something that was neither being nor not-being? The covering of the body, the covering of matter, had been torn from me, and the hallucinations of companionship and security. Everything was black and silent. I had ceased to be. I was nothing. There was nothing, save only that infinitesimal dot of light that dwindled in the gulf. I strained myself to hear and see, and for a while there was naught but infinite silence, intolerable darkness, horror, and despair.

Then I saw that about the spot of light into which the whole world of matter had shrunk there was a faint glow. And in a band on either side of that the darkness was not absolute. I watched it for ages, as it seemed to me, and through the long waiting the haze grew imperceptibly more distinct. And then about the band appeared an irregular cloud of the faintest, palest brown. I felt a passionate impatience; but the things grew brighter so slowly that they scarce seemed to change. What was unfolding itself? What was this strange reddish dawn in the interminable night of space?

The cloud's shape was grotesque. It seemed to be looped along its lower side into four projecting masses, and, above, it ended in a straight line. What phantom was it? I felt assured I had seen that figure before; but I could not think what, nor where, nor when it was. Then the realisation rushed upon me. *It was a clenched Hand.* I was alone in space, alone with this huge, shadowy Hand, upon which the whole Universe of Matter lay like an unconsidered speck of dust. It seemed as though I watched it through vast periods of time. On the forefinger glittered a ring; and the universe from which I had come was but a spot of light upon the ring's curvature. And the thing that the hand gripped had the likeness of a black rod. Through a long eternity I watched this Hand, with the ring and the rod, marvelling and fearing and waiting helplessly on what might follow. It seemed as though nothing could follow: that I should watch for ever, seeing only the Hand and the thing it held, and understanding nothing of its import. Was the whole universe but a refracting speck upon some greater Being? Were our worlds but the atoms of another universe, and those again of another, and so on through an endless progression? And what was I? Was I indeed immaterial? A vague persuasion of a body gathering about me came into my suspense. The abysmal darkness about the Hand filled with impalpable suggestions, with uncertain, fluctuating shapes.

Then, suddenly, came a sound, like the sound of a tolling bell: faint, as if infinitely far; muffled, as though heard through thick swathings of darkness: a deep, vibrating resonance, with vast gulfs of silence between each stroke. And the Hand appeared to tighten on the rod. And I saw far above the Hand, towards the apex of the darkness, a circle of dim phosphorescence, a ghostly sphere whence these sounds came throbbing; and at the last stroke the Hand vanished, for the hour had come, and I heard a noise of many waters. But the black rod remained as a great band across the sky. And then a voice, which seemed to run to the uttermost parts of space, spoke, saying, 'There will be no more pain.'

At that an almost intolerable gladness and radiance rushed in upon me, and I saw the circle shining white and bright, and the rod black and shining, and many things else distinct and clear. And the circle was the face of the clock, and the rod the rail of my bed. Haddon was standing at the foot, against the rail, with a small pair of scissors on his fingers; and the hands of my clock on the mantel over his shoulder were clasped together over the hour of twelve. Mowbray was washing something in a basin at the octagonal table, and at my side I felt a subdued feeling that could scarce be spoken of as pain.

The operation had not killed me. And I perceived, suddenly, that the dull melancholy of half a year was lifted from my mind.

The Flowering of the Strange Orchid

The buying of orchids always has in it a certain speculative flavour. You have before you the brown shrivelled lump of tissue, and for the rest you must trust your judgment, or the auctioneer, or your good luck, as your taste may incline. The plant may be moribund or dead, or it may be just a respectable purchase, fair value for your money, or perhaps – for the thing has happened again and again – there slowly unfolds before the delighted eyes of the happy purchaser, day after day, some new variety, some novel richness, a strange twist of the labellum, or some subtler colouration or unexpected mimicry. Pride, beauty, and profit blossom together on one delicate green spike, and, it may be, even immortality. For the new miracle of nature may stand in need of a new specific name, and what so convenient as that of its discoverer? 'Johnsmithia'! There have been worse names.

It was perhaps the hope of some such happy discovery that made Winter-Wedderburn such a frequent attendant at these sales – that hope, and also, maybe, the fact that he had nothing else of the slightest interest to do in the world. He was a shy, lonely, rather ineffectual man, provided with just enough income to keep off the spur of necessity, and not enough nervous energy to make him seek any exacting employments. He might have collected stamps or coins, or translated Horace, or bound books, or invented new species of diatoms. But, as it happened, he grew orchids, and had one ambitious little hothouse.

'I have a fancy,' he said over his coffee, 'that something is going to happen to me today.' He spoke – as he moved and thought – slowly.

'Oh, don't say *that!*' said his housekeeper – who was also his remote cousin. For 'something happening' was a euphemism that meant only one thing to her.

'You misunderstand me. I mean nothing unpleasant ... though what I do mean I scarcely know.

'Today,' he continued, after a pause. 'Peters' are going to sell a batch of plants from the Andamans and the Indies. I shall go up and see what they have. It may be I shall buy something good unawares. That may be it.'

He passed his cup for his second cupful of coffee.

'Are these the things collected by that poor young fellow you told me of the other day?' asked his cousin, as she filled his cup.

'Yes,' he said, and became meditative over a piece of toast.

'Nothing ever does happen to me,' he remarked presently, beginning to think aloud. 'I wonder why? Things enough happen to other people. There is Harvey. Only the other week; on Monday he picked up six-pence, on Wednesday his chicks all had the staggers, on Friday his cousin came home from Australia, and on Saturday he broke his ankle. What a whirl of excitement! – compared to me.'

'I think I would rather be without so much excitement,' said his housekeeper. 'It can't be good for you.'

'I suppose it's troublesome. Still ... you see, nothing ever happens to me. When I was a little boy I never had accidents. I never fell in love as I grew up. Never married.... I wonder how it feels to have something happen to you, something really remarkable.

'That orchid-collector was only thirty-six – twenty years younger than myself – when he died. And he had been married twice and divorced once; he had had malarial fever four times, and once he broke his thigh. He killed a Malay once, and once he was wounded by a poisoned dart. And in the end he was killed by jungle-leeches. It must have all been very troublesome, but then it must have been very interesting, you know – except, perhaps, the leeches.'

'I am sure it was not good for him,' said the lady with conviction.

'Perhaps not.' And then Wedderburn looked at his watch. 'Twenty-three minutes past eight. I am going up by the quarter to twelve train, so that there is plenty of time. I think I shall wear my alpaca jacket – it is quite warm enough – and my grey felt hat and brown shoes. I suppose—'

He glanced out of the window at the serene sky and sunlit garden, and then nervously at his cousin's face.

'I think you had better take an umbrella if you are going to London,' she said in a voice that admitted of no denial. 'There's all between here and the station coming back.'

When he returned he was in a state of mild excitement. He had made a purchase. It was rare that he could make up his mind quickly enough to buy, but this time he had done so.

'There are Vandas,' he said, 'and a Dendrobe and some Palæonophis.' He surveyed his purchases lovingly as he consumed his soup. They were laid out on the spotless tablecloth before him, and he was telling his cousin all about them as he slowly meandered through his dinner. It was his custom to live all his visits to London over again in the evening for her and his own entertainment.

'I knew something would happen today. And I have bought all these. Some of them – some of them – I feel sure, do you know, that some of them will be remarkable. I don't know how it is, but I feel just as sure as if some one had told me that some of these will turn out remarkable.

'That one' – he pointed to a shrivelled rhizome – 'was not identified. It may be a Palæonophis – or it may not. It may be a new species, or even a new genus. And it was the last that poor Batten ever collected.'

'I don't like the look of it,' said his housekeeper. 'It's such an ugly shape.'

'To me it scarcely seems to have a shape.'

'I don't like those things that stick out,' said his housekeeper.

'It shall be put away in a pot tomorrow.'

'It looks,' said the housekeeper, 'like a spider shamming dead.'

Wedderburn smiled and surveyed the root with his head on one side. 'It is certainly not a pretty lump of stuff. But you can never judge of these things from their dry appearance. It may turn out to be a very beautiful orchid indeed. How busy I shall be to-morrow! I must see tonight just exactly what to do with these things, and tomorrow I shall set to work.'

'They found poor Batten lying dead, or dying, in a mangrove swamp – I forget which,' he began again presently, 'with one of these very orchids crushed up under his body. He had been unwell for some days with some kind of native fever, and I suppose he fainted. These mangrove swamps are very unwholesome. Every drop of blood, they say, was taken out of him by the jungle-leeches. It may be that very plant that cost him his life to obtain.'

'I think none the better of it for that.'

'Men must work though women may weep,' said Wedderburn with profound gravity.

'Fancy dying away from every comfort in a nasty swamp! Fancy being ill of fever with nothing to take but chlorodyne and quinine – if men were left to themselves they would live on chlorodyne and quinine – and no one round you but horrible natives! They say the Andaman islanders are most disgusting wretches – and, anyhow, they can scarcely make good nurses, not having the necessary training. And just for people in England to have orchids!'

'I don't suppose it was comfortable, but some men seem to enjoy that kind of thing,' said Wedderburn. 'Anyhow, the natives of his party were sufficiently civilised to take care of all his collection until his colleague, who was an ornithologist, came back again from the interior; though they could not tell the species of the orchid, and had let it wither. And it makes these things more interesting.'

'It makes them disgusting. I should be afraid of some of the malaria clinging to them. And just think, there has been a dead body lying across that ugly thing! I never thought of that before. There! I declare I cannot eat another mouthful of dinner.'

'I will take them off the table if you like, and put them in the window-seat. I can see them just as well there.'

The next few days he was indeed singularly busy in his steamy little hothouse, fussing about with charcoal, lumps of teak, moss, and all the other mysteries of the orchid cultivator. He considered he was having a wonderfully eventful time. In the evening he would talk about these new orchids to his friends, and over and over again he reverted to his expectation of something strange.

Several of the Vandas and the Dendrobium died under his care, but presently the strange orchid began to show signs of life. He was delighted, and took his housekeeper right away from jam-making to see it at once, directly he made the discovery.

'That is a bud,' he said, 'and presently there will be a lot of leaves there, and those little things coming out here are aërial rootlets.'

'They look to me like little white fingers poking out of the brown,' said his housekeeper. 'I don't like them.'

'Why not?'

'I don't know. They look like fingers trying to get at you. I can't help my likes and dislikes.'

'I don't know for certain, but I don't *think* there are any orchids I know that have aërial rootlets quite like that. It may be my fancy, of course. You see they are a little flattened at the ends.'

'I don't like 'em,' said his housekeeper, suddenly shivering and turning away. 'I know it's very silly of me – and I'm very sorry, particularly as you like the thing so much. But I can't help thinking of that corpse.'

'But it may not be that particular plant. That was merely a guess of mine.'

His housekeeper shrugged her shoulders. 'Anyhow I don't like it,' she said.

Wedderburn felt a little hurt at her dislike to the plant. But that did not prevent his talking to her about orchids generally, and this orchid in particular, whenever he felt inclined.

'There are such queer things about orchids,' he said one day; 'such possibilities of surprises. You know, Darwin studied their fertilisation, and showed that the whole structure of an ordinary orchid flower was contrived in order that moths might carry the pollen from plant to plant. Well, it seems that there are lots of orchids known the flower of which cannot possibly be used for fertilisation in that way. Some of the Cypripediums, for instance; there are no insects known that can possibly fertilise them, and some of them have never been found with seed.'

'But how do they form new plants?'

'By runners and tubers, and that kind of outgrowth. That is easily explained. The puzzle is, what are the flowers for?

'Very likely,' he added, '*my* orchid may be something extraordinary in that way. If so I shall study it. I have often thought of making researches as Darwin did. But hitherto I have not found the time, or something else has happened to prevent it. The leaves are beginning to unfold now. I do wish you would come and see them!'

But she said that the orchid-house was so hot it gave her the headache. She had seen the plant once again, and the aërial rootlets, which were now some of them more than a foot long, had unfortunately reminded her of tentacles reaching out after something; and they got into her dreams, growing after her with incredible rapidity. So that she had settled to her entire satisfaction that she would not see that plant again, and Wedderburn had to admire its leaves alone. They were of the ordinary broad form, and a deep glossy green, with splashes and dots of deep red towards the base. He knew of no other leaves quite like them. The plant was placed on a low bench near the thermometer, and close by was a simple arrangement by which a tap dripped on the hot-water pipes and kept the air steamy. And he spent his afternoons now with some regularity meditating on the approaching flowering of this strange plant.

And at last the great thing happened. Directly he entered the little glass house he knew that the spike had burst out, although his great *Palæonophis Lowii* hid the corner where his new darling stood. There was a new odour in the air, a rich, intensely sweet scent, that overpowered every other in that crowded, steaming little greenhouse.

Directly he noticed this he hurried down to the strange orchid. And, behold! the trailing green spikes bore now three great splashes of blossom, from which this overpowering sweetness proceeded. He stopped before them in an ecstasy of admiration.

The flowers were white, with streaks of golden orange upon the petals; the heavy labellum was coiled into an intricate projection, and a wonderful bluish purple mingled there with the gold. He could see at once that the genus was altogether a new one. And the insufferable scent! How hot the place was! The blossoms swam before his eyes.

He would see if the temperature was right. He made a step towards the thermometer. Suddenly everything appeared unsteady. The bricks on the floor were dancing up and down. Then the white blossoms, the green leaves behind them, the whole greenhouse, seemed to sweep sideways, and then in a curve upward.

At half-past four his cousin made the tea, according to their invariable custom. But Wedderburn did not come in for his tea.

'He is worshipping that horrid orchid,' she told herself, and waited ten minutes. 'His watch must have stopped. I will go and call him.'

She went straight to the hothouse, and, opening the door, called his name. There was no reply. She noticed that the air was

very close, and loaded with an intense perfume. Then she saw
something lying on the bricks between the hot-water pipes.

For a minute, perhaps, she stood motionless.

He was lying, face upward, at the foot of the strange orchid.
The tentacle-like aërial rootlets no longer swayed freely in the air,
but were crowded together, a tangle of grey ropes, and stretched
tight, with their ends closely applied to his chin and neck and
hands.

She did not understand. Then she saw from under one of the
exultant tentacles upon his cheek there trickled a little thread of
blood.

With an inarticulate cry she ran towards him, and tried to pull
him away from the leech-like suckers. She snapped two of these
tentacles, and their sap dripped red.

Then the overpowering scent of the blossom began to make
her head reel. How they clung to him! She tore at the tough
ropes, and he and the white inflorescence swam about her. She
felt she was fainting, knew she must not. She left him and hastily
opened the nearest door, and, after she had panted for a moment
in the fresh air, she had a brilliant inspiration. She caught up a
flower-pot and smashed in the windows at the end of the
greenhouse. Then she re-entered. She tugged now with renewed
strength at Wedderburn's motionless body, and brought the
strange orchid crashing to the floor. It still clung with the
grimmest tenacity to its victim. In a frenzy, she lugged it and him
into the open air.

Then she thought of tearing through the sucker rootlets one by
one, and in another minute she had released him and was
dragging him away from the horror.

He was white and bleeding from a dozen circular patches.

The odd-job man was coming up the garden, amazed at the
smashing of glass, and saw her emerge, hauling the inanimate
body with red-stained hands. For a moment he thought impossible things.

'Bring some water!' she cried, and her voice dispelled his
fancies. When, with unnatural alacrity, he returned with the
water, he found her weeping with excitement, and with Wedderburn's head upon her knee, wiping the blood from his face.

'What's the matter?' said Wedderburn, opening his eyes feebly,
and closing them again at once.

'Go and tell Annie to come out here to me, and then go for Dr Haddon at once,' she said to the odd-job man so soon as he brought the water; and added, seeing he hesitated, 'I will tell you all about it when you come back.'

Presently Wedderburn opened his eyes again, and, seeing that he was troubled by the puzzle of his position, she explained to him, 'You fainted in the hothouse.'

'And the orchid?'

'I will see to that,' she said.

Wedderburn had lost a good deal of blood, but beyond that he had suffered no very great injury. They gave him brandy mixed with some pink extract of meat, and carried him upstairs to bed. His housekeeper told her incredible story in fragments to Dr Haddon. 'Come to the orchid-house and see,' she said.

The cold outer air was blowing in through the open door, and the sickly perfume was almost dispelled. Most of the torn aërial rootlets lay already withered amidst a number of dark stains upon the bricks. The stem of the inflorescence was broken by the fall of the plant, and the flowers were growing limp and brown at the edges of the petals. The doctor stooped towards it, then saw that one of the aërial rootlets still stirred feebly, and hesitated.

The next morning the strange orchid still lay there, black now and putrescent. The door banged intermittently in the morning breeze, and all the array of Wedderburn's orchids was shrivelled and prostrate. But Wedderburn himself was bright and garrulous upstairs in the glory of his strange adventure.

The Red Room

'I can assure you,' said I, 'that it will take a very tangible ghost to frighten me.' And I stood up before the fire with my glass in my hand.

'It is your own choosing,' said the man with the withered arm, and glanced at me askance.

'Eight-and-twenty years,' said I, 'I have lived, and never a ghost have I seen as yet.'

The old woman sat staring hard into the fire, her pale eyes wide open. 'Ay,' she broke in; 'and eight-and-twenty years you have lived and never seen the likes of this house, I reckon. There's a many things to see, when one's still but eight-and-twenty.' She swayed her head slowly from side to side. 'A many things to see and sorrow for.'

I half suspected the old people were trying to enhance the spiritual terrors of their house by their droning insistence. I put down my empty glass on the table and looked about the room, and caught a glimpse of myself, abbreviated and broadened to an impossible sturdiness, in the queer old mirror at the end of the room. 'Well,' I said, 'if I see anything tonight, I shall be so much the wiser. For I come to the business with an open mind.'

'It's your own choosing,' said the man with the withered arm once more.

I heard the sound of a stick and a shambling step on the flags in the passage outside, and the door creaked on its hinges as a second old man entered, more bent, more wrinkled, more aged even than the first. He supported himself by a single crutch, his eyes were covered by a shade, and his lower lip, half averted, hung pale and pink from his decaying yellow teeth. He made straight for an armchair on the opposite side of the table, sat down clumsily, and began to cough. The man with the withered arm gave this new-comer a short glance of positive dislike; the old woman took no notice of his arrival, but remained with her eyes fixed steadily on the fire.

'I said – it's your own choosing,' said the man with the withered arm, when the coughing had ceased for a while.

'It's my own choosing,' I answered.

The man with the shade became aware of my presence for the first time, and threw his head back for a moment and sideways, to see me. I caught a momentary glimpse of his eyes, small and bright and inflamed. Then he began to cough and splutter again.

'Why don't you drink?' said the man with the withered arm, pushing the beer towards him. The man with the shade poured out a glassful with a shaky hand that splashed half as much again on the deal table. A monstrous shadow of him crouched upon the wall and mocked his action as he poured and drank. I must confess I had scarce expected these grotesque custodians. There is to my mind something inhuman in senility, something crouching and atavistic; the human qualities seem to drop from old people insensibly day by day. The three of them made me feel uncomfortable, with their gaunt silences, their bent carriage, their evident unfriendliness to me and to one another.

'If,' said I, 'you will show me to this haunted room of yours, I will make myself comfortable there.'

The old man with the cough jerked his head back so suddenly that it startled me, and shot another glance of his red eyes at me from under the shade; but no one answered me. I waited a minute, glancing from one to the other.

'If,' I said a little louder, 'if you will show me to this haunted room of yours, I will relieve you from the task of entertaining me.'

'There's a candle on the slab outside the door,' said the man with the withered arm, looking at my feet as he addressed me. 'But if you go to the red room to-night—'

('This night of all nights!' said the old woman.)

'You go alone.'

'Very well,' I answered. 'And which way do I go?'

'You go along the passage for a bit,' said he, 'until you come to a door, and through that is a spiral staircase, and half-way up that is a landing and another door covered with baize. Go through that and down the long corridor to the end, and the red room is on your left up the steps.'

'Have I got that right?' I said, and repeated his directions. He corrected me in one particular.

'And are you really going?' said the man with the shade, looking at me again for the third time, with that queer, unnatural tilting of the face.

('This night of all nights!' said the old woman.)

'It is what I came for,' I said, and moved towards the door. As I did so, the old man with the shade rose and staggered round the table, so as to be closer to the others and to the fire. At the door I turned and looked at them, and saw they were all close together, dark against the firelight, staring at me over their shoulders, with an intent expression on their ancient faces.

'Goodnight,' I said, setting the door open.

'It's your own choosing,' said the man with the withered arm.

I left the door wide open until the candle was well alight, and then I shut them in and walked down the chilly, echoing passage.

I must confess that the oddness of these three old pensioners in whose charge her ladyship had left the castle, and the deep-toned, old-fashioned furniture of the housekeeper's room in which they foregathered, affected me in spite of my efforts to keep myself at a matter-of-fact phase. They seemed to belong to another age, an older age, an age when things spiritual were different from this of ours, less certain; an age when omens and witches were credible, and ghosts beyond denying. Their very existence was spectral; the cut of their clothing, fashions born in dead brains. The ornaments and conveniences of the room about them were ghostly – the thoughts of vanished men, which still haunted rather than participated in the world of today. But with an effort I sent such thoughts to the right-about. The long, draughty subterranean passage was chilly and dusty, and my candle flared and made the shadows cower and quiver. The echoes rang up and down the spiral staircase, and a shadow came sweeping up after me, and one fled before me into the darkness overhead. I came to the landing and stopped there for a moment, listening to a rustling that I fancied I heard; then, satisfied of the absolute silence, I pushed open the baize-covered door and stood in the corridor.

The effect was scarcely what I expected, for the moonlight, coming in by the great window on the grand staircase, picked out everything in vivid black shadow or silvery illumination. Every-thing was in its place: the house might have been deserted on the yesterday instead of eighteen months ago. There were candles in the sockets of the sconces, and whatever dust had gathered on the carpets or upon the polished flooring was distributed so evenly as to be invisible in the moonlight. I was about to advance, and stopped abruptly. A bronze group stood upon the landing, hidden from me by the corner of the wall, but its shadow fell with marvellous distinctness upon the white panelling, and gave me the impression of someone crouching to waylay me. I stood rigid for half a minute perhaps. Then, with my hand in the pocket that held my revolver, I advanced, only to discover a Ganymede and Eagle glistening in the moonlight. That incident for a time restored my nerve, and a porcelain Chinaman on a buhl table, whose head rocked silently as I passed him, scarcely startled me.

The door to the red room and the steps up to it were in a shadowy corner. I moved my candle from side to side, in order to see clearly the nature of the recess in which I stood before opening the door. Here it was, thought I, that my predecessor was found, and the memory of that story gave me a sudden twinge of apprehension. I glanced over my shoulder at the Ganymede in the moonlight, and opened the door of the red room rather hastily, with my face half turned to the pallid silence of the landing.

I entered, closed the door behind me at once, turned the key I found in the lock within, and stood with the candle held aloft, surveying the scene of my vigil, the great red room of Lorraine Castle, in which the young duke had died. Or, rather, in which he had begun his dying, for he had opened the door and fallen headlong down the steps I had just ascended. That had been the end of his vigil, of his gallant attempt to conquer the ghostly tradition of the place, and never, I thought, had apoplexy better served the ends of superstition. And there were other and older stories that clung to the room, back to the half-credible beginning of it all, the tale of a timid wife and the tragic end that came to her husband's jest of frightening her. And looking around that large sombre room, with its shadowy window bays, its recesses and alcoves, one could well understand the legends that had sprouted in its black corners, its germinating darkness. My candle was a little tongue of light in its vastness, that failed to pierce the opposite end of the room, and left an ocean of mystery and suggestion beyond its island of light.

I resolved to make a systematic examination of the place at once, and dispel the fanciful suggestions of its obscurity before they obtained a hold upon me. After satisfying myself of the fastening of the door, I began to walk about the room, peering round each article of furniture, tucking up the valances of the bed, and opening its curtains wide. I pulled up the blinds and examined the fastenings of the several windows before closing the shutters, leant forward and looked up the blackness of the wide chimney, and tapped the dark oak panelling for any secret opening. There were two big mirrors in the room, each with a pair of sconces bearing candles, and on the mantelshelf, too, were more candles in china candlesticks. All these I lit one after the other. The fire was laid, an unexpected consideration from the old housekeeper, – and I lit it, to keep down any disposition to shiver, and when it was burning well, I stood round with my back to it and regarded the room again. I had pulled up a chintz-covered arm-chair and a table, to form a kind of barricade before me, and on this lay my revolver ready to hand. My precise examination had done me good, but I still found the remoter darkness of the place, and its perfect stillness, too stimulating for the imagination. The echoing of the stir and crackling of the fire was no sort of comfort to me. The shadow in the alcove at the end in particular, had that undefinable quality of a presence, that odd suggestion of a lurking, living thing, that comes so easily in silence and solitude. At last, to reassure myself, I walked with a candle into it, and satisfied myself that there was nothing tangible there. I stood that candle upon the floor of the alcove, and left it in that position.

By this time I was in a state of considerable nervous tension, although to my reason there was no adequate cause for the condition. My mind, however, was perfectly clear. I postulated quite unreservedly that nothing supernatural could happen, and to pass the time I began to string some rhymes together, Ingoldsby fashion, of the original legend of the place. A few I spoke aloud, but the echoes were not pleasant. For the same reason I also abandoned, after a time, a conversation with myself upon the impossibility of ghosts and haunting. My mind reverted to the three old and distorted people downstairs, and I tried to keep it upon that topic. The sombre reds and blacks of the room troubled me; even with seven candles the place was merely dim. The one in the alcove flared in a draught, and the fire-flickering kept the shadows and penumbra perpetually shifting and stirring. Casting about for a remedy, I recalled the candles I had seen in the passage, and, with a slight effort, walked out into the moonlight, carrying a candle and leaving the door open, and presently returned with as many as ten. These I put in various knick-knacks of china with which the room was sparsely adorned, lit and placed where the shadows had lain deepest, some on the floor, some in the window recesses, until at last my seventeen candles were so arranged that not an inch of the room but had the direct light of at least one of them. It occurred to me that when the ghost came, I could warn him not to trip over them. The room was now quite brightly illuminated. There was something very cheery and reassuring in these little streaming flames, and snuffing them gave me an occupation, and afforded a helpful sense of the passage of time.

Even with that, however, the brooding expectation of the vigil weighed heavily upon me. It was after midnight that the candle in the alcove suddenly went out, and the black shadow sprang back to its place there. I did not see the candle go out; I simply turned and saw that the darkness was there, as one might start and see the unexpected presence of a stranger. 'By Jove!' said I aloud; 'that draught's a strong one!' and, taking the matches from the table, I walked across the room in a leisurely manner, to relight the corner again. My first match would not strike, and as I succeeded with the second, something seemed to blink on the wall before me. I turned my head involuntarily, and saw that the two candles on the little table by the fireplace were extinguished. I rose at once to my feet.

'Odd!' I said. 'Did I do that myself in a flash of absent-mindedness?'

I walked back, relit one, and as I did so, I saw the candle in the right sconce of one of the mirrors wink and go right out, and almost immediately its companion followed it. There was no mistake about it. The flame vanished, as if the wicks had been suddenly nipped between a finger and a thumb, leaving the wick neither glowing nor smoking, but black. While I stood gaping, the candle at the foot of the bed went out, and the shadows seemed to take another step towards me.

'This won't do!' said I, and first one and then another candle on the mantelshelf followed.

'What's up?' I cried, with a queer high note getting into my voice somehow. At that the candle on the wardrobe went out, and the one I had relit in the alcove followed.

'Steady on!' I said. 'These candles are wanted,' speaking with a half-hysterical facetiousness, and scratching away at a match the while for the mantel candlesticks. My hands trembled so much that twice I missed the rough paper of the matchbox. As the mantel emerged from darkness again, two candles in the remoter end of the window were eclipsed. But with the same match I also relit the larger mirror candles, and those on the floor near the doorway, so that for the moment I seemed to gain on the extinctions. But then in a volley there vanished four lights at once in different corners of the room, and I struck another match in quivering haste, and stood hesitating whither to take it.

As I stood undecided, an invisible hand seemed to sweep out the two candles on the table. With a cry of terror, I dashed at the alcove, then into the corner, and then into the window, relighting three, as two more vanished by the fireplace; then, perceiving a better way, I dropped the matches on the iron-bound deed-box in the corner, and caught up the bedroom candlestick. With this I avoided the delay of striking matches; but for all that the steady process of extinction went on, and the shadows I feared and fought against returned, and crept in upon me, first a step gained on this side of me and then on that. It was like a ragged storm-cloud sweeping out the stars. Now and then one returned for a minute, and was lost again. I was now almost frantic with the horror of the coming darkness, and my self-possession deserted me. I leaped panting and dishevelled from candle to candle, in a vain struggle against that remorseless advance.

I bruised myself on the thigh against the table, I sent a chair headlong, I stumbled and fell and whisked the cloth from the table in my fall. My candle rolled away from me, and I snatched another as I rose. Abruptly this was blown out, as I swung it off the table by the wind of my sudden movement, and immediately the two remaining candles followed. But there was light still in the room, a red light that staved off the shadows from me. The fire! Of course I could still thrust my candle between the bars and relight it!

I turned to where the flames were still dancing between the glowing coals, and splashing red reflections upon the furniture, made two steps towards the grate, and incontinently the flames dwindled and vanished, the glow vanished, the reflections rushed together and vanished, and as I thrust the candle between the bars darkness closed upon me like the shutting of an eye, wrapped about me in a stifling embrace, sealed my vision, and crushed the last vestiges of reason from my brain. The candle fell from my hand. I flung out my arms in a vain effort to thrust that ponderous blackness away from me, and, lifting up my voice, screamed with all my might – once, twice, thrice. Then I think I must have staggered to my feet. I know I thought suddenly of the moonlit corridor, and, with my head bowed and my arms over my face, made a run for the door.

But I had forgotten the exact position of the door, and struck myself heavily against the corner of the bed. I staggered back, turned, and was either struck or struck myself against some other bulky furniture. I have a vague memory of battering myself thus, to and fro in the darkness, of a cramped struggle, and of my own wild crying as I darted to and fro, of a heavy blow at last upon my forehead, a horrible sensation of falling that lasted an age, of my last frantic effort to keep my footing, and then I remember no more.

I opened my eyes in daylight. My head was roughly bandaged, and the man with the withered arm was watching my face. I looked about me, trying to remember what had happened, and for a space I could not recollect. I rolled my eyes into the corner, and saw the old woman, no longer abstracted, pouring out some drops of medicine from a little blue phial into a glass. 'Where am I?' I asked; 'I seem to remember you, and yet I cannot remember who you are.'

They told me then, and I heard of the haunted Red Room as one who hears a tale. 'We found you at dawn,' said he, 'and there was blood on your forehead and lips.'

It was very slowly I recovered my memory of my experience. 'You believe now,' said the old man, 'that the room is haunted?'

He spoke no longer as one who greets an intruder, but as one who grieves for a broken friend.

'Yes,' said I; 'the room is haunted.'

'And you have seen it. And we, who have lived here all our lives, have never set eyes upon it. Because we have never dared.... Tell us, is it truly the old earl who—'

'No,' said I; 'it is not.'

'I told you so,' said the old lady, with the glass in her hand. 'It is his poor young countess who was frightened—'

'It is not,' I said. 'There is neither ghost of earl nor ghost of countess in that room, there is no ghost there at all; but worse, far worse—'

'Well?' they said.

'The worst of all the things that haunt poor mortal man,' said I; 'and that is, in all its nakedness – *Fear!* Fear that will not have light nor sound, that will not bear with reason, that deafens and darkens and overwhelms. It followed me through the corridor, it fought against me in the room—'

I stopped abruptly. There was an interval of silence. My hand went up to my bandages.

Then the man with the shade sighed and spoke. 'That is it,' said he. 'I knew that was it. A power of darkness. To put such a curse upon a woman! It lurks there always. You can feel it even in the daytime, even of a bright summer's day, in the hangings, in the curtains keeping behind you however you face about. In the dusk it creeps along the corridor and follows you, so that you dare not turn. There is Fear in that room of hers – black Fear, and there will be – so long as this house of sin endures.'

The Cone

The night was hot and overcast, the sky red-rimmed with the lingering sunset of midsummer. They sat at the open window, trying to fancy the air was fresher there. The trees and shrubs of the garden stood stiff and dark; beyond in the roadway a gas-lamp burnt, bright orange against the hazy blue of the evening. Farther were the three lights of the railway signal against the lowering sky. The man and woman spoke to one another in low tones.

'He does not suspect?' said the man, a little nervously.

'Not he,' she said peevishly, as though that too irritated her. 'He thinks of nothing but the works and the prices of fuel. He has no imagination, no poetry.'

'None of these men of iron have,' he said sententiously. 'They have no hearts.'

'*He* has not,' she said. She turned her discontented face towards the window. The distant sound of a roaring and rushing drew nearer and grew in volume; the house quivered; one heard the metallic rattle of the tender. As the train passed, there was a glare of light above the cutting and a driving tumult of smoke; one, two, three, four, five, six, seven, eight black oblongs – eight trucks – passed across the dim grey of the embankment, and were suddenly extinguished one by one in the throat of the tunnel, which, with the last, seemed to swallow down train, smoke, and sound in one abrupt gulp.

'This country was all fresh and beautiful once,' he said; 'and now – it is Gehenna. Down that way – nothing but pot-banks and chimneys belching fire and dust into the face of heaven.... But what does it matter? An end comes, an end to all this cruelty.... *Tomorrow.*' He spoke the last word in a whisper.

'*Tomorrow,*' she said, speaking in a whisper too, and still staring out of the window.

'Dear!' he said, putting his hand on hers.

She turned with a start, and their eyes searched one another's. Hers softened to his gaze. 'My dear one!' she said, and then: 'It seems so strange – that you should have come into my life like this – to open—' She paused.

'To open?' he said.

'All this wonderful world' – she hesitated, and spoke still more softly –' this world of *love* to me.'

Then suddenly the door clicked and closed. They turned their heads, and he started violently back. In the shadow of the room stood a great shadowy figure – silent. They saw the face dimly in the half-light, with unexpressive dark patches under the pent-house brows. Every muscle in Raut's body suddenly became tense. When could the door have opened? What had he heard? Had he heard all? What had he seen? A tumult of questions.

The newcomer's voice came at last, after a pause that seemed interminable. 'Well?' he said.

'I was afraid I had missed you, Horrocks,' said the man at the window, gripping the window-ledge with his hand. His voice was unsteady.

The clumsy figure of Horrocks came forward out of the shadow. He made no answer to Raut's remark. For a moment he stood above them.

The woman's heart was cold within her. 'I told Mr Raut it was just possible you might come back,' she said in a voice that never quivered.

Horrocks, still silent, sat down abruptly in the chair by her little work-table. His big hands were clenched; one saw now the fire of his eyes under the shadow of his brows. He was trying to get his breath. His eyes went from the woman he had trusted to the friend he had trusted, and then back to the woman.

By this time and for the moment all three half understood one another. Yet none dared say a word to ease the pent-up things that choked them.

It was the husband's voice that broke the silence at last.

'You wanted to see me?' he said to Raut.

Raut started as he spoke. 'I came to see you,' he said, resolved to lie to the last.

'Yes,' said Horrocks.

'You promised,' said Raut, 'to show me some fine effects of moonlight and smoke.'

'I promised to show you some fine effects of moonlight and smoke,' repeated Horrocks in a colourless voice.

'And I thought I might catch you tonight before you went down to the works,' proceeded Raut, 'and come with you.'

There was another pause. Did the man mean to take the thing coolly? Did he, after all, know? How long had he been in the room? Yet even at the moment when they heard the door, their attitudes ... Horrocks glanced at the profile of the woman, shadowy pallid in the half-light. Then he glanced at Raut, and seemed to recover himself suddenly. 'Of course,' he said, 'I promised to show you the works under their proper dramatic conditions. It's odd how I could have forgotten.'

'If I am troubling you—' began Raut.

Horrocks started again. A new light had suddenly come into the sultry gloom of his eyes. 'Not in the least,' he said.

'Have you been telling Mr Raut of all these contrasts of flame and shadow you think so splendid?' said the woman, turning now to her husband for the first time, her confidence creeping back again, her voice just one half-note too high – 'that dreadful theory of yours that machinery is beautiful, and everything else in the world ugly. I thought he would not spare you, Mr Raut. It's his great theory, his one discovery in art.'

'I am slow to make discoveries,' said Horrocks grimly, damping her suddenly. 'But what I discover ...' He stopped.

'Well?' she said.

'Nothing;' and suddenly he rose to his feet.

'I promised to show you the works,' he said to Raut, and put his big, clumsy hand on his friend's shoulder. 'And you are ready to go?'

'Quite,' said Raut, and stood up also.

There was another pause. Each of them peered through the indistinctness of the dusk at the other two. Horrocks' hand still rested on Raut's shoulder. Raut half fancied still that the incident was trivial after all. But Mrs Horrocks knew her husband better, knew that grim quiet in his voice, and the confusion in her mind took a vague shape of physical evil. 'Very well,' said Horrocks, and, dropping his hand, turned towards the door.

'My hat?' Raut looked round in the half-light.

'That's my work-basket,' said Mrs Horrocks with a gust of hysterical laughter. Their hands came together on the back of the chair. 'Here it is!' he said. She had an impulse to warn him in an undertone, but she could not frame a word. 'Don't go!' and

'Beware of him!' struggled in her mind, and the swift moment passed.

'Got it?' said Horrocks, standing with the door half open.

Raut stepped towards him. 'Better say goodbye to Mrs Horrocks,' said the ironmaster, even more grimly quiet in his tone than before.

Raut started and turned. 'Good-evening, Mrs Horrocks,' he said, and their hands touched.

Horrocks held the door open with a ceremonial politeness unusual in him towards men. Raut went out, and then, after a wordless look at her, her husband followed. She stood motionless while Raut's light footfall and her husband's heavy tread, like bass and treble, passed down the passage together. The front door slammed heavily. She went to the window, moving slowly, and stood watching, leaning forward. The two men appeared for a moment at the gateway in the road, passed under the street lamp, and were hidden by the black masses of the shrubbery. The lamplight fell for a moment on their faces, showing only unmeaning pale patches, telling nothing of what she still feared, and doubted, and craved vainly to know. Then she sank down into a crouching attitude in the big arm-chair, her eyes wide open and staring out at the red lights from the furnaces that flickered in the sky. An hour after she was still there, her attitude scarcely changed.

The oppressive stillness of the evening weighed heavily upon Raut. They went side by side down the road in silence, and in silence turned into the cinder-made byway that presently opened out the prospect of the valley.

A blue haze, half dust, half mist, touched the long valley with mystery. Beyond were Hanley and Etruria, grey and dark masses, outlined thinly by the rare golden dots of the street lamps, and here and there a gas-lit window, or the yellow glare of some late-working factory or crowded public-house. Out of the masses, clear and slender against the evening sky, rose a multitude of tall chimneys, many of them reeking, a few smokeless during a season of 'play'. Here and there a pallid patch and ghostly stunted beehive shapes showed the position of a pot-bank or a wheel, black and sharp against the hot lower sky, marked some colliery where they raise the iridescent coal of the place. Nearer at hand was the broad stretch of railway, and half-invisible trains shunted – a steady puffing and rumbling, with every run a ringing concussion and a rhymthic series of impacts, and a passage of intermittent puffs of white steam across the further view. And to the left, between the railway and the dark mass of the low hill beyond, dominating the whole view, colossal, inky-black, and crowned with smoke and fitful flames, stood the great cylinders of the Jeddah Company Blast Furnaces, the central edifices of the big ironworks of which Horrocks was the manager. They stood heavy and threatening, full of an incessant turmoil of flames and seething molten iron, and about the feet of them rattled the rolling-mills, and the steam-hammer beat heavily and splashed the white iron sparks hither and thither. Even as they looked, a truckful of fuel was shot into one of the giants, and the red flames gleamed out, and a confusion of smoke and black dust came boiling upwards towards the sky.

'Certainly you get some colour with your furnaces,' said Raut, breaking a silence that had become apprehensive.

Horrocks grunted. He stood with his hands in his pockets, frowning down at the dim steaming railway and the busy ironworks beyond, frowning as if he were thinking out some knotty problem.

Raut glanced at him and away again. 'At present your moonlight effect is hardly ripe,' he continued, looking upward; 'the moon is still smothered by the vestiges of daylight.'

Horrocks stared at him with the expression of a man who has suddenly awakened. 'Vestiges of daylight? ... Of course, of course.' He too looked up at the moon, pale still in the midsummer sky. 'Come along,' he said suddenly, and gripping Raut's arm in his hand, made a move towards the path that dropped from them to the railway.

Raut hung back. Their eyes met and saw a thousand things in a moment that their lips came near to say. Horrocks's hand tightened and then relaxed. He let go, and before Raut was aware of it, they were arm in arm, and walking, one unwillingly enough, down the path.

'You see the fine effect of the railway signals towards Burslem,' said Horrocks, suddenly breaking into loquacity, striding fast and tightening the grip of his elbow the while – 'little green lights and red and white lights, all against the haze. You have an eye for effect, Raut. It's fine. And look at those furnaces of mine, how they rise upon us as we come down the hill. That to the right is my pet – seventy feet of him. I packed him myself, and he's boiled away cheerfully with iron in his guts for five long years. I've a particular fancy for *him*. That line of red there – a lovely bit of warm orange you'd call it, Raut – that's the puddlers' furnaces, and there, in the hot light, three black figures – did you see the white splash of the steam-hammer then? – that's the rolling mills. Come along! Clang, clatter, how it goes rattling across the floor! Sheet tin, Raut, – amazing stuff. Glass mirrors are not in it when that stuff comes from the mill. And, squelch! there goes the hammer again. Come along!'

He had to stop talking to catch at his breath. His arm twisted into Raut's with benumbing tightness. He had come striding down the black path towards the railway as though he was possessed. Raut had not spoken a word, had simply hung back against Horrocks's pull with all his strength.

'I say,' he said now, laughing nervously, but with an undertone of snarl in his voice, 'why on earth are you nipping my arm off, Horrocks, and dragging me along like this?'

At length Horrocks released him. His manner changed again. 'Nipping your arm off?' he said. 'Sorry. But it's you taught me the trick of walking in that friendly way.'

'You haven't learnt the refinements of it yet then,' said Raut, laughing artificially again. 'By Jove! I'm black and blue.' Horrocks offered no apology. They stood now near the bottom of the hill, close to the fence that bordered the railway. The ironworks had grown larger and spread out with their approach. They looked up to the blast furnaces now instead of down; the further view of Etruria and Hanley had dropped out of sight with their descent. Before them, by the stile, rose a notice-board, bearing, still dimly visible, the words, 'BEWARE OF THE TRAINS,' half hidden by splashes of coaly mud.

'Fine effects,' said Horrocks, waving his arm. 'Here comes a train. The puffs of smoke, the orange glare, the round eye of light in front of it, the melodious rattle. Fine effects! But these furnaces of mine used to be finer, before we shoved cones in their throats, and saved the gas.'

'How?' said Raut. 'Cones?'

'Cones, my man, cones. I'll show you one nearer. The flames used to flare out of the open throats, great – what is it? – pillars of cloud by day, red and black smoke, and pillars of fire by night. Now we run it off in pipes, and burn it to heat the blast, and the top is shut by a cone. You'll be interested in that cone.'

'But every now and then,' said Raut, 'you get a burst of fire and smoke up there.'

'The cone's not fixed, it's hung by a chain from a lever, and balanced by an equipoise. You shall see it nearer. Else, of course, there'd be no way of getting fuel into the thing. Every now and then the cone dips, and out comes the flare.'

'I see,' said Raut. He looked over his shoulder. 'The moon gets brighter,' he said.

'Come along,' said Horrocks abruptly, gripping his shoulder again, and moving him suddenly towards the railway crossing. And then came one of those swift incidents, vivid, but so rapid that they leave one doubtful and reeling. Half-way across, Horrocks's hand suddenly clenched upon him like a vice, and swung him backward and through a half-turn, so that he looked up the line. And there a chain of lamp-lit carriage windows telescoped swiftly as it came towards them, and the red and yellow lights of an engine grew larger and larger, rushing down upon them. As he grasped what this meant, he turned his face to Horrocks, and pushed with all his strength against the arm that held him back between the rails. The struggle did not last a moment. Just as certain as it was that Horrocks held him there, so certain was it that he had been violently lugged out of danger.

'Out of the way,' said Horrocks with a gasp, as the train came rattling by, and they stood panting by the gate into the ironworks.

'I did not see it coming,' said Raut, still, even in spite of his own apprehensions, trying to keep up an appearance of ordinary intercourse.

Horrocks answered with a grunt. 'The cone,' he said, and then, as one who recovers himself. 'I thought you did not hear.'

'I didn't,' said Raut.

'I wouldn't have had you run over then for the world,' said Horrocks.

'For a moment I lost my nerve,' said Raut.

Horrocks stood for half a minute, then turned abruptly towards the ironworks again. 'See how fine these great mounds of mine, these clinker-heaps, look in the night! That truck yonder, up above there! Up it goes, and out-tilts the slag. See the palpitating red stuff go sliding down the slope. As we get nearer, the heap rises up and cuts the blast furnaces. See the quiver up above the big one. Not that way! This way, between the heaps. That goes to the puddling furnaces, but I want to show you the canal first.' He came and took Raut by the elbow, and so they went along side by side. Raut answered Horrocks vaguely. What, he asked himself, had really happened on the line? Was he deluding himself with his own fancies, or had Horrocks actually held him back in the way of the train? Had he just been within an ace of being murdered?

Suppose this slouching, scowling monster *did* know anything? For a minute or two then Raut was really afraid for his life, but the mood passed as he reasoned with himself. After all, Horrocks might have heard nothing. At any rate, he had pulled him out of the way in time. His odd manner might be due to the mere vague jealousy he had shown once before. He was talking now of the ash-heaps and the canal. 'Eigh?' said Horrocks.

'What?' said Raut. 'Rather! The haze in the moonlight. Fine!'

'Our canal,' said Horrocks, stopping suddenly. 'Our canal by moonlight and firelight is immense. You've never seen it? Fancy that! You've spent too many of your evenings philandering up in Newcastle there. I tell you, for real florid quality—But you shall see. Boiling water ...'

As they came out of the labyrinth of clinker-heaps and mounds of coal and ore, the noises of the rolling-mill sprang upon them suddenly, loud, near, and distinct. Three shadowy workmen went by and touched their caps to Horrocks. Their faces were vague in the darkness. Raut felt a futile impulse to address them, and before he could frame his words they passed into the shadows. Horrocks pointed to the canal close before them now: a weird-looking place it seemed, in the blood-red reflections of the furnaces. The hot water that cooled the tuyères came into it, some fifty yards up – a tumultuous, almost boiling affluent, and the steam rose up from the water in silent white wisps and streaks, wrapping damply about them, an incessant succession of ghosts coming up from the black and red eddies, a white uprising that made the head swim. The shining black tower of the larger blast-furnace rose overhead out of the mist, and its tumultuous riot filled their ears. Raut kept away from the edge of the water, and watched Horrocks.

'Here it is red,' said Horrocks, 'blood-red vapour as red and hot as sin; but yonder there, where the moonlight falls on it, and it drives across the clinker-heaps, it is as white as death.'

Raut turned his head for a moment, and then came back hastily to his watch on Horrocks. 'Come along to the rolling-mills,' said Horrocks. The threatening hold was not so evident that time, and Raut felt a little reassured. But all the same, what on earth did Horrocks mean about 'white as death' and 'red as sin'? Coincidence, perhaps?

They went and stood behind the puddlers for a little while, and then through the rolling-mills, where amidst an incessant din the deliberate steam-hammer beat the juice out of the succulent iron, and black, half-naked Titans rushed the plastic bars, like hot sealing-wax, between the wheels. 'Come on,' said Horrocks in Raut's ear; and they went and peeped through the little glass hole behind the tuyères, and saw the tumbled fire writhing in the pit of the blast-furnace. It left one eye blinded for a while. Then, with green and blue patches dancing across the dark, they went to the lift by which the trucks of ore and fuel and lime were raised to the top of the big cylinder.

And out upon the narrow rail that overhung the furnace Raut's doubts came upon him again. Was it wise to be here? If Horrocks did know – everything! Do what he would, he could not resist a violent trembling. Right under foot was a sheer depth of seventy feet. It was a dangerous place. They pushed by a truck of fuel to get to the railing that crowned the thing. The reek of the furnace, a sulphurous vapour streaked with pungent bitterness, seemed to make the distant hillside of Hanley quiver. The moon was riding out now from among a drift of clouds, half-way up the sky above the undulating wooded outlines of Newcastle. The steaming canal ran away from below them under an indistinct bridge, and vanished into the dim haze of the flat fields towards Burslem.

'That's the cone I've been telling you of,' shouted Horrocks; 'and, below that, sixty feet of fire and molten metal, with the air of the blast frothing through it like gas in soda-water.'

Raut gripped the hand-rail tightly, and stared down at the cone. The heat was intense. The boiling of the iron and the tumult of the blast made a thunderous accompaniment to Horrocks's voice. But the thing had to be gone through now. Perhaps, after all ...

'In the middle,' bawled Horrocks, 'temperature near a thousand degrees. If *you* were dropped into it ... flash into flame like a pinch of gunpowder in a candle. Put your hand out and feel the heat of his breath. Why, even up here I've seen the rain-water boiling off the trucks. And that cone there. It's a damned sight too hot for roasting cakes. The top side of it's three hundred degrees.'

'Three hundred degrees!' said Raut.

'Three hundred centigrade, mind!' said Horrocks. 'It will boil the blood out of you in no time.'

'Eigh?' said Raut, and turned.

'Boil the blood out of you in ... No, you don't!'

'Let me go!' screamed Raut. 'Let go my arm!'

With one hand he clutched at the hand-rail, then with both. For a moment the two men stood swaying. Then suddenly, with a violent jerk, Horrocks had twisted him from his hold. He clutched at Horrocks and missed, his foot went back into empty air; in mid-air he twisted himself, and then cheek and shoulder and knee struck the hot cone together.

He clutched the chain by which the cone hung, and the thing sank an infinitesimal amount as he struck it. A circle of glowing red appeared about him, and a tongue of flame, released from the chaos within, flickered up towards him. An intense pain assailed him at the knees, and he could smell the singeing of his hands. He raised himself to his feet, and tried to climb up the chain, and then something struck his head. Black and shining with the moonlight, the throat of the furnace rose about him.

Horrocks, he saw, stood above him by one of the trucks of fuel on the rail. The gesticulating figure was bright and white in the moonlight, and shouting, 'Fizzle, you fool! Fizzle, you hunter of women! You hot-blooded hound! Boil! boil! boil!'

Suddenly he caught up a handful of coal out of the truck, and flung it deliberately, lump after lump, at Raut.

'Horrocks!' cried Raut. 'Horrocks!'

He clung, crying, to the chain, pulling himself up from the burning of the cone. Each missile Horrocks flung hit him. His clothes charred and glowed, and as he struggled the cone dropped, and a rush of hot, suffocating gas whooped out and burned round him in a swift breath of flame.

His human likeness departed from him. When the momentary red had passed, Horrocks saw a charred, blackened figure, its head streaked with blood, still clutching and fumbling with the chain, and writhing in agony – a cindery animal, an inhuman, monstrous creature that began a sobbing, intermittent shriek.

Abruptly at the sight the ironmaster's anger passed. A deadly sickness came upon him. The heavy odour of burning flesh came drifting up to his nostrils. His sanity returned to him.

'God have mercy upon me!' he cried. 'O God! what have I done?'

He knew the thing below him, save that it still moved and felt, was already a dead man – that the blood of the poor wretch must be boiling in his veins. An intense realisation of that agony came to his mind, and overcame every other feeling. For a moment he stood irresolute, and then, turning to the truck, he hastily tilted its contents upon the struggling thing that had once been a man. The mass fell with a thud, and went radiating over the cone. With the thud the shriek ended, and a boiling confusion of smoke, dust, and flame came rushing up towards him. As it passed, he saw the cone clear again.

Then he staggered back, and stood trembling, clinging to the rail with both hands. His lips moved, but no words came to them.

Down below was the sound of voices and running steps. The clangour of rolling in the shed ceased abruptly.

The Diamond Maker

Some business had detained me in Chancery Lane until nine in the evening, and thereafter, having some inkling of a headache, I was disinclined either for entertainment or further work. So much of the sky as the high cliffs of that narrow cañon of traffic left visible spoke of a serene night, and I determined to make my way down to the Embankment, and rest my eyes and cool my head by watching the variegated lights upon the river. Beyond comparison the night is the best time for this place; a merciful darkness hides the dirt of the waters, and the lights of this transition age, red, glaring orange, gas-yellow, and electric white, are set in shadowy outlines of every possible shade between grey and deep purple. Through the arches of Waterloo Bridge a hundred points of light mark the sweep of the Embankment, and above its parapet rise the towers of Westminster, warm grey against the starlight. The black river goes by with only a rare ripple breaking its silence, and disturbing the reflections of the lights that swim upon its surface.

'A warm night,' said a voice at my side.

I turned my head, and saw the profile of a man who was leaning over the parapet beside me. It was a refined face, not unhandsome, though pinched and pale enough, and the coat collar turned up and pinned round the throat marked his status in life as sharply as a uniform. I felt I was committed to the price of a bed and breakfast if I answered him.

I looked at him curiously. Would he have anything to tell me worth the money, or was he the common incapable – incapable even of telling his own story? There was a quality of intelligence in his forehead and eyes, and a certain tremulousness in his nether lip that decided me.

'Very warm,' said I; 'but not too warm for us here.'

'No,' he said, still looking across the water, 'it is pleasant enough here ... just now.'

'It is good,' he continued after a pause, 'to find anything so restful as this in London. After one has been fretting about business all day, about getting on, meeting obligations, and parrying dangers, I do not know what one would do if it were not for such pacific corners.' He spoke with long pauses between the sentences. 'You must know a little of the irksome labour of the world, or you would not be here. But I doubt if you can be so brain-weary and footsore as I am ... Bah! Sometimes I doubt if the game is worth the candle. I feel inclined to throw the whole thing over – name, wealth, and position – and take to some modest trade. But I know if I abandoned my ambition – hardly as she uses me – I should have nothing but remorse left for the rest of my days.'

He became silent. I looked at him in astonishment. If ever I saw a man hopelessly hard-up it was the man in front of me. He was ragged and he was dirty, unshaven and unkempt; he looked as though he had been left in a dust-bin for a week. And he was talking to *me* of the irksome worries of a large business. I almost laughed outright. Either he was mad or playing a sorry jest on his own poverty.

'If high aims and high positions,' said I, 'have their drawbacks of hard work and anxiety, they have their compensations. Influence, the power of doing good, of assisting those weaker and poorer than ourselves; and there is even a certain gratification in display....'

My banter under the circumstances was in very vile taste. I spoke on the spur of the contrast of his appearance and speech. I was sorry even while I was speaking.

He turned a haggard but very composed face upon me. Said he: 'I forget myself. Of course you would not understand.'

He measured me for a moment. 'No doubt it is very absurd. You will not believe me even when I tell you, so that it is fairly safe to tell you. And it will be a comfort to tell someone. I really have a big business in hand, a very big business. But there are troubles just now. The fact is ... I make diamonds.'

'I suppose,' said I, 'you are out of work just at present?'

'I am sick of being disbelieved,' he said impatiently, and suddenly unbuttoning his wretched coat he pulled out a little canvas bag that was hanging by a cord round his neck. From this he produced a brown pebble. 'I wonder if you know enough to know what that is?' He handed it to me.

Now, a year or so ago, I had occupied my leisure in taking a

London science degree, so that I have a smattering of physics and mineralogy. The thing was not unlike an uncut diamond of the darker sort, though far too large, being almost as big as the top of my thumb. I took it, and saw it had the form of a regular octahedron, with the carved faces peculiar to the most precious of minerals. I took out my penknife and tried to scratch it – vainly. Leaning forward towards the gas-lamp, I tried the thing on my watch-glass, and scored a white line across that with the greatest ease.

I looked at my interlocutor with rising curiosity. 'It certainly is rather like a diamond. But, if so, it is a Behemoth of diamonds. Where did you get it?'

'I tell you I made it,' he said. 'Give it back to me.'

He replaced it hastily and buttoned his jacket. 'I will sell it you for one hundred pounds,' he suddenly whispered eagerly. With that my suspicions returned. The thing might, after all, be merely a lump of that almost equally hard substance, corundum, with an accidental resemblance in shape to the diamond. Or if it was a diamond, how came he by it, and why should he offer it at a hundred pounds?

We looked into one another's eyes. He seemed eager, but honestly eager. At that moment I believed it was a diamond he was trying to sell. Yet I am a poor man, a hundred pounds would leave a visible gap in my fortunes and no sane man would buy a diamond by gaslight from a ragged tramp on his personal warranty only. Still, a diamond that size conjured up a vision of many thousands of pounds. Then, thought I, such a stone could scarcely exist without being mentioned in every book on gems, and again I called to mind the stories of contraband and light-fingered Kaffirs at the Cape. I put the question of purchase on one side.

'How did you get it?' said I.

'I made it.'

I had heard something of Moissan, but I knew his artificial diamonds were very small. I shook my head.

'You seem to know something of this kind of thing. I will tell you a little about myself. Perhaps then you may think better of the purchase.' He turned round with his back to the river, and put his hands in his pockets. He sighed. 'I know you will not believe me.'

'Diamonds,' he began – and as he spoke his voice lost its faint flavour of the tramp and assumed something of the easy tone of an educated man – 'are to be made by throwing carbon out of combination in a suitable flux and under a suitable pressure; the carbon crystallises out, not as black-lead or charcoal-powder, but as small diamonds. So much has been known to chemists for years, but no one yet has hit upon exactly the right flux in which to melt up the carbon, or exactly the right pressure for the best results. Consequently the diamonds made by chemists are small and dark, and worthless as jewels. Now I, you know, have given up my life to this problem – given my life to it.

'I began to work at the conditions of diamond making when I was seventeen, and now I am thirty-two. It seemed to me that it might take all the thought and energies of a man for ten years, or twenty years, but, even if it did, the game was still worth the candle. Suppose one to have at last just hit the right trick, before the secret got out and diamonds became as common as coal, one might realise millions. Millions!'

He paused and looked for my sympathy. His eyes shone hungrily. 'To think,' said he, 'that I am on the verge of it all, and here!

'I had,' he proceeded, 'about a thousand pounds when I was twenty-one, and this, I thought, eked out by a little teaching, would keep my researches going. A year or two was spent in study, at Berlin chiefly, and then I continued on my own account. The trouble was the secrecy. You see, if once I had let out what I was doing, other men might have been spurred on by my belief in the practicability of the idea; and I do not pretend to be such a genius as to have been sure of coming in first, in the case of a race for the discovery. And you see it was important that if I really meant to make a pile, people should not know it was an artificial process and capable of turning out diamonds by the ton. So I had to work all alone. At first I had a little laboratory, but as my resources began to run out I had to conduct my experiments in a wretched unfurnished room in Kentish Town, where I slept at last on a straw mattress on the floor among all my apparatus. The money simply flowed away. I grudged myself everything except scientific appliances. I tried to keep things going by a little teaching, but I am not a very good teacher, and I have no university degree, nor very much education except in chemistry, and I found I had to give a lot of time and labour for precious little money. But I got nearer and nearer the thing. Three years ago I settled the problem of the composition of the flux, and got near the pressure by putting this flux of mine and a certain carbon composition into a closed-up gun-barrel, filling up with water, sealing tightly, and heating.'

He paused.

'Rather risky,' said I.

'Yes. It burst, and smashed all my windows and a lot of my apparatus; but I got a kind of diamond powder nevertheless. Following out the problem of getting a big pressure upon the molten mixture from which the things were to crystallise, I hit upon some researches of Daubrée's at the Paris *Laboratorie des Poudres et Salpêtres*. He exploded dynamite in a tightly screwed steel cylinder, too strong to burst, and I found he could crush rocks into a muck not unlike the South African bed in which diamonds are found. It was a tremendous strain on my resources, but I got a steel cylinder made for my purpose after his pattern. I put in all my stuff and my explosives, built up a fire in my furnace, put the whole concern in, and – went out for a walk.'

I could not help laughing at his matter-of-fact manner. 'Did you not think it would blow up the house? Were there other people in the place?'

'It was in the interest of science,' he said ultimately. 'There was a costermonger family on the floor below, a begging-letter writer in the room behind mine, and two flower-women were upstairs. Perhaps it was a bit thoughtless. But possibly some of them were out.

'When I came back the thing was just where I left it, among the white-hot coals. The explosive hadn't burst the case. And then I had a problem to face. You know time is an important element in crystallisation. If you hurry the process the crystals are small – it is only by prolonged standing that they grow to any size. I resolved to let this apparatus cool for two years, letting the temperature go down slowly during that time. And I was now quite out of money; and with a big fire and the rent of my room, as well as my hunger to satisfy, I had scarcely a penny in the world.

'I can hardly tell you all the shifts I was put to while I was making the diamonds. I have sold newspapers, held horses, opened cab-doors. For many weeks I addressed envelopes. I had a place as assistant to a man who owned a barrow, and used to call down one side of the road while he called down the other. Once for a week I had absolutely nothing to do, and I begged. What a week that was! One day the fire was going out and I had eaten nothing all day, and a little chap taking his girl out, gave me sixpence – to show-off. Thank heaven for vanity! How the fish-shops smelt! But I went and spent it all on coals, and had the furnace bright red again, and then—Well, hunger makes a fool of a man.

'At last, three weeks ago, I let the fire out. I took my cylinder and unscrewed it while it was still so hot that it punished my hands, and I scraped out the crumbling lava-like mass with a chisel, and hammered it into a powder upon an iron plate. And I found three big diamonds and five small ones. As I sat on the floor hammering, my door opened, and my neighbour, the begging-letter writer, came in. He was drunk – as he usually is. "'Nerchist," said he. "You're drunk," said I. "'Structive scoun-drel," said he. "Go to your father," said I, meaning the Father of Lies. "Never you mind," said he, and gave me a cunning wink, and hiccupped, and leaning up against the door, with his other eye against the door-post, began to babble of how he had been prying in my room, and how he had gone to the police that morning, and how they had taken down everything he had to say – "'siffiwas a ge'm," said he. Then I suddenly realised I was in a hole. Either I should have to tell these police my little secret, and get the whole thing blown upon, or be lagged as an Anarchist. So I went up to my neighbour and took him by the collar, and rolled him about a bit, and then I gathered up my diamonds and cleared out. The evening newspapers called my den the Kentish-Town Bomb Factory. And now I cannot part with the things for love or money.

'If I go in to respectable jewellers they ask me to wait, and go and whisper to a clerk to fetch a policeman, and then I say I cannot wait. And I found out a receiver of stolen goods, and he simply stuck to the one I gave him and told me to prosecute if I wanted it back. I am going about now with several hundred thousand pounds-worth of diamonds round my neck, and without either food or shelter. You are the first person I have taken into my confidence. But I like your face and I am hard-driven.'

He looked into my eyes.

'It would be madness,' said I, 'for me to buy a diamond under the circumstances. Besides, I do not carry hundreds of pounds about in my pocket. Yet I more than half believe your story. I will, if you like, do this: come to my office tomorrow ...'

'You think I am a thief!' said he keenly. 'You will tell the police. I am not coming into a trap.'

'Somehow I am assured you are no thief. Here is my card. Take that, anyhow. You need not come to any appointment. Come when you will.'

He took the card, and an earnest of my good-will.

'Think better of it and come,' said I.

He shook his head doubtfully. 'I will pay back your half-crown with interest some day – such interest as will amaze you,' said he. 'Anyhow, you will keep the secret? ... Don't follow me.'

He crossed the road and went into the darkness towards the little steps under the archway leading into Essex Street, and I let him go. And that was the last I ever saw of him.

Afterwards I had two letters from him asking me to send bank-notes – not cheques – to certain addresses. I weighed the matter over, and took what I conceived to be the wisest course. Once he called upon me when I was out. My urchin described him as a very thin, dirty, and ragged man, with a dreadful cough. He left no message. That was the finish of him so far as my story goes. I wonder sometimes what has become of him. Was he an ingenious monomaniac, or a fraudulent dealer in pebbles, or has he really made diamonds as he asserted? The latter is just sufficiently credible to make me think at times that I have missed the most brilliant opportunity of my life. He may of course be dead, and his diamonds carelessly thrown aside – one, I repeat, was almost as big as my thumb. Or he may be still wandering about trying to sell the things. It is just possible he may yet emerge upon society, and, passing athwart my heavens in the serene altitude sacred to the wealthy and the well-advertised, reproach me silently for my want of enterprise. I sometimes think I might at least have risked five pounds.

The Remarkable Case of Davidson's Eyes

1

The transitory mental aberration of Sidney Davidson, remarkable enough in itself, is still more remarkable if Wade's explanation is to be credited. It sets one dreaming of the oddest possibilities of intercommunication in the future, of spending an intercalary five minutes on the other side of the world, or being watched in our most secret operations by unsuspected eyes. It happened that I was the immediate witness of Davidson's seizure, and so it falls naturally to me to put the story upon paper.

When I say that I was the immediate witness of his seizure, I mean that I was the first on the scene. The thing happened at the Harlow Technical College, just beyond the Highgate Archway. He was alone in the larger laboratory when the thing happened. I was in a smaller room, where the balances are, writing up some notes. The thunderstorm had completely upset my work, of course. It was just after one of the louder peals that I thought I heard some glass smash in the other room. I stopped writing, and turned round to listen. For a moment I heard nothing; the hail was playing the devil's tattoo on the corrugated zinc of the roof. Then came another sound, a smash – no doubt of it this time. Something heavy had been knocked off the bench. I jumped up at once and went and opened the door leading into the big laboratory.

I was surprised to hear a queer sort of laugh, and saw Davidson standing unsteadily in the middle of the room, with a dazzled look on his face. My first impression was that he was drunk. He did not notice me. He was clawing out at something invisible a yard in front of his face. He put out his hand, slowly, rather hesitatingly, and then clutched nothing. 'What's come to it?' he said. He held up his hands to his face, fingers spread out. 'Great Scott!' he said. The thing happened three or four years ago, when every one swore by that personage. Then he began raising his feet clumsily, as though he had expected to find them glued to the floor.

'Davidson!' cried I. 'What's the matter with you?' He turned round in my direction and looked about for me. He looked over me and at me and on either side of me, without the slightest sign of seeing me. 'Waves,' he said; 'and a remarkably neat schooner. I'd swear that was Bellow's voice. *Hullo!*' He shouted suddenly at the top of his voice.

I thought he was up to some foolery. Then I saw littered about his feet the shattered remains of the best of our electrometers. 'What's up, man?' said I. 'You've smashed the electrometer!'

'Bellows again!' said he. 'Friends left, if my hands are gone. Something about electrometers. Which way *are* you, Bellows?' He suddenly came staggering towards me. 'The damned stuff cuts like butter,' he said. He walked straight into the bench and recoiled. 'None so buttery that!' he said, and stood swaying.

I felt scared. 'Davidson,' said I, 'what on earth's come over you?'

He looked round him in every direction. 'I could swear that was Bellows. Why don't you show yourself like a man, Bellows?'

It occurred to me that he must be suddenly struck blind. I walked round the table and laid my hand upon his arm. I never saw a man more startled in my life. He jumped away from me, and came round into an attitude of self-defence, his face fairly distorted with terror. 'Good God!' he cried. 'What was that?'

'It's I – Bellows. Confound it, Davidson!'

He jumped when I answered him and stared – how can I express it? – right through me. He began talking, not to me, but to himself. 'Here in broad daylight on a clear beach. Not a place to hide in.' He looked about him wildly. 'Here! I'm *off.*' He suddenly turned and ran headlong into the big electro-magnet – so violently that, as we found afterwards, he bruised his shoulder and jawbone cruelly. At that he stepped back a pace, and cried out with almost a whimper, 'What, in Heaven's name, has come over me?' He stood, blanched with terror and trembling violently, with his right arm clutching his left, where that had collided with the magnet.

By that time I was excited and fairly scared. 'Davidson,' said I, 'don't be afraid.'

He was startled at my voice, but not so excessively as before.

I repeated my words in as clear and as firm a tone as I could assume. 'Bellows,' he said, 'is that you?'

'Can't you see it's me?'

He laughed. 'I can't even see it's myself. Where the devil are we?'

'Here,' said I, 'in the laboratory.'

'The laboratory!' he answered in a puzzled tone, and put his hand to his forehead. 'I *was* in the laboratory – till that flash came, but I'm hanged if I'm there now. What ship is that?'

'There's no ship,' said I. 'Do be sensible, old chap.'

'No ship!' he repeated, and seemed to forget my denial forthwith. 'I suppose,' said he slowly, 'we're both dead. But the rummy part is I feel just as though I still had a body. Don't get used to it all at once, I suppose. The old shop was struck by lightning, I suppose. Jolly quick thing, Bellows – eigh?'

'Don't talk nonsense. You're very much alive. You are in the laboratory, blundering about. You've just smashed a new electrometer. I don't envy you when Boyce arrives.'

He stared away from me towards the diagrams of cryohydrates. 'I must be deaf,' said he. 'They've fired a gun, for there goes the puff of smoke, and I never heard a sound.'

I put my hand on his arm again, and this time he was less alarmed. 'We seem to have a sort of invisible bodies,' said he. 'By Jove! there's a boat coming round the headland. It's very much like the old life after all – in a different climate.'

I shook his arm. 'Davidson,' I cried, 'wake up!'

2

It was just then that Boyce came in. So soon as he spoke Davidson exclaimed: 'Old Boyce! Dead too! What a lark!' I hastened to explain that Davidson was in a kind of somnambulistic trance. Boyce was interested at once. We both did all we could to rouse the fellow out of his extraordinary state. He answered our questions, and asked us some of his own, but his attention seemed distracted by his hallucination about a beach and a ship. He kept interpolating observations concerning some boat and the davits, and sails filling with the wind. It made one feel queer, in the dusky laboratory, to hear him saying such things.

He was blind and helpless. We had to walk him down the

passage, one at each elbow, to Boyce's private room, and while Boyce talked to him there, and humoured him about this ship idea, I went along the corridor and asked old Wade to come and look at him. The voice of our Dean sobered him a little, but not very much. He asked where his hands were, and why he had to walk about up to his waist in the ground. Wade thought over him a long time – you know how he knits his brows – and then made him feel the couch, guiding his hands to it. 'That's a couch,' said Wade. 'The couch in the private room of Professor Boyce. Horse-hair stuffing.'

Davidson felt about, and puzzled over it, and answered presently that he could feel it all right, but he couldn't see it.

'What *do* you see?' asked Wade. Davidson said he could see nothing but a lot of sand and broken-up shells. Wade gave him some other things to feel, telling him what they were, and watching him keenly.

'The ship is almost hull down,' said Davidson presently, *apropos* of nothing.

'Never mind the ship,' said Wade. 'Listen to me, Davidson. Do you know what hallucination means?'

'Rather,' said Davidson.

'Well, everything you see is hallucinatory.'

'Bishop Berkeley,' said Davidson.

'Don't mistake me,' said Wade. 'You are alive and in this room of Boyce's. But something has happened to your eyes. You cannot see; you can feel and hear, but not see. Do you follow me?'

'It seems to me that I see too much.' Davidson rubbed his knuckles into his eyes. 'Well?' he said.

'That's all. Don't let it perplex you. Bellows here and I will take you home in a cab.'

'Wait a bit.' Davidson thought. 'Help me to sit down,' said he presently; 'and now – I'm sorry to trouble you – but will you tell me all that over again?'

Wade repeated it very patiently. Davidson shut his eyes, and pressed his hands upon his forehead. 'Yes,' said he. 'It's quite right. Now my eyes are shut I know you're right. That's you, Bellows, sitting by me on the couch. I'm in England again. And we're in the dark.'

Then he opened his eyes. 'And there,' said he, 'is the sun just rising, and the yards of the ship, and a tumbled sea, and a couple of birds flying. I never saw anything so real. And I'm sitting up to my neck in a bank of sand.'

He bent forward and covered his face with his hands. Then he opened his eyes again. 'Dark sea and sunrise! And yet I'm sitting on a sofa in old Boyce's room! ... God help me!'

3

That was the beginning. For three weeks this strange affection of Davidson's eyes continued unabated. It was far worse than being blind. He was absolutely helpless, and had to be fed like a newly-hatched bird, and led about and undressed. If he attempted to move, he fell over things or struck himself against walls or doors. After a day or so he got used to hearing our voices without seeing us, and willingly admitted he was at home, and that Wade was right in what he told him. My sister, to whom he was engaged, insisted on coming to see him, and would sit for hours every day while he talked about this beach of his. Holding her hand seemed to comfort him immensely. He explained that when we left the College and drove home – he lived in Hampstead village – it appeared to him as if we drove right through a sandhill – it was perfectly black until he emerged again – and through rocks and trees and solid obstacles, and when he was taken to his own room it made him giddy and almost frantic with the fear of falling, because going upstairs seemed to lift him thirty or forty feet above the rocks of his imaginary island. He kept saying he should smash all the eggs. The end was that he had to be taken down into his father's consulting room and laid upon a couch that stood there.

He described the island as being a bleak kind of place on the whole, with very little vegetation, except some peaty stuff, and a lot of bare rock. There were multitudes of penguins, and they made the rocks white and disagreeable to see. The sea was often rough, and once there was a thunderstorm, and he lay and shouted at the silent flashes. Once or twice seals pulled up on the beach, but only on the first two or three days. He said it was very funny the way in which the penguins used to waddle right through him, and how he seemed to lie among them without disturbing them.

I remember one odd thing, and that was when he wanted very badly to smoke. We put a pipe in his hands – he almost poked his eye out with it – and lit it. But he couldn't taste anything. I've since found it's the same with me – I don't know if it's the usual case – that I cannot enjoy tobacco at all unless I can see the smoke.

But the queerest part of his vision came when Wade sent him out in a Bath-chair to get fresh air. The Davidsons hired a chair, and got that deaf and obstinate dependant of theirs, Widgery, to attend to it. Widgery's ideas of healthy expeditions were peculiar. My sister, who had been to the Dogs' Home, met them in Camden Town, towards King's Cross, Widgery trotting along complacently, and Davidson, evidently most distressed, trying in his feeble, blind way to attract Widgery's attention.

He positively wept when my sister spoke to him. 'Oh, get me out of this horrible darkness!' he said, feeling for her hand. 'I must get out of it, or I shall die.' He was quite incapable of explaining what was the matter, but my sister decided he must go home, and presently, as they went uphill towards Hampstead, the horror seemed to drop from him. He said it was good to see the stars again, though it was then about noon and a blazing day.

'It seemed,' he told me afterwards, 'as if I was being carried irresistibly towards the water. I was not very much alarmed at first. Of course it was night there – a lovely night.'

'Of course?' I asked, for that struck me as odd.

'Of course,' said he. 'It's always night there when it is day here.... Well, we went right into the water, which was calm and shining under the moonlight – just a broad swell that seemed to grow broader and flatter as I came down into it. The surface glistened just like a skin – it might have been empty space underneath for all I could tell to the contrary. Very slowly, for I rode slanting into it, the water crept up to my eyes. Then I went under and the skin seemed to break and heal again about my eyes. The moon gave a jump up in the sky and grew green and dim, and fish, faintly glowing, came darting round me – and things that seemed made of luminous glass; and I passed through a tangle of seaweeds that shone with an oily lustre. And so I drove down into the sea, and the stars went out one by one, and the moon grew greener and darker, and the seaweed became a luminous purple-red. It was all very faint and mysterious, and everything seemed to quiver. And all the while I could hear the wheels of the Bath-chair creaking, and the footsteps of people going by, and a man in the distance selling the special *Pall Mall*.

'I kept sinking down deeper and deeper into the water. It became inky black about me, not a ray from above came down into that darkness, and the phosphorescent things grew brighter and brighter. The snaky branches of the deeper weeds flickered like the flames of spirit-lamps; but, after a time, there were no more weeds. The fishes came staring and gaping towards me, and into me and through me. I never imagined such fishes before. They had lines of fire along the sides of them as though they had been outlined with a luminous pencil. And there was a ghastly thing swimming backwards with a lot of twining arms. And then I saw, coming very slowly towards me through the gloom, a hazy mass of light that resolved itself as it drew nearer into multitudes of fishes, struggling and darting round something that drifted. I drove on straight towards it, and presently I saw in the midst of the tumult, and by the light of the fish, a bit of splintered spar looming over me, and a dark hull tilting over, and some glowing phosphorescent forms that were shaken and writhed as the fish bit at them. Then it was I began to try to attract Widgery's attention. A horror came upon me. Ugh! I should have driven right into those half-eaten—things. If your sister had not come! They had great holes in them, Bellows, and ... Never mind. But it was ghastly!'

4

For three weeks Davidson remained in this singular state, seeing what at the time we imagined was an altogether phantasmal world, and stone blind to the world around him. Then, one Tuesday, when I called I met old Davidson in the passage. 'He can see his thumb!' the old gentleman said, in a perfect transport. He was struggling into his overcoat. 'He can see his thumb, Bellows!' he said, with the tears in his eyes. 'The lad will be all right yet.'

I rushed in to Davidson. He was holding up a little book before his face, and looking at it and laughing in a weak kind of way.

'It's amazing,' said he. 'There's a kind of patch come there.' He pointed with his finger. 'I'm on the rocks as usual, and the penguins are staggering and flapping about as usual, and there's been a whale showing every now and then, but it's got too dark now to make him out. But put something *there*, and I see it – I do see it. It's very dim and broken in places, but I see it all the same, like a faint spectre of itself. I found it out this morning while they were dressing me. It's like a hole in this infernal phantom world. Just put your hand by mine. No – not there. Ah! Yes! I see it. The base of your thumb and a bit of cuff! It looks like the ghost of a bit of your hand sticking out of the darkling sky. Just by it there's a group of stars like a cross coming out.'

From that time Davidson began to mend. His account of the change, like his account of the vision, was oddly convincing. Over patches of his field of vision, the phantom world grew fainter, grew transparent, as it were, and through these translucent gaps he began to see dimly the real world about him. The patches grew in size and number, ran together and spread until only here and there were blind spots left upon his eyes. He was able to get up and steer himself about, feed himself once more, read, smoke, and behave like an ordinary citizen again. At first it was very confusing to him to have these two pictures overlapping each other like the changing views of a lantern, but in a little while he began to distinguish the real from the illusory.

At first he was unfeignedly glad, and seemed only too anxious to complete his cure by taking exercise and tonics. But as that odd island of his began to fade away from him, he became queerly interested in it. He wanted particularly to go down into the deep sea again, and would spend half his time wandering about the low lying parts of London, trying to find the water-logged wreck he had seen drifting. The glare of real daylight very soon impressed him so vividly as to blot out everything of his shadowy world, but of a night-time, in a darkened room, he could still see the white-splashed rocks of the island, and the clumsy penguins staggering to and fro. But even these grew fainter and fainter, and, at last, soon after he married my sister, he saw them for the last time.

5

And now to tell of the queerest thing of all. About two years after his cure I dined with the Davidsons, and after dinner a man named Atkins called in. He is a lieutenant in the Royal Navy, and a pleasant, talkative man. He was on friendly terms with my brother-in-law, and was soon on friendly terms with me. It came out that he was engaged to Davidson's cousin, and incidentally he took out a kind of pocket photograph case to show us a new rendering of his *fiancée*. 'And, by-the-by,' said he, 'here's the old *Fulmar*.'

Davidson looked at it casually. Then suddenly his face lit up. 'Good heavens!' said he. 'I could almost swear—'

'What?' said Alkins.

'That I had seen that ship before.'

'Don't see how you can have. She hasn't been out of the South Seas for six years, and before then—'

'But,' began Davidson, and then, 'Yes – that's the ship I dreamt of; I'm sure that's the ship I dreamt of. She was standing off an island that swarmed with penguins, and she fired a gun.'

'Good Lord!' said Atkins, who had now heard the particulars of the seizure. 'How the deuce could you dream that?'

And then, bit by bit, it came out that on the very day Davidson was seized, HMS *Fulmar* had actually been off a little rock to the south of Antipodes Island. A boat had landed overnight to get penguins' eggs, had been delayed, and a thunderstorm drifting up, the boat's crew had waited until the morning before rejoining the ship. Atkins had been one of them, and he corroborated, word for word, the descriptions Davidson had given of the island and the boat. There is not the slightest doubt in any of our minds that Davidson has really seen the place. In some unaccountable way, while he moved hither and thither in London, his sight moved hither and thither in a manner that corresponded, about this distant island. *How* is absolutely a mystery.

That completes the remarkable story of Davidson's eyes. It's perhaps the best authenticated case in existence of real vision at a distance. Explanation there is none forthcoming, except what Professor Wade has thrown out. But his explanation invokes the Fourth Dimension, and a dissertation on theoretical kinds of space. To talk of there being 'a kink in space' seems mere nonsense to me; it may be because I am no mathematician. When I said that nothing would alter the fact that the place is eight thousand miles away, he answered that two points might be a yard away on a sheet of paper, and yet be brought together by bending the paper round. The reader may grasp his argument, but I certainly do not. His idea seems to be that Davidson, stooping between the poles of the big electro-magnet, had some extraordinary twist given to his retinal elements through the sudden change in the field of force due to the lightning.

He thinks, as a consequence of this, that it may be possible to live visually in one part of the world, while one lives bodily in another. He has even made some experiments in support of his views; but, so far, he has simply succeeded in blinding a few dogs. I believe that is the net result of his work, though I have not seen him for some weeks. Latterly I have been so busy with my work in connection with the Saint Pancras installation that I have had little opportunity of calling to see him. But the whole of his theory seems fantastic to me. The facts concerning Davidson stand on an altogether different footing, and I can testify personally to the accuracy of every detail I have given.

The Story of the Late Mr Elvesham

I set this story down, not expecting it will be believed, but, if possible, to prepare a way of escape for the next victim. He, perhaps, may profit by my misfortune. My own case, I know, is hopeless, and I am now in some measure prepared to meet my fate.

My name is Edward George Eden. I was born at Trentham, in Staffordshire, my father being employed in the gardens there. I lost my mother when I was three years old, and my father when I was five, my uncle, George Eden, then adopting me as his own son. He was a single man, self-educated, and well known in Birmingham as an enterprising journalist; he educated me generously, fired my ambition to succeed in the world, and at his death, which happened four years ago, left me his entire fortune, a matter of about five hundred pounds after all outgoing charges were paid. I was then eighteen. He advised me in his will to expend the money in completing my education. I had already chosen the profession of medicine, and through his posthumous generosity and my good fortune in a scholarship competition, I became a medical student at University College, London. At the time of the beginning of my story I lodged at 11A University Street in a little upper room, very shabbily furnished and draughty, overlooking the back of Shoolbred's premises. I used this little room both to live in and sleep in, because I was anxious to eke out my means to the very last shillings-worth.

I was taking a pair of shoes to be mended at a shop in the Tottenham Court Road when I first encountered the little old man with the yellow face, with whom my life has now become so inextricably entangled. He was standing on the kerb, and staring at the number on the door in a doubtful way, as I opened it. His eyes – they were dull grey eyes, and reddish under the rims – fell to my face, and his countenance immediately assumed an expression of corrugated amiability.

'You come,' he said, 'apt to the moment. I had forgotten the number of your house. How do you do, Mr Eden?'

I was a little astonished at his familiar address, for I had never set eyes on the man before. I was a little annoyed, too, at his catching me with my boots under my arm. He noticed my lack of cordiality.

'Wonder who the deuce I am, eh? A friend, let me assure you. I have seen you before, though you haven't seen me. Is there anywhere where I can talk to you?'

I hesitated. The shabbiness of my room upstairs was not a matter for every stranger. 'Perhaps,' said I, 'we might walk down the street. I'm unfortunately prevented—' My gesture explained the sentence before I had spoken it.

'The very thing,' he said, and faced this way, and then that. 'The street? Which way shall we go?' I slipped my boots down in the passage. 'Look here!' he said abruptly; 'this business of mine is a rigmarole. Come and lunch with me, Mr Eden. I'm an old man, a very old man, and not good at explanations, and what with my piping voice and the clatter of the traffic—'

He laid a persuasive skinny hand that trembled a little upon my arm.

I was not so old that an old man might not treat me to a lunch. Yet at the same time I was not altogether pleased by this abrupt invitation. 'I had rather—' I began. 'But I had rather,' he said, catching me up, 'and a certain civility is surely due to my grey hairs.'

And so I consented, and went with him.

He took me to Blavitiski's; I had to walk slowly to accommodate myself to his paces; and over such a lunch as I had never tasted before, he fended off my leading question, and I took a better note of his appearance. His clean-shaven face was lean and wrinkled, his shrivelled lips fell over a set of false teeth, and his white hair was thin and rather long; he seemed small to me, – though indeed, most people seemed small to me, – and his shoulders were rounded and bent. And watching him, I could not help but observe that he too was taking note of me, running his eyes, with a curious touch of greed in them, over me, from my broad shoulders to my suntanned hands, and up to my freckled face again. 'And now,' said he, as we lit our cigarettes, 'I must tell you of the business in hand.

'I must tell you, then, that I am an old man, a very old man.' He paused momentarily. 'And it happens that I have money that

I must presently be leaving, and never a child have I to leave it to.' I thought of the confidence trick, and resolved I would be on the alert for the vestiges of my five hundred pounds. He proceeded to enlarge on his loneliness, and the trouble he had to find a proper disposition of his money. 'I have weighed this plan and that plan, charities, institutions, and scholarships, and libraries, and I have come to this conclusion at last,' – he fixed his eyes on my face, – 'that I will find some young fellow, ambitious, pure-minded, and poor, healthy in body and healthy in mind, and, in short, make him my heir, give him all that I have.' He repeated, 'Give him all that I have. So that he will suddenly be lifted out of all the trouble and struggle in which his sympathies have been educated, to freedom and influence.'

I tried to seem disinterested. With a transparent hypocrisy I said, 'And you want my help, my professional services maybe, to find that person.'

He smiled, and looked at me over his cigarette, and I laughed at his quiet exposure of my modest pretence.

'What a career such a man might have!' he said. 'It fills me with envy to think how I have accumulated that another man may spend—

'But there are conditions, of course, burdens to be imposed. He must, for instance, take my name. You cannot expect everything without some return. And I must go into all the circumstances of his life before I can accept him. He *must* be sound. I must know his heredity, how his parents and grandparents died, have the strictest inquiries made into his private morals.'

This modified my secret congratulations a little.

'And do I understand,' said I, 'that I—'

'Yes,' he said, almost fiercely. 'You. *You.*'

I answered never a word. My imagination was dancing wildly, my innate scepticism was useless to modify its transports. There was not a particle of gratitude in my mind – I did not know what to say nor how to say it. 'But why me in particular?' I said at last.

He had chanced to hear of me from Professor Haslar, he said, as a typically sound and sane young man, and he wished, as far as possible, to leave his money where health and integrity were assured.

That was my first meeting with the little old man. He was mysterious about himself; he would not give his name yet, he said, and after I had answered some questions of his, he left me at the Blavitiski portal. I noticed that he drew a handful of gold coins from his pocket when it came to paying for the lunch. His insistence upon bodily health was curious. In accordance with an arrangement we had made I applied that day for a life policy in the Loyal Insurance Company for a large sum, and I was exhaustively overhauled by the medical advisers of that company in the subsequent week. Even that did not satisfy him, and he insisted I must be re-examined by the great Doctor Henderson.

It was Friday in Whitsun week before he came to a decision. He called me down, quite late in the evening, – nearly nine it was, – from cramming chemical equations for my Preliminary Scientific examination. He was standing in the passage under the feeble gas-lamp, and his face was a grotesque interplay of shadows. He seemed more bowed than when I had first seen him, and his cheeks had sunk in a little.

His voice shook with emotion. 'Everything is satisfactory, Mr Eden,' he said. 'Everything is quite, quite satisfactory. And this night of all nights, you must dine with me and celebrate your – accession.' He was interrupted by a cough. 'You won't have long to wait, either,' he said, wiping his handkerchief across his lips, and gripping my hand with his long bony claw that was disengaged. 'Certainly not very long to wait.'

We went into the street and called a cab. I remember every incident of that drive vividly, the swift, easy motion, the vivid contrast of gas and oil and electric light, the crowds of people in the streets, the place in Regent Street to which we went, and the sumptuous dinner we were served with there. I was disconcerted at first by the well-dressed waiter's glances at my rough clothes, bothered by the stones of the olives, but as the champagne warmed my blood, my confidence revived. At first the old man talked of himself. He had already told me his name in the cab; he was Egbert Elvesham, the great philosopher, whose name I had known since I was a lad at school. It seemed incredible to me that this man, whose intelligence had so early dominated mine, this great abstraction, should suddenly realise itself as this decrepit, familiar figure. I daresay every young fellow who has suddenly fallen among celebrities has felt something of my disappointment. He told me now of the future that the feeble streams of his life would presently leave dry for me, houses, copyrights, investments; I had never suspected that philosophers were so rich. He watched me drink and eat with a touch of envy. 'What a capacity for living you have!' he said; and then with a sigh, a sigh of relief I could have thought it, 'it will not be long.'

'Ay,' said I, my head swimming now with champagne; 'I have a future perhaps – of a passing agreeable sort, thanks to you. I shall now have the honour of your name. But you have a past. Such a past as is worth all my future.'

He shook his head and smiled, as I thought, with half sad appreciation of my flattering admiration. 'That future,' he said, 'would you in truth change it?' The waiter came with liqueurs. 'You will not perhaps mind taking my name, taking my position, but would you indeed – willingly – take my years?'

'With your achievements,' said I gallantly.

He smiled again. 'Kümmel – both,' he said to the waiter, and turned his attention to a little paper packet he had taken from his pocket. 'This hour,' said he, 'this after-dinner hour is the hour of small things. Here is a scrap of my unpublished wisdom.' He opened the packet with his shaking yellow fingers, and showed a little pinkish powder on the paper. 'This,' said he – 'well, you must guess what it is. But Kümmel – put but a dash of this powder in it – is Himmel.'

His large greyish eyes watched mine with an inscrutable expression.

It was a bit of a shock to me to find this great teacher gave his mind to the flavour of liqueurs. However, I feigned an interest in his weakness, for I was drunk enough for such small sycophancy.

He parted the powder between the little glasses, and, rising suddenly, with a strange unexpected dignity, held out his hand towards me. I imitated his action, and the glasses rang. 'To a quick succession,' said he, and raised his glass towards his lips.

'Not that,' I said hastily. 'Not that.'

He paused with the liqueur at the level of his chin, and his eyes blazing into mine.

'To a long life,' said I.

He hesitated. 'To a long life,' said he, with a sudden bark of laughter, and with eyes fixed on one another we tilted the little glasses. His eyes looked straight into mine, and as I drained the stuff off, I felt a curiously intense sensation. The first touch of it set my brain in a furious tumult; I seemed to feel an actual physical stirring in my skull, and a seething humming filled my ears. I did not notice the flavour in my mouth, the aroma that filled my throat; I saw only the grey intensity of his gaze that burnt into mine. The draught, the mental confusion, the noise and stirring in my head, seemed to last an interminable time. Curious vague impressions of half-forgotten things danced and vanished on the edge of my consciousness. At last he broke the spell. With a sudden explosive sigh he put down his glass.

'Well?' he said.

'It's glorious,' said I, though I had not tasted the stuff.

My head was spinning. I sat down. My brain was chaos. Then my perception grew clear and minute as though I saw things in a concave mirror. His manner seemed to have changed into something nervous and hasty. He pulled out his watch and grimaced at it. 'Eleven-seven! And to-night I must – Seven-twenty-five. Waterloo! I must go at once.' He called for the bill, and struggled with his coat. Officious waiters came to our assistance. In another moment I was wishing him goodbye, over the apron of a cab, and still with an absurd feeling of minute distinctness, as though – how can I express it? – I not only saw but *felt* through an inverted opera-glass.

'That stuff,' he said. He put his hand to his forehead. 'I ought not to have given it to you. It will make your head split tomorrow. Wait a minute. Here.' He handed me out a little flat thing like a seidlitz-powder. 'Take that in water as you are going to bed. The other thing was a drug. Not till you're ready to go to bed, mind. It will clear your head. That's all. One more shake – Futurus!'

I gripped his shrivelled claw. 'Goodbye,' he said, and by the droop of his eyelids I judged he too was a little under the influence of that brain-twisting cordial.

He recollected something else with a start, felt in his breast-pocket, and produced another packet, this time a cylinder the size and shape of a shaving-stick. 'Here,' said he. 'I'd almost forgotten. Don't open this until I come tomorrow – but take it now.'

It was so heavy that I wellnigh dropped it. 'All ri'!' said I, and he grinned at me through the cab window as the cabman flicked his horse into wakefulness. It was a white packet he had given me, with red seals at either end and along its edge. 'If this isn't money,' said I, 'it's platinum or lead.'

I stuck it with elaborate care into my pocket, and with a whirling brain walked home through the Regent Street loiterers and the dark back streets beyond Portland Road. I remember the sensations of that walk very vividly, strange as they were. I was still so far myself that I could notice my strange mental state, and wonder whether this stuff I had had was opium – a drug beyond my experience. It is hard now to describe the peculiarity of my mental strangeness – mental doubling vaguely expresses it. As I was walking up Regent Street I found in my mind a queer persuasion that it was Waterloo Station, and had an odd impulse to get into the Polytechnic as a man might get into a train. I put a knuckle in my eye, and it was Regent Street. How can I express it? You see a skilful actor looking quietly at you, he pulls a grimace, and lo! – another person. Is it too extravagant if I tell you that it seemed to me as if Regent Street had, for the moment, done that? Then, being persuaded it was Regent Street again, I was oddly muddled about some fantastic reminiscences that cropped up. 'Thirty years ago,' thought I, 'it was here that I quarrelled with my brother.' Then I burst out laughing, to the astonishment and encouragement of a group of night prowlers. Thirty years ago I did not exist, and never in my life had I boasted a brother. The stuff was surely liquid folly, for the poignant regret for that lost brother still clung to me. Along Portland Road the madness took another turn. I began to recall vanished shops, and to compare the street with what it used to be. Confused, troubled thinking is comprehensible enough after the drink I had taken, but what puzzled me were these curiously vivid phantasm memories that had crept into my mind, and not only the memories that had crept in, but also the memories that had slipped out. I stopped opposite Stevens', the natural history dealer's, and cudgelled my brains to think what he had to do with me. A 'bus went by, and sounded exactly like the rumbling of a train. I seemed to be dipping into some dark, remote pit for the recollection. 'Of course,' said I, at last, 'he has promised me three frogs tomorrow. Odd I should have forgotten.'

Do they still show children dissolving views? In those I remember one view would begin like a faint ghost, and grow and oust another. In just that way it seemed to me that a ghostly set of new sensations was struggling with those of my ordinary self.

I went on through Euston Road to Tottenham Court Road, puzzled, and a little frightened, and scarcely noticed the unusual way I was taking, for commonly I used to cut through the intervening network of back streets. I turned into University Street, to discover that I had forgotten my number. Only by a strong effort did I recall 11A, and even then it seemed to me that it was a thing some forgotten person had told me. I tried to steady my mind by recalling the incidents of the dinner, and for the life of me I could conjure up no picture of my host's face; I saw him only as a shadowy outline, as one might see oneself reflected in a window through which one was looking. In his place, however, I had a curious exterior vision of myself, sitting at a table, flushed, bright-eyed, and talkative.

'I must take this other powder,' said I. 'This is getting impossible.'

I tried the wrong side of the hall for my candle and the matches, and had a doubt of which landing my room might be on. 'I'm drunk,' I said, 'that's certain,' and blundered needlessly on the staircase to sustain the proposition.

At the first glance my room seemed unfamiliar. 'What rot!' I said, and stared about me. I seemed to bring myself back by the effort, and the odd phantasmal quality passed into the concrete familiar. There was the old glass still, with my notes on the albumens stuck in the corner of the frame, my old everyday suit of clothes pitched about the floor. And yet it was not so real after all. I felt an idiotic persuasion trying to creep into my mind, as it were, that I was in a railway carriage in a train just stopping, that I was peering out of the window at some unknown station. I gripped the bed-rail firmly to reassure myself. 'It's clairvoyance, perhaps,' I said. 'I must write to the Psychical Research Society.'

I put the rouleau on my dressing-table, sat on my bed, and began to take off my boots. It was as if the picture of my present sensations was painted over some other picture that was trying to show through. 'Curse it!' said I; 'my wits are going, or am I in two places at once?' Half-undressed, I tossed the powder into a glass and drank it off. It effervesced, and became a fluorescent amber colour. Before I was in bed my mind was already tranquillised. I felt the pillow at my cheek, and thereupon I must have fallen asleep.

I awoke abruptly out of a dream of strange beasts, and found myself lying on my back. Probably every one knows that dismal, emotional dream from which one escapes, awake indeed, but strangely cowed. There was a curious taste in my mouth, a tired feeling in my limbs, a sense of cutaneous discomfort. I lay with my head motionless on my pillow, expecting that my feeling of strangeness and terror would pass away, and that I should then doze off again to sleep. But instead of that, my uncanny sensations increased. At first I could perceive nothing wrong about me. There was a faint light in the room, so faint that it was the very next thing to darkness, and the furniture stood out in it as vague blots of absolute darkness. I stared with my eyes just over the bedclothes.

It came into my mind that some one had entered the room to rob me of my rouleau of money, but after lying for some moments, breathing regularly to simulate sleep, I realised this was mere fancy. Nevertheless, the uneasy assurance of something wrong kept fast hold of me. With an effort I raised my head from the pillow, and peered about me at the dark. What it was I could not conceive. I looked at the dim shapes around me, the greater and lesser darknesses that indicated curtains, table, fireplace, bookshelves, and so forth. Then I began to perceive something unfamiliar in the forms of the darkness. Had the bed turned round? Yonder should be the bookshelves, and something shrouded and pallid rose there, something that would not answer to the bookshelves, however I looked at it. It was far too big to be my shirt thrown on a chair.

Overcoming a childish terror, I threw back the bedclothes and thrust my leg out of bed. Instead of coming out of my truckle-bed upon the floor, I found my foot scarcely reached the edge of the mattress. I made another step, as it were, and sat up on the edge of the bed. By the side of my bed should be the candle, and the matches upon the broken chair. I put out my hand and touched – nothing. I waved my hand in the darkness, and it came against some heavy hanging, soft and thick in texture, which gave a rustling noise at my touch. I grasped this and pulled it; it appeared to be a curtain suspended over the head of my bed.

I was now thoroughly awake, and beginning to realise that I was in a strange room. I was puzzled. I tried to recall the overnight circumstances, and I found them now, curiously enough, vivid in my memory: the supper, my reception of the little packages, my wonder whether I was intoxicated, my slow undressing, the coolness to my flushed face of my pillow. I felt a sudden distrust. Was that last night, or the night before? At any rate, this room was strange to me, and I could not imagine how I had got into it. The dim, pallid outline was growing paler, and I perceived it was a window, with the dark shape of an oval toilet-glass against the weak intimation of the dawn that filtered through the blind. I stood up, and was surprised by a curious feeling of weakness and unsteadiness. With trembling hands outstretched, I walked slowly towards the window, getting, nevertheless, a bruise on the knee from a chair by the way. I fumbled round the glass, which was large, with handsome brass sconces, to find the blindcord. I could not find any. By chance I took hold of the tassel, and with the click of a spring the blind ran up.

I found myself looking out upon a scene that was altogether strange to me. The night was overcast, and through the flocculent grey of the heaped clouds there filtered a faint half-light of dawn. Just at the edge of the sky the cloud-canopy had a blood-red rim. Below, everything was dark and indistinct, dim hills in the distance, a vague mass of buildings running up into pinnacles, trees like spilt ink, and below the window a tracery of black bushes and pale grey paths. It was so unfamiliar that for the moment I thought myself still dreaming. I felt the toilet-table; it appeared to be made of some polished wood, and was rather elaborately furnished – there were little cut-glass bottles and a brush upon it. There was also a queer little object, horse-shoe shape it felt, with smooth, hard projections, lying in a saucer. I could find no matches nor candlestick.

I turned my eyes to the room again. Now the blind was up, faint spectres of its furnishing came out of the darkness. There was a huge curtained bed, and the fireplace at its foot had a large white mantel with something of the shimmer of marble.

I leant against the toilet-table, shut my eyes and opened them again, and tried to think. The whole thing was far too real for dreaming. I was inclined to imagine there was still some hiatus in my memory, as a consequence of my draught of that strange liqueur; that I had come into my inheritance perhaps, and suddenly lost my recollection of everything since my good fortune had been announced. Perhaps if I waited a little, things would be clearer to me again. Yet my dinner with old Elvesham was now singularly vivid and recent. The champagne, the observant waiters, the powder, and the liqueurs – I could have staked my soul it all happened a few hours ago.

And then occurred a thing so trivial and yet so terrible to me that I shiver now to think of that moment. I spoke aloud. I said, 'How the devil did I get here?' ... *And the voice was not my own.*

It was not my own, it was thin, the articulation was slurred, the resonance of my facial bones was different. Then, to reassure myself I ran one hand over the other, and felt loose folds of skin, the bony laxity of age. 'Surely,' I said, in that horrible voice that had somehow established itself in my throat, 'surely this thing is a dream!' Almost as quickly as if I did it involuntarily, I thrust my fingers into my mouth. My teeth had gone. My finger-tips ran on the flaccid surface of an even row of shrivelled gums. I was sick with dismay and disgust.

I felt then a passionate desire to see myself, to realise at once in its full horror the ghastly change that had come upon me. I tottered to the mantel, and felt along it for matches. As I did so, a barking cough sprang up in my throat, and I clutched the thick flannel nightdress I found about me. There were no matches there, and I suddenly realised that my extremities were cold. Sniffing and coughing, whimpering a little, perhaps, I fumbled back to bed. 'It is surely a dream,' I whispered to myself as I clambered back, 'surely a dream.' It was a senile repetition. I pulled the bedclothes over my shoulders, over my ears, I thrust my withered hand under the pillow, and determined to compose myself to sleep. Of course it was a dream. In the morning the dream would be over, and I should wake up strong and vigorous again to my youth and studies. I shut my eyes, breathed regularly, and, finding myself wakeful, began to count slowly through the powers of three.

But the thing I desired would not come. I could not get to sleep. And the persuasion of the inexorable reality of the change that had happened to me grew steadily. Presently I found myself with my eyes wide open, the powers of three forgotten, and my skinny fingers upon my shrivelled gums. I was, indeed, suddenly and abruptly, an old man. I had in some unaccountable manner fallen through my life and come to old age, in some way I had been cheated of all the best of my life, of love, of struggle, of strength, and hope. I grovelled into the pillow and tried to persuade myself that such hallucination was possible. Imperceptibly, steadily, the dawn grew clearer.

At last, despairing of further sleep, I sat up in bed and looked about me. A chill twilight rendered the whole chamber visible. It was spacious and well-furnished, better furnished than any room I had ever slept in before. A candle and matches became dimly visible upon a little pedestal in a recess. I threw back the bedclothes, and, shivering with the rawness of the early morning, albeit it was summer-time, I got out and lit the candle. Then, trembling horribly, so that the extinguisher rattled on its spike, I tottered to the glass and saw – *Elvesham's face!* It was none the less horrible because I had already dimly feared as much. He had already seemed physically weak and pitiful to me, but seen now, dressed only in a coarse flannel nightdress, that fell apart and showed the stringy neck, seen now as my own body, I cannot describe its desolate decrepitude. The hollow cheeks, the straggling tail of dirty grey hair, the rheumy bleared eyes, the quivering, shrivelled lips, the lower displaying a gleam of the pink interior lining, and those horrible dark gums showing. You who are mind and body together, at your natural years, cannot imagine what this fiendish imprisonment meant to me. To be young and full of the desire and energy of youth, and to be caught, and presently to be crushed in this tottering ruin of a body....

But I wander from the course of my story. For some time I must have been stunned at this change that had come upon me. It was daylight when I did so far gather myself together as to think. In some inexplicable way I had been changed, though how, short of magic, the thing had been done, I could not say. And as I thought, the diabolical ingenuity of Elvesham came home to me. It seemed plain to me that as I found myself in his, so he must be in possession of *my* body, of my strength, that is, and my future. But how to prove it? Then, as I thought, the thing became so incredible, even to me, that my mind reeled, and I had to pinch myself, to feel my toothless gums, to see myself in the glass, and touch the things about me, before I could steady myself to face the facts again. Was all life hallucination? Was I indeed Elvesham, and he me? Had I been dreaming of Eden overnight? Was there any Eden? But if I was Elvesham, I should remember where I was on the previous morning, the name of the town in which I lived, what happened before the dream began. I struggled with my thoughts. I recalled the queer doubleness of my memories overnight. But now my mind was clear. Not the ghost of any memories but those proper to Eden could I raise.

'This way lies insanity!' I cried in my piping voice. I staggered to my feet, dragged my feeble, heavy limbs to the washhand-stand, and plunged my grey head into a basin of cold water. Then, towelling myself, I tried again. It was no good. I felt beyond all question that I was indeed Eden, not Elvesham. But Eden in Elvesham's body!

Had I been a man of any other age, I might have given myself up to my fate as one enchanted. But in these sceptical days miracles do not pass current. Here was some trick of psychology. What a drug and a steady stare could do, a drug and a steady stare, or some similar treatment, could surely undo. Men have lost their memories before. But to exchange memories as one does umbrellas! I laughed. Alas! not a healthy laugh, but a wheezing, senile titter. I could have fancied old Elvesham laughing at my plight, and a gust of petulant anger, unusual to me, swept across my feelings. I began dressing eagerly in the clothes I found lying about on the floor, and only realised when I was dressed that it was an evening suit I had assumed. I opened the wardrobe and found some more ordinary clothes, a pair of plaid trousers, and an old-fashioned dressing-gown. I put a venerable smoking-cap on my venerable head, and, coughing a little from my exertions, tottered out upon the landing.

It was then, perhaps, a quarter to six, and the blinds were closely drawn and the house quite silent. The landing was a spacious one, a broad, richly-carpeted staircase went down into the darkness of the hall below, and before me a door ajar showed me a writing-desk, a revolving bookcase, the back of a study chair, and a fine array of bound books, shelf upon shelf.

'My study,' I mumbled, and walked across the landing. Then at the sound of my voice a thought struck me, and I went back to the bedroom and put in the set of false teeth. They slipped in with the ease of old habit. 'That's better,' said I, gnashing them, and so returned to the study.

The drawers of the writing-desk were locked. Its revolving top was also locked. I could see no indications of the keys, and there were none in the pockets of my trousers. I shuffled back at once to the bedroom, and went through the dress suit, and afterwards the pockets of all the garments I could find. I was very eager, and one might have imagined that burglars had been at work, to see my room when I had done. Not only were there no keys to be found, but not a coin, nor a scrap of paper – save only the receipted bill of the overnight dinner.

A curious weariness asserted itself. I sat down and stared at the garments flung here and there, their pockets turned inside out. My first frenzy had already flickered out. Every moment I was beginning to realise the immense intelligence of the plans of my enemy, to see more and more clearly the hopelessness of my position. With an effort I rose and hurried hobbling into the study again. On the staircase was a housemaid pulling up the blinds. She stared, I think, at the expression of my face. I shut the door of the study behind me, and, seizing a poker, began an attack upon the desk. That is how they found me. The cover of the desk was split, the lock smashed, the letters torn out of the pigeon-holes, and tossed about the room. In my senile rage I had flung about the pens and other such light stationery, and overturned the ink. Moreover, a large vase upon the mantel had got broken – I do not know how. I could find no cheque-book, no money, no indications of the slightest use for the recovery of my body. I was battering madly at the drawers, when the butler, backed by two women-servants, intruded upon me.

That simply is the story of my change. No one will believe my frantic assertions. I am treated as one demented, and even at this moment I am under restraint. But I am sane, absolutely sane, and to prove it I have sat down to write this story minutely as the things happened to me. I appeal to the reader, whether there is any trace of insanity in the style or method of the story he has been reading. I am a young man locked away in an old man's body. But the clear fact is incredible to everyone. Naturally I appear demented to those who will not believe this, naturally I do not know the names of my secretaries, of the doctors who come to see me, of my servants and neighbours, of this town (wherever it is) where I find myself. Naturally I lose myself in my own house, and suffer inconveniences of every sort. Naturally I ask the oddest questions. Naturally I weep and cry out, and have paroxysms of despair. I have no money and no cheque-book. The bank will not recognise my signature, for I suppose that, allowing for the feeble muscles I now have, my handwriting is still Eden's. These people about me will not let me go to the bank personally. It seems, indeed, that there is no bank in this town, and that I have an account in some part of London. It seems that Elvesham kept the name of his solicitor secret from all his household. I can ascertain nothing. Elvesham was, of course, a profound student of mental science, and all my declarations of the facts of the case merely confirm the theory that my insanity is the outcome of overmuch brooding upon psychology. Dreams of the personal identity indeed! Two days ago I was a healthy youngster, with all life before me; now I am a furious old man, unkempt, and desperate, and miserable, prowling about a great, luxurious, strange house, watched, feared, and avoided as a lunatic by everyone about me. And in London is Elvesham beginning life again in a vigorous body, and with all the accumulated knowledge and wisdom of threescore and ten. He has stolen my life.

What has happened I do not clearly know. In the study are volumes of manuscript notes referring chiefly to the psychology of memory, and parts of what may be either calculations or ciphers in symbols absolutely strange to me. In some passages there are indications that he was also occupied with the philosophy of mathematics. I take it he has transferred the whole of his memories, the accumulation that makes up his personality, from this old withered brain of his to mine, and, similarly, that he has transferred mine to his discarded tenement. Practically, that is, he has changed bodies. But how such a change may be possible is without the range of my philosophy. I have been a materialist for all my thinking life, but here, suddenly, is a clear case of man's detachability from matter.

One desperate experiment I am about to try. I sit writing here before putting the matter to issue. This morning, with the help of a table-knife that I had secreted at breakfast, I succeeded in breaking open a fairly obvious secret drawer in this wrecked writing-desk. I discovered nothing save a little green glass phial containing a white powder. Round the neck of the phial was a label, and thereon was written this one word, 'Release.' This may be – is most probably – poison. I can understand Elvesham placing poison in my way, and I should be sure that it was his intention so to get rid of the only living witness against him, were it not for this careful concealment. The man has practically solved the problem of immortality. Save for the spite of chance, he will live in my body until it has aged, and then, again, throwing that aside, he will assume some other victim's youth and strength. When one remembers his heartlessness, it is terrible to think of the ever-growing experience that ... How long has he been leaping from body to body? ... But I tire of writing. The powder appears to be soluble in water. The taste is not unpleasant.

There the narrative found upon Mr Elvesham's desk ends. His dead body lay between the desk and the chair. The latter had been pushed back, probably by his last convulsions. The story was written in pencil, and in a crazy hand, quite unlike his usual minute characters. There remain only two curious facts to record. Indisputably there was some connection between Eden and Elvesham, since the whole of Elvesham's property was bequeathed to the young man. But he never inherited. When Elvesham committed suicide, Eden was, strangely enough, already dead. Twenty-four hours before, he had been knocked down by a cab and killed instantly, at the crowded crossing at the intersection of Gower Street and Euston Road. So that the only human being who could have thrown light upon this fantastic narrative is beyond the reach of questions. Without further comment I leave this extraordinary matter to the reader's individual judgment.

How Gabriel Became Thompson

After the pact matrimonial there are nine possible events. All post-matrimonial stories belong to one or other of these nine classes indicated by these possibilities; the characters, the accessories, may vary indefinitely, but the tale is always to be classified under one of these heads. For each party to the marriage says one of these three things. First: 'It is not as I expected, but it will do very well' (contentment). Secondly: 'It is not as I expected, but we must manage' (compromise). Or, lastly: 'It is not as I expected, and I will not endure it' (catastrophe). The permutations of these three formulae taken two at a time are nine, forming the diapason of marriage.

Now the best stories, as stories, are to be made by taking number three in its five possible combinations, and solving your situation by the method of murder or elopement. Number one with itself gives only a nauseating spectacle of married people kissing in company; number two, alone or with one, affords no vivid sensations. Stories on these lines are but sunset pieces at the best. The young people go hither and thither buying furniture, receiving and returning cards, and the like, while the clouds of glory they trailed after them from the romantic time fade by imperceptible degrees. At last they look round and remark, or do not remark, that the light is out of the sky, and the world blue and cold. The change, indeed, is sometimes so steady and so gradual that I doubt if some of them ever know the extent of their loss.

But what a splendid time is that of the pre-matrimonial flights, before the ephemeris of the human imagination accomplishes its destiny! How the world glows! Only the untried know the infinite strength of the untried. There are innumerable things to be done, and no one has done them; the tale of those who have failed and died has no meaning in our ears. What ambitious student has not sat and talked with his sympathetic friend, lending and borrowing ears in a fair commerce of boasting of the great deeds germinating? This boasting of the future is the cement of all youthful friendships, as boasting of the past is of those of age. But the former have a divine warmth of emotion which the latter lack.

Gabriel, my own friend, was a splendid exemplification of this romance period of life. Gabriel Thompson was his name, but at first it was juster to call him Gabriel. For he had golden hair that flowed over his collar, and a beardless angelic face, his soul was full of the love of great deeds and justice, and our common conversation was the entire reform, by a few simple expedients, of human society. Later, however, it became necessary to call him Thompson. That will explain the title: it is a story of compromise, of the clipping or shedding of the archangelic pinions by which he soared.

I remember the evening when Gabriel told me he was in love. We had discoursed of the mystical woman soul that sways men – Gabriel with divine warmth, and I in colder strain. Indeed, as regards that particular fire, I have always been a bit of a salamander. Presently, however, Gabriel swooped down to the concrete. I felt more than one twinge of jealousy as he rushed into details with a transient nervousness of manner unusual to him. He gave no names or dates.

'Is she beautiful?' I said, perceiving he raved little in that direction.

'Her features are not regularly beautiful –'

'Plain?'

'Oh dear no! Indeed, she has the greatest of all beauty, the beauty of expression. You need to talk to her.'

A kind of upward adoring look, I thought. 'Is she cultured?'

'She had read very few books, and yet she had a most wonderful insight into things. Several times as I have been timidly feeling my way to this or that advanced view of ours she has come out to meet me, as it were, and I found that in the seclusion of her quiet country town she had thought out things and arrived at the very same ends as we, with all our advantages, have done.'

'She must be quick-witted?'

'She is indeed; a more subtle and yet a purer mind I never met. I am giving her some of Ruskin's books now. He is a revelation to her, she says. She finds so much in him that has been in her own mind dimly, perfectly expressed. Carlyle she must read; after that Wordsworth, Browning –'

And so he went on. She was quite 'womanly'. Gabriel was very insistent upon that. She entirely agreed with him that a woman's sphere was her home. She did not want votes. At that time he was smarting a little from a controversy with Miss Gowland (M.B.), who did. This wonderful girl was quite content to accompany his song, so he was assured, to be the 'complement of his existence', his 'good angel', and his 'armour-bearer' in that fight for the righting of the world which his soul craved after. He was to be her teacher, servant – as a king is the servant of his people – and true knight.

I felt more and more jealous. Scarcely two months before we had agreed that a new Reformation was needed, and I was cast in the role of Erasmus, and Gabriel as Luther. This arrangement, arrived at over our youthful pipes solemnly enough, was all forgotten now. My share was to hear of this absolutely new manifestation of the feminine. I was interested only in her imperfections, as they showed dimly through Gabriel's panegyric. For once, Gabriel with his bright face, his shining eyes, his rhetorical gestures, and his buoyant flow of words, absolutely bored and pained me. I cared for him a lot at that time, and had promised myself a creditable career by his side. I had, indeed, forgotten the feminine until Gabriel remembered it.

Perhaps that evening, or at any rate some evening about that time, two other friends discussed this same love affair of Gabriel's.

'I think Gabriel is a pretty name, dear,' said one.

'Now, dearest,' said the other, holding up one dainty finger with an air of great solemnity, 'I want you to tell me just exactly what you think of him.'

'He has a lovely profile. You must make him grow a moustache.' 'And cut his hair, you want to say, and dare not. Minnie, you have no moral courage. Yes; he does look a little effeminate now, but he is awfully clever. He writes, you know, and he sends me such dreadfully difficult books to read. I am getting quite learned.'

'It must be jolly to have a really clever husband, one that is well known, and has people running after his autograph, and all that. You will be cutting poor me – sunk to the besotted condition of a wine-merchant's wife – dead.'

'You shall always come to see me, dear – on my domestic days. But really, Minnie, I am going to be dreadfully happy. You know Gabriel is going to do all kinds of scientific researches, and I shall help him copy his things out, and put his experiments out for him, and all that. I shall make him be an F.R.S., and he will give performances at soirées, like that handsome man we saw who did something clever in a bottle. Gabriel's shadow would look splendid in profile on a white screen.'

'Isn't he a Socialist or Anarchist or something?'

'All young men with anything in them are like that now. It is a kind of intellectual measles, dear. I don't think any the worse of a young man for that. It is like his smoking pipes instead of cigars or cigarettes, and not wearing gloves. You must see Gabriel after I have polished him for a year.'

'Yes,' said Minnie, 'that is a woman's work. We cut and polish these rough diamonds, and they take all the credit for the flash and sparkle. But if it were not for us there would be no gentlemen in the world.'

'Oh! Gabriel, dear, is naturally a gentleman.'

'Unpolished, dear, as you admit.'

Well, so they talked, sitting cosily in dainty chairs. Long before the marriage this little Delilah of his cut his hair. He came to me less frequently, and one evening he explained that he thought he was clearer headed when he smoked less. Besides which, the smell of tobacco hung about one so much.

Thereafter he ceased to be Gabriel to me, and became Gabriel Thompson. And one memorable day I had a kind of 'Phantasm of the Living', a vision of a fairhaired man with a bees-waxed moustache, dressed in an ample frock coat, and light gloves. It was my prophet – curled and scented. The vision fluttered between me and my bookshelves for a moment and vanished, and I knew at once that my Gabriel, the world-mender, was lost to me for ever. Soon after came the visiting cards of the happy pair.

I understand that the correct thing to do is to call upon your newly-married friends when they are settled, and see what kind of furniture they have. I did this. By way of quiet sarcasm I wore my old velveteen jacket. Mrs Thompson said I looked 'quite

Bohemian', and the only consolation I had was to think that Thompson had a conscience. I asked him point-blank about the new Reformation, and she answered for him that he was dreadfully busy at research.

I saw Thompson look across at me with a dumb request not to press the matter. But I had no particular kindness for Thompson. Was he not the man who had murdered my Prophet Gabriel and buried him away in himself? I insisted upon social evils, the need of leaders for the people, and all our old themes. Presently my Gabriel awoke in Thompson again, and began to talk.

'There is a passage,' he said presently, 'in "Sesame and Lilies", the book you liked so much dear. How does it go? I am sure you know it. Ah, here is the book.'

It lay on the table, one of the many volumes he had bought for her, one, I remembered, that had 'come like a revelation' to her. He took it up and turned over the pages.

When I saw the pages were all uncut I felt sorry for the man. He stared at the book as though he hardly grasped the import of the thing. Then he put it down again with force and an expletive.

'Gabriel!' said his wife.

I rose to go. But Gabriel was white with anger. 'You never opened that book,' he said to his wife, 'and you told me you had read it.'

Mrs Thompson turned to me. 'Must you go?' she said.

So I left them face to face with each other.

It was what one might call their real introduction to one another. Each had played to the other of being what the other dreamt, and now that little comedy was over. Mrs Thompson had repeated Gabriel's conclusions after him to please him, and he had acted as a gentleman according to her lights. But that unfortunate book had ended it.

As I went out I heard her begin: 'To think, Gabriel, that in the second month of our marriage, you should curse me.'

And he: 'Why did you only pretend to read my book?'

I suppose she did it to please him, but I do not know if she made this excuse. It is for a womanly woman a perfectly adequate excuse for any little duplicity she commits.

I fancy there must have been a long discussion that afternoon. Practically it amounted to this, that each had married a stranger in mistake for an imaginary person. Such a complication, though common enough, requires very deliberate consideration and considerable mutual forbearance. On the contrary, their talk that afternoon was heated, and it ended with domestic thunder – which is the slamming of doors. Mrs Thompson was calm and reasonable throughout, but Gabriel did a deal of walking to and fro, throwing books with violence on to the floor, and invective generally.

He had imagined that his marriage was to be an idyllic episode, from which he was to return presently to his dream of a new Reformation – Gabriel well to the fore, wife inspiring, helpful, and advisatory. He felt himself cut off from all this at once, and first he tried to vent his dismay and displeasure on his wife, and being defeated by her polite coolness, he took it out of the books, the carpet, and the front door.

She was dreadfully pained at his temper and unreasonableness, and annoyed more particularly at his letting the servants hear the quarrel. She could not help asking herself what they would say. Moreover she was afraid he might do something rash or ridiculous. So that she decided to talk the matter over with Minnie, who was now a wine-merchant's wife.

'I told him he could hardly expect me to read all the books he inundated the house with, especially when I had all my things to see to, and he simply raved; he went on dreadfully, dear – swore at me and insulted me, asked me if I thought it was fair treatment towards a man with a mission in the world to marry him under false pretences. I said there were no false pretences, except that he had behaved like a gentleman, and that when I trusted myself in his hands I thought he would always do so. He almost cried when he said that he had looked to me to be his help and inspiration, just as if he had been going abroad as a missionary or something of that kind. I do think that kind of talk silly. If I had behaved really badly to him, Minnie, he could not have been worse. All this ranting and bother because I did not read his silly old books! Rather than have had this scene, dear, I would have read every one from cover to cover. You can't think how I have reproached myself for not cutting those leaves.'

So Mrs Thompson.

Minnie judiciously heard her through two or three times before she attempted any consolation or advice.

'He is certainly going on badly, my dear, but we all have our troubles. It is quite enough to make you really ill.'

'I should have been if I had not kept so cool.'

'You bear up wonderfully. He does not deserve it. Of course, dear, if you were ill – when he comes home again – really ill, I mean, not just a headache – so that all the house would be hushed – he might have the grace to feel ashamed of himself. You are too brave. It only makes a man rave worse than ever to stand up to him. They all hate to be told the truth about themselves, and they shout and bully you down. But your Gabriel – any real man – would not hit a really sick woman.'

'It is almost a pity I am so well then,' said Mrs Thompson, scarcely grasping the new idea yet.

'It's the excitement, you poor dear,' said Minnie. 'That keeps you up now, but you will find the reaction presently, mark my words.'

And sure enough, Mrs Thompson had hardly reached home when this reaction came upon her, and she was helped upstairs by the sympathetic and half-confidential parlour-maid. And all the blinds were straightway drawn and the house hushed.

Meanwhile Gabriel had been with me.

'Don't speak about it to me,' I said; 'I will not be the man to come between husband and wife – especially when the wife is Mrs Thompson.'

'For Heaven's sake, don't mock me,' said Gabriel; 'I have been cruelly deceived. Here am I at five-and-twenty, with all my card castles in a heap. It is not only that about "Sesame and Lilies", I have been finding her out ever since the marriage. That book – with you there – was the last straw. She is no helpmeet for me. Her ideas are shallow and vain, her ways are always crooked; she is just a commonplace woman of the world. What can a man do for others, what can he do for himself, with a woman like that?'

So he raved. I did not join him, but I must own my silence was sympathetic. Presently, however, after a pause, he started to his feet, and flung his chair headlong.

'I will not endure it,' he shouted, repeating, as the attentive reader will notice, formula three. 'Why should the error of three months dwarf and ruin a life? I will not live with her. I will go abroad. What are these customs and ceremonies, these flimsy ordinances, that they should chain me back from all my possibilities? I tell you I will part from her. I never married her. I married my ideal, and she is no ideal of mine.'

He caught up his hat in his hand. He stood splendid, almost heroic, holding his right hand for mine.

'Gabriel,' I said to him, calling him that for the last time, 'you have had a bitter disappointment. I cannot advise you. The law of matrimony, like the law of gravitation, no respectable man disputes. Whatever you do, may you fare well.'

'No cat and dog compromise for me,' said Gabriel; and so went out right valiantly, with my secret blessing.

He noticed the blinds in the front of the house were all down, but, being a man, he did not grasp the full symbolism of this. He knocked for admission – a firm, clear knock. Mrs Thompson, at that moment, was upstairs hurriedly putting away her bonnet, which she had thought of – happily – in time.

The parlour-maid let him in noiselessly, with a funereal expression of face. This startled him, for she was a flourishing, noisy sort of girl.

'Please, sir,' she said, in a whisper, holding out his bath slippers; 'do you mind putting these on? Missis is very ill indeed.'

'Why! what is the matter?' asked Gabriel in his natural voice, trying to keep up his militant front.

'She regular broke down, sir, after you left her,' said the parlour-maid reproachfully, in an almost noiseless whisper, and therewith handing him the slippers, she glided away, leaving him 'to his conscience'. Needless to say, she did not mention Mrs Thompson's visit to Minnie. Gabriel stood in confused thought for a minute, and then sat down on one of the hall chairs and quietly changed his boots. He had not expected this.

He sat meditating vaguely over his discarded boots for some time. He would have to postpone his climax after all. Nuisance! Then his chivalry began to awake. Perhaps he had been hitting unnecessarily hard. She was only a weak woman, and he had come home to do battle and finish with her, as if she were a dragon. Certainly his ways were violent. She had seemed cool enough during their quarrel, but then women, he had read, are clever at hiding their pain, though the dart, nevertheless, may have gone well home. What if she really cared for him? He

remembered all the wrath, sorrow, and bitterness of his denunci-
ation. Had he been heedlessly carried away?

Presently he rose and stole upstairs. He would look at her. It
was a fatal resolution.

His wife was lying dressed upon the bed, in the darkened room.
Her pale cheeks were wet, and her eyes were closed so that the
damp long lashes lay upon her cheek. Her hair, which was
abundant and beautiful, indeed her chief beauty, was down. In
one hand she held her smelling-salts, and the other lay limp and
extended. There was an expression of pain on her face; she
seemed to have cried herself to sleep. Gabriel could hardly realise
that this sorrowful little figure was the human being he had
raged against ten minutes ago.

There came over my Gabriel, I suppose, a great wave of
generous emotion. I admit – though it worked to my hurt – that
there was some greatness in his forgetting his world-mending at
that moment. Had he not held her in his arms? Had not she
trusted the happiness of her life to him? He was not one of those
intellectual prigs who will pass their dearest through the fire for
some Moloch of an idea. He had thought his career was to be
stifled by his wife. He had not realised how his assertion of this
would break her down. Poor little girl with the dishevelled hair!
Poor little Sissie! The New Reformation receded through an
illimitable perspective to the smallest speck.

She sighed in her sleep. 'Oh, Gabriel!' she said, with a sob in
her voice.

Gabriel could scarcely imagine why he had just been so angry.
She was dreaming of him. The New Reformation vanished. He
knelt by the bed, full of self-reproach, and took her hand.

Her eyes slowly opened. She looked in his face and saw she had
conquered.

'I have been a brute,' he said – this emancipator of his sex.

'Gabriel,' she whispered faintly, 'Gabriel, dear,' and closed her
eyes again.

'I have been a brute,' repeated Gabriel.

'Gabriel,' she said, 'promise me something.'

'Anything dear,' said Gabriel.

'Promise me you will never speak to that horrid man again.'
Now, the horrid man referred to was myself. And – will you

believe it, dear reader? – Gabriel, who had left my home scarcely ten minutes, vowing he would do or die, *promised*.

This is the plain and simple story of how Gabriel became Thompson, so that there was no Gabriel any more for me. I and the New Reformation were buried under the foundation-stone of their compromise, and there was, in spite of Gabriel's repetition of formula three, no catastrophe. From that day to this Thompson and I have met and crossed one another in highways and by-ways, but never a word has passed between us after my first rebuff. But I understand, through a friend – and it is a curious example of the metaboly of memory – that Thompson is under the impression that I incited him to desert his wife.

The health of Mrs Thompson is, and has been, very uncertain since that day. It has been a tactical necessity. Thompson has to be gentle and careful in all his doings; he takes her to church regularly, they have a prominent pew, and he keeps all the observances. However, the scientific research languished some-how, and he is not a Fellow of the Royal Society yet, though it led to several profitable patents. He has one of the best houses on Putney Hill, and Mrs Thompson bears up bravely against her uncertain health and gives really very brilliant garden-parties. She has dropped Minnie, because she is deceitful, and lives in one of the smaller houses in the Upper Richmond road.

Thompson is said to be apathetic in society, and irritable in business. His health has been poor lately, through an excessive consumption of cigars.

How Pingwill Was Routed

Pingwill was a nuisance. He married a respectable young woman of mature years, and lives on her sufficiency, and he goes about pretending to be a literary character on the strength of an edition of a classic, an examination success at some university place or other, and occasional reviewing. He likes to talk about books, and is offensively familiar with all the masterpieces and most of the rest of English literature. He considers gabble about books intellectual conversation. He regards a quiet man smoking in a chair as fair game for his scraps of quotation – which he is as eager to void as he is greedy to acquire – and he cannot understand that people who write books never read them, and are full of bitter memories of their own adventures in authorship. He wears a *pince-nez*, and Mrs Pingwill (when present) echoes all his quavering severities with the explanation that 'George is *so* satirical'. He is exasperatingly reliable in the matter of names and dates. And at first, perhaps, we made the mistake of encouraging Pingwill.

Heydinger was the chief encourager of Pingwill. He is a humorist, a kind of person who sees jokes in things that rouse the passions of ordinary people, and he found an unaccountable pleasure in developing one particular aspect of the Pingwill constitution. No retired pork-butcher's lady, no wife of a village rector who has married beneath him, could be more punctilious of her intimacy, than Pingwill among his authors. And Pingwill was just as intensely sensitive to the breath of scandal – which in matters literary is called criticism. No one could be thicker with a really *chic* author; no one readier to 'cut' the writer who fell under the shadow of adverse comment. He was, in fact, a literary snob – a by no means rare variety – and he had an almost passionate dread of admiring the wrong man. He took reviews in the weeklies quite seriously. Naturally, he had nothing but serene contempt for Dickens and Jerome and Mark Twain, and 'people of that stamp'. And Heydinger never tired of drawing him out upon Kipling. In a careless moment he had informed us that Kipling's style was rough and unfinished – it seems he tried for once to form a judgment for himself, and had happened upon really quite vulgar and coarse expressions. After he had learnt better from a review, the mere name filled him with uncomfortable memories. It was as if the rector's wife had cut the Duchess by mistake. Horrible! Then he was privately in great trouble about Besant and Hall Caine. 'Ought I to know them?' was the attitude. The oracles differed. He was deliciously guarded upon these authors under Heydinger's most searching questions. But his face flushed guiltily. Le Gallienne, Zangwill, and most of the younger men, who have warm friends and animated critics, bothered him more or less, and he had a horrible dread, I know, that Ruskin, whom he had committed himself to admire, was not quite all that he should be. 'One has to be so *very* particular,' was Pingwill's attitude.

However, after a while, we tired of this creature's odd way with books, and his proximity then became, as I say, a nuisance. But Heydinger, who had formed an adequate conception of his character, suggested the remedy, and together we routed him. Both Heydinger and I had got through a morning's work, and in he came, fresh, and freshly primed. He dropped into a chair, and emitted some indifferent remarks.

'I have heard,' he said, 'that these delicious child-sketches of Kenneth Graham's are out in a book by themselves.'

'Read 'em?' said Heydinger, brutally.

'No – hardly – yet,' said Pingwill: 'but they're good, aren't they?'

'Very,' said I, 'but that's no reason why you should go about calling them delicious before you have read them.'

'Perhaps not,' said Pingwill. 'Perhaps not.'

'They remind me very much of Wendle Hooper,' said Heydinger. 'You know him, Bellows?'

'Intimately,' I said. 'I have one of his first editions at home.'

'You will be reminded very much of Wendle Hooper,' said Heydinger, turning to Pingwill.

'Indeed!' said Pingwill, stepping into the trap.

'The same subtle suggestiveness of phrase,' said Heydinger. 'The same delicate yet penetrating sympathy.'

'I must certainly read him,' said Pingwill, evidently searching his mind for the name of Wendle Hooper, and flushing slightly.

'I know of no man,' said Heydinger, 'except, perhaps, Lant, who comes so near to Hooper as Graham. You know Lant's style, Pingwill?'

Pingwill flushed a little deeper, and his ears grew pink. 'I can't say,' said he 'that I've read –'

'He is not so well known as Hooper,' he admitted. 'He was in the little set that clustered round Leigh Hunt –'

Pingwill suddenly felt hotter again. 'I think Leigh Hunt –' he began, evidently ready with a fragment of text-book.

'He borrowed from Lant,' interrupted Heydinger. 'Certainly he borrowed from Lant. That essay on the chimney-pot hat –'

'Pure Lant,' I said.

'I've neglected Lant a little, I am afraid,' mumbled Pingwill, horribly bothered by this unknown name.

'You should read him,' said I. 'He's a perfect mine of good things. That passage in Browning, for instance ... You were pointing out the resemblance only this morning, Heydinger.'

'About the chattering discs,' said Heydinger. 'You remember *that*, Pingwill?'

'I think so,' said Pingwill. 'Chattering discs ... I seem to recollect. How does it go?'

'The chattering discs go reeling,' said Heydinger, inventing boldly. 'You *must* remember.'

Pingwill was now really very uncomfortable. But he was having a lively lesson in priggish conversation. 'I wish I had my Lant here,' said I.

'You surely remember about the chattering discs?' said Heydinger, turning as he pretended to search for a book on the shelf.

'The phrase is quite familiar to me,' said Pingwill, 'but for the life of me I can't recall the context! It's queer what tricks one's memory plays ...'

Heydinger quietly resumed his seat.

'Have you written anything lately?' said Pingwill to change the subject.

'Yes,' said Heydinger, and seeing some further question threatened, added, as if in explanation, '*Alvarados*.'

It pulled Pingwill up abruptly. '*Alvarados*! Ah!' he repeated after Heydinger, with an air of comprehension. If he understood he was certainly wiser than I. His ears were now bright red. We remained tranquil, watching him. It was not my affair.

He returned to conversation presently with an air of having found and grasped the thing firmly. 'Will you make them into a book?' he said, bravely. A just perceptible dew was on his face. Heydinger evidently expected as much. 'Them!' he answered. 'What?'

'Well – it. Alvarados.'

'It!' said Heydinger, raising his eyebrows. 'I don't know,' he said, and became silent. Pingwill was evidently baffled. Very awkwardly, and after a pause, he said he hoped that would be the case. Heydinger thanked him drily. There was an interval while we watched one another. Then he discovered his pipe was out – it always is – and asked me for the matches. He talked incoherently upon indifferent topics for a few minutes after that, and all the time I could see the trouble in his eyes, the awful doubt of his own omniscience that had arisen ... Alvarados! Presently he rose to go. Routed.

As he went out I heard him whisper to himself very softly, 'Alvarados!'

He has not been near us since. I can imagine the dismal times he has had hunting through Rabelais, Gil Blas, Hudibras, the Dictionary of Phrase and Fable, for Alvarados, going through the British Museum catalogue for Wendle Hooper, and hunting all Browning for the 'Chattering Discs', feeling most horribly ashamed of himself all the time. I like to think of his flush of shame, the overthrow of his frail apparatus of knowledge. And ever and again Heydinger and I break the friendly silences which constitute our intercourse by saying casually. 'Pingwill seems to be dropping us altogether,' or, 'Don't seem to see so much of Pingwill as we used to do, Bellows.' Such reflections are the olives of life.

Pollock and the Porroh Man

It was in a swampy village on the lagoon river behind the Turner Peninsula that Pollock's first encounter with the Porroh man occurred. The women of that country are famous for their good looks – they are Gallinas with a dash of European blood that dates from the days of Vasco de Gama and the English slave-traders, and the Porroh man, too, was possibly inspired by a faint Caucasian taint in his composition. (It's a curious thing to think that some of us may have distant cousins eating men on Sherboro Island or raiding with the Sofas.) At anyrate, the Porroh man stabbed the woman to the heart as though he had been a mere low-class Italian, and very narrowly missed Pollock. But Pollock, using his revolver to parry the lightning stab which was aimed at his deltoid muscle, sent the iron dagger flying, and, firing, hit the man in the hand.

He fired again and missed, knocking a sudden window out of the wall of the hut. The Porroh man stooped in the doorway, glancing under his arm at Pollock. Pollock caught a glimpse of his inverted face in the sunlight, and then the Englishman was alone, sick and trembling with the excitement of the affair, in the twilight of the place. It had all happened in less time than it takes to read about it.

The woman was quite dead, and having ascertained this, Pollock went to the entrance of the hut and looked out. Things outside were dazzling bright. Half a dozen of the porters of the expedition were standing up in a group near the green huts they occupied, and staring towards him, wondering what the shots might signify. Behind the little group of men was the broad stretch of black fetid mud by the river, a green carpet of rafts of papyrus and water-grass, and then the leaden water. The mangroves beyond the stream loomed indistinctly through the blue haze. There were no signs of excitement in the squat village, whose fence was just visible above the cane-grass.

Pollock came out of the hut cautiously and walked towards the river, looking over his shoulder at intervals. But the Porroh man had vanished. Pollock clutched his revolver nervously in his hand.

One of his men came to meet him, and as he came, pointed to the bushes behind the hut in which the Porroh man had disappeared. Pollock had an irritating persuasion of having made an absolute fool of himself; he felt bitter, savage, at the turn things had taken. At the same time, he would have to tell Waterhouse – the moral, exemplary, cautious Waterhouse – who would inevitably take the matter seriously. Pollock cursed bitterly at his luck, at Waterhouse, and especially at the West Coast of Africa. He felt consummately sick of the expedition. And in the back of his mind all the time was a speculative doubt where precisely within the visible horizon the Porroh man might be.

It is perhaps rather shocking, but he was not at all upset by the murder that had just happened. He had seen so much brutality during the last three months, so many dead women, burnt huts, drying skeletons, up the Kittam River in the wake of the Sofa cavalry, that his senses were blunted. What disturbed him was the persuasion that this business was only beginning.

He swore savagely at the black, who ventured to ask a question, and went on into the tent under the orange-trees where Waterhouse was lying, feeling exasperatingly like a boy going into the headmaster's study.

Waterhouse was still sleeping off the effects of his last dose of chlorodyne, and Pollock sat down on a packing-case beside him, and, lighting his pipe, waited for him to awake. About him were scattered the pots and weapons Waterhouse had collected from the Mendi people, and which he had been repacking for the canoe voyage to Sulyma.

Presently Waterhouse woke up, and after judicial stretching, decided he was all right again. Pollock got him some tea. Over the tea the incidents of the afternoon were described by Pollock, after some preliminary beating about the bush. Waterhouse took the matter even more seriously than Pollock had anticipated. He did not simply disapprove, he scolded, he insulted.

'You're one of those infernal fools who think a black man isn't a human being,' he said. 'I can't be ill a day without you must get into some dirty scrape or other. This is the third time in a month that you have come crossways-on with a native, and this time you're in for it with a vengance. Porroh, too! They're down

upon you enough as it is, about that idol you wrote your silly
name on. And they're the most vindictive devils on earth! You
make a man ashamed of civilisation. To think you come of a
decent family! If ever I cumber myself up with a vicious, stupid
young lout like you again' –

'Steady on, now,' snarled Pollock, in the tone that always
exasperated Waterhouse; 'steady on.'

At that Waterhouse became speechless. He jumped to his feet.
'Look here, Pollock,' he said, after a struggle to control his
breath. 'You must go home. I won't have you any longer. I'm ill
enough as it is through you' –

'Keep your hair on,' said Pollock, staring in front of him. 'I'm
ready enough to go.'

Waterhouse became calmer again. He sat down on the camp-
stool. 'Very well,' he said. 'I don't want a row, Pollock, you know,
but it's confoundedly annoying to have one's plans put out by
this kind of thing. I'll come to Sulyma with you, and see you safe
aboard' –

'You needn't,' said Pollock. 'I can go alone. From here.'

'Not far,' said Waterhouse. 'You don't understand this Porroh
business.'

'How should *I* know she belonged to a Porroh man?' said
Pollock, bitterly.

'Well, she did,' said Waterhouse; 'and you can't undo the
thing. Go alone, indeed! I wonder what they'd do to you. You
don't seem to understand that this Porroh hokey-pokey rules this
country, is its law, religion, constitution, medicine, magic.... They
appoint the chiefs. The Inquisition, at its best, couldn't hold a
candle to these chaps. He will probably set Awajale, the chief
here, on to us. It's lucky our porters are Mendis. We shall have to
shift this little settlement of ours.... Confound you, Pollock! And,
of course, you must go and miss him.'

He thought, and his thoughts seemed disagreeable. Presently
he stood up and took his rifle. 'I'd keep close for a bit, if I were
you,' he said, over his shoulder, as he went out. 'I'm going out to
see what I can find out about it.'

Pollock remained sitting in the tent, meditating. 'I was meant
for a civilised life,' he said to himself, regretfully, as he filled his
pipe. 'The sooner I get back to London or Paris the better for me.'

His eye fell on the sealed case in which Waterhouse had put

the featherless poisoned arrows they had bought in the Mendi country. 'I wish I had hit the beggar somewhere vital,' said Pollock viciously.

Waterhouse came back after a long interval. He was not communicative, though Pollock asked him questions enough. The Porroh man, it seems, was a prominent member of that mystical society. The village was interested, but not threatening. No doubt the witch-doctor had gone into the bush. He was a great witch-doctor. 'Of course, he's up to something,' said Waterhouse, and became silent.

'But what can he do?' asked Pollock, unheeded.

'I must get you out of this. There's something brewing, or things would not be so quiet,' said Waterhouse, after a gap of silence. Pollock wanted to know what the brew might be. 'Dancing in a circle of skulls,' said Waterhouse; 'brewing a stink in a copper pot,' Pollock wanted particulars. Waterhouse was vague, Pollock pressing. At last Waterhouse lost his temper. 'How the devil should I know?' he said to Pollock's twentieth inquiry what the Porroh man would do. 'He tried to kill you off-hand in the hut. *Now*, I fancy he will try something more elaborate. But you'll see fast enough. I don't want to help unnerve you. It's probably all nonsense.'

That night, as they were sitting at their fire, Pollock again tried to draw Waterhouse out on the subject of Porroh methods. 'Better get to sleep,' said Waterhouse, when Pollock's bent became apparent; 'we start early to-morrow. You may want all your nerve about you.'

'But what line will he take?'

'Can't say. They're versatile people. They know a lot of rum dodges. You'd better get that copper-devil, Shakespear, to talk.'

There was a flash and a heavy bang out of the darkness behind the huts, and a clay bullet came whistling close to Pollock's head. This, at least, was crude enough. The blacks and half-breeds sitting and yarning round their own fire jumped up, and someone fired into the dark.

'Better go into one of the huts,' said Waterhouse quietly, still sitting unmoved.

Pollock stood up by the fire and drew his revolver. Fighting, at least, he was not afraid of. But a man in the dark is in the best of armour. Realising the wisdom of Waterhouse's advice, Pollock went into the tent and lay down there.

What little sleep he had was disturbed by dreams, variegated dreams, but chiefly of the Porroh man's face, upside down, as he went out of the hut, and looked up under his arm. It was odd that this transitory impression should have stuck so firmly in Pollock's memory. Moreover, he was troubled by queer pains in his limbs.

In the white haze of the early morning, as they were loading the canoes, a barbed arrow suddenly appeared quivering in the ground close to Pollock's foot. The boys made a perfunctory effort to clear out the thicket, but it led to no capture.

After these two occurrences, there was a disposition on the part of the expedition to leave Pollock to himself, and Pollock became, for the first time in his life, anxious to mingle with blacks. Waterhouse took one canoe, and Pollock, in spite of a friendly desire to chat with Waterhouse, had to take the other. He was left all alone in the front part of the canoe, and he had the greatest trouble to make the men – who did not love him – keep to the middle of the river, a clear hundred yards or more from either shore. However, he made Shakespear, the Freetown half-breed, come up to his own end of the canoe and tell him about Porroh, which Shakespear, failing in his attempts to leave Pollock alone, presently did with considerable freedom and gusto.

The day passed. The canoe glided swiftly along the ribbon of lagoon water, between the drift of water-figs, fallen trees, papyrus, and palm-wine palms, and with the dark mangrove swamp to the left, through which one could hear now and then the roar of the Atlantic surf. Shakespear told in his soft, blurred English of how the Porroh could cast spells; how men withered up under their malice; how they could send dreams and devils; how they tormented and killed the sons of Ijibu; how they kidnapped a white trader from Sulyma who had maltreated one of the sect, and how his body looked when it was found. And Pollock after each narrative cursed under his breath at the want of missionary enterprise that allowed such things to be, and at the inert British Government that ruled over this dark heathendom of Sierra Leone. In the evening they came to the Kasi Lake, and sent a score of crocodiles lumbering off the island on which the expedition camped for the night.

The next day they reached Sulyma, and smelt the sea breeze,

but Pollock had to put up there for five days before he could get on to Freetown. Waterhouse, considering him to be comparatively safe here, and within the pale of Freetown influence, left him and went back with the expedition to Gbemma, and Pollock became very friendly with Perera, the only resident white trader at Sulyma – so friendly, indeed, that he went about with him everywhere. Perera was a little Portuguese Jew, who had lived in England, and he appreciated the Englishman's friendliness as a great compliment.

For two days nothing happened out of the ordinary; for the most part Pollock and Perera played Nap – the only game they had in common – and Pollock got into debt. Then, on the second evening, Pollock had a disagreeable intimation of the arrival of the Porroh man in Sulyma by getting a flesh-wound in the shoulder from a lump of filed iron. It was a long shot, and the missile had nearly spent its force when it hit him. Still it conveyed its message plainly enough. Pollock sat up in his hammock, revolver in hand, all that night, and next morning confided, to some extent, in the Anglo-Portuguese.

Perera took the matter seriously. He knew the local customs pretty thoroughly. 'It is a personal question, you must know. It is revenge. And of course he is hurried by your leaving de country. None of de natives or half-breeds will interfere wid him very much – unless you make it wort deir while. If you come upon him suddenly, you might shoot him. But den he might shoot you.

'Den dere's dis – infernal magic,' said Perera. 'Of course, I don't believe in it – superstition – but still it's not nice to tink dat wherever you are, dere is a black man, who spends a moonlight night now and den a dancing about a fire to send you bad dreams.... Had any bad dreams?'

'Rather,' said Pollock. 'I keep on seeing the beggar's head upside down grinning at me and showing all his teeth as he did in the hut, and coming close up to me, and then going ever so far off, and coming back. It's nothing to be afraid of, but somehow it simply paralyses me with terror in my sleep. Queer things – dreams. I know it's a dream all the time, and I can't wake up from it.'

'It's probably only fancy,' said Perera. 'Den my niggers say Porroh men can send snakes. Seen any snakes lately?'

'Only one. I killed him this morning, on the floor near my hammock. Almost trod on him as I got up.'

'*Ah!*' said Perera, and then, reassuringly, 'Of course it is a – coincidence. Still I would keep my eyes open. Den dere's pains in de bones.'

'I thought they were due to miasma,' said Pollock.

'Probably dey are. When did dey begin?'

Then Pollock remembered that he first noticed them the night after the fight in the hut. 'It's my opinion he don't want to kill you,' said Perera – 'at least not yet. I've heard deir idea is to scare and worry a man wid deir spells, and narrow misses, and rheumatic pains, and bad dreams, and all dat, until he's sick of life. Of course, it's all talk, you know. You mustn't worry about it.... But I wonder what he'll be up to next.'

'*I* shall have to be up to something first,' said Pollock, staring gloomily at the greasy cards that Perera was putting on the table. 'It don't suit my dignity to be followed about, and shot at, and blighted in this way. I wonder if Porroh hokey-pokey upsets your luck at cards.'

He looked at Perera suspiciously.

'Very likely it does,' said Perera warmly, shuffling. 'Dey are wonderful people.'

That afternoon Pollock killed two snakes in his hammock, and there was also an extraordinary increase in the number of red ants that swarmed over the place; and these annoyances put him in a fit temper to talk over business with a certain Mendi rough he had interviewed before. The Mendi rough showed Pollock a little iron dagger, and demonstrated where one struck in the neck, in a way that made Pollock shiver, and in return for certain considerations Pollock promised him a double-barrelled gun with an ornamental lock.

In the evening, as Pollock and Perera were playing cards, the Mendi rough came in through the doorway, carrying something in a blood-soaked piece of native cloth.

'Not here!' said Pollock very hurriedly. 'Not here!'

But he was not quick enough to prevent the man, who was anxious to get to Pollock's side of the bargain, from opening the cloth and throwing the head of the Porroh man upon the table. It bounded from there on to the floor, leaving a red trail on the cards, and rolled into a corner, where it came to rest upside down, but glaring hard at Pollock.

Perera jumped up as the thing fell among the cards, and began in his excitement to gabble in Portuguese. The Mendi was bowing, with the red cloth in his hand. 'De gun!' he cried. Pollock stared back at the head in the corner. It bore exactly the expression it had in his dreams. Something seemed to snap in his own brain as he looked at it.

Then Perera found his English again.

'You got him killed?' he said. 'You did not kill him yourself?'

'Why should I?' said Pollock.

'But he will not be able to take it off now!'

'Take *what* off?' said Pollock.

'And all dese cards are spoiled!'

'*What* do you mean by taking off?' said Pollock.

'You must send me a new pack from Freetown. You can buy dem dere.'

'But – "take it off"?'

'It is only superstition. I forgot. De niggers say dat if de witches – he was a witch – But it is rubbish.... You must make de Porroh man take it off, or kill him yourself.... It is very silly.'

Pollock swore under his breath, still staring hard at the head in the corner.

'I can't stand that glare,' he said. Then suddenly he rushed at the thing and kicked it. It rolled some yards or so, and came to rest in the same position as before, upside down, and looking at him.

'He is ugly,' said the Anglo-Portuguese. 'Very ugly. Dey do it on deir faces with little knives.'

Pollock would have kicked the head again, but the Mendi man touched him on the arm. 'De gun?' he said, looking nervously at the head.

'Two – if you will take that beastly thing away,' said Pollock.

The Mendi shook his head, and intimated that he only wanted one gun now due to him, and for which he would be obliged. Pollock found neither cajolery nor bullying any good with him. Perera had a gun to sell (at a profit of three hundred per cent), and with that the man presently departed. Then Pollock's eyes, against his will, were recalled to the thing on the floor.

'It is funny dat his head keeps upside down,' said Perera, with an uneasy laugh. 'His brains must be heavy, like de weight in de little images one sees dat keep always upright wid lead in dem. You will take him wiv you when you go presently. You might take him now. De cards are all spoilt. Dere is a man sell dem in Freetown. De room is in a filthy mess as it is. You should have killed him yourself.'

Pollock pulled himself together, and went and picked up the head. He would hang it up by the lamp-hook in the middle of the ceiling of his room, and dig a grave for it at once. He was under the impression that he hung it up by the hair, but that must have been wrong, for when he returned for it, it was hanging by the neck upside down.

He buried it before sunset on the north side of the shed he occupied, so that he should not have to pass the grave after dark when he was returning from Perera's. He killed two snakes before he went to sleep. In the darkest part of the night he awoke with a start, and heard a pattering sound and something scraping on the floor. He sat up noiselessly, and felt under his pillow for his revolver. A mumbling growl followed, and Pollock fired at the sound. There was a yelp, and something dark passed for a moment across the hazy blue of the doorway. 'A dog!' said Pollock, lying down again.

In the early dawn he awoke again with a peculiar sense of unrest. The vague pain in his bones had returned. For some time he lay watching the red ants that were swarming over the ceiling, and then, as the light grew brighter, he looked over the edge of his hammock and saw something dark on the floor. He gave such a violent start that the hammock overset and flung him out.

He found himself lying, perhaps, a yard away from the head of the Porroh man. It had been disinterred by the dog, and the nose was grievously battered. Ants and flies swarmed over it. By an odd coincidence, it was still upside down, and with the same diabolical expression in the inverted eyes.

Pollock sat paralysed, and stared at the horror for some time. Then he got up and walked round it – giving it a wide berth – and out of the shed. The clear light of the sunrise, the living stir of vegetation before the breath of the dying land-breeze, and the empty grave with the marks of the dog's paws, lightened the weight upon his mind a little.

He told Perera of the business as though it was a jest – a jest to be told with white lips. 'You should not have frighten de dog,' said Perera, with poorly simulated hilarity.

The next two days, until the steamer came, were spent by Pollock in making a more effectual disposition of his possession. Overcoming his aversion to handling the thing, he went down to the river mouth and threw it into the sea-water, but by some miracle it escaped the crocodiles, and was cast up by the tide on the mud a little way up the river, to be found by an intelligent Arab half-breed, and offered for sale to Pollock and Perera as a curiosity, just on the edge of night. The native hung about in the brief twilight, making lower and lower offers, and at last, getting scared in some way by the evident dread these wise white men had for the thing, went off, and, passing Pollock's shed, threw his burden in there for Pollock to discover in the morning.

At this Pollock got into a kind of frenzy. He would burn the thing. He went out straightway into the dawn, and had constructed a big pyre of brushwood before the heat of the day. He was interrupted by the hooter of the little paddle steamer from Monrovia to Bathurst, which was coming through the gap in the bar. 'Thank Heaven!' said Pollock, with infinite piety, when the meaning of the sound dawned upon him. With trembling hands he lit his pile of wood hastily, threw the head upon it, and went away to pack his portmanteau and make his adieux to Perera.

That afternoon, with a sense of infinite relief, Pollock watched the flat swampy foreshore of Sulyma grow small in the distance. The gap in the long line of white surge became narrower and narrower. It seemed to be closing in and cutting him off from his trouble. The feeling of dread and worry began to slip from him bit by bit. At Sulyma belief in Porroh malignity and Porroh magic had been in the air, his sense of Porroh had been vast, pervading, threatening, dreadful. Now manifestly the domain of Porroh was only a little place, a little black band between the sea and the blue cloudy Mendi uplands.

'Goodbye, Porroh!' said Pollock. 'Goodbye – certainly not *au revoir.*'

The captain of the steamer came and leant over the rail beside him, and wished him good-evening, and spat at the froth of the wake in token of friendly ease.

'I picked up a rummy curio on the beach this go,' said the captain. 'It's a thing I never saw done this side of Indy before.'

'What might that be?' said Pollock.

'Pickled 'ed,' said the captain.

'*What!*' said Pollock.

"Ed – smoked. 'Ed of one of these Porroh chaps, all ornamented with knife-cuts. Why! What's up? Nothing? I shouldn't have took you for a nervous chap. Green in the face. By gosh! you're a bad sailor. All right, eh? Lord, how funny you went! ... Well, this 'ed I was telling you of is a bit rum in a way. I've got it, along with some snakes, in a jar of spirit in my cabin what I keeps for such curios, and I'm hanged if it don't float upsy down. Hullo!'

Pollock had given an incoherent cry, and had his hands in his hair. He ran towards the paddle-boxes with a half-formed idea of jumping into the sea, and then he realised his position and turned back towards the captain.

'Here!' said the captain. 'Jack Philips, just keep him off me! Stand off! No nearer, mister! What's the matter with you? Are you mad?'

Pollock put his hand to his head. It was no good explaining. 'I believe I am pretty nearly mad at times,' he said. 'It's a pain I have here. Comes suddenly. You'll excuse me, I hope.'

He was white and in a perspiration. He saw suddenly very clearly all the danger he ran of having his sanity doubted. He forced himself to restore the captain's confidence, by answering his sympathetic inquiries, noting his suggestions, even trying a spoonful of neat brandy in his cheek, and, that matter settled, asking a number of questions about the captain's private trade in curiosities. The captain described the head in detail. All the while Pollock was struggling to keep under a preposterous persuasion that the ship was as transparent as glass, and that he could distinctly see the inverted face looking at him from the cabin beneath his feet.

Pollock had a worse time almost on the steamer than he had at Sulyma. All day he had to control himself in spite of his intense perception of the imminent presence of that horrible head that was overshadowing his mind. At night his old nightmare returned, until, with a violent effort, he would force himself awake, rigid with the horror of it, and with the ghost of a hoarse scream in his throat.

He left the actual head behind at Bathurst, where he changed
ship for Teneriffe, but not his dreams nor the dull ache in his
bones. At Teneriffe Pollock transferred to a Cape liner, but the
head followed him. He gambled, he tried chess, he even read
books, but he knew the danger of drink. Yet whenever a round
black shadow, a round black object came into his range, there he
looked for the head, and – saw it. He knew clearly enough that
his imagination was growing traitor to him, and yet at times it
seemed the ship he sailed in, his fellow-passengers, the sailors,
the wide sea, was all part of a filmy phantasmagoria that hung,
scarcely veiling it, between him and a horrible real world. Then
the Porroh man, thrusting his diabolical face through that
curtain, was the one real and undeniable thing. At that he would
get up and touch things, taste something, gnaw something, burn
his hand with a match, or run a needle into himself.

So, struggling grimly and silently with his excited imagination,
Pollock reached England. He landed at Southampton, and went
on straight from Waterloo to his banker's in Cornhill in a cab.
There he transacted some business with the manager in a private
room, and all the while the head hung like an ornament under
the black marble mantel and dripped upon the fender. He could
hear the drops fall, and see the red on the fender.

'A pretty fern,' said the manager, following his eyes. 'But it
makes the fender rusty.'

'Very,' said Pollock; 'a *very* pretty fern. And that reminds me.
Can you recommend me a physician for mind troubles? I've got a
little – what is it? – hallucination.'

The head laughed savagely, wildly. Pollock was surprised the
manager did not notice it. But the manager only stared at his
face.

With the address of a doctor, Pollock presently emerged in
Cornhill. There was no cab in sight, and so he went on down to
the western end of the street, and essayed the crossing opposite
the Mansion House. The crossing is hardly easy even for the
expert Londoner; cabs, vans, carriages, mail-carts, omnibuses go
by in one incessant stream; to anyone fresh from the malarious
solitudes of Sierra Leone it is a boiling, maddening confusion. But
when an inverted head suddenly comes bouncing, like an
indiarubber ball, between your legs, leaving distinct smears of
blood every time it touches the ground, you can scarcely hope to

avoid an accident. Pollock lifted his feet convulsively to avoid it, and then kicked at the thing furiously. Then something hit him violently in the back, and a hot pain ran up his arm.

He had been hit by the pole of an omnibus, and three of the fingers of his left hand smashed by the hoof of one of the horses – the very fingers, as it happened, that he shot from the Porroh man. They pulled him out from between the horses' legs, and found the address of the physician in his crushed hand.

For a couple of days Pollock's sensations were full of the sweet, pungent smell of chloroform, of painful operations that caused him no pain, of lying still and being given food and drink. Then he had a slight fever, and was very thirsty, and his old nightmare came back. It was only when it returned that he noticed it had left him for a day.

'If my skull had been smashed instead of my fingers, it might have gone altogether,' said Pollock, staring thoughtfully at the dark cushion that had taken on for the time the shape of the head.

Pollock at the first opportunity told the physician of his mind trouble. He knew clearly that he must go mad unless something should intervene to save him. He explained that he had witnessed a decapitation in Dahomey, and was haunted by one of the heads. Naturally, he did not care to state the actual facts. The physician looked grave.

Presently he spoke hesitatingly. 'As a child, did you get very much religious training?'

'Very little,' said Pollock.

A shade passed over the physician's face. 'I don't know if you have heard of the miraculous cures – it may be, of course, they are not miraculous – at Lourdes.'

'Faith-healing will hardly suit me, I am afraid,' said Pollock, with his eye on the dark cushion.

The head distorted its scarred features in an abominable grimace. The physician went upon a new track. 'It's all imagination,' he said, speaking with sudden briskness. 'A fair case for faith-healing, anyhow. Your nervous system has run down, you're in that twilight state of health when the bogles come easiest. The strong impression was too much for you. I must make you up a little mixture that will strengthen your nervous system – especially your brain. And you must take exercise.'

'I'm no good for faith-healing,' said Pollock.

'And therefore we must restore tone. Go in search of stimulating air – Scotland, Norway, the Alps' –

'Jericho, if you like,' said Pollock – 'where Naaman went.'

However, so soon as his fingers would let him, Pollock made a gallant attempt to follow out the doctor's suggestion. It was now November. He tried football, but to Pollock the game consisted in kicking a furious inverted head about a field. He was no good at the game. He kicked blindly, with a kind of horror, and when they put him back into goal, and the ball came swooping down upon him, he suddenly yelled and got out of its way. The discreditable stories that had driven him from England to wander in the tropics shut him off from any but men's society, and now his increasingly strange behaviour made even his man friends avoid him. The thing was no longer a thing of the eye merely; it gibbered at him, spoke to him. A horrible fear came upon him that presently, when he took hold of the apparition, it would no longer become some mere article of furniture, but would *feel* like a real dissevered head. Alone, he would curse at the thing, defy it, entreat it; once or twice, in spite of his grim self-control, he addressed it in the presence of others. He felt the growing suspicion in the eyes of the people that watched him – his landlady, the servant, his man.

One day early in December his cousin Arnold – his next of kin – came to see him and draw him out, and watch his sunken yellow face with narrow eager eyes. And it seemed to Pollock that the hat his cousin carried in his hand was no hat at all, but a Gorgon head that glared at him upside down, and fought with its eyes against his reason. However, he was still resolute to see the matter out. He got a bicycle, and, riding over the frosty road from Wandsworth to Kingston, found the thing rolling along at his side, and leaving a dark trail behind it. He set his teeth and rode faster. Then suddenly, as he came down the hill towards Richmond Park, the apparition rolled in front of him and under his wheel, so quickly that he had no time for thought, and, turning quickly to avoid it, was flung violently against a heap of stones and broke his left wrist.

The end came on Christmas morning. All night he had been in

a fever, the bandages encircling his wrist like a band of fire, his dreams more vivid and terrible than ever. In the cold, colourless, uncertain light that came before the sunrise, he sat up in his bed, and saw the head upon the bracket in the place of the bronze jar that had stood there overnight.

'I know that is a bronze jar,' he said, with a chill doubt at his heart. Presently the doubt was irresistible. He got out of bed slowly, shivering, and advanced to the jar with his hand raised. Surely he would see now his imagination had deceived him, recognise the distinctive sheen of bronze. At last, after an age of hesitation, his fingers came down on the patterned cheek of the head. He withdrew them spasmodically. The last stage was reached. His sense of touch had betrayed him.

Trembling, stumbling against the bed, kicking against his shoes with his bare feet, a dark confusion eddying round him, he groped his way to the dressing-table, took his razor from the drawer, and sat down on the bed with this in his hand. In the looking-glass he saw his own face, colourless, haggard, full of the ultimate bitterness of despair.

He beheld in swift succession the incidents in the brief tale of his experience. His wretched home, his still more wretched schooldays, the years of vicious life he had led since then, one act of selfish dishonour leading to another; it was all clear and pitiless now, all its squalid folly, in the cold light of the dawn. He came to the hut, to the fight with the Porroh man, to the retreat down the river to Sulyma, to the Mendi assassin and his red parcel, to his frantic endeavours to destroy the head, to the growth of his hallucination. It was a hallucination! He *knew* it was. A hallucination merely. For a moment he snatched at hope. He looked away from the glass, and on the bracket, the inverted head grinned and grimaced at him.... With the stiff fingers of his bandaged hand he felt at his neck for the throb of his arteries. The morning was very cold, the steel blade felt like ice.

The Valley of Spiders

Towards midday the three pursuers came abruptly round a bend in the torrent bed upon the sight of a very broad and spacious valley. The difficult and winding trench of pebbles along which they had tracked the fugitives for so long expanded to a broad slope, and with a common impulse the three men left the trail, and rode to a little eminence set with olive-dun trees, and there halted, the two others, as became them, a little behind the man with the silver-studded bridle.

For a space they scanned the great expanse below them with eager eyes. It spread remoter and remoter, with only a few clusters of sere thorn bushes here and there, and the dim suggestions of some now waterless ravine to break its desolation of yellow grass. Its purple distances melted at last into the bluish slopes of the further hills – hills it might be of a greener kind – and above them, invisibly supported, and seeming indeed to hang in the blue, were the snow-clad summits of mountains – that grew larger and bolder to the north-westward as the sides of the valley drew together. And westward the valley opened until a distant darkness under the sky told where the forests began. But the three men looked neither east nor west, but only steadfastly across the valley.

The gaunt man with the scarred lip was the first to speak. 'Nowhere,' he said, with a sigh of disappointment in his voice. 'But, after all, they had a full day's start.'

'They don't know we are after them,' said the little man on the white horse.

'*She* would know,' said the leader bitterly, as if speaking to himself.

'Even then they can't go fast. They've got no beast but the mule, and all today the girl's foot has been bleeding—'

The man with the silver bridle flashed a quick intensity of rage on him. 'Do you think I haven't seen that?' he snarled.

'It helps, anyhow,' whispered the little man to himself. The gaunt man with the scarred lip stared impassively. 'They can't be over the valley,' he said. 'If we ride hard—'

He glanced at the white horse and paused.

'Curse all white horses!' said the man with the silver bridle, and turned to scan the beast his curse included.

The little man looked down between the melancholy ears of his steed.

'I did my best,' he said.

The two others stared again across the valley for a space. The gaunt man passed the back of his hand across the scarred lip.

'Come up!' said the man who owned the silver bridle, suddenly. The little man started and jerked his rein, and the horse hoofs of the three made a multitudinous faint pattering upon the withered grass as they turned back towards the trail....

They rode cautiously down the long slope before them, and so came through a waste of prickly twisted bushes and strange dry shapes of thorny branches that grew amongst the rocks, into the levels below. And there the trail grew faint, for the soil was scanty, and the only herbage was this scorched dead straw that lay upon the ground. Still, by hard scanning, by leaning beside the horses' necks and pausing ever and again, even these white men could contrive to follow after their prey.

There were trodden places, bent and broken blades of the coarse grass, and ever and again the sufficient intimation of a footmark. And once the leader saw a brown smear of blood where the half-caste girl may have trod. And at that under his breath he cursed her for a fool.

The gaunt man checked his leader's tracking, and the little man on the white horse rode behind, a man lost in a dream. They rode one after another, the man with the silver bridle led the way, and they spoke never a word. After a time it came to the little man on the white horse that the world was very still. He started out of his dream. Besides the little noises of their horses and equipment, the whole great valley kept the brooding quiet of a painted scene.

Before him went his master and his fellow, each intently leaning forward to the left, each impassively moving with the paces of his horse; their shadows went before them – still, noiseless, tapering attendants; and nearer a crouched cool shape was his own. He looked about him. What was it had gone? Then he remembered the reverberation from the banks of the gorge and the perpetual accompaniment of shifting, jostling pebbles. And, moreover—? There was no breeze. That was it! What a vast, still place it was, a monotonous afternoon slumber! And the sky open and blank except for a sombre veil of haze that had gathered in the upper valley.

He straightened his back, fretted with his bridle, puckered his lips to whistle, and simply sighed. He turned in his saddle for a time, and stared at the throat of the mountain gorge out of which they had come. Blank! Blank slopes on either side, with never a sign of a decent beast or tree – much less a man. What a land it was! What a wilderness! He dropped again into his former pose.

It filled him with a momentary pleasure to see a wry stick of purple black flash out into the form of a snake, and vanish amidst the brown. After all, the infernal valley *was* alive. And then, to rejoice him still more, came a little breath across his face, a whisper that came and went, the faintest inclination of a stiff black-antlered bush upon a little crest, the first intimations of a possible breeze. Idly he wetted his finger, and held it up.

He pulled up sharply to avoid a collision with the gaunt man, who had stopped at fault upon the trail. Just at that guilty moment he caught his master's eye looking towards him.

For a time he forced an interest in the tracking. Then, as they rode on again, he studied his master's shadow and hat and shoulder, appearing and disappearing behind the gaunt man's nearer contours. They had ridden four days out of the very limits of the world into this desolate place, short of water, with nothing but a strip of dried meat under their saddles, over rocks and mountains, where surely none but these fugitives had ever been before – for *that*!

And all this was for a girl, a mere wilful child! And the man had whole cityfuls of people to do his basest bidding – girls, women! Why in the name of passionate folly *this* one in particular? asked the little man, and scowled at the world, and licked his parched lips with a blackened tongue. It was the way of the master, and that was all he knew. Just because she sought to evade him ...

His eye caught a whole row of high-plumed canes bending in unison, and then the tails of silk that hung before his neck flapped and fell. The breeze was growing stronger. Somehow it took the stiff stillness out of things – and that was well.

'Hullo!' said the gaunt man.

All three stopped abruptly.

'What?' asked the master. 'What?'

'Over there,' said the gaunt man, pointing up the valley.

'What?'

'Something coming towards us.'

And as he spoke a yellow animal crested a rise and came bearing down upon them. It was a big wild dog, coming before the wind, tongue out, at a steady pace, and running with such an intensity of purpose that he did not seem to see the horsemen he approached. He ran with his nose up, following, it was plain, neither scent nor quarry. As he drew nearer the little man felt for his sword. 'He's mad,' said the gaunt rider.

'Shout!' said the little man, and shouted.

The dog came on. Then when the little man's blade was already out, it swerved aside and went panting by them and passed. The eyes of the little man followed its flight. 'There was no foam,' he said. For a space the man with the silver-studded bridle stared up the valley. 'Oh, come on!' he cried at last. 'What does it matter?' and jerked his horse into movement again.

The little man left the insoluble mystery of a dog that fled from nothing but the wind, and lapsed into profound musings on human character. 'Come on!' he whispered to himself. 'Why should it be given to one man to say "Come on!" with that stupendous violence of effect? Always, all his life, the man with the silver bridle has been saying that. If *I* said it—!' thought the little man. But people marvelled when the master was disobeyed even in the wildest things. This half-caste girl seemed to him, seemed to every one, mad – blasphemous almost. The little man, by way of comparison, reflected on the gaunt rider with the scarred lip, as stalwart as his master, as brave and, indeed, perhaps braver, and yet for him there was obedience, nothing but to give obedience duly and stoutly....

Certain sensations of the hands and knees called the little man back to more immediate things. He became aware of something. He rode up beside his gaunt fellow. 'Do you notice the horses?' he said in an undertone.

The gaunt face looked interrogation.

'They don't like this wind,' said the little man, and dropped behind as the man with the silver bridle turned upon him.

'It's all right,' said the gaunt-faced man.

They rode on again for a space in silence. The foremost two rode downcast upon the trail, the hindmost man watched the haze that crept down the vastness of the valley, nearer and nearer, and noted how the wind grew in strength moment by moment. Far away on the left he saw a line of dark bulks – wild hog, perhaps, galloping down the valley, but of that he said nothing, nor did he remark again upon the uneasiness of the horses.

And then he saw first one and then a second great white ball, a great shining white ball like a gigantic head of thistledown, that drove before the wind athwart the path. These balls soared high in the air, and dropped and rose again and caught for a moment, and hurried on and passed, but at the sight of them the restlessness of the horses increased.

Then presently he saw that more of these drifting globes – and then soon very many more – were hurrying towards him down the valley.

They became aware of a squealing. Athwart the path a huge boar rushed, turning his head but for one instant to glance at them, and then hurling on down the valley again. And at that all three stopped and sat in their saddles, staring into the thickening haze that was coming upon them.

'If it were not for this thistle-down—' began the leader.

But now a big globe came drifting past within a score of yards of them. It was really not an even sphere at all, but a vast, soft, ragged, filmy thing, a sheet gathered by the corners, an aerial jelly-fish, as it were, but rolling over and over as it advanced, and trailing long cobwebby threads and streamers that floated in its wake.

'It isn't thistle-down,' said the little man.

'I don't like the stuff,' said the gaunt man.

And they looked at one another.

'Curse it!' cried the leader. 'The air's full of it up there. If it keeps on at this pace long, it will stop us altogether.'

An instinctive feeling, such as lines out a herd of deer at the approach of some ambiguous thing, prompted them to turn their horses to the wind, ride forward for a few paces, and stare at that advancing multitude of floating masses. They came on before the wind with a sort of smooth swiftness, rising and falling noiselessly, sinking to earth, rebounding high, soaring – all with a perfect unanimity, with a still, deliberate assurance.

Right and left of the horsemen the pioneers of this strange army passed. At one that rolled along the ground, breaking shapelessly and trailing out reluctantly into long grappling ribbons and bands, all three horses began to shy and dance. The master was seized with a sudden, unreasonable impatience. He cursed the drifting globes roundly. 'Get on!' he cried; 'get on! What do these things matter? How *can* they matter? Back to the trail!' He fell swearing at his horse and sawed the bit across its mouth.

He shouted aloud with rage. 'I will follow that trail, I tell you,' he cried. 'Where is the trail?'

He gripped the bridle of his prancing horse and searched amidst the grass. A long and clinging thread fell across his face, a grey streamer dropped about his bridle arm, some big, active thing with many legs ran down the back of his head. He looked up to discover one of those grey masses anchored as it were above him by these things and flapping out ends as a sail flaps when a boat comes about – but noiselessly.

He had an impression of many eyes, of a dense crew of squat bodies, of long, many-jointed limbs hauling at their mooring ropes to bring the thing down upon him. For a space he stared up, reining in his prancing horse with the instinct born of years of horsemanship. Then the flat of a sword smote his back, and a blade flashed overhead and cut the drifting balloon of spider-web free, and the whole mass lifted softly and drove clear and away.

'Spiders!' cried the voice of the gaunt man. 'The things are full of big spiders! Look, my lord!'

The man with the silver bridle still followed the mass that drove away.

'Look, my lord!'

The master found himself staring down at a red smashed thing on the ground that, in spite of partial obliteration, could still wriggle unavailing legs. Then, when the gaunt man pointed to another mass that bore down upon them, he drew his sword hastily. Up the valley now it was like a fog bank torn to rags. He tried to grasp the situation.

'Ride for it!' the little man was shouting. 'Ride for it down the valley.'

What happened then was like the confusion of a battle. The man with the silver bridle saw the little man go past him, slashing furiously at imaginary cobwebs, saw him cannon into the horse of the gaunt man and hurl it and its rider to earth. His own horse went a dozen paces before he could rein it in. Then he looked up to avoid imaginary dangers, and then back again to see a horse rolling on the ground, the gaunt man standing and slashing over it at a rent and fluttering mass of grey that streamed and wrapped about them both. And thick and fast as thistle down on waste land on a windy day in July the cobweb masses were coming on.

The little man had dismounted, but he dared not release his horse. He was endeavouring to lug the struggling brute back with the strength of one arm, while with the other he slashed aimlessly. The tentacles of a second grey mass had entangled themselves with the struggle, and this second grey mass came to its moorings, and slowly sank.

The master set his teeth, gripped his bridle, lowered his head, and spurred his horse forward. The horse on the ground rolled over, there was blood and moving shapes upon the flanks, and the gaunt man suddenly leaving it, ran forward towards his master, perhaps ten paces. His legs were swathed and encumbered with grey; he made ineffectual movements with his sword. Grey streamers waved from him; there was a thin veil of grey across his face. With his left hand he beat at something on his body, and suddenly he stumbled and fell. He struggled to rise, and fell again, and suddenly, horribly, began to howl, 'Oh – ohoo, ohooh!'

The master could see the great spiders upon him, and others upon the ground.

As he strove to force his horse nearer to this gesticulating, screaming grey object that struggled up and down, there came a clatter of hoofs, and the little man, in act of mounting, swordless, balanced on his belly athwart the white horse, and clutching its mane, whirled past. And again a clinging thread of grey gossamer swept across the master's face. All about him, and over him, it seemed this drifting, noiseless cobweb circled and drew nearer him....

To the day of his death he never knew just how the event of that moment happened. Did he, indeed, turn his horse, or did it really of its own accord stampede after its fellow? Suffice it that in another second he was galloping full tilt down the valley with his sword whirling furiously overhead. And all about him on the quickening breeze, the spiders' air-ships, their air bundles and air sheets, seemed to him to hurry in a conscious pursuit.

Clatter, clatter, thud, thud, – the man with the silver bridle rode, heedless of his direction, with his fearful face looking up now right, now left, and his sword arm ready to slash. And a few hundred yards ahead of him, with a tail of torn cobweb trailing behind him, rode the little man on the white horse, still but imperfectly in the saddle. The reeds bent before them, the wind blew fresh and strong, over his shoulder the master could see the webs hurrying to overtake....

He was so intent to escape the spiders' webs that only as his horse gathered together for a leap did he realise the ravine ahead. And then he realised it only to misunderstand and interfere. He was leaning forward on his horse's neck and sat up and back all too late.

But if in his excitement he had failed to leap, at any rate he had not forgotten how to fall. He was horseman again in mid-air. He came off clear with a mere bruise upon his shoulder, and his horse rolled, kicking spasmodic legs, and lay still. But the master's sword drove its point into the hard soil, and snapped clean across, as though Chance refused him any longer as her Knight, and the splintered end missed his face by an inch or so.

He was on his feet in a moment, breathlessly scanning the on-rushing spider-webs. For a moment he was minded to run, and then thought of the ravine, and turned back. He ran aside once to dodge one drifting terror, and then he was swiftly clambering down the precipitous sides, and out of the touch of the gale.

There, under the lee of the dry torrent's steeper banks, he might crouch and watch these strange, grey masses pass and pass in safety till the wind fell, and it became possible to escape. And there for a long time he crouched, watching the strange, grey ragged masses trail their streamers across his narrowed sky.

Once a stray spider fell into the ravine close beside him – a full foot it measured from leg to leg and its body was half a man's hand – and after he had watched its monstrous alacrity of search and escape for a little while and tempted it to bite his broken sword, he lifted up his iron-heeled boot and smashed it into a pulp. He swore as he did so, and for a time sought up and down for another.

Then presently, when he was surer these spider swarms could not drop into the ravine, he found a place where he could sit down, and sat and fell into deep thought and began, after his manner, to gnaw his knuckles and bite his nails. And from this he was moved by the coming of the man with the white horse.

He heard him long before he saw him, as a clattering of hoofs, stumbling footsteps, and a reassuring voice. Then the little man appeared, a rueful figure, still with a tail of white cobweb trailing behind him. They approached each other without speaking, without a salutation. The little man was fatigued and shamed to the pitch of hopeless bitterness, and came to a stop at last, face to face with his seated master. The latter winced a little under his dependent's eye. 'Well?' he said at last, with no pretence of authority.

'You left him?'

'My horse bolted.'

'I know. So did mine.'

He laughed at his master mirthlessly.

'I say my horse bolted,' said the man who once had a silver-studded bridle.

'Cowards both,' said the little man.

The other gnawed his knuckle through some meditative moments, with his eye on his inferior.

'Don't call me a coward,' he said at length.

'You are a coward, like myself.'

'A coward possibly. There is a limit beyond which every man must fear. That I have learnt at last. But not like yourself. That is where the difference comes in.'

'I never could have dreamt you would have left him. He saved your life two minutes before.... Why are you our lord?'

The master gnawed his knuckles again, and his countenance was dark.

'No man calls me a coward,' he said. 'No.... A broken sword is better than none.... One spavined white horse cannot be expected to carry two men a four days' journey. I hate white horses, but this time it cannot be helped. You begin to understand me? I perceive that you are minded, on the strength of what you have seen and fancy, to taint my reputation. It is men of your sort who unmake kings. Besides which – I never liked you.'

'My lord!' said the little man.

'No,' said the master. '*No!*'

He stood up sharply as the little man moved. For a minute perhaps they faced one another. Overhead the spiders' balls went driving. There was a quick movement among the pebbles; a running of feet, a cry of despair, a gasp and a blow....

Towards nightfall the wind fell. The sun set in a calm serenity, and the man who had once possessed the silver bridle came at last very cautiously and by an easy slope out of the ravine again; but now he led the white horse that once belonged to the little man. He would have gone back to his horse to get his silver-mounted bridle again, but he feared night and a quickening breeze might still find him in the valley, and besides, he disliked greatly to think he might discover his horse all swathed in cobwebs and perhaps unpleasantly eaten.

And as he thought of those cobwebs, and of all the dangers he had been through, and the manner in which he had been preserved that day, his hand sought a little reliquary that hung about his neck, and he clasped it for a moment with heartfelt gratitude. As he did so his eyes went across the valley.

'I was hot with passion,' he said, 'and now she has met her reward. They also, no doubt—'

And behold! far away out of the wooded slopes across the valley, but in the clearness of the sunset, distinct and unmistakable, he saw a little spire of smoke.

At that his expression of serene resignation changed to an amazed anger. Smoke? He turned the head of the white horse about, and hesitated. And as he did so a little rustle of air went through the grass about him. Far away upon some reeds swayed a tattered sheet of grey. He looked at the cobwebs; he looked at the smoke.

'Perhaps, after all, it is not them,' he said at last.

But he knew better.

After he had stared at the smoke for some time, he mounted the white horse.

As he rode, he picked his way amidst stranded masses of web.

For some reason there were many dead spiders on the ground, and those that lived feasted guiltily on their fellows. At the sound of his horse's hoofs they fled.

Their time had passed. From the ground, without either a wind to carry them or a winding-sheet ready, these things, for all their poison, could do him little evil.

He flicked with his belt at those he fancied came too near. Once, where a number ran together over a bare place, he was minded to dismount and trample them with his boots, but this impulse he overcame. Ever and again he turned in his saddle, and looked back at the smoke.

'Spiders,' he muttered over and over again. 'Spiders. Well, well ... The next time I must spin a web.'

Mr Skelmersdale in Fairyland

There's a man in that shop,' said the Doctor, 'who has been in Fairyland.'

'Nonsense!' I said, and stared back at the shop. It was the usual village shop, post-office, telegraph wire on its brow, zinc pans and brushes outside, boots, shirtings, and potted meats in the window. 'Tell me about it,' I said, after a pause.

'*I* don't know,' said the Doctor. 'He's an ordinary sort of lout – Skelmersdale is his name. But everybody about here believes it like Bible truth.'

I reverted presently to the topic.

'I know nothing about it,' said the Doctor, 'and I don't *want* to know. I attended him for a broken finger – Married and Single cricket match – and that's when I struck the nonsense. That's all. But it shows you the sort of stuff I have to deal with, anyhow, eh? Nice to get modern sanitary ideas into a people like this!'

'Very,' I said in a mildly sympathetic tone, and he went on to tell me about that business of the Bonham drain. Things of that kind, I observe, are apt to weigh on the minds of Medical Officers of Health. I was as sympathetic as I knew how, and when he called the Bonham people 'asses', I said they were 'thundering asses', but even that did not allay him.

Afterwards, later in the summer, an urgent desire to seclude myself, while finishing my chapter on Spiritual Pathology – it was really, I believe, stiffer to write than it is to read – took me to Bignor. I lodged at a farmhouse, and presently found myself outside that little general shop again, in search of tobacco. 'Skelmersdale,' said I to myself at the sight of it, and went in.

I was served by a short, but shapely, young man, with a fair downy complexion, good, small teeth, blue eyes, and a languid manner. I scrutinised him curiously. Except for a touch of melancholy in his expression, he was nothing out of the common. He was in the shirt-sleeves and tucked-up apron of his trade, and a pencil was thrust behind his inoffensive ear. Athwart his black waistcoat was a gold chain, from which dangled a bent guinea.

'Nothing more today, sir?' he inquired. He leant forward over my bill as he spoke.

'Are you Mr Skelmersdale?' said I.

'I am, sir,' he said, without looking up.

'Is it true that you have been in Fairyland?'

He looked up at me for a moment with wrinkled brows, with an aggrieved, exasperated face. 'O shut it!' he said, and, after a moment of hostility, eye to eye, he went on adding up my bill. 'Four, six and a half,' he said, after a pause. 'Thank you, sir.'

So, unpropitiously, my acquaintance with Mr Skelmersdale began.

Well, I got from that to confidence – through a series of toilsome efforts. I picked him up again in the Village Room, where of a night I went to play billiards after my supper, and mitigate the extreme seclusion from my kind that was so helpful to work during the day. I contrived to play with him and afterwards to talk with him. I found the one subject to avoid was Fairyland. On everything else he was open and amiable in a commonplace sort of way, but on that he had been worried – it was a manifest taboo. Only once in the room did I hear the slightest allusion to his experience in his presence, and that was by a cross-grained farm hand who was losing to him. Skelmersdale had run a break into double figures, which, by the Bignor standards, was uncommonly good play. 'Steady on!' said his adversary. 'None of your fairy flukes!'

Skelmersdale stared at him for a moment, cue in hand, then flung it down and walked out of the room.

'Why can't you leave 'im alone?' said a respectable elder who had been enjoying the game, and in the general murmur of disapproval, the grin of satisfied wit faded from the ploughboy's face.

I scented my opportunity. 'What's this joke,' said I, 'about Fairyland?'

''Taint no joke about Fairyland, not to young Skelmersdale,' said the respectable elder, drinking.

A little man with rosy cheeks was more communicative. 'They *do* say, sir,' he said, 'that they took him into Aldington Knoll an' kep' him there a matter of three weeks.'

And with that the gathering was well under weigh. Once one sheep had started, others were ready enough to follow, and in a little time I had at least the exterior aspect of the Skelmersdale affair. Formerly, before he came to Bignor, he had been in that very similar little shop at Aldington Corner, and there whatever it was did happen had taken place. The story was clear that he had stayed out late one night on the Knoll and vanished for three weeks from the sight of men, and had returned with 'his cuffs as clean as when he started', and his pockets full of dust and ashes. He returned in a state of moody wretchedness that only slowly passed away, and for many days he would give no account of where it was he had been. The girl he was engaged to at Clapton Hill tried to get it out of him, and threw him over partly because he refused, and partly because, as she said, he fairly gave her the "ump'. And then when, some time after, he let out to some one carelessly that he had been in Fairyland and wanted to go back, and when the thing spread and the simple badinage of the countryside came into play, he threw up his situation abruptly, and came to Bignor to get out of the fuss. But as to what had happened in Fairyland none of these people knew. There the gathering in the Village Room went to pieces like a pack at fault. One said this, and another said that.

Their air in dealing with this marvel was ostensibly critical and sceptical, but I could see a considerable amount of belief showing through their guarded qualifications. I took a line of intelligent interest, tinged with a reasonable doubt of the whole story.

'If Fairyland's inside Aldington Knoll,' I said, 'why don't you dig it out?'

'That's what I says,' said the young ploughboy.

'There's a-many have tried to dig on Aldington Knoll,' said the respectable elder, solemnly, 'one time and another. But there's none as goes about today to tell what they got by digging.'

The unanimity of vague belief that surrounded me was rather impressive; I felt there must surely be *something* at the root of so much conviction, and the already pretty keen curiosity I felt about the real facts of the case was distinctly whetted. If these real facts were to be got from any one, they were to be got from Skelmersdale himself; and I set myself, therefore, still more assiduously to efface the first bad impression I had made and win

his confidence to the pitch of voluntary speech. In that endeav-
our I had a social advantage. Being a person of affability and no
apparent employment, and wearing tweeds and knickerbockers, I
was naturally classed as an artist in Bignor, and in the
remarkable code of social precedence prevalent in Bignor an
artist ranks considerably higher than a grocer's assistant.
Skelmersdale, like too many of his class, is something of a snob;
he had told me to 'SHUT it' only under sudden, excessive
provocation, and with, I am certain, a subsequent repentance; he
was, I knew, quite glad to be seen walking about the village with
me. In due course, he accepted the proposal of a pipe and whisky
in my rooms readily enough, and there, scenting by some happy
instinct that there was trouble of the heart in this, and knowing
that confidences beget confidences, I plied him with much of
interest and suggestion from my real and fictitious past. And it
was after the third whisky of the third visit of that sort, if I
remember rightly, that *àpropos* of some artless expansion of a
little affair that had touched and left me in my teens, that he did
at last, of his own free will and motion, break the ice. 'It was like
that with me,' he said, 'over there at Aldington. It's just that
that's so rum. First I didn't care a bit and it was all her, and
afterwards, when it was too late, it was, in a manner of speaking,
all me.'

I forbore to jump upon this allusion, and so he presently threw
out another, and in a little while he was making it as plain as
daylight that the one thing he wanted to talk about now was this
Fairyland adventure he had sat tight upon for so long. You see,
I'd done the trick with him, and from being just another half-
incredulous, would-be facetious stranger, I had, by all my wealth
of shameless self-exposure, become the possible confidant. He had
been bitten by the desire to show that he, too, had lived and felt
many things, and the fever was upon him.

He was certainly confoundedly allusive at first, and my
eagerness to clear him up with a few precise questions was only
equalled and controlled by my anxiety not to get to this sort of
thing too soon. But in another meeting or so the basis of
confidence was complete; and from first to last I think I got most
of the items and aspects – indeed, I got quite a number of times
over almost everything that Mr Skelmersdale, with his very
limited powers of narration, will ever be able to tell. And so I

come to the story of his adventure, and I piece it all together
again. Whether it really happened, whether he imagined it or
dreamt it, or fell upon it in some strange hallucinatory trance, I
do not profess to say. But that he invented it I will not for one
moment entertain. The man simply and honestly believes the
thing happened as he says it happened; he is transparently
incapable of any lie so elaborate and sustained, and in the belief
of the simple, yet often keenly penetrating, rustic minds about
him I find a very strong confirmation of his sincerity. He believes
– and nobody can produce any positive fact to falsify his belief. As
for me, with this much of endorsement, I transmit his story – I
am a little old now to justify or explain.

He says he went to sleep on Aldington Knoll about ten o'clock
one night – it was quite possibly Midsummer night, though he
has never thought of the date, and he cannot be sure within a
week or so – and it was a fine night and windless, with a rising
moon. I have been at the pains to visit this Knoll thrice since his
story grew up under my persuasions, and once I went there in
the twilight summer moonrise on what was, perhaps, a similar
night to that of his adventure. Jupiter was great and splendid
above the moon, and in the north and north-west the sky was
green and vividly bright over the sunken sun. The Knoll stands
out bare and bleak under the sky, but surrounded at a little
distance by dark thickets, and as I went up towards it there was a
mighty starting and scampering of ghostly or quite invisible
rabbits. Just over the crown of the Knoll, but nowhere else, was a
multitudinous thin trumpeting of midges. The Knoll is, I believe,
an artificial mound, the tumulus of some great prehistoric
chieftain, and surely no man ever chose a more spacious prospect
for a sepulchre. Eastward one sees along the hills to Hythe, and
thence across the Channel to where, thirty miles and more,
perhaps, away, the great white lights by Gris Nez and Boulogne
wink and pass and shine. Westward lies the whole tumbled valley
of the Weald, visible as far as Hindhead and Leith Hill, and the
valley of the Stour opens the Downs in the north to interminable
hills beyond Wye. All Romney Marsh lies southward at one's feet,
Dymchurch and Romney and Lydd, Hastings and its hill are in
the middle distance, and the hills multiply vaguely far beyond
where Eastbourne rolls up to Beachy Head.

And out upon all this it was that Skelmersdale wandered,

being troubled in his earlier love affair, and as he says, 'not caring *where* he went'. And there he sat down to think it over, and so, sulking and grieving, was overtaken by sleep. And so he fell into the fairies' power.

The quarrel that had upset him was some trivial matter enough between himself and the girl at Clapton Hill to whom he was engaged. She was a farmer's daughter, said Skelmersdale, and 'very respectable', and no doubt an excellent match for him; but both girl and lover were very young and with just that mutual jealousy, that intolerantly keen edge of criticism, that irrational hunger for a beautiful perfection, that life and wisdom do presently and most mercifully dull. What the precise matter of quarrel was I have no idea. She may have said she liked men in gaiters when he hadn't any gaiters on, or he may have said he liked her better in a different sort of hat, but however it began, it got by a series of clumsy stages to bitterness and tears. She no doubt got tearful and smeary, and he grew dusty and drooping, and she parted with invidious comparisons, grave doubts whether she ever had *really* cared for him, and a clear certainty she would never care again. And with this sort of thing upon his mind he came out upon Aldington Knoll grieving, and presently, after a long interval, perhaps, quite inexplicably, fell asleep.

He woke to find himself on a softer turf than ever he had slept on before, and under the shade of very dark trees that completely hid the sky. Always, indeed, in Fairyland the sky is hidden, it seems. Except for one night when the fairies were dancing, Mr Skelmersdale, during all his time with them, never saw a star. And of that night I am in doubt whether he was in Fairyland proper or out where the rings and rushes are, in those low meadows near the railway line at Smeeth.

But it was light under these trees for all that, and on the leaves and amidst the turf shone a multitude of glow-worms, very bright and fine. Mr Skelmersdale's first impression was that he was *small*, and the next that quite a number of people still smaller were standing all about him. For some reason, he says, he was neither surprised nor frightened, but sat up quite deliberately and rubbed the sleep out of his eyes. And there all about him stood the smiling elves who had caught him sleeping under their privileges and had brought him into Fairyland.

What these elves were like I have failed to gather, so vague and imperfect is his vocabulary, and so unobservant of all minor detail does he seem to have been. They were clothed in something very light and beautiful, that was neither wool, nor silk, nor leaves, nor the petals of flowers. They stood all about him as he sat and waked, and down the glade towards him, down a glow-worm avenue and fronted by a star, came at once that Fairy Lady who is the chief personage of his memory and tale. Of her I gathered more. She was clothed in filmy green, and about her little waist was a broad silver girdle. Her hair waved back from her forehead on either side; there were curls not too wayward and yet astray, and on her brow was a little tiara, set with a single star. Her sleeves were some sort of open sleeves that gave little glimpses of her arms; her throat, I think, was a little displayed, because he speaks of the beauty of her neck and chin. There was a necklace of coral about her white throat, and in her breast a coral-coloured flower. She had the soft lines of a little child in her chin and cheeks and throat. And her eyes, I gather, were of a kindled brown, very soft and straight and sweet under her level brows. You see by these particulars how greatly this lady must have loomed in Mr Skelmersdale's picture. Certain things he tried to express and could not express; 'the way she moved', he said several times; and I fancy a sort of demure joyousness radiated from this Lady.

And it was in the company of this delightful person, as the guest and chosen companion of this delightful person, that Mr Skelmersdale set out to be taken into the intimacies of Fairyland. She welcomed him gladly and a little warmly – I suspect a pressure of his hand in both of hers and a lit face to his. After all, ten years ago young Skelmersdale may have been a very comely youth. And once she took his arm, and once, I think, she led him by the hand adown the glade that the glow-worms lit.

Just how things chanced and happened there is no telling from Mr Skelmersdale's disarticulated skeleton of description. He gives little unsatisfactory glimpses of strange corners and doings, of places where there were many fairies together, of 'toadstool things that shone pink', of fairy food, of which he could only say 'you should have tasted it!' and of fairy music, 'like a little musical box', that came out of nodding flowers. There was a great open place where fairies rode and raced on 'things', but what Mr Skelmersdale meant by 'these here things they rode', there is no telling. Larvæ, perhaps, or crickets, or the little beetles that elude us so abundantly. There was a place where water splashed and gigantic king-cups grew, and there in the hotter times the fairies bathed together. There were games being played and dancing and much elvish love-making, too, I think, among the moss branch thickets. There can be no doubt that the Fairy Lady made love to Mr Skelmersdale, and no doubt either that this young man set himself to resist her. A time came, indeed, when she sat on a bank beside him, in a quiet secluded place 'all smelling of vi'lets', and talked to him of love.

'When her voice went low and she whispered,' said Mr Skelmersdale, 'and laid 'er 'and on my 'and, you know, and came close with a soft, warm friendly way she 'ad, it was as much as I could do to keep my 'ead.'

It seems he kept his head to a certain limited unfortunate extent. He saw "ow the wind was blowing', he says, and so, sitting there in a place all smelling of violets, with the touch of this lovely Fairy Lady about him, Mr Skelmersdale broke it to her gently – that he was engaged!

She had told him she loved him dearly, that he was a sweet human lad for her, and whatever he would ask of her he should have – even his heart's desire.

And Mr Skelmersdale, who, I fancy, tried hard to avoid looking at her little lips as they just dropped apart and came together, led up to the more intimate question by saying he would like enough capital to start a little shop. He'd just like to feel, he said, he had money enough to do that. I imagine a little surprise in those brown eyes he talked about, but she seemed sympathetic for all that, and she asked him many questions about the little shop, 'laughing like' all the time. So he got to the complete statement of his affianced position, and told her all about Millie.

'All?' said I.

'Everything,' said Mr Skelmersdale, 'just who she was, and where she lived, and everything about her. I sort of felt I 'ad to all the time, I did.'

'"Whatever you want you shall have," said the Fairy Lady. "That's as good as done. You *shall* feel you have the money just as you wish. And now, you know – *you must kiss me.*"'

And Mr Skelmersdale pretended not to hear the latter part of her remark, and said she was very kind. That he really didn't deserve she should be so kind. And—

The Fairy Lady suddenly came quite close to him and whispered 'Kiss me!'

'And,' said Mr Skelmersdale, 'like a fool, I did.'

There are kisses and kisses, I am told, and this must have been quite the other sort from Millie's resonant signals of regard. There was something magic in that kiss; assuredly it marked a turning point. At any rate, this is one of the passages that he thought sufficiently important to describe most at length. I have tried to get it right, I have tried to disentangle it from the hints and gestures through which it came to me, but I have no doubt that it was all different from my telling and far finer and sweeter, in the soft filtered light and the subtly stirring silences of the fairy glades. The Fairy Lady asked him more about Millie, and was she very lovely, and so on – a great many times. As to Millie's loveliness, I conceive him answering that she was 'all right'. And then, or on some such occasion, the Fairy Lady told him she had fallen in love with him as he slept in the moonlight, and so he had been brought into Fairyland, and she had thought, not knowing of Millie, that perhaps he might chance to love her. 'But now you know you can't,' she said, 'so you must stop with me just a little while, and then you must go back to Millie.' She told him that, and you know Skelmersdale was already in love with her, but the pure inertia of his mind kept him in the way he was going. I imagine him sitting in a sort of stupefaction amidst all these glowing beautiful things, answering about his Millie and the little shop he projected and the need of a horse and cart.... And that absurd state of affairs must have gone on for days and days. I see this little lady, hovering about him and trying to amuse him, too dainty to understand his complexity and too tender to let him go. And he, you know, hypnotised as it were by his earthly position, went his way with her hither and thither, blind to everything in Fairyland but this wonderful intimacy that had come to him. It is hard, it is impossible, to give in print the effect of her radiant sweetness shining through the jungle of poor Skelmersdale's rough and broken sentences. To me, at least, she shone clear amidst the muddle of his story like a glow-worm in a tangle of weeds.

There must have been many days of things while all this was

happening – and once, I say, they danced under the moonlight in the fairy rings that stud the meadows near Smeeth – but at last it all came to an end. She led him into a great cavernous place, lit by 'a red nightlight sort of thing', where there were coffers piled on coffers, and cups and golden boxes, and a great heap of what certainly seemed to all Mr Skelmersdale's senses – coined gold. There were little gnomes amidst this wealth, who saluted her at her coming, and stood aside. And suddenly she turned on him there with brightly shining eyes.

'And now,' she said, 'you have been kind to stay with me so long, and it is time I let you go. You must go back to your Millie. You must go back to your Millie, and here – just as I promised you – they will give you gold.'

'She choked like,' said Mr Skelmersdale. 'At that, I had a sort of feeling—' (he touched his breastbone) 'as though I was fainting here. I felt pale, you know, and shivering, and even then – I 'adn't a thing to say.'

He paused. 'Yes,' I said.

The scene was beyond his describing. But I know that she kissed him goodbye.

'And you said nothing?'

'Nothing,' he said. 'I stood like a stuffed calf. She just looked back once, you know, and stood smiling like and crying – I could see the shine of her eyes – and then she was gone, and there was all these little fellows bustling about me, stuffing my 'ands and my pockets and the back of my collar and everywhere with gold.'

And then it was, when the Fairy Lady had vanished, that Mr Skelmersdale really understood and knew. He suddenly began plucking out the gold they were thrusting upon him, and shouting out at them to prevent their giving him more. '"I don't *want* yer gold," I said. "I 'aven't done yet. I'm not going. I want to speak to that Fairy Lady again." I started off to go after her and they held me back. Yes, stuck their little 'ands against my middle and shoved me back. They kept giving me more and more gold until it was running all down my trouser legs and dropping out of my 'ands. "I don't *want* yer gold," I says to them, "I want just to speak to the Fairy Lady again."'

'And did you?'

'It came to a tussle.'

'Before you saw her?'

'I didn't see her. When I got out from them she wasn't anywhere to be seen.'

So he ran in search of her out of this red-lit cave, down a long grotto, seeking her, and thence he came out in a great and desolate place athwart which a swarm of will-o'-the-wisps were flying to and fro. And about him elves were dancing in derision, and the little gnomes came out of the cave after him, carrying gold in handfuls and casting it after him, shouting, 'Fairy love and fairy gold! Fairy love and fairy gold!'

And when he heard these words, came a great fear that it was all over, and he lifted up his voice and called to her by her name, and suddenly set himself to run down the slope from the mouth of the cavern, through a place of thorns and briers, calling after her very loudly and often. The elves danced about him unheeded, pinching him and pricking him, and the will-o'-the-wisps circled round him and dashed into his face, and the gnomes pursued him shouting and pelting him with fairy gold. As he ran with all this strange rout about him and distracting him, suddenly he was knee-deep in a swamp, and suddenly he was amidst thick twisted roots, and he caught his foot in one and stumbled and fell....

He fell and he rolled over, and in that instant he found himself sprawling upon Aldington Knoll, all lonely under the stars.

He sat up sharply at once, he says, and found he was very stiff and cold, and his clothes were damp with dew. The first pallor of dawn and a chilly wind were coming up together. He could have believed the whole thing a strangely vivid dream until he thrust his hand into his side pocket and found it stuffed with ashes. Then he knew for certain it was fairy gold they had given him. He could feel all their pinches and pricks still, though there was never a bruise upon him. And in that manner, and so suddenly, Mr Skelmersdale came out of Fairyland back into this world of men. Even then he fancied the thing was but the matter of a night until he returned to the shop at Aldington Corner and discovered amidst their astonishment that he had been away three weeks.

'Lor! the trouble I 'ad!' said Mr Skelmersdale.

'How?'

'Explaining. I suppose you've never had anything like that to explain.'

'Never,' I said, and he expatiated for a time on the behaviour of this person and that. One name he avoided for a space.

'And Millie?' said I at last.

'I didn't seem to care a bit for seeing Millie,' he said.

'I expect she seemed changed?'

'Every one was changed. Changed for good. Every one seemed big, you know, and coarse. And their voices seemed loud. Why, the sun, when it rose in the morning, fair hit me in the eye!'

'And Millie?'

'I didn't want to see Millie.'

'And when you did?'

'I came up against her Sunday, coming out of church. "Where you been?" she said, and I saw there was a row. I didn't care if there was. I seemed to forget about her even while she was there a-talking to me. She was just nothing. I couldn't make out whatever I 'ad seen in 'er ever, or what there could 'ave been. Sometimes when she wasn't about, I did get back a little, but never when she was there. Then it was always the other came up and blotted her out.... Any'ow, it didn't break her heart.'

'Married?' I asked.

'Married 'er cousin,' said Mr Skelmersdale, and reflected on the pattern of the tablecloth for a space.

When he spoke again it was clear that his former sweetheart had clean vanished from his mind, and that the talk had brought back the Fairy Lady triumphant in his heart. He talked of her – soon he was letting out the oddest things, queer love secrets it would be treachery to repeat. I think, indeed, that was the queerest thing in the whole affair, to hear that neat little grocer man after his story was done, with a glass of whisky beside him and a cigar between his fingers, witnessing, with sorrow still, though now, indeed, with a time blunted anguish, of the inappeasable hunger of the heart that presently came upon him. 'I couldn't eat,' he said, 'I couldn't sleep. I made mistakes in orders and got mixed with change. There she was day and night, drawing me and drawing me. Oh, I wanted her. Lord! how I wanted her! I was up there, most evenings I was up there on the Knoll, often even when it rained. I used to walk over the Knoll and round it and round it, calling for them to let me in. Shouting. Near blubbering I was at times. Daft I was and miserable. I kept on saying it was all a mistake. And every Sunday afternoon I went up there, wet and fine, though I knew as well as you do it wasn't no good by day. And I've tried to go to sleep there.'

He stopped sharply and decided to drink some whisky.

'I've tried to go to sleep there,' he said, and I could swear his lips trembled. 'I've tried to go to sleep there, often and often. And, you know, I couldn't, sir – never. I've thought if I could go to sleep there, there might be something.... But I've sat up there and laid up there, and I couldn't – not for thinking and longing. It's the longing.... I've tried—'

He blew, drank up the rest of his whisky spasmodically, stood up suddenly and buttoned his jacket, staring closely and critically at the cheap oleographs beside the mantel meanwhile. The little black notebook in which he recorded the orders of his daily round projected stiffly from his breast pocket. When all the buttons were quite done, he patted his chest and turned on me suddenly. 'Well,' he said, 'I must be going.'

There was something in his eyes and manner that was too difficult for him to express in words. 'One gets talking,' he said at last at the door, and smiled wanly, and so vanished from my eyes. And that is the tale of Mr Skelmersdale in Fairyland just as he told it to me.

The Apple

'I must get rid of it,' said the man in the corner of the carriage, abruptly breaking the silence.

Mr Hinchcliff looked up, hearing imperfectly. He had been lost in the rapt contemplation of the college cap tied by a string to his portmanteau handles – the outward and visible sign of his newly-gained pedagogic position – in the rapt appreciation of the college cap and the pleasant anticipations it excited. For Mr Hinchcliff had just matriculated at London University, and was going to be junior assistant at the Holmwood Grammar School – a very enviable position. He stared across the carriage at his fellow-traveller.

'Why not give it away?' said this person. 'Give it away! Why not?'

He was a tall, dark, sunburnt man with a pale face. His arms were folded tightly, and his feet were on the seat in front of him. He was pulling at a lank black moustache. He stared hard at his toes.

'Why not?' he said.

Mr Hinchcliff coughed.

The stranger lifted his eyes – they were curious, dark-grey eyes – and stared blankly at Mr Hinchcliff for the best part of a minute, perhaps. His expression grew to interest.

'Yes,' he said slowly. 'Why not? And end it.'

'I don't quite follow you, I'm afraid,' said Mr Hinchcliff, with another cough.

'You don't quite follow me?' said the stranger quite mechanically, his singular eyes wandering from Mr Hinchcliff to the bag with its ostentatiously displayed cap, and back to Mr Hinchcliff's downy face.

'You're so abrupt, you know,' apologised Mr Hinchcliff.

'Why shouldn't I?' said the stranger, following his thoughts. 'You are a student?' he said, addressing Mr Hinchcliff.

'I am – by Correspondence – of the London University,' said Mr

Hinchcliff, with irrepressible pride, and feeling nervously at his tie.

'In pursuit of knowledge,' said the stranger, and suddenly took his feet off the seat, put his fist on his knees, and stared at Mr Hinchcliff as though he had never seen a student before. 'Yes,' he said, and flung out an index finger. Then he rose, took a bag from the hat-rack, and unlocked it. Quite silently he drew out something round and wrapped in a quantity of silver-paper, and unfolded this carefully. He held it out towards Mr Hinchcliff – a small, very smooth, golden-yellow fruit.

Mr Hinchcliff's eyes and mouth were open. He did not offer to take this object – if he was intended to take it.

'That,' said this fantastic stranger, speaking very slowly, 'is the Apple of the Tree of Knowledge. Look at it – small, and bright, and wonderful – Knowledge – and I am going to give it to you.'

Mr Hinchcliff's mind worked painfully for a minute, and then the sufficient explanation, 'Mad!' flashed across his brain, and illuminated the whole situation. One humoured madmen. He put his head a little on one side.

'The Apple of the Tree of Knowledge, eigh!' said Mr Hinchcliff, regarding it with a finely assumed air of interest, and then looking at the interlocutor. 'But don't you want to eat it yourself? And besides – how did you come by it?'

'It never fades. I have had it now three months. And it is ever bright and smooth and ripe and desirable, as you see it.' He laid his hand on his knee and regarded the fruit musingly. Then he began to wrap it again in the papers, as though he had abandoned his intention of giving it away.

'But how did you come by it?' said Mr Hinchcliff, who had his argumentative side. 'And how do you know that it *is* the Fruit of the Tree?'

'I bought this fruit,' said the stranger, 'three months ago – for a drink of water and a crust of bread. The man who gave it to me – because I kept the life in him – was an Armenian. Armenia! that wonderful country, the first of all countries, where the ark of the Flood remains to this day, buried in the glaciers of Mount Ararat. This man, I say, fleeing with others from the Kurds who had come upon them, went up into desolate places among the mountains – places beyond the common knowledge of men. And fleeing from imminent pursuit, they came to a slope high among the mountain-peaks, green with a grass like knife-blades, that cut and slashed most pitilessly at anyone who went into it. The Kurds were close behind, and there was nothing for it but to plunge in, and the worst of it was that the paths they made through it at the price of their blood served for the Kurds to follow. Every one of the fugitives was killed save this Armenian and another. He heard the screams and cries of his friends, and the swish of the grass about those who were pursuing them – it was tall grass rising overhead. And then a shouting and answers, and when presently he paused, everything was still. He pushed out again, not understanding, cut and bleeding, until he came out on a steep slope of rocks below a precipice, and then he saw the grass was all on fire, and the smoke of it rose like a veil between him and his enemies.'

The stranger paused. 'Yes?' said Mr Hinchcliff. 'Yes?'

'There he was, all torn and bloody from the knife-blades of the grass, the rocks blazing under the afternoon sun – the sky molten brass – and the smoke of the fire driving towards him. He dared not stay there. Death he did not mind, but torture! Far away beyond the smoke he heard shouts and cries. Women screaming. So he went clambering up a gorge in the rocks – everywhere were bushes with dry branches that stuck like thorns among the leaves – until he clambered over the brow of a ridge that hid him. And then he met his companion, a shepherd, who had also escaped. And, counting cold and famine and thirst as nothing against the Kurds, they went on into the heights, and among the snow and ice. They wandered three whole days.

'The third day came the vision. I suppose hungry men often do see visions, but then there is this fruit.' He lifted the wrapped globe in his hand. 'And I have heard it, too, from other mountaineers who have known something of the legend. It was in the evening time, when the stars were increasing, that they came down a slope of polished rock into a huge dark valley all set about with strange, contorted trees, and in these trees hung little globes like glow-worm spheres, strange round yellow lights.

'Suddenly this valley was lit far away, many miles away, far down it, with a golden flame marching slowly athwart it, that made the stunted trees against it black as night, and turned the slopes all about them and their figures to the likeness of fiery gold. And at the vision they, knowing the legends of the mountains, instantly knew that it was Eden they saw, or the sentinel of Eden, and they fell upon their faces like men struck dead.

'When they dared to look again the valley was dark for a space, and then the light came again – returning, a burning amber.

'At that the shepherd sprang to his feet, and with a shout began to run down towards the light, but the other man was too fearful to follow him. He stood stunned, amazed, and terrified, watching his companion recede towards the marching glare. And hardly had the shepherd set out when there came a noise like thunder, the beating of invisible wings hurrying up the valley, and a great and terrible fear; and at that the man who gave me the fruit turned – if he might still escape. And hurrying headlong up the slope again, with that tumult sweeping after him, he stumbled against one of these stunted bushes, and a ripe fruit came off it into his hand. This fruit. Forthwith, the wings and the thunder rolled all about him. He fell and fainted, and when he came to his senses, he was back among the blackened ruins of his own village, and I and the others were attending to the wounded. A vision? But the golden fruit of the tree was still clutched in his hand. There were others there who knew the legend, knew what that strange fruit might be.' He paused. 'And this is it,' he said.

It was a most extraordinary story to be told in a third-class carriage on a Sussex railway. It was as if the real was a mere veil to the fantastic, and here was the fantastic poking through. 'Is it?' was all Mr Hinchcliff could say.

'The legend,' said the stranger, 'tells that those thickets of dwarfed trees growing about the garden sprang from the apple that Adam carried in his hand when he and Eve were driven forth. He felt something in his hand, saw the half-eaten apple, and flung it petulantly aside. And there they grow, in that desolate valley, girdled round with the everlasting snows, and there the fiery swords keep ward against the Judgment Day.'

'But I thought these things were' – Mr Hinchcliff paused – 'fables – parables rather. Do you mean to tell me that there in Armenia' –

The stranger answered the unfinished question with the fruit in his open hand.

'But you don't know,' said Mr Hinchcliff, 'that that *is* the fruit of the Tree of Knowledge. The man may have had – a sort of mirage, say. Suppose' –

'Look at it,' said the stranger.

It was certainly a strange-looking globe, not really an apple, Mr Hinchcliff saw, and a curious glowing golden colour, almost as though light itself was wrought into its substance. As he looked at it, he began to see more vividly the desolate valley among the mountains, the guarding swords of fire, the strange antiquities of the story he had just heard. He rubbed a knuckle into his eye. 'But' – said he.

'It has kept like that, smooth and full, three months. Longer than that it is now by some days. No drying, no withering, no decay.'

'And you yourself,' said Mr Hinchcliff, 'really believe that' –

'Is the Forbidden Fruit.'

There was no mistaking the earnestness of the man's manner and his perfect sanity. 'The Fruit of Knowledge,' he said.

'Suppose it was?' said Mr Hinchcliff, after a pause, still staring at it. 'But after all,' said Mr Hinchcliff, 'it's not my kind of knowledge – not the sort of knowledge. I mean, Adam and Eve have eaten it already.'

'We inherit their sins – not their knowledge,' said the stranger. 'That would make it all clear and bright again. We should see into everything, through everything, into the deepest meaning of everything' –

'Why don't you eat it, then?' said Mr Hinchcliff, with an inspiration.

'I took it intending to eat it,' said the stranger. 'Man has fallen. Merely to eat again could scarcely' –

'Knowledge is power,' said Mr Hinchcliff.

'But is it happiness? I am older than you – more than twice as old. Time after time I have held this in my hand, and my heart has failed me at the thought of all that one might know, that terrible lucidity – Suppose suddenly all the world became pitilessly clear?'

'That, I think, would be a great advantage,' said Mr Hinchcliff, 'on the whole.'

'Suppose you saw into the hearts and minds of everyone about you, into their most secret recesses – people you loved, whose love you valued?'

'You'd soon find out the humbugs,' said Mr Hinchcliff, greatly struck by the idea.

'And worse – to know yourself, bare of your most intimate illusions. To see yourself in your place. All that your lusts and weaknesses prevented your doing. No merciful perspective.'

'That might be an excellent thing too. "Know thyself", you know.'

'You are young,' said the stranger.

'If you don't care to eat it, and it bothers you, why don't you throw it away?'

'There again, perhaps, you will not understand me. To me, how could one throw away a thing like that, glowing, wonderful? Once one has it, one is bound. But, on the other hand, to *give* it away! To give it away to someone who thirsted after knowledge, who found no terror in the thought of that clear perception' –

'Of course,' said Mr Hinchcliff thoughtfully, 'it might be some sort of poisonous fruit.'

And then his eye caught something motionless, the end of a white board black-lettered outside the carriage window. '–MWOOD', he saw. He started convulsively. 'Gracious!' said Mr Hinchcliff. 'Holmwood!' – and the practical present blotted out the mystic realisations that had been stealing upon him.

In another moment he was opening the carriage-door, port-manteau in hand. The guard was already fluttering his green flag. Mr Hinchcliff jumped out. 'Here!' said a voice behind him, and he saw the dark eyes of the stranger shining and the golden fruit, bright and bare, held out of the open carriage-door. He took it instinctively, the train was already moving.

'No!' shouted the stranger, and made a snatch at it as if to take it back.

'Stand away,' cried a country porter, thrusting forward to close the door. The stranger shouted something Mr Hinchcliff did not catch, head and arm thrust excitedly out of the window, and then the shadow of the bridge fell on him, and in a trice he was hidden. Mr Hinchcliff stood astonished, staring at the end of the last waggon receding round the bend, and with the wonderful fruit in his hand. For the fraction of a minute his mind was confused, and then he became aware that two or three people on

the platform were regarding him with interest. Was he not the
new Grammar School master making his début? It occurred to
him that, so far as they could tell, the fruit might very well be the
naïve refreshment of an orange. He flushed at the thought, and
thrust the fruit into his side pocket, where it bulged undesirably.
But there was no help for it, so he went towards them,
awkwardly concealing his sense of awkwardness, to ask the way
to the Grammar School, and the means of getting his portmanteau and the two tin boxes which lay up the platform thither. Of
all the odd and fantastic yarns to tell a fellow!

His luggage could be taken on a truck for sixpence, he found,
and he could precede it on foot. He fancied an ironical note in the
voices. He was painfully aware of his contour.

The curious earnestness of the man in the train, and the
glamour of the story he told, had, for a time, diverted the current
of Mr Hinchcliff's thoughts. It drove like a mist before his
immediate concerns. Fires that went to and fro! But the
preoccupation of his new position, and the impression he was to
produce upon Holmwood generally, and the school people in
particular, returned upon him with reinvigorating power before
he left the station and cleared his mental atmosphere. But it is
extraordinary what an inconvenient thing the addition of a soft
and rather brightly-golden fruit, not three inches in diameter,
may prove to a sensitive youth on his best appearance. In the
pocket of his black jacket it bulged dreadfully, spoilt the lines
altogether. He passed a little old lady in black, and he felt her eye
drop upon the excrescence at once. He was wearing one glove
and carrying the other, together with his stick, so that to bear the
fruit openly was impossible. In one place, where the road into the
town seemed suitably secluded, he took his encumbrance out of
his pocket and tried it in his hat. It was just too large, the hat
wobbled ludicrously, and just as he was taking it out again, a
butcher's boy came driving round the corner.

'Confound it!' said Mr Hinchcliff.

He would have eaten the thing, and attained omniscience
there and then, but it would seem so silly to go into the town
sucking a juicy fruit – and it certainly felt juicy. If one of the boys
should come by, it might do him a serious injury with his
discipline so to be seen. And the juice might make his face sticky

and get upon his cuffs – or it might be an acid juice as potent as lemon, and take all the colour out of his clothes.

Then round a bend in the lane came two pleasant sunlit girlish figures. They were walking slowly towards the town and chattering – at any moment they might look round and see a hot-faced young man behind them carrying a kind of phosphorescent yellow tomato! They would be sure to laugh.

'*Hang!*' said Mr Hinchcliff, and with a swift jerk sent the encumbrance flying over the stone wall of an orchard that there abutted on the road. As it vanished, he felt a faint twinge of loss that lasted scarcely a moment. He adjusted the stick and glove in his hand, and walked on, erect and self-conscious, to pass the girls.

But in the darkness of the night Mr Hinchcliff had a dream, and saw the valley, and the flaming swords, and the contorted trees, and knew that it really was the Apple of the Tree of Knowledge that he had thrown regardlessly away. And he awoke very unhappy.

In the morning his regret had passed, but afterwards it returned and troubled him; never, however, when he was happy or busily occupied. At last, one moonlight night about eleven, when all Holmwood was quiet, his regrets returned with redoubled force, and therewith an impulse to adventure. He slipped out of the house and over the playground wall, went through the silent town to Station Lane, and climbed into the orchard where he had thrown the fruit. But nothing was to be found of it there among the dewy grass and the faint intangible globes of dandelion down.

The Country of the Blind

Three hundred miles and more from Chimborazo, one hundred from the snows of Cotopaxi, in the wildest wastes of Ecuador's Andes, there lies that mysterious mountain valley, cut off from the world of men, the Country of the Blind. Long years ago that valley lay so far open to the world that men might come at last through frightful gorges and over an icy pass into its equable meadows; and thither indeed men came, a family or so of Peruvian half-breeds fleeing from the lust and tyranny of an evil Spanish ruler. Then came the stupendous outbreak of Mindobamba, when it was night in Quito for seventeen days, and the water was boiling at Yaguachi and all the fish floating dying even as far as Guayaquil; everywhere along the Pacific slopes there were land-slips and swift thawings and sudden floods, and one whole side of the old Arauca crest slipped and came down in thunder, and cut off the Country of the Blind for ever from the exploring feet of men. But one of these early settlers had chanced to be on the hither side of the gorges when the world had so terribly shaken itself, and he perforce had to forget his wife and his child and all the friends and possessions he had left up there, and start life over again in the lower world. He started it again but ill, blindness overtook him, and he died of punishment in the mines; but the story he told begot a legend that lingers along the length of the Cordilleras of the Andes to this day.

He told of his reason for venturing back from that fastness, into which he had first been carried lashed to a llama, beside a vast bale of gear, when he was a child. The valley, he said, had in it all that the heart of man could desire – sweet water, pasture, and even climate, slopes of rich brown soil with tangles of a shrub that bore an excellent fruit, and on one side great hanging forests of pine that held the avalanches high. Far overhead, on three sides, vast cliffs of grey-green rock were capped by cliffs of ice; but the glacier stream came not to them but flowed away by the farther slopes, and only now and then huge ice masses fell on the valley side. In this valley it neither rained nor snowed, but the abundant springs gave a rich green pasture, that irrigation would spread over all the valley space. The settlers did well indeed there. Their beasts did well and multiplied, and but one thing marred their happiness. Yet it was enough to mar it greatly. A strange disease had come upon them, and had made all the children born to them there – and indeed, several older children also – blind. It was to seek some charm or antidote against this plague of blindness that he had with fatigue and danger and difficulty returned down the gorge. In those days, in such cases, men did not think of germs and infections but of sins; and it seemed to him that the reason of this affliction must lie in the negligence of these priestless immigrants to set up a shrine so soon as they entered the valley. He wanted a shrine – a handsome, cheap, effectual shrine – to be erected in the valley; he wanted relics and such-like potent things of faith, blessed objects and mysterious medals and prayers. In his wallet he had a bar of native silver for which he would not account; he insisted there was none in the valley with something of the insistence of an inexpert liar. They had all clubbed their money and ornaments together, having little need for such treasure up there, he said, to buy them holy help against their ill. I figure this dim-eyed young mountaineer, sunburnt, gaunt, and anxious, hat-brim clutched feverishly, a man all unused to the ways of the lower world, telling this story to some keen-eyed, attentive priest before the great convulsion; I can picture him presently seeking to return with pious and infallible remedies against that trouble, and the infinite dismay with which he must have faced the tumbled vastness where the gorge had once come out. But the rest of his story of mischances is lost to me, save that I know of his evil death after several years. Poor stray from that remoteness! The stream that had once made the gorge now bursts from the mouth of a rocky cave, and the legend his poor, ill-told story set going developed into the legend of a race of blind men somewhere 'over there' one may still hear today.

And amidst the little population of that now isolated and forgotten valley the disease ran its course. The old became groping and purblind, the young saw but dimly, and the children that were born to them saw never at all. But life was very easy in that snow-rimmed basin, lost to all the world, with neither thorns nor briars, with no evil insects nor any beasts save the gentle breed of llamas they had lugged and thrust and followed up the beds of the shrunken rivers in the gorges up which they had come. The seeing had become purblind so gradually that they scarcely noted their loss. They guided the sightless youngsters hither and thither until they knew the whole valley marvellously, and when at last sight died out among them the race lived on. They had even time to adapt themselves to the blind control of fire, which they made carefully in stoves of stone. They were a simple strain of people at the first, unlettered, only slightly touched with the Spanish civilisation, but with something of a tradition of the arts of old Peru and of its lost philosophy. Generation followed generation. They forgot many things; they devised many things. Their tradition of the greater world they came from became mythical in colour and uncertain. In all things save sight they were strong and able, and presently the chance of birth and heredity sent one who had an original mind and who could talk and persuade among them, and then afterwards another. These two passed, leaving their effects, and the little community grew in numbers and in understanding, and met and settled social and economic problems that arose. Generation followed generation. Generation followed generation. There came a time when a child was born who was fifteen generations from that ancestor who went out of the valley with a bar of silver to seek God's aid, and who never returned. Thereabouts it chanced that a man came into this community from the outer world. And this is the story of that man.

He was a mountaineer from the country near Quito, a man who had been down to the sea and had seen the world, a reader of books in an original way, an acute and enterprising man, and he was taken on by a party of Englishmen who had come out to Ecuador to climb mountains, to replace one of their three Swiss guides who had fallen ill. He climbed here and he climbed there, and then came the attempt on Parascotopetl, the Matterhorn of the Andes, in which he was lost to the outer world. The story of the accident has been written a dozen times. Pointer's narrative is the best. He tells how the little party worked their difficult and almost vertical way up to the very foot of the last and greatest precipice, and how they built a night shelter amidst the snow upon a little shelf of rock, and, with a touch of real dramatic power, how presently they found Nunez had gone from them.

They shouted, and there was no reply; shouted and whistled, and for the rest of that night they slept no more.

As the morning broke they saw the traces of his fall. It seems impossible he could have uttered a sound. He had slipped eastward towards the unknown side of the mountain; far below he had struck a steep slope of snow, and ploughed his way down it in the midst of a snow avalanche. His track went straight to the edge of a frightful precipice, and beyond that everything was hidden. Far, far below, and hazy with distance, they could see trees rising out of a narrow, shut-in valley – the lost Country of the Blind. But they did not know it was the lost Country of the Blind, nor distinguish it in any way from any other narrow streak of upland valley. Unnerved by this disaster, they abandoned their attempt in the afternoon, and Pointer was called away to the war before he could make another attack. To this day Parascotopetl lifts an unconquered crest, and Pointer's shelter crumbles unvisited amidst the snows.

And the man who fell survived.

At the end of the slope he fell a thousand feet, and came down in the midst of a cloud of snow upon a snow slope even steeper than the one above. Down this he was whirled, stunned and insensible, but without a bone broken in his body; and then at last came to gentler slopes, and at last rolled out and lay still, buried amidst a softening heap of the white masses that had accompanied and saved him. He came to himself with a dim fancy that he was ill in bed; then realised his position with a mountaineer's intelligence, and worked himself loose and, after a rest or so, out until he saw the stars. He rested flat upon his chest for a space, wondering where he was and what had happened to him. He explored his limbs, and discovered that several of his buttons were gone and his coat turned over his head. His knife had gone from his pocket and his hat was lost, though he had tied it under his chin. He recalled that he had been looking for loose stones to raise his piece of the shelter wall. His ice-axe had disappeared.

He decided he must have fallen, and looked up to see, exaggerated by the ghastly light of the rising moon, the tremendous flight he had taken. For a while he lay, gazing blankly at that vast pale cliff towering above, rising moment by moment out of a subsiding tide of darkness. Its phantasmal, mysterious beauty held him for a space, and then he was seized with a paroxysm of sobbing laughter....

After a great interval of time he became aware that he was near the lower edge of the snow. Below, down what was now a moonlit and practicable slope, he saw the dark and broken appearance of rock-strewn turf. He struggled to his feet, aching in every joint and limb, got down painfully from the heaped loose snow about him, went downward until he was on the turf, and there dropped rather than lay beside a boulder, drank deep from the flask in his inner pocket, and instantly fell asleep....

He was awakened by the singing of birds in the trees far below.

He sat up and perceived he was on a little alp at the foot of a vast precipice, that was grooved by the gully down which he and his snow had come. Over against him another wall of rock reared itself against the sky. The gorge between these precipices ran east and west and was full of the morning sunlight, which lit to the westward the mass of fallen mountain that closed the descending gorge. Below him it seemed there was a precipice equally steep, but behind the snow in the gully he found a sort of chimney-cleft dripping with snow-water down which a desperate man might venture. He found it easier than it seemed, and came at last to another desolate alp, and then after a rock climb of no particular difficulty to a steep slope of trees. He took his bearings and turned his face up the gorge, for he saw it opened out above upon green meadows, among which he now glimpsed quite distinctly a cluster of stone huts of unfamiliar fashion. At times his progress was like clambering along the face of a wall, and after a time the rising sun ceased to strike along the gorge, the voices of the singing birds died away, and the air grew cold and dark about him. But the distant valley with its houses was all the brighter for that. He came presently to talus, and among the rocks he noted – for he was an observant man – an unfamiliar fern that seemed to clutch out of the crevices with intense green hands. He picked a frond or so and gnawed its stalk and found it helpful.

About midday he came at last out of the throat of the gorge into the plain and the sunlight. He was stiff and weary; he sat down in the shadow of a rock, filled up his flask with water from a spring and drank it down, and remained for a time resting before he went on to the houses.

They were very strange to his eyes, and indeed the whole

aspect of that valley became, as he regarded it, queerer and more unfamiliar. The greater part of its surface was lush green meadow, starred with many beautiful flowers, irrigated with extraordinary care, and bearing evidence of systematic cropping piece by piece. High up and ringing the valley about was a wall, and what appeared to be a circumferential water-channel, from which the little trickles of water that fed the meadow plants came, and on the higher slopes above this flocks of llamas cropped the scanty herbage. Sheds, apparently shelters or feeding-places for the llamas, stood against the boundary wall here and there. The irrigation streams ran together into a main channel down the centre of the valley, and this was enclosed on either side by a wall breast high. This gave a singularly urban quality to this secluded place, a quality that was greatly enhanced by the fact that a number of paths paved with black and white stones, and each with a curious little kerb at the side, ran hither and thither in an orderly manner. The houses of the central village were quite unlike the casual and higgledy-piggledy agglomeration of the mountain villages he knew; they stood in a continuous row on either side of a central street of astonishing cleanness; here and there their particoloured façade was pierced by a door, and not a solitary window broke their even frontage. They were parti-coloured with extraordinary irregularity, smeared with a sort of plaster that was sometimes grey, sometimes drab, sometimes slate-coloured or dark brown; and it was the sight of this wild plastering first brought the word 'blind' into the thoughts of the explorer. 'The good man who did that,' he thought, 'must have been as blind as a bat.'

He descended a steep place, and so came to the wall and channel that ran about the valley, near where the latter spouted out its surplus contents into the deeps of the gorge in a thin and wavering thread of cascade. He could now see a number of men and women resting on piled heaps of grass, as if taking a siesta, in the remoter part of the meadow, and nearer the village a number of recumbent children, and then nearer at hand three men carrying pails on yokes along a little path that ran from the encircling wall towards the houses. These latter were clad in garments of llama cloth and boots and belts of leather, and they wore caps of cloth with back and ear flaps. They followed one another in single file, walking slowly and yawning as they walked, like men who have been up all night. There was something so reassuringly prosperous and respectable in their bearing that after a moment's hesitation Nunez stood forward as conspicuously as possible upon his rock, and gave vent to a mighty shout that echoed round the valley.

The three men stopped, and moved their heads as though they were looking about them. They turned their faces this way and that, and Nunez gesticulated with freedom. But they did not appear to see him for all his gestures, and after a time, directing themselves towards the mountains far away to the right, they shouted as if in answer. Nunez bawled again, and then once more, and as he gestured ineffectually the word 'blind' came up to the top of his thoughts. 'The fools must be blind,' he said.

When at last, after much shouting and wrath, Nunez crossed the stream by a little bridge, came through a gate in the wall, and approached them, he was sure that they were blind. He was sure that this was the Country of the Blind of which the legends told. Conviction had sprung upon him, and a sense of great and rather enviable adventure. The three stood side by side, not looking at him, but with their ears directed towards him, judging him by his unfamiliar steps. They stood close together like men a little afraid, and he could see their eyelids closed and sunken, as though the very balls beneath had shrunk away. There was an expression near awe on their faces.

'A man,' one said, in hardly recognisable Spanish – 'a man it is – a man or a spirit – coming down from the rocks.'

But Nunez advanced with the confident steps of a youth who enters upon life. All the old stories of the lost valley and the Country of the Blind had come back to his mind, and through his thoughts ran this old proverb, as if it were a refrain –

'In the Country of the Blind the One-eyed Man is King.'

'In the Country of the Blind the One-eyed Man is King.'

And very civilly he gave them greeting. He talked to them and used his eyes.

'Where does he come from, brother Pedro?' asked one.

'Down out of the rocks.'

'Over the mountains I come,' said Nunez, 'out of the country beyond there – where men can see. From near Bogota, where there are a hundred thousands of people, and where the city passes out of sight.'

'Sight?' muttered Pedro. 'Sight?'

'He comes,' said the second blind man, 'out of the rocks.'

The cloth of their coats Nunez saw was curiously fashioned, each with a different sort of stitching.

They startled him by a simultaneous movement towards him, each with a hand outstretched. He stepped back from the advance of these spread fingers.

'Come hither,' said the third blind man, following his motion and clutching him neatly.

And they held Nunez and felt him over, saying no word further until they had done so.

'Carefully,' he cried, with a finger in his eye, and found they thought that organ, with its fluttering lids, a queer thing in him. They went over it again.

'A strange creature, Correa,' said the one called Pedro. 'Feel the coarseness of his hair. Like a llama's hair.'

'Rough he is as the rocks that begot him,' said Correa, investigating Nunez's unshaven chin with a soft and slightly moist hand. 'Perhaps he will grow finer.' Nunez struggled a little under their examination, but they gripped him firm.

'Carefully,' he said again.

'He speaks,' said the third man. 'Certainly he is a man.'

'Ugh!' said Pedro, at the roughness of his coat.

'And you have come into the world?' asked Pedro.

'*Out* of the world. Over mountains and glaciers; right over above there, half-way to the sun. Out of the great big world that goes down, twelve days' journey to the sea.'

They scarcely seemed to heed him. 'Our fathers have told us men may be made by the forces of Nature,' said Correa. 'It is the warmth of things and moisture, and rottenness – rottenness.'

'Let us lead him to the elders,' said Pedro.

'Shout first,' said Correa, 'lest the children be afraid. This is a marvellous occasion.'

So they shouted, and Pedro went first and took Nunez by the hand to lead him to the houses.

He drew his hand away. 'I can see,' he said.

'See ?' said Correa.

'Yes, see,' said Nunez, turning towards him, and stumbled against Pedro's pail.

'His senses are still imperfect,' said the third blind man. 'He stumbles, and talks unmeaning words. Lead him by the hand.'

'As you will,' said Nunez, and was led along, laughing.

It seemed they knew nothing of sight.

Well, all in good time he would teach them.

He heard people shouting, and saw a number of figures gathering together in the middle roadway of the village.

He found it tax his nerve and patience more than he had anticipated, that first encounter with the population of the Country of the Blind. The place seemed larger as he drew near to it, and the smeared plasterings queerer, and a crowd of children and men and women (the women and girls, he was pleased to note, had some of them quite sweet faces, for all that their eyes were shut and sunken) came about him, holding on to him, touching him with soft, sensitive hands, smelling at him, and listening at every word he spoke. Some of the maidens and children, however, kept aloof as if afraid, and indeed his voice seemed coarse and rude beside their softer notes. They mobbed him. His three guides kept close to him with an effect of proprietorship, and said again and again, 'A wild man out of the rocks.'

'Bogota,' he said. 'Bogota. Over the mountain crests.'

'A wild man – using wild words,' said Pedro. 'Did you hear that – *Bogota?* His mind is hardly formed yet. He has only the beginnings of speech.'

A little boy nipped his hand. 'Bogota!' he said mockingly.

'Ay! A city to your village. I come from the great world – where men have eyes and see.'

'His name's Bogota,' they said.

'He stumbled,' said Correa, 'stumbled twice as we came hither.'

'Bring him to the elders.'

And they thrust him suddenly through a doorway into a room as black as pitch, save at the end there faintly glowed a fire. The crowd closed in behind him and shut out all but the faintest glimmer of day, and before he could arrest himself he had fallen headlong over the feet of a seated man. His arm, outflung, struck the face of someone else as he went down; he felt the soft impact of features and heard a cry of anger, and for a moment he struggled against a number of hands that clutched him. It was a one-sided fight. An inkling of the situation came to him, and he lay quiet.

'I fell down,' he said; 'I couldn't see in this pitchy darkness.'

There was a pause as if the unseen persons about him tried to understand his words. Then the voice of Correa said: 'He is but newly formed. He stumbles as he walks and mingles words that mean nothing with his speech.'

Others also said things about him that he heard or understood imperfectly.

'May I sit up?' he asked, in a pause. 'I will not struggle against you again.'

They consulted and let him rise.

The voice of an older man began to question him, and Nunez found himself trying to explain the great world out of which he had fallen, and the sky and mountains and sight and such-like marvels, to these elders who sat in darkness in the Country of the Blind. And they would believe and understand nothing whatever he told them, a thing quite outside his expectation. They would not even understand many of his words. For fourteen generations these people had been blind and cut off from all the seeing world; the names for all the things of sight had faded and changed; the story of the outer world was faded and changed to a child's story; and they had ceased to concern themselves with anything beyond the rocky slopes above their circling wall. Blind men of genius had arisen among them and questioned the shreds of belief and tradition they had brought with them from their seeing days, and had dismissed all these things as idle fancies, and replaced them with new and saner explanations. Much of their imagination had shrivelled with their eyes, and they had made for themselves new imaginations with their ever more sensitive ears and finger-tips. Slowly Nunez realised this; that his expectation of wonder and reverence at his origin and his gifts was not to be borne out; and after his poor attempt to explain sight to them had been set aside as the confused version of a new-made being describing the marvels of his incoherent sensations, he subsided, a little dashed, into listening to their instruction. And the eldest of the blind men explained to him life and philosophy and religion, how that the world (meaning their valley) had been first an empty hollow in the rocks, and then had come, first, inanimate things without the gift of touch, and llamas and a few other creatures that had little sense, and then men, and at last angels, whom one could hear singing and making fluttering sounds, but whom no one could touch at all, which puzzled Nunez greatly until he thought of the birds.

He went on to tell Nunez how this time had been divided into the warm and the cold, which are the blind equivalents of day and night, and how it was good to sleep in the warm and work during the cold, so that now, but for his advent, the whole town of the blind would have been asleep. He said Nunez must have been specially created to learn and serve the wisdom they had acquired, and that for all his mental incoherency and stumbling behaviour he must have courage, and do his best to learn, and at that all the people in the door-way murmured encouragingly. He said the night – for the blind call their day night – was now far gone, and it behoved every one to go back to sleep. He asked Nunez if he knew how to sleep, and Nunez said he did, but that before sleep he wanted food.

They brought him food – llama's milk in a bowl, and rough salted bread – and led him into a lonely place to eat out of their hearing, and afterwards to slumber until the chill of the mountain evening roused them to begin their day again. But Nunez slumbered not at all.

Instead, he sat up in the place where they had left him, resting his limbs and turning the unanticipated circumstances of his arrival over and over in his mind.

Every now and then he laughed, sometimes with amusement, and sometimes with indignation.

'Unformed mind!' he said. 'Got no senses yet! They little know they've been insulting their heaven-sent king and master. I see I must bring them to reason. Let me think – let me think.'

He was still thinking when the sun set.

Nunez had an eye for all beautiful things, and it seemed to him that the glow upon the snowfields and glaciers that rose about the valley on every side was the most beautiful thing he had ever seen. His eyes went from that inaccessible glory to the village and irrigated fields, fast sinking into the twilight, and suddenly a wave of emotion took him, and he thanked God from the bottom of his heart that the power of sight had been given him.

He heard a voice calling to him from out of the village. 'Ya ho there, Bogota! Come hither!'

At that he stood up smiling. He would show these people once and for all what sight would do for a man. They would seek him, but not find him.

'You move not, Bogota,' said the voice.

He laughed noiselessly, and made two stealthy steps aside from the path.

'Trample not on the grass, Bogota; that is not allowed.'

Nunez had scarcely heard the sound he made himself. He stopped amazed.

The owner of the voice came running up the piebald path towards him.

He stepped back into the pathway. 'Here I am,' he said.

'Why did you not come when I called you?' said the blind man. 'Must you be led like a child? Cannot you hear the path as you walk?'

Nunez laughed. 'I can see it,' he said.

'There is no such word as *see*,' said the blind man, after a pause. 'Cease this folly, and follow the sound of my feet.'

Nunez followed, a little annoyed.

'My time will come,' he said.

'You'll learn,' the blind man answered. 'There is much to learn in the world.'

'Has no one told you, "In the Country of the Blind the One-eyed Man is King"?'

'What is blind?' asked the blind man carelessly over his shoulder.

Four days passed, and the fifth found the King of the Blind still incognito, as a clumsy and useless stranger among his subjects.

It was, he found, much more difficult to proclaim himself than he had supposed, and in the meantime, while he meditated his *coup d'état*, he did what he was told and learnt the manners and customs of the Country of the Blind. He found working and going about at night a particularly irksome thing, and he decided that that should be the first thing he would change.

They led a simple, laborious life, these people, with all the elements of virtue and happiness, as these things can be understood by men. They toiled, but not oppressively; they had food and clothing sufficient for their needs; they had days and seasons of rest; they made much of music and singing, and there was love among them, and little children.

It was marvellous with what confidence and precision they went about their ordered world. Everything, you see, had been made to fit their needs; each of the radiating paths of the valley area had a constant angle to the others, and was distinguished by a special notch upon its kerbing; all obstacles and irregularities of path or meadow had long since been cleared away; all their methods and procedure arose naturally from their special needs. Their senses had become marvellously acute; they could hear and judge the slightest gesture of a man a dozen paces away – could hear the very beating of his heart. Intonation had long replaced expression with them, and touches gesture, and their work with hoe and spade and fork was as free and confident as garden work can be. Their sense of smell was extraordinarily fine; they could distinguish individual differences as readily as a dog can, and they went about the tending of the llamas, who lived among the rocks above and came to the wall for food and shelter, with ease and confidence. It was only when at last Nunez sought to assert himself that he found how easy and confident their movements could be.

He rebelled only after he had tried persuasion.

He tried at first on several occasions to tell them of sight. 'Look you here, you people,' he said. 'There are things you do not understand in me.'

Once or twice one or two of them attended to him; they sat with faces downcast and ears turned intelligently towards him, and he did his best to tell them what it was to see. Among his hearers was a girl, with eyelids less red and sunken than the others, so that one could almost fancy she was hiding eyes, whom especially he hoped to persuade. He spoke of the beauties of sight, of watching the mountains, of the sky and the sunrise, and they heard him with amused incredulity that presently became condemnatory. They told him there were indeed no mountains at all, but that the end of the rocks where the llamas grazed was indeed the end of the world; thence sprang a cavernous roof of the universe, from which the dew and the avalanches fell; and when he maintained stoutly the world had neither end nor roof such as they supposed, they said his thoughts were wicked. So far as he could describe sky and clouds and stars to them it seemed to them a hideous void, a terrible blankness in the place of the smooth roof to things in which they believed – it was an article of faith with them that the cavern roof was exquisitely smooth to the touch. He saw that in some manner he shocked them, and gave up that aspect of the matter altogether, and tried to show them the practical value of sight. One morning he saw Pedro in the path called Seventeen and coming towards the central houses, but still too far off for hearing or scent, and he told them as much. 'In a little while,' he prophesied, 'Pedro will be here.' An old man remarked that Pedro had no business on path Seventeen, and then, as if in confirmation, that individual as he drew near turned and went transversely into path Ten, and so back with nimble paces towards the outer wall. They mocked Nunez when Pedro did not arrive, and afterwards, when he asked Pedro questions to clear his character, Pedro denied and outfaced him, and was afterwards hostile to him.

Then he induced them to let him go a long way up the sloping meadows towards the wall with one complacent individual, and to him he promised to describe all that happened among the houses. He noted certain goings and comings, but the things that really seemed to signify to these people happened inside of or behind the windowless houses – the only things they took note of to test him by – and of these he could see or tell nothing; and it was after the failure of this attempt, and the ridicule they could not repress, that he resorted to force. He thought of seizing a spade and suddenly smiting one or two of them to earth, and so in fair combat showing the advantage of eyes. He went so far with that resolution as to seize his spade, and then he discovered a new thing about himself, and that was that it was impossible for him to hit a blind man in cold blood.

He hesitated, and found them all aware that he had snatched up the spade. They stood alert, with their heads on one side, and bent ears towards him for what he would do next.

'Put that spade down,' said one, and he felt a sort of helpless horror. He came near obedience.

Then he thrust one backwards against a house wall, and fled past him and out of the village.

He went athwart one of their meadows, leaving a track of trampled grass behind his feet, and presently sat down by the side of one of their ways. He felt something of the buoyancy that comes to all men in the beginning of a fight, but more perplexity.

He began to realise that you cannot even fight happily with creatures who stand upon a different mental basis to yourself. Far away he saw a number of men carrying spades and sticks come out of the street of houses, and advance in a spreading line along the several paths towards him.

They advanced slowly, speaking frequently to one another, and ever and again the whole cordon would halt and sniff the air and listen.

The first time they did this Nunez laughed. But afterwards he did not laugh.

One struck his trail in the meadow grass, and came stooping and feeling his way along it.

For five minutes he watched the slow extension of the cordon, and then his vague disposition to do something forthwith became frantic. He stood up, went a pace or so towards the circumferential wall, turned, and went back a little way. There they all stood in a crescent, still and listening.

He also stood still, gripping his spade very tightly in both hands. Should he charge them?

The pulse in his ears ran into the rhythm of 'In the Country of the Blind the One-eyed Man is King!'

Should he charge them?

He looked back at the high and unclimbable wall behind – unclimbable because of its smooth plastering, but withal pierced with many little doors, and at the approaching line of seekers. Behind these others were now coming out of the street of houses.

Should he charge them?

'Bogota!' called one. 'Bogota! where are you?'

He gripped his spade still tighter, and advanced down the meadows towards the place of habitations, and directly he moved they converged upon him. 'I'll hit them if they touch me,' he swore; 'by Heaven, I will. I'll hit.' He called aloud, 'Look here, I'm going to do what I like in this valley. Do you hear? I'm going to do what I like and go where I like!'

They were moving in upon him quickly, groping, yet moving rapidly. It was like playing blind man's buff, with everyone blindfolded except one. 'Get hold of him!' cried one. He found himself in the arc of a loose curve of pursuers. He felt suddenly he must be active and resolute.

'You don't understand,' he cried in a voice that was meant to be great and resolute, and which broke. 'You are blind, and I can see. Leave me alone!'

'Bogota! Put down that spade, and come off the grass!'

The last order, grotesque in its urban familiarity, produced a gust of anger.

'I'll hurt you,' he said, sobbing with emotion. 'By Heaven, I'll hurt you. Leave me alone!'

He began to run, not knowing clearly where to run. He ran from the nearest blind man, because it was a horror to hit him. He stopped, and then made a dash to escape from their closing ranks. He made for where a gap was wide, and the men on either side, with a quick perception of the approach of his paces, rushed in on one another. He sprang forward, and then saw he must be caught, and *swish!* the spade had struck. He felt the soft thud of hand and arm, and the man was down with a yell of pain, and he was through.

Through! And then he was close to the street of houses again, and blind men, whirling spades and stakes, were running with a sort of reasoned swiftness hither and thither.

He heard steps behind him just in time, and found a tall man rushing forward and swiping at the sound of him. He lost his nerve, hurled his spade a yard wide at his antagonist, and whirled about and fled, fairly yelling as he dodged another.

He was panic-stricken. He ran furiously to and fro, dodging when there was no need to dodge, and in his anxiety to see on every side of him at once, stumbling. For a moment he was down and they heard his fall. Far away in the circumferential wall a little doorway looked like heaven, and he set off in a wild rush for it. He did not even look round at his pursuers until it was gained, and he had stumbled across the bridge, clambered a little way among the rocks, to the surprise and dismay of a young llama, who went leaping out of sight, and lay down sobbing for breath.

And so his *coup d'état* came to an end.

He stayed outside the wall of the valley of the Blind for two nights and days without food or shelter, and meditated upon the unexpected. During these meditations he repeated very frequently and always with a profounder note of derision the exploded proverb: 'In the Country of the Blind the One-Eyed Man is King.' He thought chiefly of ways of fighting and conquering these people, and it grew clear that for him no practicable way was possible. He had no weapons, and now it would be hard to get one.

The canker of civilisation had got to him even in Bogota, and he could not find it in himself to go down and assassinate a blind man. Of course, if he did that, he might then dictate terms on the threat of assassinating them all. But – sooner or later he must sleep! ...

He tried also to find food among the pine trees, to be comfortable under pine boughs while the frost fell at night, and – with less confidence – to catch a llama by artifice in order to try to kill it – perhaps by hammering it with a stone – and so finally, perhaps, to eat some of it. But the llamas had a doubt of him and regarded him with distrustful brown eyes, and spat when he drew near. Fear came on him the second day and fits of shivering. Finally he crawled down to the wall of the Country of the Blind and tried to make terms. He crawled along by the stream, shouting, until two blind men came out to the gate and talked to him.

'I was mad,' he said. 'But I was only newly made.'

They said that was better.

He told them he was wiser now, and repented of all he had done.

Then he wept without intention, for he was very weak and ill now, and they took that as a favourable sign.

They asked him if he still thought he could '*see*'.

'No,' he said. 'That was folly. The word means nothing – less than nothing!'

They asked him what was overhead.

'About ten times ten the height of a man there is a roof above the world – of rock – and very, very smooth.' ... He burst again into hysterical tears. 'Before you ask me any more, give me some food or I shall die.'

He expected dire punishments, but these blind people were capable of toleration. They regarded his rebellion as but one more proof of his general idiocy and inferiority; and after they had whipped him they appointed him to do the simplest and heaviest work they had for anyone to do, and he, seeing no other way of living, did submissively what he was told.

He was ill for some days, and they nursed him kindly. That refined his submission. But they insisted on his lying in the dark, and that was a great misery. And blind philosophers came and talked to him of the wicked levity of his mind, and reproved him so impressively for his doubts about the lid of rock that covered their cosmic casserole that he almost doubted whether indeed he was not the victim of hallucination in not seeing it overhead.

So Nunez became a citizen of the Country of the Blind, and these people ceased to be a generalised people and became individualities and familiar to him, while the world beyond the mountains became more and more remote and unreal. There was Yacob, his master, a kindly man when not annoyed; there was Pedro, Yacob's nephew; and there was Medina-saroté, who was the youngest daughter of Yacob. She was little esteemed in the world of the blind, because she had a clear-cut face, and lacked that satisfying, glossy smoothness that is the blind man's ideal of feminine beauty; but Nunez thought her beautiful at first, and presently the most beautiful thing in the whole creation. Her closed eyelids were not sunken and red after the common way of the valley, but lay as though they might open again at any moment; and she had long eyelashes, which were considered a grave disfigurement. And her voice was strong, and did not satisfy the acute hearing of the valley swains. So that she had no lover.

There came a time when Nunez thought that, could he win her, he would be resigned to live in the valley for all the rest of his days.

He watched her; he sought opportunities of doing her little services, and presently he found that she observed him. Once at a rest-day gathering they sat side by side in the dim starlight, and the music was sweet. His hand came upon hers and he dared to clasp it. Then very tenderly she returned his pressure. And one day, as they were at their meal in the darkness, he felt her hand very softly seeking him, and as it chanced the fire leapt then and he saw the tenderness of her face.

He sought to speak to her.

He went to her one day when she was sitting in the summer moonlight spinning. The light made her a thing of silver and mystery. He sat down at her feet and told her he loved her, and told her how beautiful she seemed to him. He had a lover's voice, he spoke with a tender reverence that came near to awe, and she had never before been touched by adoration. She made him no definite answer, but it was clear his words pleased her.

After that he talked to her whenever he could take an opportunity. The valley became the world for him, and the world beyond the mountains where men lived in sunlight seemed no more than a fairy tale he would some day pour into her ears. Very tentatively and timidly he spoke to her of sight.

Sight seemed to her the most poetical of fancies, and she listened to his description of the stars and the mountains and her own sweet white-lit beauty as though it was a guilty indulgence. She did not believe, she could only half understand, but she was mysteriously delighted, and it seemed to him that she completely understood.

His love lost its awe and took courage. Presently he was for demanding her of Yacob and the elders in marriage, but she became fearful and delayed. And it was one of her elder sisters who first told Yacob that Medina saroté and Nunez were in love.

There was from the first very great opposition to the marriage of Nunez and Medina-saroté; not so much because they valued her as because they held him as a being apart, an idiot, incompetent thing below the permissible level of a man. Her sisters opposed it bitterly as bringing discredit on them all; and old Yacob, though he had formed a sort of liking for his clumsy, obedient serf, shook his head and said the thing could not be. The young men were all angry at the idea of corrupting the race, and one went so far as to revile and strike Nunez. He struck back. Then for the first time he found an advantage in seeing, even by twilight, and after that fight was over no one was disposed to raise a hand against him. But they still found his marriage impossible.

Old Yacob had a tenderness for his last little daughter, and was grieved to have her weep upon his shoulder.

'You see, my dear, he's an idiot. He has delusions; he can't do anything right.'

'I know,' wept Medina-saroté. 'But he's better than he was. He's getting better. And he's strong, dear father, and kind – stronger and kinder than any other man in the world. And he loves me – and, father, I love him.'

Old Yacob was greatly distressed to find her inconsolable, and, besides – what made it more distressing – he liked Nunez for many things. So he went and sat in the windowless council-chamber with the other elders and watched the trend of the talk, and said, at the proper time, 'He's better than he was. Very likely, some day, we shall find him as sane as ourselves.'

Then afterwards one of the elders, who thought deeply, had an idea. He was the great doctor among these people, their medicine-man, and he had a very philosophical and inventive mind, and the idea of curing Nunez of his peculiarities appealed to him. One day when Yacob was present he returned to the topic of Nunez.

'I have examined Bogota,' he said, 'and the case is clearer to me. I think very probably he might be cured.'

'That is what I have always hoped,' said old Yacob.

'His brain is affected,' said the blind doctor.

The elders murmured assent.

'Now, *what* affects it?'

'Ah!' said old Yacob.

'*This*,' said the doctor, answering his own question. 'Those queer things that are called the eyes, and which exist to make an agreeable soft depression in the face, are diseased, in the case of Bogota, in such a way as to affect his brain. They are greatly distended, he has eyelashes, and his eyelids move, and consequently his brain is in a state of constant irritation and distraction.'

'Yes?' said old Yacob. 'Yes?'

'And I think I may say with reasonable certainty that, in order to cure him completely, all that we need do is a simple and easy surgical operation – namely, to remove these irritant bodies.'

'And then he will be sane?'

'Then he will be perfectly sane, and a quite admirable citizen.'

'Thank Heaven for science!' said old Yacob, and went forth at once to tell Nunez of his happy hopes.

But Nunez's manner of receiving the good news struck him as being cold and disappointing.

'One might think,' he said, 'from the tone you take, that you did not care for my daughter.'

It was Medina-saroté who persuaded Nunez to face the blind surgeons.

'*You* do not want me,' he said, 'to lose my gift of sight?'

She shook her head.

'My world is sight.'

Her head drooped lower.

'There are the beautiful things, the beautiful little things – the flowers, the lichens among the rocks, the lightness and softness on a piece of fur, the far sky with its drifting down of clouds, the sunsets and the stars. And there is *you*. For you alone it is good to have sight, to see your sweet, serene face, your kindly lips, your dear, beautiful hands folded together.... It is these eyes of mine you won, these eyes that hold me to you, that these idiots seek. Instead, I must touch you, hear you, and never see you again. I must come under that roof of rock and stone and darkness, that horrible roof under which your imagination stoops ... No; you would not have me do that?'

A disagreeable doubt had arisen in him. He stopped, and left the thing a question.

'I wish,' she said, 'sometimes—' She paused.

'Yes,' said he, a little apprehensively.

'I wish sometimes – you would not talk like that.'

'Like what?'

'I know it's pretty – it's your imagination. I love it, but *now*—'

He felt cold. '*Now?*' he said faintly.

She sat quite still.

'You mean – you think – I should be better, better perhaps—'

He was realising things very swiftly. He felt anger, indeed, anger at the dull course of fate, but also sympathy for her lack of understanding – a sympathy near akin to pity.

'*Dear*,' he said, and he could see by her whiteness how intensely her spirit pressed against the things she could not say. He put his arms about her, he kissed her ear, and they sat for a time in silence.

'If I were to consent to this?' he said at last, in a voice that was very gentle.

She flung her arms about him, weeping wildly. 'Oh, if you would,' she sobbed, 'if only you would!'

For a week before the operation that was to raise him from his servitude and inferiority to the level of a blind citizen, Nunez knew nothing of sleep, and all through the warm sunlit hours, while the others slumbered happily, he sat brooding or wandered aimlessly, trying to bring his mind to bear on his dilemma. He had given his answer, he had given his consent, and still he was not sure. And at last work-time was over, the sun rose in splendour over the golden crests, and his last day of vision began for him. He had a few minutes with Medina-saroté before she went apart to sleep.

'Tomorrow,' he said, 'I shall see no more.'

'Dear heart!' she answered, and pressed his hands with all her strength.

'They will hurt you but little,' she said; 'and you are going through this pain – you are going through it, dear lover, for *me*.... Dear, if a woman's heart and life can do it, I will repay you. My dearest one, my dearest with the tender voice, I will repay.'

He was drenched in pity for himself and her.

He held her in his arms, and pressed his lips to hers, and looked on her sweet face for the last time. 'Goodbye!' he whispered at that dear sight, 'goodbye!'

And then in silence he turned away from her.

She could hear his slow retreating footsteps, and something in the rhythm of them threw her into a passion of weeping.

He had fully meant to go to a lonely place where the meadows were beautiful with white narcissus, and there remain until the hour of his sacrifice should come, but as he went he lifted up his eyes and saw the morning, the morning like an angel in golden armour, marching down the steeps ...

It seemed to him that before this splendour he, and this blind world in the valley, and his love, and all, were no more than a pit of sin.

He did not turn aside as he had meant to do, but went on, and passed through the wall of the circumference and out upon the rocks, and his eyes were always upon the sunlit ice and snow.

He saw their infinite beauty, and his imagination soared over them to the things beyond he was now to resign for ever.

He thought of that great free world he was parted from, the world that was his own, and he had a vision of those further slopes, distance beyond distance, with Bogota, a place of multitudinous stirring beauty, a glory by day, a luminous mystery by night, a place of palaces and fountains and statues and white houses, lying beautifully in the middle distance. He thought how for a day or so one might come down through passes, drawing ever nearer and nearer to its busy streets and ways. He thought of the river journey, day by day, from great Bogota to the still vaster world beyond, through towns and villages, forest and desert places, the rushing river day by day, until its banks receded and the big steamers came splashing by, and one had reached the sea – the limitless sea, with its thousand islands, its thousands of islands, and its ships seen dimly far away in their incessant journeyings round and about that greater world. And there, unpent by mountains, one saw the sky – the sky, not such a disc as one saw it here, but an arch of immeasurable blue, a deep of deeps in which the circling stars were floating....

His eyes scrutinised the great curtain of the mountains with a keener inquiry.

For example, if one went so, up that gully and to that chimney there, then one might come out high among those stunted pines that ran round in a sort of shelf and rose still higher and higher as it passed above the gorge. And then? That talus might be managed. Thence perhaps a climb might be found to take him up to the precipice that came below the snow; and if that chimney failed, then another farther to the east might serve his purpose better. And then? Then one would be out upon the amber-lit snow there, and half-way up to the crest of those beautiful desolations.

He glanced back at the village, then turned right round and regarded it steadfastly.

He thought of Medina-saroté, and she had become small and remote.

He turned again towards the mountain wall, down which the day had come to him.

Then very circumspectly he began to climb.

When sunset came he was no longer climbing, but he was far and high. He had been higher, but he was still very high. His clothes were torn, his limbs were blood-stained, he was bruised in many places, but he lay as if he were at his ease, and there was a smile on his face.

From where he rested the valley seemed as if it were in a pit and nearly a mile below. Already it was dim with haze and shadow, though the mountain summits around him were things of light and fire, and the little details of the rocks near at hand were drenched with subtle beauty – a vein of green mineral piercing the grey, the flash of crystal faces here and there, a minute, minutely-beautiful orange lichen close beside his face. There were deep mysterious shadows in the gorge, blue deepening into purple, and purple into a luminous darkness, and overhead was the illimitable vastness of the sky. But he heeded these things no longer, but lay quite inactive there, smiling as if he were satisfied merely to have escaped from the valley of the Blind in which he had thought to be King.

The glow of the sunset passed, and the night came, and still he lay peacefully contented under the cold clear stars.

The Door in the Wall

1

One confidential evening, not three months ago, Lionel Wallace told me this story of the Door in the Wall. And at the time I thought that so far as he was concerned it was a true story.

He told it me with such a direct simplicity of conviction that I could not do otherwise than believe in him. But in the morning, in my own flat, I woke to a different atmosphere, and as I lay in bed and recalled the things he had told me, stripped of the glamour of his earnest slow voice, denuded of the focussed, shaded table light, the shadowy atmosphere that wrapped about him and me, and the pleasant bright things, the dessert and glasses and napery of the dinner we had shared, making them for the time a bright little world quite cut off from everyday realities, I saw it all as frankly incredible. 'He was mystifying!' I said, and then: 'How well he did it! ... It isn't quite the thing I should have expected him, of all people, to do well.'

Afterwards as I sat up in bed and sipped my morning tea, I found myself trying to account for the flavour of reality that perplexed me in his impossible reminiscences, by supposing they did in some way suggest, present, convey – I hardly know which word to use – experiences it was otherwise impossible to tell.

Well, I don't resort to that explanation now. I have got over my intervening doubts. I believe now, as I believed at the moment of telling, that Wallace did to the very best of his ability strip the truth of his secret for me. But whether he himself saw, or only thought he saw, whether he himself was the possessor of an inestimable privilege or the victim of a fantastic dream, I cannot pretend to guess. Even the facts of his death, which ended my doubts for ever, throw no light on that.

That much the reader must judge for himself.

I forget now what chance comment or criticism of mine moved so reticent a man to confide in me. He was, I think, defending himself against an imputation of slackness and unreliability I had made in relation to a great public movement, in which he had disappointed me. But he plunged suddenly. 'I have,' he said, 'a preoccupation—

'I know,' he went on, after a pause, 'I have been negligent. The fact is – it isn't a case of ghosts or apparitions – but – it's an odd thing to tell of, Redmond – I am haunted. I am haunted by something – that rather takes the light out of things, that fills me with longings ...'

He paused, checked by that English shyness that so often overcomes us when we would speak of moving or grave or beautiful things. 'You were at Saint Æthelstan's all through,' he said, and for a moment that seemed to me quite irrelevant. 'Well' – and he paused. Then very haltingly at first, but afterwards more easily, he began to tell of the thing that was hidden in his life, the haunting memory of a beauty and a happiness that filled his heart with insatiable longings, that made all the interests and spectacle of worldly life seem dull and tedious and vain to him.

Now that I have the clue to it, the thing seems written visibly in his face. I have a photograph in which that look of detachment has been caught and intensified. It reminds me of what a woman once said of him – a woman who had loved him greatly. 'Suddenly,' she said, 'the interest goes out of him. He forgets you. He doesn't care a rap for you – under his very nose ...'

Yet the interest was not always out of him, and when he was holding his attention to a thing Wallace could contrive to be an extremely successful man. His career, indeed, is set with successes. He left me behind him long ago: he soared up over my head, and cut a figure in the world that I couldn't cut – anyhow. He was still a year short of forty, and they say now that he would have been in office and very probably in the new Cabinet if he had lived. At school he always beat me without effort – as it were by nature. We were at school together at Saint Æthelstan's College in West Kensington for almost all our school-time. He came into the school as my co-equal, but he left far above me, in a blaze of scholarships and brilliant performance. Yet I think I made a fair average running. And it was at school I heard first of the 'Door in the Wall' – that I was to hear of a second time only a month before his death.

To him at least the Door in the Wall was a real door, leading

through a real wall to immortal realities. Of that I am now quite
assured.

And it came into his life quite early, when he was a little fellow
between five and six. I remember how, as he sat making his
confession to me with a slow gravity, he reasoned and reckoned
the date of it. 'There was,' he said, 'a crimson Virginia creeper in
it – all one bright uniform crimson, in a clear amber sunshine
against a white wall. That came into the impression somehow,
though I don't clearly remember how, and there were horse-
chestnut leaves upon the clean pavement outside the green door.
They were blotched yellow and green, you know, not brown nor
dirty, so that they must have been new fallen. I take it that
means October. I look out for horse-chestnut leaves every year
and I ought to know.

'If I'm right in that, I was about five years and four months
old.'

He was, he said, rather a precocious little boy – he learnt to
talk at an abnormally early age, and he was so sane and 'old-
fashioned', as people say, that he was permitted an amount of
initiative that most children scarcely attain by seven or eight. His
mother died when he was two, and he was under the less vigilant
and authoritative care of a nursery governess. His father was a
stern, preoccupied lawyer, who gave him little attention, and
expected great things of him. For all his brightness he found life a
little grey and dull, I think. And one day he wandered.

He could not recall the particular neglect that enabled him to
get away, nor the course he took among the West Kensington
roads. All that had faded among the incurable blurs of memory.
But the white wall and the green door stood out quite distinctly.

As his memory of that childish experience ran, he did at the
very first sight of that door experience a peculiar emotion, an
attraction, a desire to get to the door and open it and walk in.
And at the same time he had the clearest conviction that either it
was unwise or it was wrong of him – he could not tell which – to
yield to this attraction. He insisted upon it as a curious thing that
he knew from the very beginning – unless memory has played
him the queerest trick – that the door was unfastened, and that
he could go in as he chose.

I seem to see the figure of that little boy, drawn and repelled.
And it was very clear in his mind, too, though why it should be

so was never explained, that his father would be very angry if he went in through that door.

Wallace described all these moments of hesitation to me with the utmost particularity. He went right past the door, and then, with his hands in his pockets and making an infantile attempt to whistle, strolled right along beyond the end of the wall. There he recalls a number of mean dirty shops, and particularly that of a plumber and decorator with a dusty disorder of earthenware pipes, sheet lead, ball taps, pattern books of wall paper, and tins of enamel. He stood pretending to examine these things, and *coveting*, passionately desiring, the green door.

Then, he said, he had a gust of emotion. He made a run for it, lest hesitation should grip him again; he went plump with outstretched hand through the green door and let it slam behind him. And so, in a trice, he came into the garden that has haunted all his life.

It was very difficult for Wallace to give me his full sense of that garden into which he came.

There was something in the very air of it that exhilarated, that gave one a sense of lightness and good happening and well-being; there was something in the sight of it that made all its colour clean and perfect and subtly luminous. In the instant of coming into it one was exquisitely glad – as only in rare moments, and when one is young and joyful one can be glad in this world. And everything was beautiful there....

Wallace mused before he went on telling me. 'You see,' he said, with the doubtful inflection of a man who pauses at incredible things, 'there were two great panthers there.... Yes, spotted panthers. And I was not afraid. There was a long wide path with marble-edged flower borders on either side, and these two huge velvety beasts were playing there with a ball. One looked up and came towards me, a little curious as it seemed. It came right up to me, rubbed its soft round ear very gently against the small hand I held out, and purred. It was, I tell you, an enchanted garden. I know. And the size? Oh! it stretched far and wide, this way and that. I believe there were hills far away. Heaven knows where West Kensington had suddenly got to. And somehow it was just like coming home.

'You know, in the very moment the door swung to behind me, I forgot the road with its fallen chestnut leaves, its cabs and tradesmen's carts, I forgot the sort of gravitational pull back to the discipline and obedience of home, I forgot all hesitations and fear, forgot discretion, forgot all the intimate realities of this life. I became in a moment a very glad and wonder-happy little boy – in another world. It was a world with a different quality, a warmer, more penetrating and mellower light, with a faint clear gladness in its air, and wisps of sun-touched cloud in the blueness of its sky. And before me ran this long wide path, invitingly, with weedless beds on either side, rich with untended flowers, and these two great panthers. I put my little hands fearlessly on their soft fur, and caressed their round ears and the sensitive corners under their ears, and played with them, and it was as though they welcomed me home. There was a keen sense of home-coming in my mind, and when presently a tall, fair girl appeared in the pathway and came to meet me, smiling, and said "Well?" to me, and lifted me, and kissed me, and put me down, and led me by the hand, there was no amazement, but only an impression of delightful rightness, of being reminded of happy things that had in some strange way been overlooked. There were broad red steps, I remember, that came into view between spikes of delphinium, and up these we went to a great avenue between very old and shady dark trees. All down this avenue, you know between the red chapped stems, were marble seats of honour and statuary, and very tame and friendly white doves ...

'Along this cool avenue my girl-friend led me, looking down – I recall the pleasant lines, the finely-modelled chin of her sweet kind face – asking me questions in a soft, agreeable voice, and telling me things, pleasant things I know, though what they were I was never able to recall.... Presently a little Capuchin monkey, very clean, with a fur of ruddy brown and kindly hazel eyes, came down a tree to us and ran beside me, looking up at me and grinning, and presently leapt to my shoulder. So we two went on our way in great happiness.'

He paused.

'Go on,' I said.

'I remember little things. We passed an old man musing among laurels, I remember, and a place gay with paroquets, and came through a broad shaded colonnade to a spacious cool palace, full of pleasant fountains, full of beautiful things, full of the quality and promise of heart's desire. And there were many things and many people, some that still seem to stand out clearly and some that are a little vague; but all these people were beautiful and kind. In some way – I don't know how – it was conveyed to me that they all were kind to me, glad to have me there, and filling me with gladness by their gestures, by the touch of their hands, by the welcome and love in their eyes. Yes—'

He mused for a while. 'Playmates I found there. That was very much to me, because I was a lonely little boy. They played delightful games in a grass-covered court where there was a sun-dial set about with flowers. And as one played one loved....

'But – it's odd – there's a gap in my memory. I don't remember the games we played. I never remembered. Afterwards, as a child, I spent long hours trying, even with tears, to recall the form of that happiness. I wanted to play it all over again – in my nursery – by myself. No! All I remember is the happiness and two dear playfellows who were most with me.... Then presently came a sombre dark woman, with a grave, pale face and dreamy eyes, a sombre woman, wearing a soft long robe of pale purple, who carried a book, and beckoned and took me aside with her into a gallery above a hall – though my playmates were loth to have me go, and ceased their game and stood watching as I was carried away. "Come back to us!" they cried. "Come back to us soon!" I looked up at her face, but she heeded them not at all. Her face was very gentle and grave. She took me to a seat in the gallery, and I stood beside her, ready to look at her book as she opened it upon her knee. The pages fell open. She pointed, and I looked, marvelling, for in the living pages of that book I saw myself; it was a story about myself, and in it were all the things that had happened to me since ever I was born....

'It was wonderful to me, because the pages of that book were not pictures, you understand, but realities.'

Wallace paused gravely – looked at me doubtfully.

'Go on,' I said. 'I understand.'

'They were realities – yes, they must have been; people moved and things came and went in them; my dear mother, whom I had near forgotten; then my father, stern and upright, the servants, the nursery, all the familiar things of home. Then the front door and the busy streets, with traffic to and fro. I looked and marvelled, and looked half doubtfully again into the woman's face and turned the pages over, skipping this and that, to see

more of this book and more, and so at last I came to myself
hovering and hesitating outside the green door in the long white
wall, and felt again the conflict and the fear.

'"And next?" I cried, and would have turned on, but the cool
hand of the grave woman delayed me.

'"Next?" I insisted, and struggled gently with her hand, pulling
up her fingers with all my childish strength, and as she yielded
and the page came over she bent down upon me like a shadow
and kissed my brow.

'But the page did not show the enchanted garden, nor the
panthers, nor the girl who had led me by the hand, nor the
playfellows who had been so loth to let me go. It showed a long
grey street in West Kensington, in that chill hour of afternoon
before the lamps are lit, and I was there, a wretched little figure,
weeping aloud, for all that I could do to restrain myself, and I was
weeping because I could not return to my dear playfellows who
had called after me, "Come back to us! Come back to us soon!" I
was there. This was no page in a book, but harsh reality; that
enchanted place and the restraining hand of the grave mother at
whose knee I stood had gone – whither had they gone?'

He halted again, and remained for a time staring into the fire.

'Oh! the woefulness of that return!' he murmured.

'Well?' I said, after a minute or so.

'Poor little wretch I was! – brought back to this grey world
again! As I realised the fulness of what had happened to me, I
gave way to quite ungovernable grief. And the shame and
humiliation of that public weeping and my disgraceful home-
coming remain with me still. I see again the benevolent-looking
old gentleman in gold spectacles who stopped and spoke to me –
prodding me first with his umbrella. "Poor little chap," said he;
"and are you lost then?" – and me a London boy of five and
more! And he must needs bring in a kindly young policeman and
make a crowd of me, and so march me home. Sobbing,
conspicuous, and frightened, I came back from the enchanted
garden to the steps of my father's house.

'That is as well as I can remember my vision of that garden –
the garden that haunts me still. Of course, I can convey nothing
of that indescribable quality of translucent unreality, that
difference from the common things of experience that hung about
it all; but that – that is what happened. If it was a dream, I am

sure it was a day-time and altogether extraordinary dream....
H'm! – naturally there followed a terrible questioning, by my
aunt, my father, the nurse, the governess – everyone....

'I tried to tell them, and my father gave me my first thrashing
for telling lies. When afterwards I tried to tell my aunt, she
punished me again for my wicked persistence. Then, as I said,
everyone was forbidden to listen to me, to hear a word about it.
Even my fairytale books were taken away from me for a time –
because I was too "imaginative". Eh? Yes, they did that! My
father belonged to the old school.... And my story was driven
back upon myself. I whispered it to my pillow – my pillow that
was often damp and salt to my whispering lips with childish
tears. And I added always to my official and less fervent prayers
this one heartfelt request: "Please God I may dream of the garden.
Oh! take me back to my garden!" Take me back to my garden! I
dreamt often of the garden. I may have added to it, I may have
changed it; I do not know.... All this, you understand, is an
attempt to reconstruct from fragmentary memories a very early
experience. Between that and the other consecutive memories of
my boyhood there is a gulf. A time came when it seemed
impossible I should ever speak of that wonder glimpse again.'

I asked an obvious question.

'No,' he said. 'I don't remember that I ever attempted to find
my way back to the garden in those early years. This seems odd
to me now, but I think that very probably a closer watch was
kept on my movements after this misadventure to prevent my
going astray. No, it wasn't till you knew me that I tried for the
garden again. And I believe there was a period – incredible as it
seems now – when I forgot the garden altogether – when I was
about eight or nine it may have been. Do you remember me as a
kid at Saint Æthelstan's?'

'Rather!'

'I didn't show any signs, did I, in those days of having a secret
dream?'

2

He looked up with a sudden smile.

'Did you ever play North-West Passage with me? ... No, of
course you didn't come my way!'

'It was the sort of game,' he went on, 'that every imaginative child plays all day. The idea was the discovery of a North-West Passage to school. The way to school was plain enough; the game consisted in finding some way that wasn't plain, starting off ten minutes early in some almost hopeless direction, and working my way round through unaccustomed streets to my goal. And one day I got entangled among some rather low-class streets on the other side of Campden Hill, and I began to think that for once the game would be against me and that I should get to school late. I tried rather desperately a street that seemed a *cul-de-sac*, and found a passage at the end. I hurried through that with renewed hope. "I shall do it yet," I said, and passed a row of frowsy little shops that were inexplicably familiar to me, and behold! there was my long white wall and the green door that led to the enchanted garden!

'The thing whacked upon me suddenly. Then, after all, that garden, that wonderful garden, wasn't a dream!'

He paused.

'I suppose my second experience with the green door marks the world of difference there is between the busy life of a schoolboy and the infinite leisure of a child. Anyhow, this second time I didn't for a moment think of going in straight away. You see— For one thing, my mind was full of the idea of getting to school in time – set on not breaking my record for punctuality. I must surely have felt *some* little desire at least to try the door – yes. I must have felt that.... But I seem to remember the attraction of the door mainly as another obstacle to my overmastering determination to get to school. I was immensely interested by this discovery I had made, of course – I went on with my mind full of it – but I went on. It didn't check me. I ran past, tugging out my watch, found I had ten minutes still to spare, and then I was going downhill into familiar surroundings. I got to school, breathless, it is true, and wet with perspiration, but in time. I can remember hanging up my coat and hat.... Went right by it and left it behind me. Odd, eh?'

He looked at me thoughtfully. 'Of course I didn't know then that it wouldn't always be there. Schoolboys have limited imaginations. I suppose I thought it was an awfully jolly thing to have it there, to know my way back to it, but there was the school tugging at me. I expect I was a good deal distraught and inattentive that morning, recalling what I could of the beautiful strange people I should presently see again. Oddly enough I had no doubt in my mind that they would be glad to see me.... Yes, I must have thought of the garden that morning just as a jolly sort of place to which one might resort in the interludes of a strenuous scholastic career.

'I didn't go that day at all. The next day was a half holiday, and that may have weighed with me. Perhaps, too, my state of inattention brought down impositions upon me, and docked the margin of time necessary for the *détour*. I don't know. What I do know is that in the meantime the enchanted garden was so much upon my mind that I could not keep it to myself.

'I told. What was his name? – a ferrety-looking youngster we used to call Squiff.'

'Young Hopkins,' said I.

'Hopkins it was. I did not like telling him. I had a feeling that in some way it was against the rules to tell him, but I did. He was walking part of the way home with me; he was talkative, and if we had not talked about the enchanted garden we should have talked of something else, and it was intolerable to me to think about any other subject. So I blabbed.

'Well, he told my secret. The next day in the play interval I found myself surrounded by half a dozen bigger boys, half teasing, and wholly curious to hear more of the enchanted garden. There was that big Fawcett – you remember him? – and Carnaby and Morley Reynolds. You weren't there by any chance? No I think I should have remembered if you were....

'A boy is a creature of odd feelings. I was, I really believe, in spite of my secret self-disgust, a little flattered to have the attention of these big fellows. I remember particularly a moment of pleasure caused by the praise of Crawshaw – you remember Crawshaw major, the son of Crawshaw the composer? – who said it was the best lie he had ever heard. But at the same time there was a really painful undertow of shame at telling what I felt was indeed a sacred secret. That beast Fawcett made a joke about the girl in green—'

Wallace's voice sank with the keen memory of that shame. 'I pretended not to hear,' he said. 'Well, then Carnaby suddenly called me a young liar, and disputed with me when I said the thing was true. I said I knew where to find the green door, could

lead them all there in ten minutes. Carnaby became outrageously
virtuous, and said I'd have to – and bear out my words or suffer.
Did you ever have Carnaby twist your arm? Then perhaps you'll
understand how it went with me. I swore my story was true.
There was nobody in the school then to save a chap from
Carnaby, though Crawshaw put in a word or so. Carnaby had
got his game. I grew excited and red-eared, and a little frightened.
I behaved altogether like a silly little chap, and the outcome of it
all was that instead of starting alone for my enchanted garden, I
led the way presently – cheeks flushed, ears hot, eyes smarting,
and my soul one burning misery and shame – for a party of six
mocking, curious, and threatening schoolfellows.

'We never found the white wall and the green door....'

'You mean—?'

'I mean I couldn't find it. I would have found it if I could.

'And afterwards when I could go alone I couldn't find it. I
never found it. I seem now to have been always looking for it
through my school-boy days, but I never came upon it – never.'

'Did the fellows – make it disagreeable?'

'Beastly.... Carnaby held a council over me for wanton lying. I
remember how I sneaked home and upstairs to hide the marks of
my blubbering. But when I cried myself to sleep at last it wasn't
for Carnaby, but for the garden, for the beautiful afternoon I had
hoped for, for the sweet friendly women and the waiting playfellows, and the game I had hoped to learn again, that beautiful
forgotten game....

'I believed firmly that if I had not told –.... I had bad times after
that – crying at night and wool-gathering by day. For two terms I
slackened and had bad reports. Do you remember? Of course you
would! It was *you* – your beating me in mathematics that
brought me back to the grind again.'

3

For a time my friend stared silently into the red heart of the fire.
Then he said: 'I never saw it again until I was seventeen.

'It leapt upon me for the third time – as I was driving to
Paddington on my way to Oxford and a scholarship. I had just
one momentary glimpse. I was leaning over the apron of my
hansom smoking a cigarette, and no doubt thinking myself no

end of a man of the world, and suddenly there was the door, the wall, the dear sense of unforgettable and still attainable things.

'We clattered by – I too taken by surprise to stop my cab until we were well past and round a corner. Then I had a queer moment, a double and divergent movement of my will: I tapped the little door in the roof of the cab, and brought my arm down to pull out my watch. "Yes, sir!" said the cabman, smartly. "Er – well – it's nothing," I cried. "*My* mistake! We haven't much time! Go on!" And he went on....

'I got my scholarship. And the night after I was told of that I sat over my fire in my little upper room, my study, in my father's house, with his praise – his rare praise – and his sound counsels ringing in my ears, and I smoked my favourite pipe – the formidable bulldog of adolescence – and thought of that door in the long white wall. "If I had stopped," I thought, "I should have missed my scholarship, I should have missed Oxford – muddled all the fine career before me! I begin to see things better!" I fell musing deeply, but I did not doubt then this career of mine was a thing that merited sacrifice.

'Those dear friends and that clear atmosphere seemed very sweet to me, very fine but remote. My grip was fixing now upon the world. I saw another door opening – the door of my career.'

He stared again into the fire. Its red light picked out a stubborn strength in his face for just one flickering moment, and then it vanished again.

'Well,' he said and sighed, 'I have served that career. I have done – much work, much hard work. But I have dreamt of the enchanted garden a thousand dreams, and seen its door, or at least glimpsed its door four times since then. Yes – four times. For a while this world was so bright and interesting, seemed so full of meaning and opportunity, that the half-effaced charm of the garden was by comparison gentle and remote. Who wants to pat panthers on the way to dinner with pretty women and distinguished men? I came down to London from Oxford, a man of bold promise that I have done something to redeem. Something – and yet there have been disappointments....

'Twice I have been in love – I will not dwell on that – but once, as I went to someone who, I knew, doubted whether I dared to come, I took a short cut at a venture through an unfrequented road near Earl's Court, and so happened on a white wall and a familiar green door. "Odd!" said I to myself, "but I thought this place was on Campden Hill. It's the place I never could find somehow – like counting Stonehenge – the place of that queer daydream of mine." And I went by it intent upon my purpose. It had no appeal to me that afternoon.

'I had just a moment's impulse to try the door, three steps aside were needed at the most – though I was sure enough in my heart that it would open to me – and then I thought that doing so might delay me on the way to that appointment in which I thought my honour was involved. Afterwards I was sorry for my punctuality – I might at least have peeped in, I thought, and waved a hand to those panthers, but I knew enough by this time not to seek again belatedly that which is not found by seeking. Yes, that time made me very sorry....

'Years of hard work after that, and never a sight of the door. It's only recently it has come back to me. With it there has come a sense as though some thin tarnish had spread itself over my world. I began to think of it as a sorrowful and bitter thing that I should never see that door again. Perhaps I was suffering a little from overwork – perhaps it was what I've heard spoken of as the feeling of forty. I don't know. But certainly the keen brightness that makes effort easy has gone out of things recently, and that just at a time – with all these new political developments – when I ought to be working. Odd, isn't it? But I do begin to find life toilsome, its rewards, as I come near them, cheap. I began a little while ago to want the garden quite badly. Yes – and I've seen it three times.'

'The garden?'

'No – the door! And I haven't gone in!'

He leant over the table to me, with an enormous sorrow in his voice as he spoke. 'Thrice I have had my chance – *thrice*! If ever that door offers itself to me again, I swore, I will go in, out of this dust and heat, out of this dry glitter of vanity, out of these toilsome futilities. I will go and never return. This time I will stay.... I swore it, and when the time came – *I didn't go*.

'Three times in one year have I passed that door and failed to enter. Three times in the last year.

'The first time was on the night of the snatch division on the Tenants' Redemption Bill, on which the Government was saved by a majority of three. You remember? No one on our side –

perhaps very few on the opposite side – expected the end that night. Then the debate collapsed like eggshells. I and Hotchkiss were dining with his cousin at Brentford; we were both unpaired, and we were called up by telephone, and set off at once in his cousin's motor. We got in barely in time, and on the way we passed my wall and door – livid in the moonlight, blotched with hot yellow as the glare of our lamps lit it, but unmistakable. "My God!" cried I. "What?" said Hotchkiss. "Nothing!" I answered, and the moment passed.

'"I've made a great sacrifice," I told the whip as I got in. "They all have," he said, and hurried by.

'I do not see how I could have done otherwise then. And the next occasion was as I rushed to my father's bedside to bid that stern old man farewell. Then, too, the claims of life were imperative. But the third time was different; it happened a week ago. It fills me with hot remorse to recall it. I was with Gurker and Ralphs – it's no secret now, you know, that I've had my talk with Gurker. We had been dining at Frobisher's, and the talk had become intimate between us. The question of my place in the reconstructed Ministry lay always just over the boundary of the discussion. Yes – yes. That's all settled. It needn't be talked about yet, but there's no reason to keep a secret from you.... Yes – thanks! thanks! But let me tell you my story.

'Then, on that night things were very much in the air. My position was a very delicate one. I was keenly anxious to get some definite word from Gurker, but was hampered by Ralphs' presence. I was using the best power of my brain to keep that light and careless talk not too obviously directed to the point that concerned me. I had to. Ralphs' behaviour since has more than justified my caution.... Ralphs, I knew, would leave us beyond the Kensington High Street, and then I could surprise Gurker by a sudden frankness. One has sometimes to resort to these little devices.... And then it was that in the margin of my field of vision I became aware once more of the white wall, the green door before us down the road.

'We passed it talking. I passed it. I can still see the shadow of Gurker's marked profile, his opera hat tilted forward over his prominent nose, the many folds of his neck wrap going before my shadow and Ralphs' as we sauntered past.

'I passed within twenty inches of the door. "If I say good-night to them, and go in," I asked myself, "what will happen?" And I was all a-tingle for that word with Gurker.

'I could not answer that question in the tangle of my other problems. "They will think me mad," I thought. "And suppose I vanish now! – Amazing disappearance of a prominent politician!" That weighed with me. A thousand inconceivably petty worldlinesses weighed with me in that crisis.'

Then he turned on me with a sorrowful smile, and, speaking slowly, 'Here I am!' he said.

'Here I am!' he repeated, 'and my chance has gone from me. Three times in one year the door has been offered me – the door that goes into peace, into delight, into a beauty beyond dreaming, a kindness no man on earth can know. And I have rejected it, Redmond, and it has gone—'

'How do you know?'

'I know. I know. I am left now to work it out, to stick to the tasks that held me so strongly when my moments came. You say I have success – this vulgar, tawdry, irksome, envied thing. I have it.' He had a walnut in his big hand. 'If that was my success,' he said, and crushed it, and held it out for me to see.

'Let me tell you something, Redmond. This loss is destroying me. For two months, for ten weeks nearly now, I have done no work at all, except the most necessary and urgent duties. My soul is full of inappeasable regrets. At nights – when it is less likely I shall be recognised – I go out. I wander. Yes. I wonder what people would think of that if they knew. A Cabinet Minister, the responsible head of that most vital of all departments, wandering alone – grieving – sometimes near audibly lamenting – for a door, for a garden!'

4

I can see now his rather pallid face, and the unfamiliar sombre fire that had come into his eyes. I see him very vividly to-night. I sit recalling his words, his tones, and last evening's *Westminster Gazette* still lies on my sofa, containing the notice of his death. At lunch today the club was busy with his death. We talked of nothing else.

They found his body very early yesterday morning in a deep excavation near East Kensington Station. It is one of two shafts that have been made in connection with an extension of the railway southward. It is protected from the intrusion of the public by a hoarding upon the high road, in which a small doorway has been cut for the convenience of some of the workmen who live in that direction. The doorway was left unfastened through a misunderstanding between two gangers, and through it he made his way....

My mind is darkened with questions and riddles.

It would seem he walked all the way from the House that night – he has frequently walked home during the past Session – and so it is I figure his dark form coming along the late and empty streets, wrapped up, intent. And then did the pale electric lights near the station cheat the rough planking into a semblance of white? Did that fatal unfastened door awaken some memory?

Was there, after all, ever any green door in the wall at all?

I do not know. I have told his story as he told it to me. There are times when I believe that Wallace was no more than the victim of the coincidence between a rare but not unprecedented type of hallucination and a careless trap, but that indeed is not my profoundest belief. You may think me superstitious, if you will, and foolish; but, indeed, I am more than half convinced that he had, in truth, an abnormal gift, and a sense, something – I know not what – that in the guise of wall and door offered him an outlet, a secret and peculiar passage of escape into another and altogether more beautiful world. At any rate, you will say, it betrayed him in the end. But did it betray him? There you touch the inmost mystery of these dreamers, these men of vision and the imagination. We see our world fair and common, the hoarding and the pit. By our daylight standard he walked out of security into darkness, danger, and death.

But did he see like that?

Bibliography

'Through a Window', *Black and White*, 25 August 1894
'The Purple Pileus', *Black and White*, December 1896
'A Catastrophe', *New Budget*, 4 April 1895
'Æpyornis Island', *Pall Mall Budget*, 13 December 1894
'The Sea Raiders', *Weekly Sun Literary Supplement*, 6 December 1896
'The Crystal Egg', *New Review*, 1897
'Under the Knife', *New Review*, January 1896
'The Flowering of the Strange Orchid', *Pall Mall Budget*, 2 August 1894
'The Red Room', *Idler*, March 1896
'The Cone', *Unicorn*, 16 September 1895
'The Diamond Maker', *Pall Mall Budget*, 16 August 1894
'The Remarkable Case of Davidson's Eyes', *Pall Mall Budget*, 28 March
    1895
'The Story of the Late Mr Elvesham', *Idler*, May 1896
'How Gabriel Became Thompson', *Truth*, 26 July 1894
'How Pingwill was Routed', *New Budget*, 27 June 1895
'Pollock and the Porroh Man', *New Budget*, 23 May 1895
'The Valley of Spiders', *Strand Magazine*, March 1903
'Mr Skelmersdale in Fairyland', *Strand Magazine*, 1901
'The Apple', *Idler*, October 1896
'The Country of the Blind', *Strand Magazine*, April 1904
'The Door in the Wall', *Daily Chronicle*, 14 July 1906